BAGRAM

A NOVEL

J.P. SPRINGETT II

COMMODORE'S RIDGE PUBLISHING, LURAY VA

This is a work of fiction. Names, characters, businesses, events, and incidents are the products of the author's imagination. Any resemblance to actual persons, living or dead, or actual events is purely coincidental.

The views expressed in this book are entirely those of the author and do not reflect any official policy or position of the Department of Defense or any part of the U.S. Government. Any representation of classified material is entirely fictional.

Commodore's Ridge Publishing, LLC

www.commodoresridge.com

Library of Congress Control Number: 2025903275

Ebook ISBN: 979-8-9905882-4-0

Paperback ISBN: 979-8-9905882-5-7

Hardcover ISBN: 979-8-9905882-6-4

Cover Design by CRP (C) 2025. Photo from the author's personal collection.

V 1.11

Dedicated to the warriors who were sent to a harsh and dangerous land to fight the nation's enemies in the name of national security. Betrayed by their leader's lack of strategic understanding, these heroes bore the burden of this foreign war with honor and courage - even when the cause was forsaken.

"Let me not then die ingloriously and without a struggle, but let me first do some great thing that shall be told among men hereafter."

The Iliad - Homer

Source: CIA World Factbook (Image is Public Domain)

Bagram Air Base. © 2025
From the author's personal collection.

PROLOGUE

ALONG THE KHOST-GARDEZ HIGHWAY - AFGHANISTAN

The rusted old Toyota pickup rumbled through the riverbed, its diesel motor barely more than a low, throaty murmur. The driver navigated carefully, threading between boulders that could flatten the bald tires or cripple the suspension, his eyes fixed on the faint tracks left by others who had come this way before. Beside him, on the cracked vinyl bench seat, sat Farid - husband to Shikha, father to Aashna. His wife and daughter rode in the open bed behind them, wrapped in their robes against the dust and wind.

Farid had scraped together what little money he could to pay for this journey, hiring the driver to take them from their remote village in the Suleiman Mountains to the hospital in Khost. Aashna needed a doctor.

THIS WASN'T the first time the girl had fought for her life. Sickly from birth, she had already endured more than most children her age. When she was three, she had fallen violently ill -

vomiting relentlessly, her tiny body wracked with uncontrollable diarrhea. No home remedy had worked. Desperate, Farid and Shikha had carried their daughter to the roadside along the Gardez-Khost Highway, waving down passing vehicles, pleading for help.

Salvation had come in the form of an Egyptian doctor, an aid worker traveling the region. The man had stepped from his truck, taken one look at the limp child in Shikha's arms, and immediately recognized the symptoms of cholera. He had moved quickly, setting up an IV, administering antibiotics, and handing over a packet of zinc powder to ease her suffering. Within hours, the little girl had turned a corner.

Since then, Aashna had blossomed. She was clever, full of laughter, and the light of Farid's life. The men in the village often teased him for doting on his daughter. Daughters were burdens meant to be dowered off as soon as possible, while sons carried the future of the family. But Farid had no sons, and Aashna filled his days with joy.

Then, a week ago, she had begun scratching at her right eye. At first, it seemed like nothing, but within days, her face had swollen so badly she could barely see. Farid knew the signs of leishmaniasis - the cruel parasite carried by sandflies. He also knew that if left untreated it could take her sight.

SHIKHA DID WHAT SHE COULD, pressing warm and cold cloths to the swelling, whispering soothing words as Aashna whimpered in pain. But it wasn't enough. The bruising worsened, and the swelling grew. After two more days of helplessly watching his daughter suffer, Farid could take no more. He had begged the village elders to use their radio to call for help. When a driver finally responded, he had gathered every coin he could find to pay for the journey.

The driver had arrived the night before, a kind old man from farther down the mountain. When he saw Aashna's swollen face, he had shaken his head, then quietly handed half the money back.

"I will only keep the cost of petrol," he had said. "It would be a sin in Allah's eyes to make a profit from this."

They had set off at dawn, bumping down rough mountain trails for hours before finally reaching the outskirts of civilization. Now, as they neared the long stretch of tarmac that would carry them the last fifty kilometers into Khost, the driver reached over and turned on the radio. A Pakistani FM station crackled to life, filling the cab with music. Despite the dust and exhaust that would creep in through the windows, he slid open the small rear pane so the family in the back could listen.

Mid-morning, they came across a Jingle truck stalled at the roadside. These towering, brightly painted trucks were a common sight - mobile works of art, adorned with intricate patterns, prayers, and images of peacocks and flowers. Their drivers lived in them, hauling goods endlessly from city to city, their colorful rigs a stark contrast to the harsh, dusty landscape.

"Aashna, look at the truck. Isn't it pretty?" Farid asked, hoping to distract her, if only for a moment.

The little girl turned her head but barely reacted, too drained by illness to admire the vibrant designs.

As they pulled closer, they saw two men struggling to change a massive front tire. The Toyota driver eased to a stop beside them.

"Do you need help?" Farid asked.

One of the men straightened, wiping sweat from his brow. "No, thank you. We're almost done." He looked exhausted, his clothes stained with dirt and grease.

Farid nodded. "God be with you."

The man offered a tired smile before bending back to his work. The Toyota rolled forward again, leaving the stranded truck behind as the road stretched out toward the city - and, with hope, the help Aashna needed.

. . .

In order to make room for the men repairing the Jingle truck, the Toyota's driver had been forced to pull off the well-traveled part of the track. As they continued the journey, the old man had to navigate the riverbed for some distance before finding a gap in the rocks that would allow a safe return. After roughly thirty meters of careful maneuvering along a less traveled path, he spotted a suitable opening in the rocky berm. As he steered across a smooth patch of sand, the pickup's left front wheel rolled over an Improvised Explosive Device, a bomb that had been buried there only a few days earlier. The device was designed to be triggered remotely and should not have exploded, but the weight of the truck crushed its flimsy plastic casing, short-circuiting the Chinese-manufactured detonator. The result was nearly a kilo of powerful plastic explosive erupting in an instant.

The charge, intended to destroy or disable a large American armored vehicle, shredded the lightweight pickup truck, bending it in half and tossing it across the rocks as if it was a toy. Farid and the driver died instantly. The woman and the girl were flung a dozen or more meters from the bed of the truck, landing among the smooth rocks of the dry riverbed.

Shocked, the two men who had been repairing the Jingle truck ran to the two bodies as the Toyota burned, sending a pillar of dark smoke into the sky. The first man arrived at the body that was closer to the flaming wreck. He stood over the woman for a moment and then turned to his companion and shook his head. The other man then reluctantly walked to a smaller bundle of smoking rags that had landed awkwardly astride one of the larger boulders in the area. As he got closer, he thought he saw the injured girl move a hand, but when he bent down to pick her up, he saw that she was gone.

1

THE TANK, PENTAGON - ARLINGTON VIRGINIA

Six four-star officers were seated in the Pentagon briefing room known as "The Tank." This was the highly secure conference room where the Joint Chiefs of Staff held their formal meetings, making critical decisions that shaped national security and military strategy. The Tank was one of the rare spaces in the sprawling Pentagon where these senior officers could engage in frank and unguarded discussions, free from the watchful eyes and ears of subordinates, staffers, and the ever-present political machinery in "the building."

The initial agenda for the meeting had centered on the challenges that all of the services were facing with the "Low Density, High Demand" units that were critical enablers for the wars in Iraq and Afghanistan but which were not large enough to cover all the required commitments. Each service chief had his own list of small units that were worn out from constant deployments and who needed a break from conflict. After a lengthy discussion about their limited options, the senior officers had come to an unsatisfactory conclusion, agreeing that the best option was to do nothing and handle issues on a unit-level basis as they inevitably emerged.

When this discussion was complete, the Chairman turned to the remaining staff. "Time for you folks to give us a minute." The handful of senior aides and briefers who had attended the meeting quietly left the room.

After the room was clear, the Chairman opened a folder and handed out a paper copy of a single PowerPoint slide to each of the men at the table. "So, I'm sure you have heard that the Afghanistan surge has been approved. We will start sending the first units over in the next ten days or so."

"Can we really call this a surge?" asked the Commandant of the Marine Corps as he looked at the sheet of paper. "Thirty-thousand troops is not really much of an increase."

"It's the most the boss would accept," replied the Chairman. "It is also important to note that the President gave us a timeline for the end of the surge as well. We have approximately two years before we begin our withdraw."

There was an uneasy silence in the room.

"A public deadline doesn't do anything more than give the enemy an understanding of how long they need to survive," said the Commandant. "Great."

"Where did that date come from?" asked the Chief of Staff of the Army, the irritation clear in his voice. "I don't remember that in the draft."

"The NSC," said the Chairman. "The President would not approve a request for forces without one."

"Don't forget that while we are sending more combat forces, CENTCOM wants us to pull thousands of supporting troops out and increase the tooth-to-tail ratio," said the Chief of Staff of the Air Force. "The new CENTCOM visited the theater a few weeks ago and was not impressed by the fact that there were burger joints, coffee shops, and an ice cream parlor at Bagram and Kandahar."

"Sure, that's the headline, but there are thousands of useful support troops that he also wants to send home," replied the Chief of Staff of the Army. "This means we potentially starve the fighting force of the services they need just when they need them the most."

"I understand the concern, but I share CENTCOM's problem with the administrative bloat in theater. We want to wrap this fight up and leave, not bed down for the long haul," said the Commandant. "The lighter we are, the better."

The conversation paused for a moment until the Chief of Staff of the Army spoke again. "So, let me see if I have this right. We really have two end states. One is based on the President's deadline for the surge, and the second is based on the mission statement." He looked down and began to read out loud from the slide. "We will disrupt, dismantle, and defeat al-Qa'ida and prevent its capacity to threaten America and our allies in the future. To accomplish this, we will pursue three objectives: deny al-Qa'ida a safe haven, reverse the Taliban's momentum, and strengthen the capacity of Afghanistan's security forces and government so that they can take lead responsibility for Afghanistan's future."

"It sounds like we fight until we are out of time or the Afghan government is ready to take the mission," said the Commandant. "Whichever comes first." He flipped the piece of paper across the table. "That's not a military objective, it's a fuse."

The room was quiet until the Chief of Naval Operations cleared his throat. "Is there any number of American troops that could enable us to achieve those objectives?" He pointed at the piece of paper lying on the table in front of him. "It doesn't matter what the surge does, our success now depends entirely on Afghanistan's government and security forces eventually being able to deny al-Qa'ida a safe haven and to hold the Taliban at bay, and to do both of these things indefinitely. Hell, we can't achieve our objective with more than a hundred and fifty thousand of the best trained and equipped soldiers, sailors, airmen, and marines in the world. How in the hell do we think the Afghan Army is going to do it? For heaven's sake, they literally can't do anything on their own."

It was quiet in the room for a long moment.

The Chairman broke the silence. "We are going to do the best we can. That's all we can do."

* * *

CENTRAL INTELLIGENCE AGENCY HEADQUARTERS - LANGLEY, VA

"We need a more effective way to expand our operation," said Dr. Marcus Reynolds, Deputy Director of the CIA's Special Activities Division. "Sending small teams out isn't scaling very well. The decision isn't public yet, but the President has decided we are going to copy the Iraq surge in order to get the war in Afghanistan back under control."

"That's interesting," replied Terrance Winters, Assistant Special Activities Division lead for Afghanistan, his tone laced with cynicism. "In my opinion, Iraq is exactly the same shit show that it was before we doubled down, so I'm not sure who is defining what control really means."

He saw his boss wince, and he held up his hand to short-circuit the reply he knew was coming. "Yeah, yeah. I know that's above my paygrade." He paused. "Anyway, I talked to JSOC on the way here, and they definitely could use some help, particularly along the border with Pakistan. Our Counter-Terrorism Pursuit Teams are doing good work, but they are gradually becoming less effective."

He checked his notes and looked up at his boss. "I think we can add some focus to our efforts in the tribal areas and perhaps conduct some more significant cross-border raids. The Pakistani ISI is getting a bit desperate as the violence spreads farther into the country."

"I would agree," said Reynolds as he reached for his cup of coffee. He hesitated for a moment before drinking, "Although I think the data shows that ISI is a more deeply involved with the Taliban than we are admitting to ourselves. We will have to do something about that before long."

THE TWO MEN were sitting in what was known as a "SCIF," or Secure Compartmented Information Facility, deep in the heart of the CIA headquarters in Langley, Virginia. One week earlier, Winters had been ordered to return from his office in Kabul and make the rounds in D.C. His job during the visit was to keep an increasingly large number of policymakers and politicians informed about the massive CIA counter-terrorism mission in the region, as well as the ongoing search for Osama bin Laden. He despised the necessity for the trip and the fact that the actions of his teams were so broadly known outside of the highly classified circles in which they were intended to operate.

"THE DRONE STRIKES ARE DOING GOOD," said Winters. "We could ramp them up."

"Already on the list," replied Reynolds. "POTUS has authorized a much more aggressive drone-strike effort in the FATA, you can expect to assist with some of the targeting."

"Great," replied Winters. "Happy to help." He looked down at his notes. "You could send some assets over from Iraq. We could fill the gap there with contract support if we needed to," said Winters.

"One assault team is already on the way," said Reynolds. "They should be on the ground soon."

"Okay," said Winters with a bit of a surprised look on his face. He made a note and went to the next thing on his list. "I'd like to place several more of those integrated surveillance systems along the ridgelines near J-Bad and west of Khost. The winter did more damage to the old ones than we predicted."

"Approved," said Reynolds. "Send the list of what types you need when you get a chance."

"Great," replied Winters, who was now truly surprised. "Well, I have an expensive option if you are interested."

"What is it?" replied Reynolds.

"We can start doing night raids ourselves," said Winters. "Plenty of targets to go around, especially along the border and around Tora Bora. We'd need to buy some MI-17s and get the logistics set up, but we could go into places that JSOC currently isn't authorized to spend time in. I'd base the unit in the northeast. Probably keep the main detachment at Bagram but send teams to Jalalabad, Khost, and maybe south to Kandahar. We could use the increased aviation support in the search for UBL as well."

"Why use MI-17s?" asked Reynolds. "It would be a lot easier for us to get a few more Blackhawks."

"I suppose we could do both," said Winters. "The thought had been to establish our cover with MI-17s painted in Afghan National Army colors, but that might not be required."

Reynolds thought for a moment. "The way things are heating up, I don't think that it is necessary. Just get some Blackhawks and fly them black." He paused and scribbled on the paper in front of him. "I guess it might be helpful to have a couple painted just in case something comes up, but it wouldn't be my first priority. How many helicopters would you need?"

Surprised his boss hadn't immediately said "No," Winters looked down to check his notes again. "I hadn't considered using Blackhawks for any of this, but based on what we are talking about, I'd say two M-model Blackhawks should get us going. We could expand from there if necessary."

"I think we could support that," replied Reynolds. He looked at Winters. "How fast could you build the capability?"

"Really? Not even going to ask about the cost?" asked Winters. His boss stayed silent. Winters looked at his notes again. "I could probably get the two Blackhawks pretty quickly if I moved them from Iraq. I would guess it would be about ninety days until we had all the people and parts on station."

"Get it moving," said Reynolds. "You have a few Blackhawks that are already in the field, right?"

"We have several in Afghanistan, but they are all just trash haulers," replied Winters. "Not equipped for NVGs or bad weather. The two I'd be bringing from Iraq are the new MH-60M models that are designed for the mission." He looked at his boss. "If we do this you know the Army isn't going to give us more people, I am going to have to recruit."

"Do what you have to do. I want you to have the unit assembled in two weeks," said Reynolds. "Let me know when you are ready to run missions."

Winters was quiet for a moment as he looked at his boss. "You already planned to do this, didn't you?"

"Let's just say great minds think alike," replied Reynolds as he swiveled back to his computer. "I've got a guy from the aviation unit on the ground taking a look at things right now."

"Shit," said Winters. Reynolds turned slightly and gave him a look. "I mean, it sounds like a plan boss. I'm on it. I leave for Bagram in the morning, I'll let you know if we need anything else."

"Good," replied Reynolds as he began typing a note on his computer. "Have a safe trip back."

* * *

LOGISTICS OFFICE, CENTCOM HEADQUARTERS - TAMPA, FL.

"Boss, I haven't seen it officially, but I hear that Option C was approved," said Major Kevin Maddox. "The President will announce it in a speech."

"So, thirty thousand new troops," said Colonel Andrew Renner. "Any idea when we can start flowing them in?"

"Not yet, sir. The timeline on the SECDEF orders-book is still close-hold," said Maddox.

"Well, Afghanistan is going to be packed, that's for sure," said Renner.

"The new troops will go to the field, so that won't be as much of an issue," said Maddox. "We just need to absorb them for a week or so at the air bases and then move them out into the country. That just means lots of tents. The difficulty is going to be bringing people home. There will be a mountain of equipment to process and decide what to do with."

"Remind me, what did Option C tell us we needed to bring back?" asked Renner.

"Four thousand supporting troops need to exit the theater," said Maddox. "The President insisted on including a cap for the number of combat troops on the ground."

"Well, that's what the General wanted anyway," said Renner. "No more Burger King in Bagram."

"No more Burger King, no Starbucks, all creature comforts must go," replied Maddox.

"As I recall, nobody said anything about the number of contractors we can use," said Renner. "Maybe we just make a trade."

"But that will cost three times as much," Maddox pointed out.

"Maybe. Maybe that won't matter," said Renner thoughtfully. "Nobody is really counting dollars, just bodies." He made a note on his computer and then looked back up at Maddox. "Okay, well, let's get the team in here. We need to smooth the current plan. I'm sure there will be some units that have issues when they hear the news." He paused. "Oh, get on the line with your buddy in the J3. See if you can get a copy of the deployment order or at least a draft. That will get us going."

"Yes, sir. Will do." Maddox began to walk out of the office.

"Major," said Renner.

Maddox stopped and turned. "Yes, sir?"

"Have the contracting officer come visit me."

* * *

S4 LOGISTICS, COMBINED JOINT TASK FORCE-82 - BAGRAM AIR BASE

Lieutenant Colonel Mark Benson, CJTF-82 supply officer, stepped into the Chief of Staff's office and closed the door behind him.

"Sir, you wanted to see me?"

Colonel David Sinclair nodded and gestured to a chair. "Mark, I assume you've heard the rumors."

"Yes, sir. Major Maddox called me from Tampa a while ago. Thirty thousand combat troops inbound. No official word yet, but it sounds like a done deal."

Sinclair sighed. "And at the same time, we are being ordered to cut back on supporting forces. We're looking at a serious space crunch."

Benson pulled out a notepad. "We can stand up tent cities at Bagram, Kandahar, and Jalalabad, but we'll need more GP Mediums and ECUs. We'll also need to add a bunch of sanitation facilities."

Sinclair rubbed his temple. "How fast can we do that?"

"If we surge engineering teams and contractors, maybe two weeks. But sir, even if we get enough to cover them in the short term, we can't keep them at Bagram for long."

"Agreed," said Sinclair. "What are we going to do with the

non-essential gear? I'm sure that won't be going back to the States."

"No, sir," said Benson. "Most everything will have to be demilitarized and destroyed," he exhaled. "The burn pit is going twenty-four hours a day already. I've also been working to triple the size of the area we are using for DRMO. We've got lots of room in those lots right now."

"Great," replied Sinclair. "What else did you get?"

"We need to send troops out to stay under the cap, but we can use more contractors for sustainment if we want. Maddox tells me that contractors won't be part of the personnel numbers," said Benson.

"That makes no sense," said Sinclair as he rubbed his forehead. "Fuck it. Run the numbers. Find me options."

Benson stood. "Yes, sir. I'll have a plan by 1900."

"Good, thanks."

2

SPECIAL OPERATIONS COMPOUND - BAGRAM AIR BASE

The door of the B-hut opened with a loud raspy squeak, letting a shockingly bright slice of dusty Afghan sunlight into the dark room. The head and shoulders of a man wearing aviator sunglasses and a Washington Nationals baseball cap appeared in the opening, harshly silhouetted by the morning sun. The man spoke with a growling, low voice. "Briggs, get your ass up." He reached for a switch next to the door and turned on the bare fluorescent overhead lights. "We brief in thirty minutes."

There was an extended moment of silence as the human shape in the bed remained totally still. As the visitor was about to step further into the room, Ward Briggs slowly rolled over, checked his G-shock, and saw that it was eight in the morning. He groaned loudly, and then blearily looked up at the man in the doorway and growled, "Kiss my ass Fletcher."

The man in the door laughed. "Yeah, yeah. Easy mission today, just a round robin. Get your ass up."

There was a pause and then another growl. "Fuck this shit."

This time, the curse seemed to be more of a general comment on the universe. "Okay, I'll be there in a minute."

Without another word, the visitor retreated, and the door closed with a bang. Briggs rolled onto his back and stared at the bare plywood ceiling of the B-hut for a minute, trying unsuccessfully to capture the dream that he'd been having. Realizing the attempt was futile, he swung his feet over the side of the bed, stood up, stretched, farted, and then grabbed the towel that was hanging on the back of his door. He shuffled tiredly over to one of the two chairs in the room, rummaged through a pile of laundry that had collected there, and pulled on a pair of gym shorts and a t-shirt. He then retrieved the shaving kit that was hanging from a hook on the wall, slid his feet into his flip-flops, and stepped out of his B-hut into the comfortably warm late-May day in Afghanistan.

While it was hardly a palace, Briggs reflected for the thousandth time that he had scored big with his room. The 18x36 plywood structure known as a B-hut typically housed eight or more men. In this case, the hut he was living in had been divided into halves, giving each resident a decent-sized space that held a single bed and whatever furniture that could be scrounged or built. The occupant of the other side of the hut was an Army Lieutenant Colonel who Briggs rarely saw. Briggs knew something about the special unit that the Colonel supported and wasn't surprised that the officer spent more time out in the field than in his B-hut.

In his room, Briggs had a desk, a couple of chairs, a mini refrigerator, and a small flat-screen television that a previous resident had mounted to the wall. Two plastic-covered windows had been filled with expanding foam and covered with a piece of plywood in an attempt to keep the room dark and ensure that the wind and sand stayed out. He didn't have a closet but had strung some parachute cord between a couple of 2x4s as a place to hang his clothes. He was also fortunate to have a pretty solid "mini-split" heat pump system. It wasn't great, but managed to keep the internal temperature of the uninsulated building about twenty degrees warmer or cooler than the ambient temperature outside.

He walked across the rough gravel between the buildings, being careful not to twist an ankle on the fist-sized rocks that were scattered everywhere. His path took him past several identical B-huts until he came to one of the large Army-style toilet trailers that dotted the compound.

He stepped inside, took care of business, and then walked back out and over to the shower trailer that was next door. There were six stalls in the trailer. One was permanently out of order. He knew from long experience that the stall in the back right had the best water pressure and the least slimy floor.

There was nobody else in the trailer, so he shaved and brushed his teeth with bottled water from a box that was kept by the sink. He then took off his trousers and shirt and hung them on a hook, went to his favorite stall, and took a decent shower with the non-potable water that smelled slightly of the chemicals that had been used by the Army engineers to make it reasonably safe.

Shower complete, Briggs dried off and began the walk back to his B-hut. He paused for a moment when he heard the sound of some A-10 "Warthogs" preparing for takeoff. He couldn't actually see the runway from his spot in the Special Operations compound but could hear the aircraft's distinctive turbofans go to maximum power for takeoff. He watched for a moment as two of the awkward-looking aircraft appeared over the tops of the nearby buildings and skimmed low over the end of the air base. The two planes appeared to hesitate for some time as they built up speed, then climbed sharply to make a sweeping turn to the east. The A-10s were awesome. The Cold War beast that had been built to kill tanks was the perfect counter-insurgency weapon. Everyone but the Air Force was happy that the chain of command had the good sense to bring them to Afghanistan.

Briggs arrived back at his hut, pulled open the door, and stepped inside.

In a smooth and frequently practiced succession, he hung the towel on the back of the door, kicked off his flip-flops, pulled off the athletic shorts, exchanged his t-shirt for a lightweight button-up shirt with rolled-up sleeves that were sold at Bass Pro Shops for fishing, and then pulled a desert-tan flight suit with no rank or name over top of everything.

He sat down on the edge of his bed for a moment, pulled on a pair of socks, and then his well-worn hiking boots. Next, he stood up, looked at a small collection of ball caps hanging from the wall, and decided that it felt like a "Caterpillar" day.

Dressed and ready to go, he threw his access badge around his neck, walked over to the chair by his desk, grabbed the leather shoulder holster and Sig Sauer P-226 pistol that were hanging there, and slung it on. He then picked up a pair of dark sunglasses from his desk, walked across the room, and grabbed his "go bag" by a strap. The bag was a medium-sized dark blue civilian back-pack that contained the gear he would need if he ended up stranded somewhere for a few days.

He turned off the overhead light and stepped outside, pausing for a moment to put his glasses on and throw a combination lock on the door.

He looked at his watch. He had five minutes to spare, so on the way to the operations office, he stopped by the small Green Beans coffee shop. He opened the door and walked into the building that had been constructed from a shipping container.

A middle-aged Asian woman who was sitting on a stool behind the counter and reading from a Kindle looked up and smiled when he walked in. "Good morning, sunshine."

"Good morning, Myra," said Briggs. "Can I get a regular coffee and a muffin?"

The woman stood up and went to one of the coffee urns that was always full and always hot, no matter what time of day it was. "I can get you the coffee, but our next shipment of snacks didn't make it in yet. Maybe later today." She poured the coffee. "One fifty-nine."

He reached into his front pocket and grabbed a handful of cardboard "pogs" that the Exchange used as a replacement for the real coins that were too heavy to ship around a combat zone. He counted them out and handed them over. "Three bucks with a tip."

She took the pogs and handed him the coffee. "Thanks. Sorry about the muffin."

"Ah, no worries," he said. He left the coffee shop and walked the last fifty yards across the compound to the operations office.

THE OFFICE WAS a B-hut with a sign on the door that said, "Detachment Kilo - Ops, Authorized Personnel Only." He pulled open the door and stepped inside. The interior of the building was lighted by a set of naked fluorescent bulbs mounted on the ceiling. There was a massive map of Afghanistan on one wall next to a whiteboard that was covered with notes about a variety of administrative issues.

In the back of the room was a long counter built from scrounged plywood. A middle-aged man was sitting behind the counter, pecking away at a computer. On the wall behind the counter were two T.V. screens; one was showing an Armed Forces Network news program, while the other displayed weather information for a range of regional air bases. All the way at the far end of the counter was a radio that was currently tuned to the Bagram Air Field's ground control frequency, with the volume turned down so that they could just barely hear the transmissions.

"Perfect timing," said a man sitting at a large table in the middle of the room.

Ty Fletcher was still wearing his Washington Nationals ballcap, now with his sunglasses perched on the brim. A few strands of reddish hair curled out from beneath the cap, catching the light as he shifted. He wore a shirt similar to Briggs's but had opted for a green flight suit instead of desert tan. As he lifted a Diet Coke, the faint scatter of freckles on his forearm stood out against his sun-weathered skin, the ink of a Special Forces tattoo partially visible beneath the folded sleeve.

Spread out in front of him were an aviation chart and a few notecards, sized perfectly for a pilot's kneeboard. Briggs dropped his bag beside another already leaning against the wall, set his coffee on the table, and sank into the chair next to Fletcher. His movements were a bit sluggish and tired. "Sorry, that mission yesterday sucked the life out of me. I was beat last night."

"I know," Fletcher said. "I'd have swapped Davidson in on this hop, but he's got that bug that is going around."

"That's all right, I'm good." Briggs took a long sip of his cooling coffee, draining half of it, then reached for a set of kneeboard cards and a printout he recognized as the Air Tasking Order. A few highlighted lines caught his eye - ATHOS 32. The callsign for their ride, a UH-60 Blackhawk.

"This mission shouldn't be bad," Fletcher said. "We take a team of six to Jalalabad, pick up two passengers and some gear, stop by FOB Chapman, drop them off, then grab three more pax and head home. Back in time for dinner."

"How's the weather?" asked Briggs.

"Not bad. Clear and dry. The only issue will be the fact that the one hundred and twenty days of wind is starting. Probably seeing gusts to thirty-five or so by the time we get to Khowst," replied Fletcher.

"Roger. Well, at least we don't have to fight the thunderstorms yet," said Briggs. He picked up one of the pieces of paper and briefly looked at the daily flight schedule that detailed all the missions that their unit, known as Detachment Kilo, was responsible for. He saw that two other crews from the detachment had already headed out for the day; one was heading to Kandahar, and the other was heading to the north to drop some supplies to a FOB in the Pech River valley. "Who is our crew chief?"

"Holland," said Fletcher. "He's out at the aircraft right now."

"Gotcha," said Briggs. He looked at his watch. "Guess we should get moving."

The two men stood up. Briggs walked to the counter and stood across from the man on the computer.

"McCoy, what in the hell are you working on?"

Arthur McCoy looked up, his florid face flushed from frustration. He was tall, with a Marine buzz cut that made his head look even broader. His worn green flight suit had its velcro straps set at their widest, and was still a bit tight around the middle, evidence that he had recently spent more time behind a desk than in the field.

"I am doing fucking paperwork, what does it look like?"

"I won't tell you what it looks like; you wouldn't think it was funny," replied Briggs. "We don't do paperwork anymore. We are civilians, remember?"

"We still work for the damn government," McCoy shot back. "And all the sneaky CIA shit we do still runs through the budget process. How the hell do you think you get paid?"

"I figured it was magic," said Briggs dryly. "But my question is, why in the hell are you doing paperwork? I know you never took a contracting class in your life. You were a Marine for heaven's sake; you can barely read. Hell, you're typing with two fingers right now."

"I'm answering fucking Terrance," McCoy replied, ignoring the jab. "He's visiting Langley. He sent me a note last night and asked me to fill some of this shit out and send it back in a hurry. The boss wants to add something to our mission."

"Oh, the hell with that," said Fletcher, his voice edged with annoyance. "We do enough as it is. We need more people if they want to add more tasking.

"Congress is sending money over here in fucking dump-truck loads," said McCoy. "Langley can get whatever it wants as long as they say we are looking for Osama-fucking-Bin-Laden." The name came out in a smooth, multi-syllable way that was indicative of its frequent usage.

"What do they want to add?" asked Briggs.

"Some night raids," said McCoy. "Langley wants to be able to do some of its own. The military Special Ops teams have a different targeting agenda here, and our lists don't quite match."

"Do night raids? With who?" asked Briggs. "That would take an entirely different setup. We'd need more helos and a lot of gear, not to mention at least a few people who know what the fuck they are doing."

"Well, you were an Army helo pilot for two decades," replied McCoy. "You even flew for the 160th. The boss knows you have some skills."

"And I was smart enough to get out when I could," said Briggs.

"And yet, here you are," replied McCoy sarcastically. "So you aren't that smart Army boy. Anyway, don't get too worked up about it. It probably won't start for months. They are looking for some of the new Blackhawks. They are also thinking about buying a couple of MI-17s and making them look like they are from the ANA, but that will take some time."

"Yeah. Well, if he asks, you can tell Winters that's a hard pass from me," said Briggs.

"If the boss says he wants us to do it, we do it. You can quit any time," replied McCoy neutrally. He looked up at the clock. "But today, you need to take a team to J-bad, and you are almost late."

"We're moving." Briggs reached for a logbook that said "Weapons" on the front. Flipped to the open page and said, "I'm waiting."

"Yeah, yeah. On it," said McCoy. He stood up and walked over to a rack of M-4 rifles, pulled one out, cleared it, and read the serial number out loud. Briggs copied the number to the book and signed his name. McCoy handed him the rifle and a plate carrier that included eight loaded magazines in the chest pockets. When Briggs was done, Fletcher stepped forward and filled out the logbook while McCoy returned to grab the second rifle and gear.

As he waited, Briggs walked to the end of the counter, where there was a large cardboard box full of random food that people had brought back from the dining facility. He rummaged around inside for a moment and found a blueberry muffin wrapped in cellophane - a small victory. He turned to McCoy. "See you this evening."

"Have a good hop," replied McCoy as he returned to his paperwork.

* * *

NEAR KHAJEH KOWT - GARDEZ-KHOST HIGHWAY

"That doesn't seem like a good idea, Dittman," said Ryan Ross. "If we go up to that village right now, we're still going to be on the road after dark."

The two men sat in an up-armored Humvee, its desert-tan paint dulled by months of dust and hard miles. Through the dirty windshield, they watched as twenty of their Afghan National Army counterparts strolled lazily across a cultivated field towards two battered cargo trucks that served as their transport.

The team had just wrapped up a meeting in Khvajeh Kowt, a small village straddling the Gardez-Khost highway. Their mission had been to gather intelligence on Taliban leadership rumored to be operating in the area, but instead, they'd picked up a lead on a bomb maker - one skilled with Radio-Controlled Improvised Explosive Devices, or RCIEDs, and active in the region around Khost.

The tip had come from a village elder, a grizzled old man who had long been known to trade information for the right price. Dittman and his team carried a bag of cash for precisely this purpose. Today's intel had cost the U.S. government a mere two hundred dollars - cheap enough that both operatives suspected personal motivation. Someone close to the elder had likely been maimed or killed by one of the bomber's devices. Religion was a factor in many of these interactions, but revenge was a currency as old as the land itself.

Peter Dittman, perched in the driver's seat, studied a map spread across the Humvee's dashboard. His sun-seared skin and deeply lined face told the story of a man who had spent two hard years working Afghanistan's shadowy underbelly. Now, he weighed the risk: leave the safety of the highway and push twenty klicks into the hills in search of a rumor, or stick to the plan and return to base.

"I don't think we'd be that late," Dittman said, his voice rasping from years of alcohol and cigarettes. "You know as soon as we leave here, the old man's going to let everyone know who we're looking for. If we move now, we might still have some surprise."

"Bullshit," Ross shot back. "First off, you know that someone from the village has already radioed a warning. Second, we're here to track Taliban leadership, not bomb-makers. That's the Special Operations Task Force's job. And even if we did go, we wouldn't catch him just rolling into his village. The only time they ever bag these guys is on night raids."

Dittman exhaled sharply. "I know," he admitted. "But when we submit this name, it's going to crawl through the intel pipeline, bounce around CENTCOM for weeks before it makes the target list. Meanwhile, this asshole keeps planting bombs on the same highway we drive every other day."

The pair sat in silence, each weighing the difficulty of their work.

After a moment, Dittman sighed tiredly. "Let's head back to

Khost for now." He tapped a finger on the map. "The road up to the valley is a few klicks away. When we get there, we'll take a look and decide then."

With that, he twisted the Humvee's ignition. The diesel engine rumbled to life, coughing a thick cloud of black exhaust into the dry Afghan air.

The armored passenger-side rear door creaked open with a piercing squeal, and Janan Quazi, their young Afghan interpreter, climbed in. He reached into a battered cardboard box full of water bottles and held one up.

"The ANA are ready to go," Quazi said. "You guys want water?"

"Nah," Ross replied. "We're good. Thanks, Quazi."

The convoy - two Humvees and a pair of ancient cargo trucks carrying ten ANA troops each - was ready to roll.

The radio crackled to life. "We've got the lead if you're ready to go," said Spencer Powell, the driver of the second Humvee. Along with Juan Martinez, he made up the rest of the CIA paramilitary team on this trip.

Ross grabbed the handset. "Let's move."

* * *

SPERA, AFGHANISTAN

Nabil Hamid looked at his new protege, seventeen-year-old Azeem, with pride. "Good job. That bomb is well constructed. Now, place it in the container with the rest of them."

The teen carefully picked up the Radio Controlled Improvised Explosive Device, or RCIED, and put it into a wooden box that was filled with straw. The box itself had been placed in a three-foot deep hole in the floor of the adobe house so that if the Americans came, it could be quickly covered by a cleverly disguised set of bricks that made it look like it was part of the floor.

Hamid had been traveling around Khost for more than a month. He had been tasked to spread his knowledge of bomb-making to as many students as he could find, and young Azeem was one of the best. Prior to the invasion, the young man had been a student at one of the region's better schools and, in other circumstances, might have eventually made it to Pakistan for college. However, now that Afghanistan was at war with America, it seemed a certainty that the young man would be more valuable to the Taliban here in his local mountains, making bombs.

Hamid moved from the low table that they had been using as a workbench, stepped to the open door of the building, and stretched - trying to shake off the stress of three hours of building explosives. He looked out across the courtyard in front of the house and up into the towering mountains. The village was as quiet and pastoral as one could imagine.

The scenery was much different than his native Quetta. He had grown up in the claustrophobic city, joined the Pakistani Army, and had learned his trade skirmishing with the Indian Army along the wide-open borders of Pakistani-administered Kashmir. When the Americans had invaded Afghanistan, he had been transferred to the Pakistani intelligence service known as the ISI and soon found himself on the border, where he had made contact with the Tehrik-e Taliban.

In what could only be described as a byzantine web of relationships, he was now helping the Taliban fight the Americans so that they would stop disrupting northern Pakistan. Hamid wasn't sure of the logic, but years of conflict were making him increasingly numb to the politics of his job; he just did what he was told.

A young boy ran across the dusty courtyard and stopped in front of Hamid. He was clearly excited to be allowed to talk to the important foreigner. "Sir, sir. There is a message for you on the radio."

Hamid turned back into the house. "Azeem, why don't you prepare two of those bombs for travel? I am going to the radio."

Azeem nodded and, without a word, began to prepare one of the special backpacks that Hamid had brought with him.

Hamid walked across the courtyard through a gate in the tall adobe wall that surrounded his compound and across the village. When he had first arrived, he had ensured that the villagers had understood that it was critically important to keep the radios as far away from the bombs as practical. He entered the village elder's hut and found three of the local farmers gathered around one of the high-powered push-to-talk handsets that provided the basis of all the communications in the region. These were simple, unencrypted radios that allowed the locals to communicate for tens of kilometers up and down the valley. Prior to the war, they were used to coordinate the essentials of village life, however, now they were the network that connected the Taliban with all of the local leaders.

Hamid nodded to the men. "What have we heard?"

"The Americans on the highway have finished their meeting and are heading to the east on the highway," replied one of the elder men. "They have been told of your presence."

Hamid considered the information. The American CIA had been working in and around Khost for years, looking for their chief enemy, Osama bin-Laden. Until recently, they hadn't spent much time worried about the bombs that were killing American soldiers and the ANA troops that worked with them, but that seemed to be changing. One of his bombs had been successful against a team of Americans a few days prior, and now there were men in the area asking about him. Hamid knew their search meant very little, the Taliban would protect him as long as he was in the mountains. It was America's sophisticated technical intelligence that created the most risk.

This was not his only challenge. Unfortunately, one of the first bombs he had prepared had killed a local family headed to

Khost in a pickup truck. A man, his wife, and their eight-year-old daughter had died when the truck had accidentally triggered an IED. Although the local Taliban had made it clear to the family's relatives that they would not tolerate any reprisals against Hamid, he knew that this would not keep the villagers from seeking revenge. Wounds like this festered for generations in the little villages that were spread across the region. He would have to watch his back.

"They will be gone by the time I can get down there to set up an ambush," said Hamid. "Why don't you see if young Azzat's team can harass them on the way east? We will set a better attack up the next time they visit."

The man nodded. Another of the men in the room got on the radio and issued the order to the five-man team that was waiting along the road for such tasking. When his short conversation was complete, he turned back to Hamid. "They will strike and, with any luck, will kill a few. Allah Akbar."

Hamid, already thinking about what he needed to do next, absently looked up and replied, "Inshallah. Allah Akbar."

* * *

SPECIAL OPERATIONS FLIGHT LINE - BAGRAM AIR BASE

Briggs and Fletcher walked out of the B-hut and made their way out of the compound.

Bagram Air Base was a massive complex. Not only was it the base for dozens of combat aircraft, but it was also the largest combat support facility in the northern half of Afghanistan and was the home of tens of thousands of American and NATO troops. While the concept was "one team, one fight," in actuality, the huge facility was divided up into dozens of different fiefdoms, defined by their nationality, service, branch, or mission. Most of these areas were separated by "Hesco" barriers or tall barbed-wire fences. The Hescos were clever expandable metal and cloth containers that were delivered flat, but when they were filled with dirt, they created effective, semi-permanent battlements. The exterior walls that ringed the entire base were at least two Hescos wide at the base, with one or more rows piled on top, resulting in a twelve-foot-tall battlement that was entirely covered by razor wire.

When it came to Aviation Detachment Kilo, they were tucked inside of the U.S. Special Operations Command compound. This had many advantages. While most of the base tended to suffer from the fact that everyone was transient, the Special Operations compound was maintained at the highest standards. The B-huts were painted a uniform brown, the green sandbags around the bomb shelters were all properly filled, the DFAC where they ate was excellent, and everything that needed to work worked. In the center of the compound was a much larger three-story building that housed the headquarters of Joint Special Operations Command, Afghanistan. The headquarters building contained an amazing amount of American technology and served as the home for the dozens of staffers who organized the missions that JSOC ran.

Briggs tried to stay out of the headquarters building as much as possible, but when he was forced to visit, he was always astonished by the amazing power displayed by JSOC. On the operations floor, there were a dozen massive screens that displayed current missions, cable news, and anything that the team on the operations floor needed to see, from satellite intelligence to drone video. It always occurred to him that if there was one thing better than the nice facilities, it was the fact that the people in the compound were all professionals, discipline was good, everyone knew that they had a mission, and they were almost all entirely focused.

. . .

THE TWO MEN walked through the well-guarded compound gate, crossed the main road that had been named "Disney Drive" after an airman who had been killed early in the base's reconstruction, and wound their way through a warren of temporary buildings and tent-like hangars to their small flight line facilities. They arrived at a security gate that surrounded the Special Operations flightline, showed their badges to the armed guard, and were waved inside. Another short walk later, they came to B-hut with "Detachment Kilo - Maintenance" on the door and stepped inside. The interior of the building had a long counter near the front door, and the rest of the building had been divided into four small offices. There were two men who barely looked up when the door opened. One was sitting at the counter typing away on a computer terminal, the other was looking intensely at a maintenance manual. There were more aircraft maintenance manuals on a shelf along the wall and numerous boxes of aircraft parts stacked neatly on the floor.

The man on the computer stopped typing and looked up. "Your helo is ready." He reached below the counter, pulled out a large three-ring binder, and slid it over. The binder was labeled "Blackhawk: Tail 05-0422."

"Thanks," said Briggs simply.

Fletcher had reached the counter first, so he opened the binder and started paging through it quickly, reading the aircraft's maintenance history. They had both flown the helicopter recently, but it always paid to see if there was anything new from a different crew or one of the constant maintenance inspections. When he was done, he slid the book over to Briggs, who looked at the last few sheets and then leaned over and signed a sheet of paper inside, taking responsibility for the aircraft.

"Try not to break it today," said a voice from the back of the building.

Briggs looked up and saw that Matt Rathbine had stepped out

of his tiny office and was leaning against the door looking at them.

"We'll do what we can Master Chief," said Briggs, knowing that it made the retired Navy senior enlisted maintenance man happy to be referred to by his old rank.

"I am sure you will Warrant," said Rathbine, referring to Briggs' rank in the Army when he retired.

PAPERWORK COMPLETE, the two aviators gathered their gear and walked from the B-hut out to the tarmac. Their small maintenance area was on the northeast side of the massive air base, hidden among the AC-130s and other Special Operations aircraft that were parked on the ramp. They passed the large multi-engine CASA 235, and a Twin Otter DHC-6 that they both also occasionally flew and then came to a stop in front of a single-engine Pilatus PC-6 that had three maintenance personnel huddled under the right wing looking up at the surface, their crossed arms indicative of quiet frustration.

"What happened this time?" asked Fletcher as they walked up.

The men turned to face the two pilots. Kody Bishop, one of their most qualified maintenance managers, and a man who always had a dip in his lower lip, replied. "Well," he began in a very southern drawl. "Davidson and Walton took a few PKM rounds through the wing on their trip back from Mazar E-Sharif yesterday. Somehow nobody seemed to notice until we tried to refuel it last night and pissed gas all over the ramp."

Briggs stepped up and looked at the aircraft. He saw that somebody had circled two holes in the underside of the wing with a grease pencil. "That's a respectable grouping. Is that repairable out here?"

"Sure," said Bishop laconically. "A little bit of duct tape, and we will be good." He laughed when he saw the look on Brigg's face. "Yeah, unfortunately, the rounds went through the fuel bladder. It is going to be out for at least two months or so while we get her repaired." He paused for a moment, "Please don't get the Blackhawk shot up today. We are running out of airplanes."

"Ah, this is just a milk run today," said Fletcher.

"Sure," said Bishop, gesturing to the wing of the damaged aircraft. "So was last night."

He turned back to the repairs, and the two pilots turned and walked another few yards down the flight line and up to the unmarked UH-60 Blackhawk that they would be flying.

As they approached the aircraft, a young man in a desert tan flight suit stepped out of the fuselage door and walked over. "She looks fine," said Kyle Holland. "The team will be back here in a couple of minutes. I already packed their gear." Holland was one of the younger men in the unit. Everyone in the detachment was a veteran, and most had extensive combat experience. Holland was the exception, he had only served a single four-year tour in the Navy as a helicopter air crewman before getting out and becoming a member of the CIA. Despite his inexperience, he was a solid team member, and Briggs liked flying with him.

"Great," said Briggs. He started at the front of the helicopter and walked around the aircraft clockwise, while Fletcher walked around counter-clockwise, a pre-flight inspection routine that they had settled on when they first began flying together.

THE UH-60 WAS the perfect aircraft for Afghanistan. The twin-engine helicopter had been designed from the ground up for combat support, and the aircraft's capability had been well proven by both the Army and the Navy in operations around the globe. It was a rugged machine that could carry ten people in its current configuration, cruise at up to 150 knots, and stay airborne for hours. While access to the highest terrain in Afghanistan could be problematic, the aircraft could land almost anywhere, and it was a good match for the requirements of the

CIA and the special operations teams that used them. Their particular aircraft was almost identical to the Army helicopters that operated from the other end of the base, with the notable exception that there was nothing but a number painted on the tail.

FINISHED WITH PREFLIGHT, Briggs climbed into the cockpit. He and Fletcher generally alternated pilot and co-pilot duties, and it was his turn to fly from the right, or pilot's seat. He stored his bag and weapon behind the cockpit and then sat down and buckled himself in. He turned on the battery and began to warm up the electronics and program the navigation computer. He had just turned on the GPS when he looked out of his windscreen and saw six men walking casually towards the aircraft.

While they weren't in uniform, the men walking towards the aircraft were clearly from a similar background. All of them were very fit and tanned, wearing ball caps and dark wrap-around sunglasses that hugged their faces. One of the men was black and one was Asian, with a surprisingly healthy beard. They all were wearing tan cargo pants, but some had camouflage shirts, while others wore light-colored sporting shirts similar to his own. All were armed, wearing tactical rigs and had pistols in a holster halfway down their thigh. A couple of the men had additional small backpacks slung over their shoulders. As he did his preflight Briggs had seen that their combat gear already had been loaded in the helicopter.

Afghanistan was filled with teams like this, and Briggs had frequently reflected that this was literally the heyday for a certain type of armed adventurer. If you were disciplined and professional, you could work for the world's wealthiest and most powerful government, use the most sophisticated technology available, and literally hunt humans in one of the harshest social and physical environments on the planet. If you just wanted to wear dark sunglasses and carry a gun, you could get hired by one of the many civilian companies that frequently made headlines for their excesses or failures. Essentially, if you wanted to shoot humans without much risk of going to jail, this was the place to be.

Briggs had seen the manifest and knew that this particular team was a paramilitary group from Langley, rotating into the Jalalabad area to continue the perpetual hunt for Osama bin Laden, OBL - or confusingly, sometimes UBL. The CIA, generally known as "the agency" or "Other Government Agency" by the military, had a large presence at Jalalabad, or J-bad. The austere base sat at the foot of the White Mountains, where OBL had made his home while conducting his war against the United States. There were new rumors every day about the location of OBL, many of which suggested that he was still hiding in one of his caves in the exceptionally rugged mountains. Teams like the one they were taking to J-bad were gradually combing all of the caves in the hills, investigating every lead. Briggs had no doubt that they would eventually find him.

FLETCHER CLIMBED INTO THE AIRCRAFT, stored his gear, and took the copilot's seat. They began working through their pre-start checklist. While either of the men could have started the aircraft in their sleep, they forced themselves to use checklists and stick to their training, because they both knew men who hadn't and had died as a result of forgetting something when tired or under stress.

After a few minutes, the paramilitary team filed onto the helicopter, sat down in the lightweight seats, and buckled in without needing to be told. Holland moved into a position outside on the tarmac where both Briggs and Fletcher could see him as they started the two turbine engines. When both engine starts were complete, he gave them a thumbs up. Next, climbed into the back of the aircraft and plugged his headset into the intercom system.

"All buttoned up and secured back here."

"Roger," replied Fletcher. He then switched to his radio, "Bagram ground, ATHOS 32, hover taxi to spot Echo."

"ATHOS 32 cleared to taxi to spot Echo. Altimeter 30.01," replied ground control.

"ATHOS 32 cleared to taxi. 30.01," replied Fletcher.

The good thing about working from the SOCOM hangar was that it kept them away from the most curious eyeballs. They were at the north end of the field, and their equipment was lost among the rest of the wide-ranging collection of aircraft that SOCOM used.

If it was a miserably hot day, they would leave the doors open while they taxied. Today, however, it was a comfortable seventy degrees or so, and extra ventilation wasn't required. It only took a few minutes to taxi to the north helicopter pad.

THEY STOPPED for a moment and watched as a gray Navy EA-6B electronic warfare aircraft lined up on the runway in preparation for takeoff. The odd-looking tactical jet was a surprising sight in Afghanistan because it was usually based on an aircraft carrier. Briggs didn't know what the Navy's electronic warfare crews were doing, but it didn't take a rocket scientist to know that they were jamming something important, as they were usually airborne around the clock. At some point, he intended to walk down the flight line and try to get a tour of the jet from one of the crews, but he never seemed to find the time.

The EA-6B went to max power, and the noise was so loud that it made the Blackhawk shudder. For Briggs, it felt as if the noise was vibrating the fillings out of his teeth. After hesitating for a moment, the Navy jet released its brakes and began to roll down the ten thousand-foot-long runway. It seemed like it took a long time for the EA-6B to get airborne, and it stayed very low to the ground for a few miles outside the field before it quickly climbed into the sky, leaving a trail of darkish exhaust behind it.

Fletcher turned around to the passengers, "You guys ready to go?"

One of the operators gave a thumbs up.

Holland answered, "All good."

"Bagram tower, ATHOS 32 for takeoff, pad Echo. Departing to the east."

"ATHOS 32 cleared for takeoff, pad Echo. Cleared to switch."

Briggs increased power, checked all the engine instruments, got a "Looks good" from Fletcher, and then pulled up on the collective and began an easy climb. Unlike the EA-6B, which had taken more than half the runway to get airborne, the Blackhawk rose quickly into the air. Now airborne, Briggs waited a few moments for the airspeed to increase and then started a slow right-hand turn towards Jalalabad.

3

JALALABAD AIR BASE

"Jalalabad Tower, ATHOS 32 is ten miles out for runway one-three," said Ty Fletcher.

"ATHOS 32, you are cleared for the approach on runway one-three and then spot Bravo. Winds are calm. Your traffic is three H-60s departing the field to the south."

"ATHOS 32 is looking for the traffic. Cleared to land runway one three, spot Bravo."

Briggs saw the three helicopters first. "Traffic in sight. Right one o'clock. No factor."

"Roger," replied Fletcher.

As they approached the field, they skimmed over the top of several clay-walled homes, flew over the stacked Hesco barriers that surrounded the base, and brought the helicopter to a low hover down the first third of the runway. After a few moments of hover taxiing, they turned off the runway.

"Jalalabad ground, ATHOS 32 is off at midfield for the terminal for Bravo," said Fletcher.

"ATHOS 32, you are cleared to Bravo."

. . .

Briggs landed and then taxied slowly towards the terminal. Eventually, he saw a man in a safety vest walk out from one of the nearby shelters. The man waved them over and directed the aircraft into one of the several marked parking spots. When they came to a stop, Fletcher said, "Brakes are set."

"Roger," said Holland, and they heard the cargo door open, letting in a blast of warmth. Holland jumped out of the open door, walked under the airplane, stepped into Briggs' vision, and gave him a thumbs up. Briggs said, "Shutting her down," and cut the fuel to each engine in turn, immediately reducing the sound. The rotors windmilled for a minute or so and gradually came to a stop.

Fletcher pulled off his headphones, turned, and looked at the passengers. "You guys are cleared to get out. Kyle will help you unload your gear."

"Thanks," said one of the men, and the nearly silent group climbed from the helicopter and waited by the door for their gear.

Briggs and Fletcher worked through the post-flight checklist, noted the hours and fuel state in a logbook, and climbed out of the Blackhawk. Holland had already begun unstrapping the various bags and gun cases and was handing gear to the team. Fletcher peeled off to help him, and Briggs got out and did a quick walk around the aircraft, mostly focusing on the tires that tended to wear out faster because of the sand and rocks that were everywhere. Everything looked good. When the cargo was clear, the three aircrew walked into the terminal with the six passengers. As they arrived outside the terminal, they were met by a bearded man in civilian clothes who nodded to the flight crew and led the passengers off into the base.

"We have time for lunch, right?" asked Holland.

Fletcher looked at his watch. "Yeah, as long as it is quick." The three walked to the small base operations office, and Briggs stepped inside while the two other men waited. He came back out after a couple of minutes. "Nothing changed. The detachment will bring the gear over in about thirty minutes. We still have two passengers, but they haven't shown up yet."

"Let's go to lunch," said Fletcher.

They walked through the small terminal and out of security onto the dusty road through the center of the northern side of the base. After about a hundred yards, they turned and walked into a large tent with a sign that said "DFAC." As they walked into the facility, they each showed their badges to the Afghan attendant at the door and then continued inside.

The DFAC wasn't particularly busy. They had all been there dozens of times. Fletcher headed straight towards the grill, where he could get one of the burgers that he apparently lived on. Briggs walked to the salad bar, made a monster salad, and grabbed a large iced tea. Holland hesitated, looked at the spaghetti that was being served on the main line for a couple of seconds, and then followed Fletcher over to the grill. Being the first one ready with his food, Briggs found an empty table, sat down, and began to eat. Within five minutes, the other two men arrived and sat down.

"Do you want to try to cut through the mountains to Khost or go all the way around?" asked Fletcher in between bites of his burger.

"It's your leg, but the weather is pretty good," replied Briggs. "I don't know why we shouldn't cut the corner today."

"Sounds good to me," said Fletcher.

* * *

NEAR KHAJEH KOWT - GARDEZ-KHOST HIGHWAY

The small convoy had stopped at the entrance to the shallow valley where they had been told that the bombmaker was working. Dittman had left the humvee running but got out of the truck with a pair of binoculars and threw the map over the hood.

Ross got out, walked over, and looked at the map with him. Dittman then stepped away from the truck and scanned the terrain. Neither man said a word for a few minutes.

Dittman turned to Ross and pulled the binoculars from his face. "We aren't going to go up there today. Next time we visit the area, we will be better prepared."

"Sounds good," said Ross as he sighed with relief. "Not gonna lie, I am glad. I think that going up there would have been trouble."

Dittman grunted and folded up the map. "How about taking a few pictures of this intersection and what we can see of the road up the valley? We'll put them in the file for when we come back." Without another word, he walked back to the driver's side door, climbed in, and pulled it closed.

"Will do," replied Ross. He walked back around the truck, leaned in, and grabbed a digital camera. He spent a few minutes taking photos of the area. When he was done, he climbed back into the Humvee and grabbed the radio. "We are RTB."

"Roger," came the response from Powell. "Moving."

The convoy started again. Ross looked at his watch, he figured that they should be back in the compound by about four p.m.

* * *

DFAC - JALALABAD AIR BASE

As they were wrapping up lunch, Briggs saw two men enter the DFAC, look around, and then head straight towards them.

"Briggs, Fletcher, you guys enjoying yourselves?" came the high-pitched voice of Michael Gray. Gray was a tall and skinny man with a patchy and thin beard that just didn't work with his face. He was wearing what the Special Operations guys called "consumer camouflage" and looked more like a tourist than a CIA paramilitary pilot.

"Well, I was until you showed up," replied Fletcher dryly. "I thought you rotated home a couple of months ago, Mike."

"I'm supporting a special project now," said Gray. He sat down too close to Briggs and didn't introduce the other man, who sat further down the table without a word.

"I don't want to hear about it," said Briggs. "I'm glad you found something to do."

"Oh, you'll hear about it soon enough," said Gray in a tone that suggested that he was almost begging for them to ask.

"I'm sure it can wait," said Briggs.

Gray looked disappointed. "We are the two passengers for your leg to FOB Chapman. You guys want to let me fly as copilot?"

"You know that would break detachment regulations, Mike," replied Briggs calmly.

"Okay, just asking," Gray said quickly. He pointed at the silent man with whom he had walked in. "That's Matt Barnes, he's here from Langley's aviation leadership to take a look at all our facilities. He is putting together a new project."

Barnes nodded at hearing his name but didn't say anything.

Briggs looked at Barnes for a long moment. "You were at Balad in 2004."

Barnes smiled. "Yeah, I was flying Chinooks. We helped you guys from the 160th a couple of times."

"That operation was a total shit show," said Briggs. "But you guys did good." He paused for a moment. "You can't have been with Langley for long."

"Nope," replied Barnes. "This is my first trip for them. I think they are taking advantage of the fact that I still have contacts in the Army."

"Yup," said Briggs wearily. "Taking advantage of people is what they do best."

* * *

VILLAGE ABOVE THE KHOST-GARDEZ HIGHWAY

Azzat was excited, the village elders had finally given him permission to attack the infidels with his own team. He motioned his small group of men to gather around. Three of the men were armed with old AK-47s and one with an PKM machine gun.

"We will attack the Americans at the lower highway curve." He paused. "I will try to trigger a bomb under one of the troop transports, perhaps we can kill a dozen or more."

He pointed at the man with the machine gun, "Batoor, we only have four hundred rounds, so you will fire carefully and defend us from counter-attack." He looked at his youngest team member. "Nangial, you have the best eyes. You will try to shoot the Americans with your rifle." He looked up. "The rest of us will make their lives difficult for some time, and then we will leave before they call in aircraft for support." He stood up. "Let's move, we have less than an hour to set up."

Nangial stood and said "Allah Akbar!"

"Allah Akbar!" replied the rest of the men in a ragged chorus.

* * *

BASE OPERATIONS - JALALABAD AIR BASE

Briggs, Fletcher, and Holland had dropped the two passengers off in base operations to wait while they prepared the aircraft. As they walked across the ramp to the Blackhawk, a forklift drove up carrying two small pallets stacked on top of one another. Both were wrapped with plastic and tightly taped.

Holland opened a side door of the chopper and pulled out some tie-down straps. Fletcher looked at the paperwork for the transfer package, noting that one of the pallets contained some Class C explosives, while the other one listed some lithium batteries. Both were going to the large CIA detachment in Khost.

While Briggs did another walk around the helicopter,

Fletcher and Holland loaded the pallets into the cargo area and strapped them down tightly. Then Holland walked back towards base operations to retrieve their passengers.

Fletcher climbed into the helicopter, took his place in the left seat, and began working through the pre-start checklist. Briggs had stopped to grab a bottle of water from a box in the back and then took the right seat. Within a few minutes, both Gray and Barnes arrived, each carrying a large backpack. Holland strapped the packs down in the rear on top of the pallets and handed them each a headset so that they could talk with the crew. The two passengers took the first two seats immediately behind the cockpit.

"I sure miss this," said Gray.

"You know that you can come back any time," said Briggs. "There is plenty of flying to go around; both here and Iraq."

"Ah, I've got some kind of inner ear problem. Can't pass a flight physical at the moment," replied Gray. "They've got me working on scheduling and stuff for a while. I'm just a tour guide for this trip."

"Copy," said Briggs. "That's too bad," he said, trying to sound sincere.

Fletcher and Briggs worked their way through the checklist and started both engines. Holland gave them a thumb's up, climbed in, and secured the doors. "I'm in."

"Jalalabad Ground, ATHOS 32 for taxi," said Briggs.

"ATHOS 32, taxi to runway 31, winds 330 at 12, gusting to 18. Altimeter 30.02,"

"ATHOS 32 is cleared to taxi, altimeter 30.02," replied Briggs.

The helicopter taxied to the hold short of runway 31. "Everybody good?" asked Fletcher.

"All good," came a couple of voices.

"Tower, ATHOS 32, ready for takeoff," said Briggs.

"ATHOS 32 is cleared to take off runway 31. Winds 340 at 10."

"ATHOS 32 is cleared to take off runway 31," replied Briggs.

Fletcher checked the instruments, advanced the throttles, and pulled up on the collective. Within moments, the Blackhawk climbed into the bright blue Afghan sky.

* * *

ON THE KHOST-GARDEZ HIGHWAY

"This is the spot where those special forces guys got hit last week," said Spencer Powell, pointing to a crater on the left side of the road surrounded by debris from the vehicle that had been hit. Powell was driving the lead humvee with Juan Martinez in the passenger seat. They were making decent time, probably averaging about fifteen miles an hour on the rugged highway. Parts of it were paved, but there were miles-long stretches that were essentially just a gravel or sandy path in a dry riverbed.

"Yeah," said Martinez. "Got it. We can slide to the right side of the riverbed if you want. We just need to try to stay in the large tracks."

Powell guided the Humvee into a wide area of the dry riverbed that had dozens of tracks from other vehicles on it. The two trucks with the ANA soldiers followed them, each spaced about twenty meters apart. In the final humvee, Dittman and Ross stayed another twenty or so meters behind the trucks and kept an eye on the group from the rear.

They had gone another six kilometers down the riverbed when most of the tire tracks led out of the riverbed to a decent stretch of pavement. The men preferred driving on tarmac, as it was harder to hide an IED, so Powell followed the tracks, turned out of the gravel, and drove the humvee over the bump at the ragged edge of the road. They had only gone about a few dozen meters further down the road when there was a massive, ear-shattering explosion from behind them.

* * *

HILLSIDE ABOVE KHOST-GARDEZ HIGHWAY

Azzat watched the four vehicles slowly crawl along the rocky riverbed from a few hundred meters away on the side of a steep mountain slope. In his heart, he wanted to strike one of the American humvees, but he knew his Taliban instructors would tell him to attack one of the trucks that was loaded with ANA troops. He carried two detonators in his pocket; they were based on key fobs that unlocked car doors, but these had been specially amplified so that a bomber could strike from a surprisingly long distance. Both were simple and used electronics that he had been told came from Iran but which had probably originated in China. Neither had any safety device, but were kept in small plastic baggies without their batteries attached until they were required for use.

Today, he had access to two bombs at this location. One of the bombs had been set on the far side of the riverbed, and the other at the transition from sand and gravel to the tarmac. Azzat had emplaced both bombs himself in the manner that he had been instructed by the foreigner, carefully leaving a few feet of very thin wire on the surface to act as an antenna.

It looked as if the Americans were going to take the route that took them back onto the tarmac, so Azzat quickly pulled a new nine-volt battery from his equipment bag and attached it to the correct detonator. The system was now live.

The first humvee rolled over the site of the bomb and onto the tarmac. The truck behind the Americans slowed for a moment, presumably so that it would not toss the soldiers in the back of the truck around. As the driver slowly drove up and onto the road, the vehicle rolled almost directly over the buried explosive.

"Allah Akbar," said Azzat quietly, and he pressed the trigger. There was a nanosecond delay that seemed to stretch for forever, and Azzat thought that the attack might have failed - then there was a gratifyingly massive explosion that lifted the front of the truck a meter into the air, before it crashed back to earth.

Azzat yelled, "Fire, fire!" to his small unit, but his command was unnecessary. He heard Batoor firing the PKM from a few meters away and the slow but steady aimed fire from Nangial lying on the ground near him. The other two men were peppering the area around the enemy. He picked up his own AK-47 and began to shoot at the ANA troops who were now running for safety, some of them without weapons, thinking to himself, "Cowards."

* * *

ON THE KHOST-GARDEZ HIGHWAY

Powell slammed the Humvee to a stop.

"IED, IED!" Martinez's voice tore through the radio. "I've got the gun mount."

He scrambled into the back, awkwardly positioning himself behind the M-240 machine-gun in the turret. A few bursts from a PKM cracked through the air, followed by the distinct, sharper pops of AK fire from the hills above. With no clear target, Martinez laid down suppressing fire, sweeping bursts along the rugged cliffs to keep the Taliban pinned down.

In the trailing Humvee, Dittman and Ross had an unbroken view of the blast. The first ANA truck erupted in a deafening explosion, its front end lifting nearly three feet before crashing back into the shallow crater. The concussion sent a wave of dust and shrapnel skyward, pebbles and jagged metal fragments clattering against the Humvee's armor like hail. Then, as the dust settled, the unmistakable chatter of an PKM and several AKs again echoed from the ridgeline.

"I'm on the gun!" Quazi shouted.

The interpreter yanked himself into the turret, chambered a

round in the M-240, and opened fire, sweeping his shots across the hillsides that might provide cover for the enemy.

Below them, chaos unfolded. ANA soldiers bailed from the backs of both trucks - some clutching their rifles, others running full-tilt, gear forgotten, desperation in every movement. They dove for a roadside ditch, vanishing into whatever cover they could find.

Dittman turned at the long burst of machine-gun fire behind him. "Quazi, don't burn up all our ammo. We might be here for a while."

"Roger!" Quazi shouted, shifting to more disciplined two- and three-round bursts.

Ross grabbed his M-4 rifle and a first-aid bag from the back. "I'm going to check the casualties."

He yanked the door open, hesitated just long enough to time his sprint, then bolted toward the wrecked ANA truck.

Dittman keyed his radio. "Powell, Martinez, you guys okay?"

"We're good up here," Powell called back over the machine gun's steady thumping. "But that first truck took a beating."

"Tell Martinez to conserve ammo; this might take some time to recover."

"Will do."

Dittman reached for the satellite phone, dialing the Joint Operations Center at FOB Salerno, the main Army hub north of FOB Chapman.

"JOC Salerno," a voice answered.

"This is CREST 8," Dittman said, voice steady. "I am declaring a Troops in Contact at the following grid." He glanced at the chart and rattled off their coordinates. "ANA truck hit an IED. Unknown casualties at this time."

"Copy all, CREST 8. You've declared a TIC. Grid received. Do you need air support?"

Dittman hesitated. The PKM still fired sporadically, but the

AKs had gone quiet. "Not yet. We'll probably need a dust-off, though. I'll call back once we assess casualties."

As he turned, his eyes locked onto a slow-moving Jingle truck that had stopped a few hundred meters up the road.

"Quazi, don't let anyone get past us. I'm going out."

He grabbed his M-4, threw open the Humvee door, and sprinted to the wrecked truck. A quick scan of the interior revealed scattered water bottles, torn uniforms, and abandoned AK-47s. No movement. He rounded the front of the truck, finding two ANA soldiers stretched out in the shade. One lay still, his head and shoulders covered with a jacket. The other moaned weakly, legs sprawled awkwardly in the dust. Ross and two ANA medics were working on him.

"What do you have?"

"One KIA from shrapnel," Ross said. "This guy probably has a broken back. Took some hits along his legs, but nothing critical that I can see. He's pretty pale, though. We need to move him somewhere stable."

Dittman crouched beside the wounded man, scanning the ridge above. "Not much fire coming down now. Think we can get out of the kill zone on our own, or do we need to call in air support?"

Ross wiped sweat from his face. "None of the guys in the truck bed were critically hurt. Maybe a couple of broken bones, lots of bruises. Let's load them in the good truck and just get the hell out of here."

"Okay. Get this guy stabilized. I'll clear the site."

Dittman keyed his radio. "Powell, we're loading everyone in the good truck and rolling out. Do you have any incendiary grenades?"

A pause.

"Yeah, got a couple."

"Dig 'em up. We're burning the truck."

He sprinted toward the ditch where the ANA troops had

hunkered down. The ones who had held onto their rifles were still firing blindly at the hillside, despite the silence from above. Dittman found Major Hakimi standing, barking commands.

"Major! Cease fire, cease fire! Save your ammo!"

Hakimi stared at him, uncomprehending.

"Stop shooting!" Dittman repeated, firm.

"Ah, okay, okay!" Hakimi turned and shouted a command. The gunfire tapered off.

"Do you have all your men?"

"Yes, Dittman," Hakimi replied in broken English. "I have them all."

"Load them into the good truck. We're getting out of here."

"Yes, we must leave," replied Hakimi. He began to signal his troops. The message took a few moments to sink in, but when the ANA truck driver finally sprinted to the cab and began to honk the horn repeatedly, the soldiers began to abandon their hiding spots, ran to the truck, and climbed aboard.

A short burst from Quazi's M-240 grabbed Dittman's attention.

"Quazi, what's up?"

"Saw movement just below the ridgeline. It stopped."

"Good. We're leaving. Keep their heads down."

Powell approached. "You want me to burn the truck?"

"Yeah. Grab any weapons first."

Dittman moved back to the injured man. "Can we put him in the first Humvee?"

"Should work," Ross said. "Got a body bag?"

"Yeah, back in my Humvee."

Dittman jogged back to his vehicle. "Quazi, grab me a body bag."

Quazi disappeared into the turret, reappearing a moment later to toss one down.

"Thanks."

As Dittman returned to the truck, another burst of AK fire

cracked through the air, sending gravel skittering across the road. The gunners on both Humvees returned fire. Dittman sprinted the last few feet to the body, handing the bag to the medics. With Ross's help, they carefully placed the dead soldier into the bag.

"I hate to say it, but the body needs to go in the back of the truck with the troops," Dittman said. "And we need to move - now. The ANA in that bed are sitting ducks."

The wounded man was secured in the back of the lead Humvee, the body bag in the crowded truck.

"Let's get on the road," Powell said, yanking the pin on an incendiary grenade. He lobbed it into the wrecked truck's cab, then tossed another into the back. Within seconds, flames licked up through the shattered frame.

Dittman and Ross were making their way back to the Humvee when the air around them cracked with accurate AK fire. Pebbles scattered from the road where bullets struck.

Ross heard Dittman curse - "Shit!" And watched as he dropped to the ground hard.

"Dittman's hit!" Ross shouted, grabbing his partner's harness and dragging him toward cover behind the Humvee.

Dittman grimaced. "Ah, fuck. Easy, Ross, easy. Just get me to cover. Took one in the leg, maybe another in the arm or chest. Hurts like hell."

Ross stretched Dittman out and quickly assessed the wounds. "Through-and-through on your thigh. It looks shallow. Upper arm's busted. I think your plate stopped the last one."

"Put me in the back with Quazi and let's get the fuck out of here."

Ross nodded. "Quazi, help me with Dittman!"

Quazi climbed down out of the Humvee and helped to place Dittman in the rear seat.

As the burning truck sent a column of thick black smoke skyward, Ross got into the driver's seat and grabbed the radio.

"Move out, move out now!"

* * *

HILLSIDE ABOVE THE KHOST-GARDEZ HIGHWAY

"Allah Akbar! Nangial, you hit an American! You hit one!" yelled Azzat. "Allah Akbar!"

The teenager looked up from where he was crouched over his rifle and smiled proudly at Azzat.

"Now, we must run. If we injured an American, they will certainly call in aircraft soon," said Azzat. He yelled across their small ambush site. "Batoor, we must go."

One of the other older men, a villager named Sial, ran over in a crouch and dropped heavily to the ground next to Azzat. "Batoor is injured."

"Ah," said Azzat, immediately deflated. "Let me come see." He stood up, crouched, and then ran a few meters to the large rocks where Batoor had set up his machine gun. His friend was slumped over the weapon, face down. Azzat crawled under the bush that Batoor had used for concealment and in an urgent whisper, "Batoor! Are you okay?"

There was no response. He reached out, grabbed his friend's shoulder, and rolled him off the gun. There was no sign of injury to his head, but Azzat saw a tremendous amount of blood pooled near the wooden stock of the machine gun, and his friend's lower chest was soaked and red. He pulled the young man out of the hiding spot and stretched him out along the rocky ground. It quickly became clear that Batoor was dead. A machine gun round had somehow skimmed between the ground and Batoor's prone body, impacted him near his collarbone, and exited through his belly. He had died nearly instantly.

"Ah Batoor, Batoor," said Azzat sadly as he stroked his friend's face. He looked up and yelled to Sial. "Sial, we must take Batoor home. You and Kushan must carry him. I will carry the weapon."

The two Afghans rushed over. The man known as Sial looked down and considered the challenge for a moment. "I will carry him alone until we get away. Help me pick him up."

Azzat and Kushan helped get the body over Sial's bony but strong shoulders. Kushan took the extra rifle.

"Let us go," said Azzat. He picked up the machine gun. "We need to get into the valley as quickly as possible."

4

OVER GARDEZ MOUNTAIN RANGE, AFGHANISTAN

The terrain of Afghanistan was breathtaking but unforgiving. Briggs had been struck by its beauty when he first arrived - steep mountains, tree-lined valleys, and rivers that looked perfect for fishing. But for pilots, it was treacherous. Towering peaks made navigation tricky, and summer storms would soon trap helicopters between brutal turbulence and the risk of gunfire from the armed men in every village below. While their Blackhawk could technically operate at a much higher altitude, they stayed low, following broader valleys for safety. When the weather allowed, however, cutting through the rugged mountain passes was one of the rare joys of flying in this war.

The Blackhawk hummed steadily, slicing through the air as the jagged snow-covered ridgelines passed beneath them.

"These fucking mountains are crazy," said Matthew Barnes on the helicopter's intercom.

"First trip to Afghanistan?" asked Briggs.

"Yeah, all my time was in Iraq," replied Barnes. "The mountains in Kurdistan and along the border with Turkey were big, but this is insane."

"Hell, these aren't even the tall ones," said Gray. "Wait until you see the mountains up north."

"Yup, the rest of the Hindu Kush is worth seeing, especially if Langley is thinking about adding any new capabilities," said Briggs.

"Thought you didn't want to talk about the new tasking," said Gray.

"I don't, but somebody has to let them know that whatever they are planning, it is going to be about three times more difficult than they think," said Briggs.

"I'm supposed to stop by Bagram before I leave the country so we can discuss it," said Barnes. "I haven't been around the agency long, but I think I can say that the boss is going into this with his eyes open. Nobody hesitated at the initial cost estimates, and they were high. The Army would have puked and thrown me out of the office."

"Not sure that makes me feel any better," said Briggs.

There was silence on the intercom until they crested a ridge, and the massive Khost valley opened up in front of them.

"Holy crap," said Barnes.

"Welcome to the Khost dust bowl," said Fletcher. "I'm sure you know, but the runway at FOB Chapman is just gravel. That means a ton of dust. While we aren't sparing any expense anywhere else, for some reason they are drawing the line at paving this place. The ground crew has to check it pretty carefully if one of the afternoon thunderstorms comes through. It washes out fast. There have been a couple of times when the water created gullies that you wouldn't want to hit."

After several more minutes of droning flight towards the air base, Briggs switched to the tower frequency.

"Chapman tower, ATHOS 32 is checking in fifteen miles northwest," said Briggs.

"ATHOS 32, runway 07 is active. Winds 100 at 25, gusts to 30. Altimeter 30.05. Continue inbound."

"Copy all. 30.05," replied Briggs.

* * *

ON THE KHOST-GARDEZ HIGHWAY

"How you doing, Dittman?" asked Ross.

"Ah, fuck. It hurts. The arm is miserable," replied Dittman. "I can feel the bones in my arm grinding together."

"Shit. Quazi, don't we have a splint anywhere?"

"Boss, I am looking. I know there are a couple in the first aid bag somewhere," replied Quazi as he looked through the medical kit.

"Keep looking. Dittman, we are probably still about an hour and a half away from the base. We can stop along the way and get that dust-off moving. What do you think?"

"Give me the radio," ordered Dittman. "Let's get a status check."

Ross handed Dittman the microphone.

"Martinez, this is Dittman. How you guys looking up there?"

There was a moment of random noise on the radio as if it was being retrieved from under a pile of gear, and then Martinez answered. "Our patient is critical up here. We just found an entry wound in his abdomen. He is bleeding now, and his vitals are getting pretty weak."

"Gotcha," replied Dittman. He thought for a moment. "I am going to ask for the QRF to roll from FOB Salerno and meet a dust-off about fifteen klicks from here." He stopped for a moment. "Hey Quazi, hand me that map."

The interpreter reached for the map that Dittman had asked for and handed it over.

Dittman looked at it for a moment and then yelled to Ross. "We can stop near the big ANA base. You know where that is?"

"Got it," replied Ross.

Dittman got back on the radio, "Martinez, turn off the highway in about ten klicks and head to the ANA base. I'll get the QRF to roll from Salerno and see if we can get a dust-off."

There was a moment's pause, and then Martinez came back on the line, "Copy all. How are you doing?"

"I am increasingly unhappy but will survive," replied Dittman. He then picked up his satellite phone. "JOC Salerno, this is CREST 8."

The response was quick. "Go ahead, CREST 8."

"I'd like to request that you roll the QRF and a dust-off to the following grid." He read the map location to the clear area that he had chosen. "Do you copy?"

"JOC Salerno copies all. We already had the QRF saddled up, they are heading out the gate now. A dust-off from Bagram may take a while, but the request is in."

"We'll take whatever we can get," replied Dittman.

* * *

FORWARD OPERATING BASE CHAPMAN - KHOST

The landing at FOB Chapman was routine. They shut down the Blackhawk and climbed out.

Gray walked over to Briggs. "Thanks for the ride. I know you don't want to talk about it, but Winters is counting on your experience with the 160th to get this new capability going as quickly as we can."

Briggs looked at Gray, "Yeah, I'll bet he is. I'm rotating out of here in seventy-four days. If they want my help, they are going to have to hurry."

"Oh, they are in a hurry," said Gray. "The boss already approved it."

"Well, if they want my input, have them get in touch through McCoy; he's my boss here," said Briggs.

"I'll make it happen," said Barnes.

Briggs and Fletcher exchanged handshakes with the two travellers.

"You guys be safe out here, this is the wild west," said Fletcher, looking pointedly at Barnes.

"We will be good," said Gray. "See you in a couple days."

The five men walked into the plywood building that served as base operations. Gray and Barnes peeled off and walked towards a desk with a phone to call their contact on base.

BRIGGS, Fletcher, and Holland stopped at an area set aside for aircrew to update their flight information. As they looked at the schedule, an Army Major and a man in civilian clothing that Briggs recognized as a CIA operative entered the building, looked across the room, and walked over to them.

"Are you Briggs?" asked the Major.

"I am. What do you need?"

The man in civilian clothes began to talk. "I don't know if you remember me, but my name is Jason Sharp," said the CIA officer. He reached out to shake Briggs' hand. "I think we met in the compound at Bagram a couple of months ago."

"You look familiar, but honestly, I would never have remembered your name," said Briggs, returning the handshake.

"No worries," replied Sharp. "So, we've got a team of four agents who were out along the highway working with the ANA today. About thirty minutes ago, they hit an IED. We have one KIA and two critically injured who need to get to the hospital in Bagram." He paused, "We are working on getting a regular dust-off, but there are a couple TICs in the area and several casualties, so it is pretty damn busy..." his voice trailed off.

Briggs interrupted, "Happy to help. Where are they?"

The Major spread out a map on a tabletop, and Fletcher and Holland gathered around.

"They are meeting with a QRF from FOB Salerno right about here," he said, pointing to a clear area a few kilometers south of a large ANA base. "The QRF will pull security for your LZ and get the rest of the team home after you go." He looked up at Briggs. "We've used this field as an LZ a few times; it is clear. It is only about twenty-five klicks from here."

Briggs looked at Fletcher, "Shouldn't be an issue. Right?"

"Well, we don't have any real medical gear onboard, but we are better than nothing. Kyle, any thoughts?" asked Fletcher, looking at Holland.

"Let's do it. They need to unload those pallets we brought," replied Holland. "We can take out some of the seats. This obviously means we can't take our scheduled passengers."

"Not a problem," said Sharp. "They are my guys. We'll send them on the next ride out."

"Okay," said Briggs. "We have the fuel. How about a medic?"

"The QRF has one that will jump aboard for the trip to Bagram," replied the Major.

"How long is the flight to Bagram?" asked Sharp.

"It's about two hundred klicks. Maybe an hour or so," said Briggs.

Sharp reached out to shake Briggs' hand again, "Thanks a ton. The injured agent is a good friend of mine named Pete Dittman. When you see him, tell him he's already out of sick days."

"Can do," said Briggs with a smile. He turned to Fletcher and Holland, "Let's go."

* * *

NADER SHAH - NEAR THE GARDEZ-KHOST HIGHWAY

"Dust-off is inbound," said Ross as he put the radio handset down. "And the QRF is about three klicks out."

"It's about time," groaned Dittman.

The convoy had come to a halt at the landing zone. The ANA

soldiers had climbed from the back of the truck and spread out to protect the area. The four CIA officers had parked their humvees together to give them some cover.

Powell and Martinez were huddled over the ANA casualty, the man was pale and breathing shallowly. They had finally been able to get him onto a backboard and Martinez was looking angrily through their first aid kit in search of an airway.

"We need to fix these kits. Someone organized them by size or something," growled Martinez. "Everything is in a little pocket, all zippered, no labels. Fucking bullshit." He angrily picked the bag up and dumped the entire contents on the ground.

The sound of diesel engines became clearer and within a few moments, they saw a convoy of ten armored humvees.

"Ah, the calvary arrives," said Ross.

The trucks rolled up. Three of the trucks took a rear guard position, while two rolled through their position and took up spots on the other end of the road. One of the vehicles stopped next to the two CIA humvees, and four men got out. A tall soldier walked up to where the operatives were huddled over the wounded man. He bent over the team. "I know this is kind of a stupid thing to say, but who's in charge?"

Dittman, who was sitting in the front seat of one of the humvees with the door propped open and an unlit cigarette in his hand, spoke up, "Hey Lieutenant, thanks for the assist. I'm Paul Dittman. I'd get up to shake your hand, but I don't think the docs would like that."

The Lieutenant straightened and walked over to the humvee. One of the other soldiers intercepted the Lieutenant, "Sir, we've got security out. The dust-off should be here in a few minutes."

"Thanks, First Sergeant," replied the Lieutenant. "Mr Dittman, I'm Damian Cobb. What do we need to know?"

"Ambush about thirty klicks back up the highway. An IED took out one of the ANA trucks. I've got one ANA killed in action, one badly wounded, and I got hit in my leg and arm.

Major Hakimi is in charge of our ANA support." He gestured to an Afghan officer sitting in the cab of the remaining cargo truck who was smoking a cigarette and silently watching the Americans.

"Got it. Sorry to hear about the casualties. It's been a busy day around the FOB. We've got two TICs to the north of here with three wounded, both hit IEDs," replied Cobb.

The men watched for a moment as a medic from the QRF leaned in to take charge of the wounded ANA soldier. Another soldier walked up to the group, "Sir, I'm Sergeant Stevens, one of the medics on the team. I understand you were wounded this morning. Mind if I take a look at you?"

"Thanks, Sergeant. I should be good for now. Honestly, I don't want to move. My arm and chest are killing me," replied Dittman.

"I'm going to have to report your condition and keep an eye on you as we fly, so let me take a look," said the Sergeant as he began to survey Dittman's wounds. After a few minutes, he looked up, "Pretty lucky you were wearing a side plate; you'd be having a real bad day if you didn't."

Dittman grimaced, "Yeah, I knew a guy who took a round right under his arm. Haven't skipped a day wearing it since."

They all looked up at the sound of an inbound helicopter.

"That was quick," said the Lieutenant. "They must have re-tasked someone, either that or you must be important."

"Pays to have friends in low places," said Dittman with a pained attempt at a smile.

* * *

VILLAGE OF SPERA, AFGHANISTAN

There was a radio conversation ending when Hamid walked into the village elder's house.

"The Americans were attacked; at least one was wounded,"

said the village elder to Hamid. "Azzat thinks that there were at least twenty casualties."

"This probably means two or three," replied Hamid. When the elder looked at him questioningly, he said, "Things like this are difficult to assess when you are in the middle of a firefight." He paused. "And our team?"

"One dead," said the elder sadly.

"Not a very good trade," said Hamid. "I will be moving in the morning. My superiors want me to train another group to the south of here."

"The Americans will be looking for you now," said the elder.

"The pressure will certainly increase," replied Hamid. "But they do not have the resources to do much. As long as I stay in motion, they will be unable to track me down."

"Inshallah," replied the old man as he fingered the prayer beads in his right hand.

"Inshallah," said Hamid.

* * *

NADER SHAH - NEAR THE GARDEZ-KHOST HIGHWAY

"I have the LZ in sight," said Briggs.

"Me too," replied Fletcher. "Wind is pretty gusty out of the west."

"It's not horrible," said Briggs. "Just requires a little extra concentration."

Both men chuckled at the quote. It was derived from the ill-timed comments of one of their fellow pilots who was rumored to have said something similar, right before a brown-out resulted in a hard landing with a two-star Marine General in the back.

"We look good from back here," said Kyle Holland over the intercom. "No vertical obstructions within three hundred meters. The terrain rises from right to left."

One of the soldiers popped red smoke. Fletcher acknowledged the color over the radio, and they analyzed the wind direction one last time. He then began to call out altitudes, "Fifty, thirty, twenty..." He paused for a moment as they lost sight of the ground in the dust. "Ten." The Blackhawk landed smoothly, and as soon as Briggs reduced power, the dust began to settle.

Holland jumped to the ground, still tethered to the machine by his headset, and began talking to one of the soldiers. After a moment, his voice came over the intercom. "There are two wounded. An ANA soldier who is in critical condition and an American with gunshot wounds who is stable. Also, one ANA killed."

"Well," said Fletcher. "Get them loaded up, and let's get out of here."

"Will do," said Holland. He waved the evacuation teams over. The ANA soldiers had been placed on stretchers. Dittman had refused being carried on and had been helped over to the copter. It took five minutes for Holland and the medics to arrange the wounded in the back of the helicopter to give them the most access.

Holland came back on the intercom. "We are set. One KIA, two WIA, and one medic."

"Only one," asked Briggs.

"Yup, they think that will be enough," said Holland.

They heard a pained voice. "The Afghani is in tough shape," said Dittman, who had found a headset and put it on. "I am going to take some time to repair, but no bleeding at the moment."

"Are you Dittman?" asked Briggs.

"That's me," replied Dittman.

"Jason Sharp wanted me to tell you that you don't have any sick days left," said Briggs.

There was a rough laugh from Dittman. "Yeah, well, I'll let him work the details out with the boss."

"It's time to leave, Briggs," said Fletcher, the stress clear in his voice.

"We are all clear back here," said Holland.

"Let's go to Bagram," replied Briggs.

A LITTLE OVER an hour of flight time later, Fletcher transmitted on the radio. "Bagram tower, this is ATHOS 32. Ten miles to the southeast with information Echo. We've been retasked as a dust-off and are heading directly to the casevac ramp."

"ATHOS 32, you are cleared inbound. Traffic is an A-10 that is on final for runway zero three."

"Traffic in sight," replied Fletcher.

"How are you guys doing back there?" asked Briggs, half turning to the back of the aircraft. "It's been quiet for a while."

"Yeah, I'm pretty sure we lost the injured Afghan," replied Holland. "The Doc is still working on him, but it doesn't look good."

"Shit," replied Briggs.

The intercom was quiet for a few moments.

"Dittman, how are you doing?" asked Briggs.

"I'm still here," replied Dittman weakly. "Hurts pretty bad at this point."

"Five minutes out," said Briggs.

"ATHOS 32, you are cleared to the casevac ramp. Do you know where it is?" asked the tower.

"We are familiar," replied Fletcher.

Briggs flew across the large runway and towards a beaten up old hangar that reputedly had been the site of a last stand by the Russians. The dedicated Army casevac squadron operated from the building, which was only thirty yards from the base hospital. He saw a group of people standing next to the casevac parking spot, clearly waiting for them, and smoothly brought the helicopter to a stop in the marked area. Kyle Holland jumped from the helicopter and talked to a medic who had stepped forward.

After a brief discussion, they waved the rest of the team over to the chopper.

Fletcher looked back to see an exhausted-looking Army medic hand his charge over to the arriving personnel. His gloved hands were covered with blood, and the back of the helicopter was littered with debris from his lifesaving efforts. As the team from the base pulled the stretcher from the chopper, the medic grabbed his gear, climbed from the chopper, and followed his patient.

"Thanks for the lift guys," said Dittman.

"Have a good time in Germany," said Briggs, knowing that Dittman would be stabilized in Bagram and quickly sent to the major hospital in Landstuhl for most of his care.

"I'll try," said Dittman. He eased the headset off with one hand and gingerly laid down on the second stretcher that the medical team had brought. Within seconds, he, too was on his way into the hospital.

Finally, the last team from the hospital gently placed the body bag of the dead Afghan soldier on a stretcher and then followed the rest of the group.

Within minutes, the helicopter was empty. Holland jumped back on board. "We are clear."

"Right," said Briggs.

"Bagram ground, ATHOS 32 to taxi from the casevac ramp to the north parking pad," said Fletcher.

"ATHOS 32 cleared as requested."

Five minutes later, they pulled into their flight line.

"Shutting her down," said Fletcher.

IT TOOK A FEW MINUTES, but when the blades had stopped, Briggs and Fletcher collected their gear and climbed from the aircraft. Fletcher began an external walk around while Brigs set his weapon and flight gear down on the tarmac, grabbed one of the garbage bags that were customarily stowed in a pocket behind his seat, and started to clear the mess in the back. He had just finished policing up the residue of the medical effort when Holland returned from the hangar with a wheeled contraption that contained fifty gallons of water, a battery, and an electric pump. Once he turned the pump on, he began to spray out the interior.

Briggs stopped what he was doing for a second and watched. Although he had seen similar things many times before, for some reason, the sight of blood and water sluicing out of the helicopter door and splashing onto the tarmac mesmerized him.

Fletcher walked back around the front of the helicopter and stopped by his friend. "You okay?"

Spell broken, Briggs looked up from the growing puddle of reddish water on the ground. "Sure."

5

JOINT COUNTER-IED TASK FORCE - BAGRAM AIR BASE

"The attacks around Khost are picking up. Our analysts think there is probably a new bomber in the area," said Special Agent Nancy Reams as she looked at her notes. She was sitting at a conference table inside the Joint Operations Center in Bagram. Reams was a tall, attractive brunette who was one of five FBI agents assigned to the Joint Counter-IED Task Force. She was wearing standard body armor over a long-sleeve shirt and khaki pants. A Sig-Sauer 9mm pistol was strapped in a thigh holster on her right leg. Reams had been in Bagram for just under a week on this trip, but was on her third deployment into the region to support the Counter IED Task Force; this time, she was the Acting Senior Agent in Charge.

There were nine other personnel at the table, all of whom were men. Three were Army officers, two were CIA, one was DIA, and the last two were contractors supporting the Counter-IED team.

At the head of the table sat a short, round Army Colonel

named Mike "Mel" Brooks, who was the Joint Counter-IED Task Force lead.

"It sure seems like it," said Brooks. "That is now two hits along the Gardez-Khost highway in two days. Three KIA and four WIA."

One of the CIA analysts, a younger man named Steve Loris, spoke up. "The CIA team that got hit yesterday was told that there is a new foreign bomber in the valley."

"Did they get a name or description?" asked Brooks.

"No, the old man they talked to said that there was a foreigner making bombs. He did give them the name of the town he was supposedly working in," replied Loris.

"Why would they give him up?" asked Brooks.

"The team thinks that the bomber probably hit some civilians, and the village is looking for revenge," said Loris. "Pretty normal, actually."

"Roger," said Brooks. He turned and looked at a Major halfway down the table. "Bob, any chance we can get another IED exploitation team into Khost? Sure would be nice to start collecting forensics. We are going to need them to help identify this guy."

Major Robert Donalds glanced down at the PowerPoint slides in his hands and then back up at Brooks. "We could send one of the teams from J-bad for a few weeks. It has slowed down there."

"Send Flynn's team," said Brooks. "He's good at this shit."

"Yes, sir. Honestly, I was trying to give his team a bit of a break," replied Donalds. "They just spent two weeks working from a FOB near the Pech River. It was a mess up there."

"Khost is no worse than J-bad as a place to catch their breath," said Brooks. "Send them."

"Got it," said Donalds.

"When they get there, let me know," said Reams. "I'd like to take my new guys out to meet Flynn and see an exploitation team in action."

"Will do," said Donalds. "It'll probably take a couple of days."

"What else do we have?" asked Brooks.

One of the new intelligence analysts raised his hand.

"Go ahead, Mark," said Brooks.

"There were night letters posted around the valley again last night. This time, they made it to nearly every mosque near the base," replied the analyst.

"What are night letters?" asked one of the other team members.

"They can be a lot of things, but here around Bagram, the Taliban use them to post warnings or threats on the neighborhood mosques. Usually, they try to keep the local populace from collaborating with us or the Afghan government," replied Major Donalds.

"Anything new in these ones?" asked Brooks.

The analyst looked at his notes. "The letters warned about an impending attack and told people to stay away from the market at the front gate and away from the walls."

"Okay," said Brooks. "I am sure headquarters staff knows, right?"

"Yes, sir," replied the analyst.

"Good." He looked up. "Anything else?" There was silence around the table. "We will skip tomorrow's update. I've got a meeting with the boss."

* * *

KHOST, AFGHANISTAN

Nabil Hamid wandered through the streets of the small city of Khost, wandering from stall to stall in the market and occasionally stopping to check his surroundings. While he had publicly let it be known that he was traveling to another town in the mountains, he had actually been directed to a meeting with his ISI handlers, both as a way to receive updated tasking, and in order to resupply. So, after saying goodbye to the village, he had driven his trusty Hilux out of the mountains, past a few new IEDs that were still waiting for victims along the highway, and across the valley.

WALKING through the dusty Afghan city was refreshing in a way. He had been living in tiny little mountain towns for a long time, and although he enjoyed the physical grandeur of the region, he missed his city home.

Hamid had made two circuits through the main market and had seen no sign of surveillance. There had been several roving Afghan Army patrols on the streets and elsewhere in town, but none of the soldiers seemed particularly alert. As the temperature rose in the late morning, he stopped at a tree-shaded restaurant next to his hotel and sat down at a table.

The owner came out after a few moments. "Good afternoon. Today's special is Kabuli Pulao."

"That will be fine," replied Hamid. "Tea, please."

"Of course," replied the owner as he turned and walked back into the restaurant.

Within moments, a young boy came out from the building with a tea kettle and a glass, along with some flat bread. He placed the glass on the table and filled it. "Thank you," said Hamid absently. He then unfolded the newspaper that he had purchased during his stroll and began to scan it. He was reading an article about Pakistan's cricket team when a shadow fell over him.

"Greetings, traveler," said a rugged-looking man in Western-style clothing who was standing next to the table. "May I join you?"

Recognizing his ISI handler, Zayan Shah, Hamid nodded.

The man sat down and leaned back in the chair. "It is good to see you, Nabil. The director congratulates you on your work."

"God has been good," replied Hamid.

"Indeed," said Shah.

The men looked up as the owner walked back to the table. Before he could speak, Shah said, "I'll just have what he is having."

The owner nodded and returned inside. Again, the boy came out, this time providing tea for Shah.

When the boy was gone, Shah began again. "How are your supplies?"

"I'm out of almost everything," replied Hamid. "The training has gone well, and there are many targets."

"Yes, we understand. Your vehicle is being loaded as we speak," replied Shah. He sipped his tea. "The CIA suspects us. This is not good. Remember, we are looking for those who are using Afghanistan as a sanctuary to attack us in the FATA."

"I am doing what I can," said Hamid. "The Taliban does not trust me. I am still an outsider."

"Your cover is impeccable," said Shah. "Let them dig."

"It is not that," replied Hamid. "They don't care that I work for ISI; if they did, you and I could never meet. They are worried I am looking for the Sheikh. Anyway, they will know of this meeting by tomorrow at the latest."

"You think so?" replied Shah with a surprised look on his face.

"The owner has already reported us," said Hamid. "I know this. That is why I chose this hotel. I must not be caught trying to hide my relationships."

Shah looked thoughtful. The conversation stopped for a while after the food was delivered. Both men ate quietly. When they were finished, the boy cleared the table, and the men sat back and finished their tea.

Shah lighted a cigarette and leaned forward. "So, if this is the case, should we still trust you?"

"Of course," said Hamid. "I am loyal to Pakistan above all."

"Even above God?" asked Shah with a raised eyebrow.

"Perhaps not, but those loyalties are woven together," said Hamid.

"I see," said Shah. "It is a complicated world."

"It is," replied Hamid. "When can I return home? I have been in the field for a long time."

"We will see," said Shah as he stubbed out his cigarette. "We want you to move towards Zangay for a few weeks. There are rumors that Akbar Khan has moved to Gardez. If you hear about him, we will want to know."

"Did you get me the blood money I need for the accident?" asked Hamid.

"No. Leadership does not like the precedent it would set," replied Shah. "This is a war, there are casualties."

Visibly irritated, Hamid replied. "The cost is so small compared to the anger it will generate among the villagers. There is no forgiveness in those mountains." He thought about it for a moment and then shrugged. "Inshallah."

"Inshallah, my friend," said Shah.

* * *

CIA SPECIAL ACTIVITIES DIVISION B-HUT - BAGRAM AIR BASE

"Briggs, you are off the fight schedule tomorrow. We need to go to a meeting about this new project," said Arthur McCoy as Briggs and Fletcher walked into the Operations B-hut.

Briggs was quiet for a moment as he set his go-bag on the ground and then walked over to the counter and placed his rifle and gear on top.

"That was fast," he said with a subdued voice.

McCoy walked to the rifle rack, talking over his shoulder as he did so. "Yeah, the way Winters tells it, he didn't even have to make a request; Reynolds just approved everything."

"Somebody isn't telling the entire truth," said Briggs. "Mike

Gray is here with a new guy from Langley. We flew them from J-Bad to Khost." He paused. "His name is Barnes, I think. He is doing reconnaissance for this new project as we speak."

"Yeah," replied McCoy. "My sense is that headquarters had already decided that we were going to be tasked with this before Winters mentioned it."

"Great," said Fletcher. "So, what you are saying is that headquarters never listens to the troops. Now that is surprising," he finished, the irony clear in his voice.

"No news there," replied McCoy. "Oh, by the way, Reynolds told Winters that we needed to get set up as soon as possible."

Fletcher placed his rifle on the counter. "As soon as possible? How the hell is that going to work?"

"I have no idea," said McCoy. "We need the right choppers, we need more pilots who have experience, and we need a strike team..."

Briggs interrupted. "And a good intelligence effort, a targeting cell, medical support, and connections to JSOC or whoever is going to be our backup. Not to mention training. None of which is happening in two weeks."

"This is why we need to have a meeting," said McCoy, grabbing Fletcher's rifle and placing it in the rack and then signing it in. "We will meet in the JSOC Headquarters at nine tomorrow. Conference room five."

"Fuck," said Briggs tiredly. "A meeting. That's all I need."

McCoy looked up and noticed that both Briggs and Fletcher looked especially grim. "You guys okay?"

"Our third leg turned into a dust-off. Picked up one agency guy and two ANA. One was KIA, and the other died on the way," said Fletcher.

"Shit, sorry," said McCoy. "Anyone we know?"

"A guy named Dittman," said Briggs. "He's got a ticket home. Took a round in the leg and one that shattered his arm."

All three men were quiet for a minute.

"That sucks," said McCoy, breaking the silence.

"Yeah," said Briggs. "I'll see you in the morning."

* * *

CHARIKAR, AFGHANISTAN

Zubair Wardak drove the old truck down Saiad Road that ran just outside the American air base in Bagram. He had driven from the northern suburbs of Kabul, where his truck had been loaded with several items for one of the local Taliban cells. After working his way through the late afternoon traffic along the main highway, he pulled up next to a mosque in the dusty town of Charikar, an old city that sat at the foot of the mountain range that surrounded the base.

As he expected, there was a covered pickup truck parked in the gravel lot. He slowly pulled up alongside the other vehicle, bringing his truck to a stop when the rear of the two vehicles were even. He kept the motor idling. In his mirrors, he watched as two men stepped from the pickup, opened the rear of his truck, and quickly unloaded the heavy materials within. He felt his truck shudder and heard the noise of the rear gate being slammed closed. One of the men walked by his driver's side door, slapping the metal twice as he did so. Zubair whispered "Allah Akbar," and then placed his truck into gear and resumed his normal route, picking up farm goods to take back into the city for the next morning's market.

THE TWO MEN from the covered pickup drove away from the mosque, headed north.

"Straight to the site," said the passenger. He was an older man with a sharp scar across the side of his head. "There were too many patrols in the area today. They must have been alerted by the notices on the mosques."

"I am heading there, old man. Just one loop around the city to see if we are being followed," replied the younger man with a smile.

"You have heard too many spy stories," said the older man. "The Americans would follow us with a drone that you can't even see."

"Yes, but the ANA are the ones setting up the patrols in the valley. Don't want them to get lucky," said the younger man condescendingly.

"Just go to the spot; it is getting dark," replied the older man, irritated. "I have no time for foolishness."

The extra circuit took twenty minutes, but eventually, they pulled up beside a decrepit old adobe-style farm building that was about three kilometers from the outer walls of the base. Knowing that they were within range of any number of potential observers, they rapidly unloaded three large Soviet 122mm rockets and took them into the shack. The launch site had been prepared in advance. The decaying hole in the roof of the building had been widened, and a rough launch ramp had been constructed from wooden poles. The men propped the rockets at a roughly calculated angle that should have an impact somewhere inside the base. The older man then opened a cardboard box that contained the rough timer and three ignition devices that he carefully attached to the rockets.

He stood up. "We are done. They will launch in four hours, plus or minus thirty minutes."

"Good," replied the younger man. "Let's go make the last drop."

The two returned to the truck and drove off into the darkening evening.

* * *

FORENSICS TEAM - JALALABAD AIR BASE

"Khost? We just fucking got back here," said Sergeant Eli Grayson angrily. "I haven't even done laundry yet."

"Don't worry, you'll have time," replied Staff Sergeant Daniel Flynn with a thin smile. "I already checked at base operations. There isn't air transport available until tomorrow. Get your laundry done, and have a good night's sleep. We will pack up in the morning."

On the other side of their small team room, Sergeant Ty Jenkins quietly said, "Fuck." He was sitting at the classified computer that gave them access to the Joint Counter IED Task Force.

"What?" asked Flynn.

"Just looking at what they have on this new bomber who is working along the highway," replied Jenkins. "Not a lot of detail, but looks like a pro."

"Great," said Grayson. "Request that the guys at Chapman set up someone to support us and see who is running the EOD team. This cross-border shit is worse than dealing with gang-bangers at home."

The three men had been working as a counter-IED forensic team for two months. In a move that Flynn acknowledged to be one of the brighter decisions by his leadership, someone had noticed that all three of the National Guard troopers were law enforcement officers in their "real lives." Flynn was a Virginia State Trooper, Grayson was a detective from Nashville, and Jenkins was on the force in Washington D.C. Their job was now to travel to locations where IEDs had been employed against Americans and collect what they could of the device, including triggers, explosives, and any forensic evidence they could find that could determine the who, what, and where of the bomb. Not only were they interested in the changing technologies used by the bombers, but they also intended to tie each bomb to a specific enemy and their local supply chain.

"I already asked," said Flynn. "We will have plenty of support.

They are ready for us to get there. For some reason, this one is high vis."

"Shit," said Jenkins as he turned from the computer and looked at Flynn. "I don't like the ones where we don't have to beg for help."

"Me neither," replied Flynn.

* * *

SPECIAL OPERATIONS COMPOUND - BAGRAM AIR BASE

Briggs and Fletcher walked back across the base and to the Special Operations Compound. They flashed their badges at the gate and walked inside.

"I need to work out," said Fletcher.

"Yeah, that sounds like a good idea," replied Briggs. "I'll see you at the gym in about ten."

The two men went separate directions. Briggs walked across the compound, nodding to a few guys that he knew. He arrived at his B-hut to find that there was no lock on the door. He pulled it open and saw a man in civilian clothes sitting on a bed that hadn't been there when he left in the morning.

Briggs noted the man's backwoods-style beard, thick and unkempt. He looked to be in his thirties, with deep lines etched around his eyes that suggested stress and a deep tan that could only come from extended exposure to the elements. Dressed in khaki cargo pants and a black t-shirt, he had a lean, wiry build. Briggs had seen plenty like him before - the kind of man who moved around the combat theater getting the really tough jobs.

"Sorry, dude," said the man as he stood up. "My unit just dropped in, and the camp mayor put me here." He reached forward to shake Briggs' hand. "I'm Hunter Scott."

Briggs stepped forward. "Briggs Ward."

"I probably won't be here a lot," said Scott. "But I appreciate having a place to keep my gear."

"No problem at all," said Briggs tiredly. He stepped into the room and sat down heavily on his bed. "This isn't the first time someone has moved in."

Scott sat back down on his bed. "You okay?"

"I'm a helo pilot," said Briggs. "It was a long day that ended with a dust-off."

"Sorry man, that's tough," replied Scott. "Anyone you knew?"

"No. Or not really, anyway. Two ANA and one SAD team member."

"Really? You know his name?" asked Scott, his interest clear. "Those are my guys."

"Dittman," said Briggs.

Scott was quiet for a moment. "He's one of the old schoolers, got here at the beginning. Don't know him personally, but I hear he is tough as they come."

"Took a couple rounds, but should be okay," said Briggs.

"Well, I work for the same guys," said Scott. "It's why they put me in here with you. My team just got pulled from Iraq on no notice. Feels like the boss is setting something up."

"Never a dull moment," said Briggs. He shook off the lethargy that threatened to overwhelm him and stood back up. "I've got to get to the gym and burn off some stress." He looked at Scott. "You find the showers and the shitters yet?"

"Yeah," replied Scott. "And the DFAC. This compound is pretty squared away compared to our old place in Ramadi."

Briggs began to change into his PT gear. "Squared away? Were you a squid?"

"Still am," said Scott. "You know, temporary assignment."

"Gotcha," said Briggs. "I'm retired Army, now civilian."

"I'm sure we will still get along," said Scott with a smile. "How's the gym?"

"Not bad," said Briggs as he looked at his watch. "Tends to be pretty busy in the morning and the evening, but there is always room to do something." He walked over to the corner of the room and reached into a box, pulling out a roll of 550 cord and a couple of old dark sheets. He handed them to Scott. "You can set up a screen, the hooks are already in the wall. It will help with sleeping."

"You are an organized man," said Scott as he accepted the gear.

"Can't take credit. The guy who was in here when I showed up put it together," replied Briggs.

"Got it," said Scott.

Briggs pushed open the door and stepped out. "See you later."

* * *

AIR FORCE FACILITIES - BAGRAM AIR BASE

"Dude, where did you find the time to get so good?" said Captain Ben "Chris" Cross as he frustratedly watched his character die in a hail of machine gun fire.

"It's not that I am good Chris," replied Captain Sarah "Noodles" Matthews, whose victorious character then tea-bagged her defeated opponent. "It's just that you suck."

There was a round of laughter from the other young aviators who were watching the two A-10 pilots play Call of Duty on one of the squadron's prized possessions, an X-box that had been bought with pooled resources. The video game was set up on a large-screen T.V. in the back of the squadron's ready room and was rarely turned off.

The ready room itself could have been mistaken for almost any Air Force squadron space anywhere in the world. While the Air Force facilities in Bagram had initially been built around the old Russian tower from the same B-huts, shipping containers, and tents as the rest of the base, they had gotten better over time. Not only had the United States built an entirely new runway, but the service had constructed modern hangars and squadron spaces on the south-eastern side of the field, a requirement for the service to be able to start rotating aircraft through Bagram like the F-16's that were not intended to operate out of such austere environments. The 104th Fighter Squadron, an A-10 unit based in Maryland, had been in-country for two weeks, and the squadron members who had been to Bagram on previous deployment were astonished at the upgrade.

THE SQUADRON DO, MAJOR JIM "BOOM" Calloway, walked to the front of the room and raised his voice just enough to be heard. "Okay, okay. Let's get moving. The faster we get this meeting done, the better off we will be."

The twenty-five pilots in the squadron dropped whatever they were doing and found seats that faced the front of the room. Calloway maintained his position by the entrance, and when he saw the CO walking down the hallway, he called, "Attention!"

The aviators all stood as Lieutenant Colonel Travis "Snake" O'Connor walked into the room. "As you were."

Everyone sat down, and Calloway found a seat that had been held for him in the center of the front row.

"Sorry about the meeting. I know we are cutting it close with crew rest, but Boom tells me we can manage," said O'Connor. He looked across the room. "Let's start with safeties. Does anybody have a good one this week?"

Captain "Bucky" Foster raised a hand.

"What you got, Bucky?" asked O'Connor.

"Yeah, Balls and I were down near Tarin Khowt on Tuesday, late afternoon. The JTAC called us in and gave us a good spot. They were taking fire, so I rushed my prep in order to get rounds on target. I rolled in for a strafing run and misjudged the terrain a bit." The aviator next to him laughed for a second, and Bucky continued. "My roll-in was perpendicular to a shadowed ridgeline that was really hard to see in the low sun angle, and I got really low on my pull-out. Hell, I could see individual sheep running in the village."

The group of aviators laughed.

"Good effects on the target?" asked O'Connor.

"Good effects, Sir," replied Bucky.

"I'd hope so," said O'Connor. The crowd laughed again.

"Thanks for the update," said O'Connor. He looked around the room. "You know my first rule: nobody goes home in a box. Any of us can make a mistake. Bucky has been here twice already and is a flight lead for a reason. This shit is dangerous. Balls, what were you doing while Bucky was trying to drag himself into the dirt?"

The new pilot looked a bit embarrassed. "I was focused on the target area. I could hear the firefight on the JTAC's frequency and got distracted."

"I can understand. We all can," said O'Connor. "What have we said a thousand times about keeping our cool under fire?"

"Our job is to be surgical, not emotional," replied Balls.

"That's right," said O'Connor. "Let's learn from this and move on." He strolled across the room. "Any more safeties?" No hands went up. "Okay, good. Well, I thought it would be important to let you know that we are building towards a surge."

The crowd of aviators was quiet.

"Apparently, this is going to be something like the surge in Iraq, but with a smaller force package." He paced back across the room. "What it means for us is that we are going to get even busier than we already are." He paused for a moment. "It sounds like a squadron of Strike Eagles from Lakenheath will be rolling in soon, so that will help." He paced to the other side of the room. "Now, there will be rumors about being extended, there will be rumors about other squadrons coming. Hell, there will be rumors about nearly everything. Don't listen to them. I won't keep secrets about our schedule, you can be sure of that."

He turned to Calloway. "Boom, what else do we have this evening?"

"Um, you know sir, there is that one thing," said Calloway with a smile as he stood up and handed something to the CO.

"Oh yeah," replied O'Connor. "Captain Matthews front and center."

There was a moment of quiet as Matthews stepped forward.

"Noodles, I hear you are pretty good at video games. I can assure you that this is not why the Air Force has seen fit to promote you to Major," said O'Connor with a smile.

"Room, attention!" said Calloway. All in the room stood up. An NCO stepped into the room with a camera.

"Raise your right hand and repeat after me," said O'Connor as he administered the oath of office. When he was done, he ripped off one of the velcroed Captain's bars on one of Matthews' shoulders while Calloway removed the other. They then replaced them with the bronze oak leaves of a Major.

"Congratulations, Major Matthews," said O'Connor, stepping back. "While we can't celebrate the way we would at home, there are few things better than being promoted in a combat zone. Especially when you are getting tax-free pay." The room busted into applause, rose to their feet, and circled around the new promotee, shaking her hand.

A few minutes later, O'Connor raised his voice over the crowd. "Hey, listen up." The squadron stopped and listened.

"It's time for at least two of you to brief for this tonight's mission, and everybody else needs to get some rest. Keep up the great work, and fly safe. Those kids on the ground out there depend on your expertise," said O'Connor. "You are dismissed."

* * *

CHARIKAR RELIGIOUS SCHOOL - OUTSIDE OF BAGRAM AIR BASE

"Rahman, Allah has chosen well. You will certainly be blessed in heaven," said the Imam that the locals knew as Naseer Rohani.

There were four men in the room: the volunteer, two guards, and the Imam.

"I pray only that my sacrifice will take a large number of Americans with me," replied the young man called Rahman. He was very thin and moved awkwardly. His right leg was permanently twisted at the knee, the result of a bullet from the Pakistani security force when he was a child. A native of Peshawar, the nineteen-year-old had been nominated by his home village and blessed by his local Imam for the special task. He had just completed six days of travel in the company of two Al Quaeda operatives, crossing the Afghanistan-Pakistan border through Torkam gate only the day before on a crowded bus.

"It will, it will," replied Rohani. He looked at the two guards. "Is everything prepared?"

The older of the two men, a sun-scarred operative who had been working in the region for decades, nodded. "It is good."

"You will be well taken care of, Rahman. Enjoy your rest," said the Imam. He nodded and left the small room, signaling for the older operative to follow him.

The two men walked through the school and into the courtyard of the Mosque that shared the compound.

"What time have you chosen?" asked Rohani.

"The day after tomorrow. In the morning, by the front gate," said the operative. "The yard will be full of trucks, and the Americans will be conducting searches."

"Good," said Rohani. "Allah Akbar."

"Allah Akbar."

* * *

THE LANDING ZONE, SPECIAL OPERATIONS COMPOUND - BAGRAM AIR BASE

The Landing Zone, or "El Zed" as it had become known, was the informal name for the Morale Welfare and Recreation Facility that had been set up inside the Special Operations Compound. It consisted of two B-huts that had been built side-by-side and connected through two doorways. It had three pool tables, a couple of large-screen televisions, and refrigerators filled with water, soda, and fake beer. On the side of the room were tables that held things that people had sent to the troops: snacks, letters, magazines, and books. There were several couches, tables, and stuffed chairs scattered around the space. Normally, there weren't many people inside the facility, especially in the evenings, because much of the primary activity of the people who worked in the compound was nocturnal.

Briggs had finished his workout, said goodnight to Fletcher, and decided that he didn't want to go to bed, especially knowing that he wasn't on the flight schedule. So he wandered to the El Zed to play some pool and de-stress in front of the T.V.

He had been rotating through pool games for about an hour when a familiar face wandered in. Special Agent Nancy Reams stepped into the room along with two other people that Briggs figured were also FBI agents. She saw Briggs and walked over.

"Hey Briggs, haven't seen you in a while," said Reams. She stepped forward, and instead of a handshake, she gave Briggs a hug. The two male agents with her looked slightly nonplussed about the nature of the greeting.

Briggs held her at arm's length for a moment. "You look good, Nancy. They got you all patched up?"

"Yup, can hardly see the scar. Right across my left ass cheek. She turned to the two agents that had come with her. "Briggs flew into a hot landing zone a couple of months ago after we got ambushed. He pulled me and several members of the Counter IED team out of trouble. He earned that hug."

She pointed out a tall, very skinny agent with short brown hair. He was wearing the same clothes as most of the civilians in the compound: khaki cargo pants and a long-sleeved shirt with an FBI logo. "This is Derek Lawson. He's been here one time before."

Lawson reached forward to shake Briggs's hand. "Nice to meet you."

Briggs returned the handshake.

Reams pointed to the other agent. He was shorter and darker but was wearing similar clothing. "This is Ethan Khawar, It's his first trip anywhere as an FBI agent, right Ethan?"

Khawar shook Briggs's hand. "Yeah, but I was here as a grunt a few years back. Did one deployment down near Khandahar and decided to use the GI bill to better myself. Can't believe I'm back."

"That's what we all say," said Briggs with a half smile. "Nice to meet you guys."

Reams turned, "There are usually sodas in the fridges, or maybe fake beers. Popcorn is next to the microwave. There is a cashbox by the door to chip in for this stuff. It's usually where I get rid of all my Pogs."

"Hell, I'll buy the first round," said Khawar. "What do you guys want?" He asked, gesturing to the group.

"Coke for me," said Reams.

"Same," said Lawson.

"I'm good, thanks," replied Briggs.

"So, how much time do you have left?" asked Reams.

"I'm down to seventy-three days on this rotation as of tomorrow," said Briggs. "But who is counting?" he finished with a smile.

"Spent a lot of time here?" asked Lawson.

"This is my second trip here as a civilian. Spent a fair amount of time in the region while I was in the Army," replied Briggs.

"Gotcha," said Lawson.

Khawar returned with the drinks and handed them out.

"We try not to talk about work here in the El Zed," said Reams to her fellow agents as she opened her soda. "Especially with people we don't know. Too many folks in the compound who can't discuss what they do. Makes things awkward."

"Understandable," said Khawar. "Anyone want to play on the open table over there?"

"I will," said Lawson.

The two agents went to the pool table to set up a game. Reams and Briggs sat down in two of the stuffed chairs that shared a small table. Briggs grabbed the soda water he was drinking and turned to Reams. He spoke quietly in order not to be overheard. "So, are we good? It's been a while."

"Yeah, it was just one of those things. We are good," replied Reams with a smile.

* * *

CIA SPECIAL ACTIVITIES DIVISION B-HUT - BAGRAM AIR BASE

The seven members of the team known as Special Activities Division Team "ATLAS" met in the B-hut that they had been provided when they had arrived. The space was empty except for a single table, ten chairs, and the large pile of pelican cases, bags, and weapon boxes that they had stacked at the rear of the building when they arrived.

"So, what the fuck are we doing here boss?" asked Jack O'Connor, the team's EOD expert. "Not that I was sorry to leave Iraq, but I didn't mind that it was mostly flat. I look at these mountains around us, and all I see is pain."

There was quiet in the room for a moment, and then Hunter Scott cleared his throat. "Well, the official line is that Dr. Reynolds convinced the boss that it was time that SAD was more deeply involved in the strategic mission set here. The Department of Defense is starting a surge, and he thinks that there will be opportunities for us to take action."

"I'm sorry," said Dan Reyes, a former Delta operator and the operations officer for the team. "What in the hell is a strategic mission set in Afghanistan? A strategic mission set is nukes, or comms, or leadership. None of that shit here."

"Maybe we are after Osama?" said O'Connor.

"Fuck that," replied Reyes. "There are tens of thousands of folks here looking for Osama. Hell, there are more paramilitary teams in this single compound alone than almost anywhere else in the world. Everyone wants his scalp. What do we add?"

"I think the answer might be plausible deniability," said Scott. "Look, I said it was the official line. I personally think we are here just in case something big happens. In the meantime, we will be operating off the record."

"Fuuuuck," said O'Connor in a long, drawn-out way. "Come on, dude, that tells us nothing. We are in SAD, that means we are always off the record."

There was another pause, and Amina Khan, the unit's intelligence officer, spoke. "I wandered around the JSOC facility for a while and checked around. Nobody officially knows that we are here. I mean, there are a few familiar faces who saw us arrive, but the action officer at the CIA desk swears he didn't know we were coming."

"So, what the hell does that mean?" asked Reyes. "Not sure I want to work in this shithole without top cover."

"Oh, shutup you wanker," said Amir Patel, the group's combat medic and veteran of the British Army. "We fucking love working without top cover."

"It depends on where we are I suppose, you British prick," said Reyes with a smile. He got serious. "I've been here before, and I know that working without backup is stupid."

"Well, I don't know if that is the case, but I know this conversation is stupid," said Emilio Delegado. A sniper and electronics specialist, he stood up from the table and went to one of the pelican cases. "I'm going to set up the satellite dish. It's time to see what we have online."

Scott's phone buzzed. He looked at it for a minute. "Well, speak of the devil. Winters is arriving tomorrow. He has a meeting with the aviation guys first and then will have a chat with us when he is done. In the meantime, he says to start setting this place up as our base." He looked at his team. "Time to unpack."

"Home sweet home," said O'Connor as he looked around the plywood-walled room. "Great."

* * *

OUTSIDE BAGRAM AIR BASE

At 2332, the crude ignition device on the three 122mm rockets fired. The first two rockets ignited nearly simultaneously and arced into the sky towards the base. The violence of their launch destroyed the temporary structure they had been leaning against, and as a result, when the third rocket ignited a tenth of a second later, it punched through the adobe wall of the hut and tumbled across the neighboring field before lying inert a few hundred meters away.

The two rockets that had successfully launched were tracked by the base's 20mm C-RAM counter-artillery system, but the automated device could not engage due to their shallow trajectory. The first rocket landed on an empty taxiway and exploded, leaving a shallow hole and no other damage. The second missile landed with a 'thud' in the dirt between the main taxiway and the runway, the remains of the projectile sticking out of the ground after the warhead failed to detonate.

IN THE EL ZED, Briggs and Reams heard the blaring alarm from "Big Voice." Multiple sets of powerful speakers that ringed the base began broadcasting a loud, klaxon-like alarm. The alert was interrupted with the words "Incoming, Incoming" in short intervals. Within a few seconds, they heard the sound of a single explosion somewhere off towards the flight line.

Lawson walked over with a concerned look on his face and asked, “Aren’t we supposed to do something? Go to shelter?”

“It is what we are supposed to do,” replied Reams. “But odds are very high that the attack is over. They shoot a few rockets, miss, and that is all the excitement you get. The alert will go for another hour or so until they have accounted for everyone.”

“You’ll need to call into whoever is keeping track of you in the Ops Center,” said Briggs. “They will send a headcount to headquarters.”

“So you aren’t heading to the bunker?” asked Lawson.

“Actually,” said Briggs tiredly. “I’m going to bed.” He stood up and looked at Reams. “Great to see you again, Nancy.” He turned to Lawson and Khawar. “Welcome to Bagram.”

6

SPECIAL OPERATIONS HEADQUARTERS - BAGRAM AIR BASE

Briggs walked toward the Ops B-hut half an hour before the meeting was set to begin. He'd woken up feeling relatively refreshed, gone for a run, and eaten breakfast with his new roommate. When they finished, Scott left to find his team, and Briggs took his customary route past the coffee shop.

He pulled open the plywood door to the Ops hut, careful not to spill the coffee in his left hand, and stepped inside.

"Good morning, sunshine," McCoy called from behind the counter, his voice dripping with fake cheer. "You ready for a couple hours of meetings?"

Briggs walked in and sat down at the briefing table. "Not particularly." He looked at McCoy. "We gonna talk about what role you want me to play in this bullshit?"

McCoy came around the counter and sat across from him. "Why do you think this is bullshit?"

Briggs took a sip of coffee. "Reynolds has had this plan in the works long enough to already have a strike team transferred from Iraq and an aviation guy surveying likely operating sites. Nobody really cares what we think, so why pretend?"

"Well, with that attitude, you'll really enjoy the fact that two MH-60Ms are showing up in the next couple of days," McCoy said. "Since you and Fletcher are the only pilots we have who were ever qualified to fly them, I expect we'll be seeing some new crew members soon."

Briggs was quiet for a moment before speaking, his voice lower. "This mission requires skills that don't just come back overnight. When I did this shit in the Army, I was younger, dumber, and my reflexes were better."

"I think that should be part of the discussion," McCoy replied. "It can help guide the missions we take on."

"Who are you kidding?" Briggs scoffed. "Before long, we'll just be taking the same units off into the dark to kill terrorists. I was completely burned out when I left. You get that, right?"

"Briggs, you've got just over two months left on this rotation," McCoy said, trying to sound reasonable. "Help us get this going, and I'll see if we can get you home early."

Briggs gave him a sharp look. "That sounds like you're offering me parole. I'm a volunteer, not an inmate. Don't fucking go there again."

"Okay, I'm sorry," McCoy said sincerely. "We're all beat. Hey, at least this time, we get to wear civvies."

Briggs didn't smile. "So, who's in this meeting?"

"Winters got in last night," McCoy replied. "He's probably worthless from jet lag, but he's leading the discussion. There'll be a Colonel from JSOC and probably a couple of his minions. One of our reps from the Combined Air Operations Center at Al Udeid will be there too."

"Right," Briggs said. "So, what do you want me to do?"

"Attend the meeting. Sit next to me. Take notes. No negative comments that make it sound like the CIA's Special Activities Division isn't working together as a team, understand?"

"Got it," Briggs said. He glanced at his watch and stood abruptly. "Let's go."

* * *

FOB CHAPMAN - KHOST

The helicopter from J-bad had dropped the forensics team off at base operations. The men had unloaded their gear and were sitting outside the waiting area smoking cigarettes.

"It seems like we were just here," said Grayson as he popped open a soda, cigarette dangling from his lip.

"Wasn't that long ago," said Flynn. "It was like the second trip for us."

"Yup," said Jenkins. "We went south along the border last time."

A large desert tan MRAP rolled to a stop outside the waiting area. The heavy armored driver-side door opened up, and a Sergeant with an EOD badge on his chest stepped out.

"You guys the forensics team?"

"That's us," said Flynn.

The Sergeant stepped forward, "I'm Marcus Blake, one of the EOD guys that you'll be working with." He stepped forward to shake hands with all three of the men.

"Is that your gear?" Blake asked, pointing to a pile of equipment that included four large Pelican cases, backpacks, and other personal gear.

"That's it," said Grayson.

"Well, let me help you load up." He pointed to the MRAP. "This will be your vehicle for the duration." He looked at the three soldiers. "One of you is qualified on the MRAP, right?"

"We all are," replied Flynn. "Trained and current."

"Great," replied Blake.

The men stubbed out or finished their cigarettes, stood up, and began loading into the MRAP.

"This fucker is brand new," said Jenkins happily as he climbed into the back of the truck. "Still smells like a new car. Much better than that rolling piece of shit they gave us in A-Bad. We should have driven over an IED on purpose and just put that dam thing out of its misery."

"You guys have been to Asadabad?" asked Blake.

"Oh, yes," said Jenkins grumpily. "Just got back from a wonderful two week experience in FOB Wright, getting shot at every damn day."

"Damn," said Blake. "Well, we get shelled every once in a while. Our patrols get hit pretty frequently, but mostly with small arms. They shoot at us and run away."

"But there is a new bomber along the highway, right?" asked Flynn.

"Oh yeah," replied Blake. "Hit a special forces team and some spooks last week."

Jenkins turned to Flynn knowingly, "That's why they rushed us here. Someone hit some of the special guys."

"Sounds like it," said Flynn noncommittally.

"The spooks pretty much run this base," said Blake. He pointed up to the north where the White Mountains were just visible in the haze. "That's Taliban country. Lots going on behind the scenes in this area."

"I'm sure there is," said Flynn. "Where are we staying?"

"Get in, and I'll take you to our part of the compound. Our supply shack has plenty of room for you guys," said Blake. "Lieutenant Johnson wants us on the road at 0430 tomorrow so we can get to the location of the last IED strike early."

"Great," replied Flynn flatly. "Let's go."

* * *

RELIGIOUS SCHOOL, CHARIKAR - OUTSIDE OF BAGRAM AIR BASE

The door to the small room opened. The young man, who had a restless night, was already awake and dressed. He was sitting on the cot placed along the wall.

"Come with me, Rahman," said the Imam. "It is time for morning prayers."

The two then walked from the school building and across the courtyard to the neighboring mosque, the two guards maintaining a discrete distance. As they stepped inside, it surprised the young man to see that the small Mosque was full; there were more than forty men already inside.

When Rahman attempted to stay in the rear of the building, the Imam shook his head and insistently walked him all the way to the front of the church. They stopped by five or six older villagers who bowed or nodded slightly to the Imam and then took turns shaking Rahman's hand somberly. "Go with God."

The Imam stepped up to the front of the room and, after saying his prayers, stood for the sermon. He delivered a fiery narrative of sacrifice and redemption that was rewarded by the low and reverent responses of "Inshallah," or "Allah Akbar." He held up his hands and the room went silent. He then stepped forward, reached for Rahman's hand, and helped the young man to his feet.

As the pair walked through the quiet room full of penitents, Rahman felt gentle hands pat him on his shoulder, or reach for his hand and shake it. For the first time in his life he felt valued, honored; his heart swelled with pride.

"We will go break our fast," said the Imam. He led Rahman back across the courtyard to a room in the school building that had been set up for the meal. There was a long wooden table set up in the middle of the room that contained a wide variety of excellent foods. "Take this seat here," said the Imam, pointing to one of the chairs. Rahman sat down, and the Imam sat next to him at the head of the table. The two guards pulled over chairs for themselves and sat at the other end of the table.

"Enjoy yourself," said the Imam gesturing to the food.

Rahman was very hungry; the meals during the trip had been very meager. He ate until he was full and then sat back in his chair. "This was wonderful."

"It was," replied the Imam. "A blessing for you." He paused for a moment. "It is time for you to go. Your guides will take you to your next step. Go with God."

All of the men stood up. The guards led Rahman out of the room and across the gravel to a black passenger van. The driver started the vehicle as Rahman sat in the back with a guard, while the other sat in the passenger seat.

The Imam walked over, and spoke through the open window. "You are God's warrior, Rahman. Have great courage, and your victory will be assured."

After the van pulled out, the Imam retrieved a cell phone from his robes and dialed. "The package is inbound." He listened for a second. "No problems here; it will be good." He listened again. "Yes, I will pick up the next one in ten days time. Inshallah."

* * *

SPECIAL OPERATIONS HEADQUARTERS - BAGRAM AIR BASE

"Good morning guys, thanks for coming. I'm Terrance Winters, the CIA's lead for the Special Activities Division here in Afghanistan."

Winters was sitting at the head of a table that seated eight. Seated around the table were an Army Colonel, a Lieutenant Colonel, McCoy, Briggs, and a younger male CIA agent who Briggs didn't know.

"I'm here to help to coordinate a new effort," said Winters. He picked up the coffee in front of him and took a drink. "We are going to start to conduct some night raids. Within a few days we will have two MH-60Ms added to our local aviation inventory. I already have a strike team forming up here in the compound as we speak. As you know, we have several trained aircrew on station to fly the current fleet of support aircraft. We are expecting more to arrive in a couple of weeks." He looked down at his notes and back up at the group, "We intend for this mission to primarily operate near Jalalabad, Khost, and the White Mountains in and around the Tora Bora area."

Colonel Matt Carter shuffled in his chair. "So, are you telling us this, or asking for assistance?"

"Maybe a little of both," said Winters. "I've already talked to Tampa and stopped by Ft Bragg just over a week ago. We all understand resources are stretched and that it is going to get worse during the surge, but that is the whole point."

"Stretched tight doesn't begin to explain how busy we are," said the Colonel. "My guys are running two or three raids a night. It doesn't sound to me like you are going to help relieve that pressure; you are just going to tie up my air support."

"We are not going to be running nightly raids, if that is what you are saying," said Winters. "Our target list is smaller." He looked at Carter. "We've been tasked with putting some pressure on the Taliban near the border while you continue your normal targeting process."

"So, you will be tying up my resources," Carter said flatly. "Did this issue come up in Tampa?"

"It did," Winters confirmed. "Leadership expects us to work it out here in theater."

"Fuck," Carter muttered tiredly.

A young CIA agent - one Briggs didn't recognize - spoke up. "We can make it work in the CAOC. There's room in the schedule for two or three extra raids a week."

Carter turned a jaundiced eye toward the speaker. "Thanks for the input. Who the hell are you?"

Without hesitation, the man replied, "I'm Alex Ramirez. I'm

the all-purpose CIA representative in the CAOC. There hasn't been much for me to do, so I've been working with the JSOC air element schedulers every night."

"Well, thanks for that, Alex," Carter said sourly. "I'm sure we all appreciate your opinion."

Silence settled over the table for a moment before the Lieutenant Colonel spoke. "What about ramp space and ground support? Have you talked to those guys yet? Lots of units are bringing gear in for the surge. That north ramp is pretty full."

"Good point," Carter said. "Is there room for you to expand here?"

"Yeah, there's space for a couple of additional birds, but it's tight. I've got my aviation rep out on a survey right now," Winters replied. "For now, I think we'll keep our maintenance effort here, but we'll probably send the new aircraft to Jalalabad for an extended period."

"That'll limit the need for aerial fuel," Briggs noted. "At most, we'll need air cover, but we can make do with TACAIR instead of the AC-130s you usually use."

"Well, that's comforting," Carter said sardonically. He turned to Briggs. "You're Briggs, right?"

"I am," Briggs replied.

"I know your background. What do you think about this?" Carter asked.

Briggs saw both Winters and McCoy watching him warily. "It depends on communication, as always," he said. "If Ramirez does a good job in the CAOC and we put someone on the operations floor here every night, the coordination for resources won't be worse than anything else we're doing."

"That didn't answer my question," Carter said.

Briggs met the Colonel's gaze. "I think there are a lot of targets to handle, especially with more troops coming in over the next few weeks. I don't see how we have any choice."

"Yeah," Carter said, exhaling. "I get that." He looked up. "I'm going to communicate my reservations back to CONUS, but we'll make shit happen like we always do." He gestured to the Lieutenant Colonel beside him. "Jay Thompson will handle this for me. Let me know if you need anything."

"Good," Winters said. "We appreciate that."

* * *

PANJ KALA - OUTSIDE BAGRAM AIR BASE

"This is your vehicle," said the older guard, pointing to a smaller Jingle truck. "You told us you know how to drive; this is true, right?"

"Yes," replied Rahman. He looked at the Jingle truck. It had a covered box on the rear that three men were loading with crates of explosives.

"We will give you a radio and follow you to the gate," said the guard. He handed Rahman a trigger. "You will hold this tightly. Once we have removed the safety, it will detonate when you release it."

Raman held the trigger in his hand and felt the odd power of it. He looked up. "How will I know when?"

"You will drive into the base as far as you can. If you can get to the headquarters, do it there. It is a large building with lots of flags out front. If you get stopped or inspected, you will do it there," said the older guard.

The guard pointed Rahman to a room where Rahman recognized the al-Qa'ida flag spread across a wall. There was a video camera set up and an AK-47 leaning against the wall.

"You can read? asked the older guard. Rahman nodded.

The younger guard led Rahman to a spot in front of the flag. He had him place one knee on the ground and look at the camera. Next, he retrieved the AK-47, checked that it was unloaded, and gave it to Rahman. The final touch was the headband of the martyr, placed around his head and tied in the back.

The older guard stepped forward and gave Rahman a sheet of paper. "Here are your words. They will live forever, as will you."

The two guards stepped behind the camera. The younger guard ensured the focus was correct and hit 'record.'

"Read the paper," said the older guard.

The first time, it took only a few minutes for Rahman to read the words. They made him do it again because he was clearly nervous and was reading too quickly.

"You are God's chosen," said the older guard. "Relax, think about the words."

The young man steadied himself, looked into the camera, and bravely read the last words of the martyr.

When he was done, the two guards led Rahman away to a little room off the side of the garage in which the truck was being worked on. The room was undecorated. There was a chair and wooden bed with a copy of the Koran sitting in the middle of the blanket.

"You can prepare yourself here," said the older guard. Rahman stepped inside, and the door closed behind him. He went to the bed and sat down.

Outside, the guards conferred. "When will the truck be ready?"

"Two hours, but we will wait until the morning as planned," said the older guard.

* * *

FOB CHAPMAN - KHOST

"You guys going to be ready to roll out tomorrow morning?" asked Lieutenant Eric Johnson. He had visited the forensics team inside the supply shack that they had been assigned for their visit. One of the original buildings on the base, it was relatively small. Half of the room was filled with supplies for the unit's MRAPs, but there were six empty cots lined up as an overflow for visitors.

"Yes, sir," replied Flynn. "We unloaded our stuff and are settled into the truck."

"Great, I appreciate it," said Johnson. "I was online with headquarters before you got here and they told me to take good care of you. I heard you've been busy."

"The business of IEDs is pretty good in Afghanistan these days," said Jenkins with a straight face.

"I suppose it is," replied Johnson. "Mind if I ask what it is you actually do?"

"Sure," said Flynn. "All three of us are cops in our day jobs," he said, pointing to Jenkins and Grayson. "We move between FOBs and help collect evidence that identifies new bombers, new tactics, and new materials for the Counter IED Task Force. Everything goes back to Bagram and sometimes all the way back to the FBI lab at Quantico."

"Cool," said Johnson. "So you can make a legal case out of this?"

"Well," said Flynn. "I don't think anyone expects that will really happen. But there are dudes being held in Guantanamo based on similar kinds of evidence. We will see what we can find over the next couple of days and help you guys track this fucker down. We will collect evidence and you or someone else will put him six feet under."

"I hope so," said Johnson. He rolled out a map on top of a stack of crates. "Tomorrow should be pretty simple, kind of a shakedown movement." He pointed to a spot along the Gardez-Khost highway. "This is where we are heading. It's where the last attack took place, one wounded and two KIA." He looked up at Flynn. "The road is pretty good along here, so we should be up there in a couple hours, let you do your thing with EOD, and then head back before it gets too late."

"Sounds good to me," replied Flynn.

* * *

SPECIAL OPERATIONS COMPOUND - BAGRAM AIR BASE

"Well, that was pointless," said Briggs.

"What do you mean, pointless?" replied McCoy.

"Nothing got done," said Briggs. "Typical D.C. style meeting. The only difference is that it took place in Bagram. We sat around a table, talked, and nothing got done."

Winters spoke up. "Shit Briggs, that was a great meeting. We told JSOC what we were doing and they agreed not to interfere as long as we didn't tie up the resources they are using. They gave us a good point of contact who is pretty senior and publicly told him to assist us."

"What in the hell are you talking about?" asked Briggs.

Winters laughed, "You'd be hopeless in D.C. All of those things happened. Ramirez here was the guy who nearly screwed things up." He turned to the junior CIA agent who was walking alongside them. "Didn't I tell you not to say shit in there?"

"It seemed like the right thing to point out," said Ramirez defensively. "I see extra assets airborne every single night."

"That is something for you and the other junior CAOC representatives to work out between each other at the action officer level. Now that Colonel Carter knows you are on the inside, expect to be removed from your little volunteer effort."

"What?" asked Ramirez, surprised. "No way."

"The Army does not want anyone from the outside questioning their resourcing decisions," said McCoy. "You just exposed the fact that there was a CIA guy keeping an eye on things. I'd bet ten dollars that you have already been kicked off the team."

"A classic counter-intelligence blunder. You burned yourself," said Winters. He saw Ramirez's glum look. "That's okay, I'm reassigning you here to Bagram anyway. You got good exposure to the process at the CAOC, and we have more friends here at the

JOC in Bagram to cover for your rookie mistakes. I've got a replacement in mind for you at Al Udied anyway."

The group was quiet for a moment as a large truck passed them on the gravel road, raising a cloud of dust.

"I know I'm changing the subject, but when do the new helicopters get here?" asked Briggs.

"Soon," said Winters. "I'll sit down with you and McCoy tomorrow to figure out a plan to get moving. Our man Barnes should also get here tomorrow." He shook his head tiredly. "Right now, I need a break. My brain is somewhere over the Atlantic trying to catch up to my body at a very slow speed. I have one more meeting to take care of right now, and then I am going to take a nap."

"Well, I've got one request for tomorrow," said Briggs.

"What's that?" asked Winters tiredly.

"Don't let Mike Gray sit in the meeting," replied Briggs. "Or any meeting for that matter."

Startled, McCoy laughed.

"Done," said Winters.

7

AL-QAEDA FIGHTERS AT THE FOOT OF THE WHITE MOUNTAINS - PARICHINAR, PAKISTAN

"Are we ready?" asked Khalil Al-Sudani.

"We are," replied Abu Hamza. "We have thirty-six fighters for the trip."

"How is our security?" asked Al-Sudani.

"Good," said Hamza. "You and I hold the only satellite phones in the group, and I have two metallic bags for us both to store them."

"That is only part of my concern," said Al-Sudani. "There are no reports of rumors or other indications of information leaking about our trip?"

"None," replied Hamza. "These are God's warriors. They are veterans and understand the cost of weakness. None of them have said a word."

"Do they understand why we are going to Tora Bora?" asked Al-Sudani.

Hamza paused for a moment. "They believe they are going to protect the Sheikh as he returns to battle."

It was Al-Sudani's turn to pause. "No, our mission is not so grand. There is a cache of material hidden in a cave that the Sheikh can not afford for the invaders to recover. We are tasked to return it to him, or destroy it."

"I see," said Hamza, scratching his beard. "It is still a righteous test."

"It is," said Al-Sudani. "We must travel quickly and avoid contact with the enemy. When we approach the caves there is little doubt that we will be discovered, but the Sheikh judges that we can complete the mission and return before the enemy responds."

"If he says it, we will do so," said Hamza. "Allah Akbar."

"Allah Akbar."

* * *

A GARAGE IN PANJ KALA - OUTSIDE BAGRAM AIR BASE

"You need to drink this," said the older guard to Rahman. He held out a small teacup to the young man. "It is part of the preparation."

Rahman took the cup and drank the two ounces of bitter fluid he found in the cup. When he was done, he shook his head. "What was that?"

"It takes the pain away and lets you float into the clouds when God calls you to heaven," said the guard.

A tough-looking man walked into the room with a bomb vest. "Hold out your arms."

Rahman held out his arms as they placed the heavy vest on him. "You can put your arms down now," said the tough man.

Rahman heard a 'click' from behind him.

"It is armed," said the tough-looking man. He looked at Rahman for a moment. "Go with God," and then walked from the room.

The older guard led Rahman to his truck. "Get in."

Rahman climbed into the vehicle. He was surprised when the

older guard handcuffed him to the wheel. He felt that he should be more surprised, but was feeling increasingly disconnected, as if this was all happening to someone else.

The younger guard brought in the handheld trigger. "This is not armed yet. We will arm it remotely. When we tell you on the radio, you must push and hold the button. When you release it, your mission will be done. Do you understand?

Rahman swallowed and nodded.

The older guard turned on a radio handset that was connected to the bomb vest. "Radio is on. We can hear you through this."

The younger guard climbed into the passenger side of the truck and turned the ignition key. The engine started quickly. He climbed back out of the truck and slammed the door shut, startling everyone in the garage.

"Ooof," said the older guard. "Be careful, no more slamming things!" He leaned in the open driver's side window of the truck. "You will follow our van. We will take you to within five kilometers of the gate, then it is up to you." He paused and put his hand on Rahman's shoulder. "Idhhab ma'a Allah."

* * *

FOB CHAPMAN - KHOST

"Mount'em up," said the voice of Lieutenant Eric Johnson over the tactical radio in the MRAP.

In their new vehicle, Jenkins looked at Flynn, "Mount'em up? Not one of those Army Cavalry nuts again. Fuck."

Grayson, who had drawn the short straw and was driving the MRAP turned to Jenkins in the passenger seat and laughed. "Should have figured when he told us we were now part of Thunder Squadron."

It was 0520 in the morning and the enthusiasm in the forensics team was remarkably high considering they had spent the night in a supply shed. The three team members had been assigned the callsign "Lancer Four" as the fourth of seven MRAPs on the mission. Lancer Three contained the Explosive Ordnance Disposal team, and the rest of the MRAPs contained troops from the 73rd Calvary Regiment.

"Let's roll," came the call from Johnson.

The men watched as the first three MRAPs rolled out of the gate, turned right, and headed towards the Gardez-Khost Highway. Jenkins put the vehicle into gear and followed.

"Well, off we go," said Grayson. "How is the system in this thing?"

"It's fucking great," said Jenkins. "Camera works, the jammer works, and the radios are all new. I want to take this back home with us."

"We'll see what we can work out," said Flynn from the back.

* * *

ON THE GARDEZ-KHOST HIGHWAY - KHOST

Nabil Hamid had enjoyed his stay in Khost, but it was time to head back into the mountains. The meeting with Zayan Shah had been marginally productive. He had gotten new tasking, more supplies, but none of the money that could have paid off the family of the villagers who had died.

As was his normal custom, he had decided to leave very early in the morning, just after morning prayers had finished. This would put him in the mountains in mid-afternoon. He had a little over a hundred kilometers to drive and was supposed to meet a Taliban contact up near the Gardez-Khost pass in the Suliman mountains. According to Shah, his new job was to begin harassing the Americans who had an outpost near the pass itself and see what he could do to create havoc there. The challenge was that the mujahedeen in that area were very wary of outsiders; not only would he need an introduction, but might perhaps require full-time support.

He got into his Hilux and started the diesel motor with a puff of dark smoke. He sat for a moment, letting the vehicle warm up. He had an AK-74 hidden under a blanket in the passenger footwell and three Russian grenades in a pouch next to it. In the cargo bed were all the materials required for a few dozen more IEDs. They fit into a surprisingly compact space among the lumber that filled most of the bed. His cargo would not pass much of an inspection if he was stopped, but the risk of a search was very small.

He placed the truck into gear and began driving through the relatively quiet city. He eventually arrived on the two-lane paved track and turned to head northeast into the mountains. As he drove, the traffic increased as the city woke up. After about five minutes of easy driving, he found himself in a traffic jam stuck behind a ragged line of vehicles; cars, motorcycles, and jingle trucks, all were motionless on the normally busy highway. He considered the likelihood of some kind of security roadblock and decided to see what he could discover. He turned off the truck, locked the door, and walked down the side of the road. He had only walked a hundred meters when he saw the issue. An American convoy had stopped traffic. One of the large armored trucks known as a MRAP stopped across the road, holding traffic while several others slowly turned onto the highway and headed east.

This was unlucky. He knew that the Americans were probably heading along the highway into the mountains or perhaps to the nearby Afghan Army base. The complication was that no traffic was allowed to pass the convoy. Anyone who tried would hear the warning shot of a machine gun. If they did not stop, they would be fired upon.

As he walked back to his pickup, he considered his options. The safest move would be to find a place to stay in town for a few hours and let the Americans get out of the way. The choice that he was leaning towards was more risky.

He started the pickup. After judiciously using his horn and urgently waving people aside with his hands, he finally managed to squeeze his truck through the line of parked vehicles and into a narrow alleyway. He picked his way through the alley, around garbage piles, past abandoned vehicles and other detritus of decades, until he came to a large street that was parallel to the highway. With some relief that he had not flattened a tire, he turned onto the street and continued driving for another ten kilometers. The road eventually ended at a "T" intersection, where he turned once again back towards the highway.

After driving three more kilometers, he found himself at the last major intersection with the highway. His timing was perfect. In the distance, he could see the line of American armored vehicles moving at a deliberate pace down the road towards him. He stopped for a moment and counted seven of the monstrous trucks. Before they could pass him once again, he turned right and back onto the highway, accelerating ahead of the convoy into the mountains. He had remembered that Zayan Shah had said that the Americans might be looking him. If this was truly the case he had an idea of where they might be heading. He was now excited. If he could get far enough ahead of them, there was a chance that he could turn this encounter into an opportunity to make them regret their patrol.

* * *

CIA SPECIAL ACTIVITIES DIVISION B-HUT - BAGRAM AIR BASE, AFGHANISTAN

"Jesus Winters, you look like shit," said Dan Reyes. "When did you get in here?"

"Thanks for that, Reyes," said Winters. "I got in a few hours ago, and this is my second meeting of the day. As soon as we are done here, I promise that I will crash for a while."

Winters was sitting in one of the folding chairs that were the only furniture in the B-hut. The gear that had once been piled in the back of the space had now been neatly organized. There was a classified computer sitting on the table and all seven members of team ATLAS were present.

"Well, we are glad you took the time to stop by," said Hunter Scott. "This situation seems a little ad hoc, even for us."

"Yeah, I understand. We are jumping through our ass right now," said Winters. "Reynolds is getting a lot of pressure from above. There are a few targets along and across the border that we need to handle."

"There are dozens of CIA paramilitary guys here already, not to mention the Counter Terrorism Pursuit Teams," said Amir Patel. "What do we add?"

"We need to conduct some clean cross-border ops," said Winters. "Everything here right now is somehow connected to the formal effort. Either through JSOC or our Pursuit Teams. We needed an off-the-record unit to take care of a few things. You know, do some real CIA shit."

"I fucking told you so," said O'Connor as he looked at Patel. "Pay up."

Patel smiled, reached down by his chair, and handed O'Connor a paper bag.

"What the hell is this?" said O'Connor. He opened the bag, reached in, and pulled out a handful of paper pogs.

"It's twenty dollars in pogs," said Patel with a grin.

"You dick," said O'Connor, the exasperation clear in his voice.

Everyone in the room laughed.

"Okay," said Winters. "I'm beat, so let's get this done." He turned to Amina Khan. "Amina, you are the only one who I want to go into the Joint Ops Center. The CIA rep will have a desk for you. Your cover is that you are working on a special project for Langley."

"Some cover," said Delgado wryly.

"It'll work," said Winters. "Anyway, you'll get targeting info via that network. You will be supported by two dedicated MH-60M aircraft that are on the way. While we wait for the aviation guys to get their shit together you have your own work to do. Go to the range. Work out. Get some sleep. Do what you need to do. Familiarize yourself with the border area near Khost and Torkam Gate. As soon as the helicopter team is ready, you'll get tasking. Expect difficult targets and long-range shots." He looked around, "And some messaging."

"Messaging?" asked Scott.

"Well, let's just say that we think that people across the border who are enabling the bombing of Americans ought to reap what they sow."

* * *

OUTSIDE THE FRONT GATE - BAGRAM AIR BASE

Rahman had followed the black van for a few kilometers through an older part of the little town. As they got closer to the big American base, the traffic increased.

He heard the voice of the older guard come from his radio. "It is up to you now, young hero. Allah Akbar." He saw a small red light illuminate on the trigger. He gripped the device tightly, knowing that if he released it too early, his mission would fail.

Ahead of him the van turned from the highway, leaving Rahman on his own. For a while he wove his way through traffic but eventually began following another container truck that was heading the same direction. After about three more kilometers, they both arrived at the first set of walls.

His guides had described the procedure several times. He would follow the other trucks through the first open gate. There were no guards there. All of the trucks would park temporarily in a large holding area, waiting to be inspected one at a time in another, smaller lot. He was not to wait for the inspection. Once he saw a clear path to the main gate, he was supposed to accelerate, break through the guards, and then drive down the road until he saw his primary target.

RAHMAN FELT NUMB. Whatever they had given him in the teacup had removed all emotion. There was an annoying roaring in his ears that seemed to be getting louder.

He drove through the outer gate, relieved that he was now inside the base. He followed the truck in front of him for a few meters and then parked side by side with about a dozen other vehicles. After he stopped, he sat, one hand clutching the wheel, the other clutching the trigger; waiting. He looked up through the windshield. He could see armed American and Afghan guards along the walls, looking down into the parking area.

Rahman watched as the other drivers got out of their trucks and gathered around, talking, joking, and smoking cigarettes. After a few minutes, he saw the first truck in the row pull forward and head towards the inspection gate.

He heard a voice from the radio on his chest, fuzzy now as if he was in a dream. "Go boy. Go now!" While he felt increasingly detached, he began to pull forward slowly. Leaving his spot took more effort than he had imagined. As he turned towards the gate he tried not to hit the confused drivers who were now yelling and waving for him to stop.

Up on the HESCO outer wall of the base, Specialist Malik James saw a truck begin to move out of order in the first inspection section. The other men with more experience were clearly trying to stop the rogue driver, but the vehicle continued to move forward slowly. This wasn't entirely uncommon; it was the first time at the base for many of the drivers and it was a more complicated process than they were used to. Once the interloper had been stopped, they would always be sent to the back of the line as a penalty for the infraction.

James lifted his rifle so that he could use the optic on his rifle to see the driver better. It took him a moment to steady his view, but when he did, he quickly saw that the driver was holding a detonation device in his right hand and seemed to be wearing a bomb vest.

"Oh shit!" He picked up his radio and yelled. "VBIED in the containment facility! VBIED in the containment facility!"

It took less than three seconds for the klaxon of Big Voice began to sound. "Take cover!"

James clicked the safety of his M-4 rifle off, steadied himself, and pulled the trigger, aiming directly at the driver of the slowly moving truck.

RAHMAN WAS PULLING towards the gate, waiting to get around one other vehicle before he accelerated. His awareness that his mission was almost complete was bursting in his brain. The other drivers had stopped trying to tell him to stay and had begun to run from him in a panic. It felt so much like he was dreaming now. He looked around in a daze, and it seemed as if time was slowing.

The urgent voice from the radio seemed to be smothered in deep cotton. "Go boy! Go faster!"

He wasn't sure what that meant. It now seemed to him as if he was already flying. The glass of the truck's windshield started to break apart. He saw bullet holes appear and was mesmerized by the way the shards of glass scattered the light as they fell. He felt a sharp moment of pain as a bullet entered his chest, and then he felt no more.

. . .

THE FIVE HUNDRED kilograms of plastic explosive in the bed of the truck went off with a crushing blast, instantly incinerating Rahman and four of the drivers who had not gotten to safety. Twelve cargo trucks burned to the ground. However, aside from the carnage inside the isolation lot, there was little damage on the base aside from some broken glass in windows within a few hundred meters, and light damage from shrapnel that landed inside the base walls; shrapnel that would later be collected by the troops inside as a curiosity.

SPECIALIST JAMES STOOD up from behind the sandbags that he had used for cover. He looked over the wall and saw the burning wreckage of several trucks. There were a variety of sirens sounding, and the klaxon of the Big Voice was still going. His ears felt as if they were filled with water from the pool. He worked his jaw and unsuccessfully tried to clear it. A Lieutenant walked up to him, "Are you okay?"

Yes sir. Or, I think so anyway. My hearing is a bit off."

"We will get you to the doc. Was that your call on the radio?"

"Yes, sir."

"You did a fucking great job soldier. You saved lives," said the Lieutenant. "CID might want to talk to you, but we have it all on tape." He patted James on the back. "Really great job," he said almost absently as he looked from James to the burning mess inside the compound.

THE WRECKAGE BURNED for some time, sending a towering pillar of black smoke into the air. However, within two hours, EOD had declared the site clear, and a bulldozer had pushed the twisted mass of metal from the parking area and out into a vacant gravel lot where it smouldered for several hours as container trucks continued to drive in, one at a time.

8

AIRBORNE - SOMEWHERE NEAR GARDEZ

"TUSK 30, your tanker TEXACO 22 is BRA 010 at 25, angels 18," called the AWACS. "With the tanker in sight, cleared to boom frequency."

"TUSK 30 copies," replied Major "Noodles" Matthews. "Looking."

MATTHEWS WAS at the controls of her trusty A-10C. She had launched from Bagram two hours earlier and had been sent to a kill box in the vicinity of Gardez, Afghanistan, where she and her wingman, Captain "Chris" Cross were waiting for tasking. After nearly two hours of flying lazy circles without being directed to a target, they now needed to refuel so that they could cover the second half of their four-hour mission.

While the troops on the ground saw Afghanistan as dusty roads, small villages, mountains and deserts, from an aviation perspective, the entire nation was divided up to a grid of boxes labeled alphanumeric characters. These were known as "kill boxes." Overlaying these kill boxes were a large number of pre-established tracks for all of the specialist aircraft that flew over the fight, tankers, AWACs, Electronic Warfare, and drones, all at different altitudes that were also assigned in the Air Tasking Order, or ATO. Since there was no air traffic radar in Afghanistan, all of the aircraft flew using "procedural deconfliction," which meant that knowing your specified altitude was important.

As she looked for her tanker, Matthews reflected on the fact that the war in Afghanistan would drastically different without the giant tankers. Every tactical aircraft or bomber that operated over Afghanistan required aerial refueling; without it, the character of the war would be different, and definitely much worse for the troops on the ground.

"TALLY, LEFT ELEVEN O'CLOCK," called Cross on their plane-to-plane frequency. The A-10C had a variety of radio capabilities. They generally maintained one UHF radio on the control frequency, one on a frequency that they used between aircraft, and had another system that enabled communication with the troops on the ground.

Matthews saw the KC-135 slightly left of her nose and made a call to her wingman, "Switching to boom freq." She then dialed in the frequency that the tanker was using.

"TEXACO 22, TUSK 30 and 31 are two A-10's, five miles out, port side."

"TUSK 30 and flight, cleared to port observation."

Matthews loved joining with the tanker. It was always gratifying to execute a smooth rendezvous. While she appreciated the fact that the F-15s and F-16s could swoop in at high speed and bring themselves to an abrupt halt next to the tanker, chasing a KC-135 was a different task for the A-10C. The KC-135 with its jet engines would be flying as slow as it could safely go with a heavy load of fuel, while the A-10s with their dual turbofans would be going nearly as fast as they could move to catch it. There was not much margin for error between the two, and an expeditious rendezvous was all about achieving the right geometry.

The KC-135 began a left turn as the A-10s got closer and made the join-up less challenging. Within minutes, Matthews and Cross were flying formation off the left wing of the big tanker.

"TUSK 30 is port observation, nose cold, switches safe," called Matthews, telling the tanker that her weapons were all safe.

"TUSK 30 cleared to pre-contact," replied the tanker, permitting the A-10 to slide behind the boom that had now partially lowered from the rear of the KC-135.

Matthews dropped back and down to a position below the tanker that was indicated by lights on the bottom of the big jet.

Stabilized, she called "Pre-contact."

While Matthews flew formation from below the tanker, an operator who was lying down in the rear of the tanker looking at the A-10 through an observation window now flew the boom to the aerial refueling port on the top of her aircraft. She felt the shudder of contact with the boom and quickly saw her fuel gauge begin to climb. "Contact. TUSK 30 good flow."

"Copy," called the boom operator.

Now, all there was to do was to continue to fly formation with the tanker, a task that got slightly more difficult as her aircraft got heavier.

After a few minutes, she saw the fuel gauge stop rising, just below what she would call full.

"Offload complete."

"Ready for disconnect."

"Disconnect."

In a moment, she was free. She then flew to a position off the tanker's right wing and watched as Cross duplicated the entire procedure. When he was complete, he slid his jet to her right wing.

"TUSK 30 is detaching to the right," called Matthews. "Thanks."

"TUSK 30 is cleared to detach." She could see the pilot in the right seat of the tanker wave. She waved back and then gently turned away from the big jet and set a course back to their holding pattern.

* * *

NEAR THE DARA BAZAR - OUTSIDE GARDEZ

"Goddamit, Hernandez! Keep your truck in the center of the road," came the voice of First Sergeant Danny Reed over the radio. "Stay in the tracks!"

"I am in the damn tracks," grumbled Sergeant Tony Hernandez as he drove the heavy MRAP on the rough dirt track. "This thing steers like a boat."

The man next to Hernandez in the passenger seat of the MRAP, Sergeant David Washington, laughed for a second and picked up the radio handset. "We got it, Danny. We are on the tracks."

"Do it better," came the brief reply from Reed.

The patrol of six MRAPS was rolling west on a dirt and gravel road outside of Gardez. Their intended destination was a village about fifty kilometers from the large American FOB that had been built outside of Gardez. Their company commander, Captain Mike Bennett, had scheduled a meeting with some village elders, and they were running late.

"We should have started earlier," said Bennett. He was riding in the passenger seat of the third MRAP in the formation, eating a bag of potato chips and idly listening to the radio conversation between his troops.

"Sir, you know the village elders don't really give a shit about the meeting, right?" asked Master Sergeant Salem "Mo" Hasan. He was sitting behind Bennett in one of the two crew seats. "In fact, they would be really happy if they never saw our sorry asses again."

"Yeah, I know. For fuck sake, I'd be happy if we never went back too," replied Bennett. "But the U.S. Army insists we be punctual for meetings that we arrange, and I will be dammed if we don't at least give it a shot."

The radio crackled. "Hey, this is Mack. You guys see those motorcycles?" asked a voice. "Two of them. Along the ridgeline, left side. They have been pacing us for a bit."

Reed, sitting in the second MRAP, used the ruggedized screen in front of him to rotate the remote camera that was mounted on the top of his vehicle. He scanned the ridgeline until he saw the motorcycles that his gunner had seen. He zoomed the stabilized camera in on the Afghan cyclists as they rolled to a halt at the top of the terrain and watched the Americans. After looking at them for a moment, he grabbed his microphone. "I don't see any weapons, but that is definitely not good. Nice spot. Let's keep a good three-sixty scan going."

Bennett ate another chip. "Twenty bucks says we get hit."

"Not taking that bet, boss," said Hasan.

"Fuck these people and their shitty desert," said Bennett. He crumpled the bag and tossed it at his feet, where it sat with the growing collection of empty water bottles and other trash.

THIS HAD BEEN the company's life for the last six months. They would drive out to a meeting with some elders, or to check on a sighting of Taliban or al-Qa'ida. There, they would visit with the villagers and hand out food, or pay small sums for useless information, let the medic hand out some ibuprofen, or just try to be friendly. Half the time they would find themselves at the sharp end of an ambush. Sometimes there would be an IED, other times a Rocket Propelled Grenade would swish by, or they would be attacked with rifle or machine gun fire. The worst were probably the mortar attacks that pinned them inside the trucks, threatening them from above - at the thinnest part of their armor.

"WHY DON'T we stop and watch for a few minutes?" said Hasan. "See if we can catch them off balance."

Bennett grabbed the microphone swinging from an elastic cord above him. "Let's stop and do some recce. Get the cameras moving. Gunners, be prepared to provide suppressive fire. I've got that itch."

Everyone in the company tightened up at the words. Bennett had gotten somewhat of a reputation among his troops for his intuition about being ambushed. All six vehicles came to a halt. Gunners rotated nervously in their gun mounts. Cameras checked the horizon. They spent ten minutes waiting for something to happen, but nothing did.

Bennett looked at his watch. "We aren't going to make it, and I don't want to be out after dark." He reached for the mic. "Good work guys, but we are going to get out of here and try another day."

"Fucking awesome!" said Hernandez nervously to the crew inside his MRAP. "If the boss thinks we are going to get hit, it's time to leave."

"Yeah, it's great except we are totally exposed out here, and this makes us tail end Charlie," said Washington.

"We will be heading the right fucking way though," said Hernandez. "Back to my rack."

Reed's voice came over the radio. "We are going to do this like we have trained. Jonesy, you move first. Remember, turn like your granny. I don't care if it takes twenty times to get heading the other way. Try to stay on the hardpack. They probably expected us to turn here, watch for bombs."

The last MRAP in the formation reversed for a few yards and then began to turn ponderously on the narrow road. The gunners and observers in the other trucks watched the hills and down the road intently, looking for the enemy that they knew was nearby.

When the first u-turn was complete, the next MRAP in the row began the same process. After five minutes, it was time for the MRAP containing Bennett and Hasan to turn around.

The driver, a Private from Alaska named Bobby Miller, who had earned the nickname "Ricky" for his driving skill, turned to the Captain. "Sir, are you ready?"

"It's our turn, Ricky. Make it happen," replied Bennett. "And don't fuck it up."

"Got it sir," said Miller. He swung the truck to the edge of the roadbed and then began the process of turning the forty-five thousand pound truck around at about ten degrees per effort.

Miller had just completed the turn when Reed's voice came over the radio. "I see a new contact along the ridge, five hundred meters. Three or four heads peeking over the hill. I am pretty sure I see weapons. Anyone else got them?"

"I see them," said the gunner from the first MRAP. "Looks like an PKM machine gun and a couple of AKs."

Bennett picked up the mic. "Hold your fire until we get everyone reversed. I want to be able to break contact in a hurry."

The driver in the second to last MRAP began to turn. The tension in the group began to rise.

"We are screwed now," said Hernandez. "We should be the first one to turn, not the last."

"Just keep it on the road, Hernandez," replied Washington.

In his vehicle, Hasan picked up the radio that was connected to the command net, "Apache HQ, this is Apache one-six."

"Apache one-six, this is Apache HQ, go."

"Apache one-six is retrograding at this time. Grid element..." he looked down at the display in front of him and provided their location. "We are being surveilled. At least three individuals with small arms. No contact yet."

"Copy retrograde at this time," replied the HQ.

The second to last MRAP completed its turn.

Hernandez began to turn the final MRAP, cutting back and forth, getting about ten degrees per effort.

"Here's when it happens," said Bennett. He reached for the mic. "Reed, you still see those guys?"

"Yes sir," replied Reed.

"Light'em up. Let's give Hernandez space to turn," said Bennett. "See if we can catch them off guard."

"Copy," said Reed. "Task Force Apache, you heard the boss. Control your fire and only shoot what you can see; let's give ourselves some time." He let go of the microphone and yelled up to the gunner in his MRAP. "Vasquez, open fire."

THE LOUD STACCATO of the roof-mounted machine guns from the neighboring MRAPs was distracting as hell, thought Bennett. His troops had opened fire on armed militants that had been surveilling his patrol from a hillside that was about five hundred meters to the north. The line of six MRAPs he was responsible for was stretched out for about a hundred meters along a road in a shallow valley. So far, there hadn't been much of a response to their covering fire. Two RPGs had impacted the hillside near the vehicles, and desultory rifle and machine gun fire peppered the convoy with random "ping" noise as they hit the armor.

"What is taking you guys so long?" asked Reed on the radio. "Get that thing turned around!"

"Fuck! Does he want me to hurry, or stay on the road?" asked Hernandez frustratedly as he wrestled the steering wheel of the big truck. "I can't do both."

"Nothing like a little machinegun fire to make everything a bit more urgent," said Sergeant Marcus Washington. "Just take your time."

Hernandez made the last cut of a twenty-point turn and victoriously turned to Washington. "Tell that asshole we are ready."

Washington picked up the radio. "Danny, we are good back here."

Hearing that all of the vehicles were now heading in the correct direction, Bennett pulled the radio handset to him. "This is Six. Let's roll west at a steady pace. Maintain fire discipline, and keep your eyes peeled."

In what was now the lead MRAP, Private "Jonesy" Mitchells put his truck in gear and began to head to the southeast. He drove at about twenty miles an hour, a pace that was intended to make it easy for the convoy to stay together. One by one, the other MRAPs followed, the trail of dust rising high into the air.

Sitting in the seat behind Bennett was Master Sergeant "Mo" Hasan. While Bennett looked at a map of the area for the ten-thousandth time, Hasan had called the Headquarters element.

"Apache HQ, this is Apache One-Six."

"Apache One-Six, go ahead."

"Apache Six is declaring a Troops in Contact at our location." Hasan looked down at his display and read off the grid coordinates. "We are heading southwest along the valley road and are taking occasional fire."

"Copy that the Six is declaring a TIC," replied headquarters. "We will see what aviation assets are in the area."

"Roger," replied Hasan. "Apache One-Six, out."

* * *

AIRBORNE - SOMEWHERE NEAR GARDEZ

Major Matthews had been daydreaming for a bit when her

radio came alive with a call from the NATO AWACS radar aircraft that was circling somewhere near Kandahar.

"TUSK 30, MAGIC."

"MAGIC, go for TUSK30."

"TUSK30, CAOC directs you to support a TIC at the following coordinates. Unit callsign Apache Six."

Matthews pulled her pen out and copied the unit name and coordinates delivered by the AWACS on her kneeboard.

"TUSK30 copies, all. Proceeding."

She typed the coordinates into her navigation system and saw that the site was about seventy miles away, to the east of Gardez. She then triggered the mic button for the radio to her wingman.

"What's your state?"

"Ten point five," replied her wingman, Captain Cross, relaying the fuel remaining in his aircraft in thousands of pounds.

"Roger." She rolled her aircraft on a heading towards the TIC and advanced the throttles.

* * *

NEAR THE DARA BAZAR - OUTSIDE GARDEZ

The formation of MRAPs drove steadily for ten more kilometers and the small arms fire stopped. The only noise to be heard was the crackle of the radio and the subdued roar of the diesel motor.

Bennet half-turned in his seat to talk to Hasan behind him. "I guess we will put that down as a missed meeting," he said jokingly.

Hasan was in the midst of a response when there was a large explosion under the left front wheel of their MRAP. The driver had been only a foot outside the tracks of the previous truck when the tire crossed a pressure plate triggered IED buried in the dirt. The crude device had been made of two strips of foil-coated wood, a battery, detonator, and about a quarter of a kilo of plastic explosive buried in an old tin can.

MRAPs were expressly designed to manage the explosion of mines and IEDs. The lower hull was angled to divert the blast and any shrapnel away from the crew compartment. The heavy seats were suspended from the frame and were mounted with shock absorbers intended to reduce or eliminate spinal fractures. The rolling chassis was designed to absorb damage, the big tires serving to separate the vehicle from the blast.

INSIDE THE MRAP, Bennett thought that it was really odd that dust had been instantaneously shaken from every surface inside the truck. It was almost stroboscopic. One second, he could see Hasan in the seat behind him; the next, it was like there was a sandstorm inside the cabin - a storm that included a mix of garbage, loose brass cartridges, water bottles, and anything else that had not been secured to the truck.

The large explosive charge lifted the vehicle a foot from the ground and blew off the front tire. The truck's momentum carried it forward for a few feet while the ragged end of the axle dragged in the dirt, spilling gear oil and forcing the remains of the front end under the truck with a loud grinding sound.

The truck shuddered to a halt. For a moment, there was no movement or sound.

In the passenger seat, Bennett shook his head and worked his jaw, it felt like he had cotton in his ears. He tried to ask Hasan and Miller if they were okay but couldn't hear his own voice. He tried again, saw them nodding in response, and only gradually realized that they were all yelling. As his hearing gradually returned, the next thing he was aware of was Reed's voice on the radio, urgently asking if they were okay.

"Fuck!" said Hasan. He grabbed the radio mic. "Reed, we are

good, I think. Give us a minute to check things. Keep an eye out for the ambush."

The truck was tilted several degrees towards the damaged front end, and when Bennett unlatched his harness, he fell awkwardly towards the driver. He caught himself on the center console and turned to Miller.

"Ricky, you all right?"

The response took a few seconds. "Yes, sir. My head hurts and so does my arm." He held his left arm up, it was noticeably bent. "My arm was resting on the door frame." He paused for a moment as he looked at his disfigured limb, the shock clear in his face. "Yeah, it's really fucking starting to hurt."

"Shit," said Bennett. "Mo, how about you?"

Hasan replied, "Hearing damage, but I think I am fine. You got any injuries?"

"No," replied Bennett. "I think I'm okay."

The sound of machine gun fire was audible from the other trucks in the convoy. They heard the "swish and boom" of an incoming RPG. A few rifle rounds "pinged" off their armor.

"We got a group of bad guys approaching from the north," said Reed over the radio. "Several pairs of dudes on motorcycles. They dropped behind some rocks about three hundred meters away."

"Of course," said Bennett to Hasan. He picked up a mic. "Keep them busy. We are going to need a medic for Ricky. Busted arm, non-critical. I am going to get some air cover while we figure this shit out."

"Copy all, sir," replied Reed.

Bennett switched radios. "Apache HQ, this is Apache Six."

"Apache Six, go for HQ."

Bennett grabbed his display. "We have an IED strike and Troops in Contact. One non-critical WIA. One disabled MRAP. Would like air support at the following grid." He called off the location.

There was a pause. "Apache Six, good copy on your TIC. Expect TUSK30 flight to be overhead in ten minutes."

"Apache Six copies," replied Bennett.

There were two or three more "pings" as rifle or machine gun rounds ricocheted off the side of the truck.

"Let's police up our gear so we can transfer to a good truck," said Bennett.

He turned to his driver. "How you doing Ricky?"

"My arm is blowing up like a balloon and hurts like hell," replied Miller. "I think I am going to puke," he said and then turned to the side and barfed half a bottle of orange Gatoraide and a Snickers bar into the space between his seat and the door.

* * *

AIRBORNE - SOMEWHERE OUTSIDE GARDEZ

Matthews and Cross thundered through the sky at 20,000 feet, the distant ridgelines of eastern Afghanistan sprawling below them. As they neared the coordinates, Matthews keyed her mic.

"Apache Six, this is TUSK30, checking in. How copy?"

Silence.

She switched frequencies and tried again. "Apache Six, TUSK30. We are on station, say situation."

Still no response.

"Comms might be down," Cross offered.

"We will give them a few minutes. Let's see what we're dealing with." Matthews slewed her SNIPER pod toward the coordinates. The infrared image resolved into a cluster of MRAPs strung out along a dirt road at the foot of a ridgeline.

She adjusted the zoom. Further up the slope, nestled into rocky outcroppings, was a large enemy position. Several figures with small arms and what looked like an RPG team crouched near the crest, were watching the convoy.

"I see them," Cross said, his own pod scanning the terrain. "Looks like at least fifteen or twenty militants, plus some guys moving along the ridge."

"Yeah. It looks like a coordinated attack." Matthews keyed the mic again.

"Apache Six, TUSK30. We have eyes on multiple enemy positions to your west. Say status. Over"

* * *

ON A GRAVEL ROAD - SOMEWHERE OUTSIDE GARDEZ

"Hey Captain, I think there are more bad guys showing up," said Reed over the radio. "Just saw five or six bodies sprint to the south trying to flank us."

Bennett, who had collected all the paper in the MRAP, looked at Hasan. "Let's transfer our shit and wait it out from a good truck."

"Concur," replied Hasan.

Bennett grabbed a mic. "Copy. We are about done in here. Apache Four, I need you to help us move our gear into your truck. I want to grab the radios, the displays, and the paperwork just in case we have to destroy this thing in place."

"Yes sir," came the response from Apache Four.

"How you doing Miller?" asked Hasan.

"My arm is fucking throbbing," said Miller. They had found a splint in their large first aid kit and wrapped the young soldier's arm as tightly as they could. His face was still pale, and he was clearly in pain.

They heard a long burst of machine gun fire from the truck in front of them, and then things went quiet. Bennett grabbed the mic. "We are coming out the rear doors. I am bringing this radio with me. No more comms from Six until we get into Apache Four. Reed, keep us covered."

"Will do, sir," came the response.

The Master Sergeant crawled into the back of the vehicle and opened the rear doors. When the doors opened, the previously muffled sounds of combat instantly were many times louder. The crack of AK rounds going overhead, along with another burst of machine gun fire from a MRAP spurred them to action. "Miller, get your ass up here. You are going with me."

Miller carefully made his way to the back of the MRAP. Along the way he hit his injured arm on a radio mount and stopped to dry heave for a moment. Hasan helped the injured soldier out of the doors and into the arms of two soldiers from Apache Four who were waiting outside the truck. Once Miller was ready, they quickly covered the distance between the two trucks in a crouching run, and placed the injured man in the other MRAP.

While the other soldiers were taking care of Miller, Bennett had stacked the classified and the electronics at the back of the truck. After four or five minutes, Hasan and the two other soldiers appeared and removed the gear, making another run to the MRAP. Bennett then removed the light machine gun from the turret above the back seats, found Miller's M-4, and stacked their spare ammunition for removal. After four transfers, they had cleaned out the vehicle. Bennett made one last sweep, climbed down and closed the rear doors, holding his rifle in one hand.

The Master Sergeant came back around the truck, "Sir, our air cover is overhead."

"Good," said Bennett. The two soldiers worked their way around the truck and then sprinted to the open doors of the MRAP that was in front of them. Bennett climbed over Miller and pulled himself to the right rear seat so he could work the radios and the displays.

He turned to the Sergeant in the other rear seat. "What is their callsign?"

"It's TUSK30, sir!"

"Got it." He grabbed the mic and switched the radio to the air coordination frequency. "TUSK30, this is Apache Six. How copy?"

There was a pause, and then the somewhat scratchy sound of a female voice replied, "Apache Six, this is TUSK30, got two hogs overhead your location. Standing by with loadout."

Bennett realized he didn't have anything to write with. "Whose got a pen?"

A pen was pushed into his hand. "Apache Six is standing by."

"Apache, TUSK30 is a flight of two A-10s. Currently overhead at angels 15, playtime 90 minutes, 2×GBU-38s, 2×AGM-65Ds, 1150 rounds of 30mm. Ready for tasking," said Matthews.

Bennett copied the A-10 loadout. "Good copy. We are currently in contact at the following grid." He looked at his map and called out grid coordinates. "Friendlies are six MRAPs. Targets are dismounts in the field. Standby for 9-line. Confirm you have eyes on the target area and are ready to copy."

"TUSK is visual," was the response from Matthews. "I see about fifteen bad guys about three hundred meters from the your location. Standing by to copy."

Bennett began to give a nine-line brief. "IP Alpha, heading 165, distance five, elevation 3200, dismounted infantry with small arms and RPGs. Friendlies 300 meters southwest. Egress south. Advise when ready for remarks. How copy."

Matthews wrote the information on her kneeboard. "TUSK copies all. Standing by for remarks."

Bennett dispensed with the formulas. "Can you work that low ridgeline with a couple of gun runs? We will save the heavy ordnance for anything else that rolls up on us."

"TUSK30 copies. We will each do a run and see what is left after that," replied Matthews. She spent a few moments searching for obstacles, looked for anything unexpected in the air near them, and then transmitted to Cross. "I'll make the first run, you follow, and then we will assess."

"Copy," came the call from Cross.

Matthews began a turn that would align her aircraft with her intended heading, switched her Master Arm switch to "Arm," and selected Gun. She then transmitted on the radio, "One's in hot."

Matthews overbanked the aircraft, letting the nose smoothly drop below the horizon while she pulled the jet around. She rolled out of the hard turn and found the nose of her Hog tracking perfectly towards the unknowing militants. Just before her pipper crossed the target area, she held the trigger down for three long seconds, sending more than a hundred 1.5-pound explosive projectiles towards the enemy at more than 3300 feet per second. She released the trigger and pulled the aircraft's nose up, simultaneously switching back to "Safe."

Behind her, Cross had watched his lead roll in. He waited for about thirty seconds before following her and engaged the enemy with equal skill, covering the area with a dispersal that was slightly more towards the east. He pulled off, safed his gun, and began to slew his SNIPER pod to the target area to record the effects for the debrief.

On the ground, the effects of the cannon runs had been catastrophic. Twelve of the fifteen militants were dead, several of whom were spattered among the rocks, bearing no resemblance to the living and breathing humans that they had been only seconds before.

Inside the MRAPs, there were a variety of grateful responses to the unmistakable "Brrrrt" sound of the incoming A-10 cannon fire, and the notable absence of any subsequent gunfire from the enemy. It was quiet for the first time in more than half an hour.

"Holy shit," said Hasan. "Nothing left after that."

Bennett, who had been watching the strike through the MRAPs optics, saw the cannon rounds destroy the insurgents. He reached for the radio.

"TUSK30 Apache Six. Good effects on target. We are going to be here for a while in order to recover our damaged vehicle, so if you have time, it would be great to keep you overhead."

Matthews smiled inside her oxygen mask. "TUSK30 copies good effects. We aren't going anywhere. We will keep an eye on you guys as long as you need it."

* * *

AIR FORCE FACILITIES - BAGRAM AIR BASE

After circling the TIC for another three hours and one more trip to the tanker, the flight was finally relieved by the AWACS overhead and cleared to detach. Matthews and Cross turned west, setting course for Bagram. After more than six and a half hours in the air, they landed uneventfully, their wheels touching down with the familiar thud of home. Taxiing to the flight line, they followed the signals of their ground crew, rolling into their designated spots before shutting down. The canopies popped open, and both pilots climbed out, stretching stiff limbs as they stepped onto the tarmac.

They took a slow walk around their aircraft, scanning for any damage. Satisfied that everything was intact, they exchanged a glance and a nod before heading toward the squadron's maintenance spaces, the deep fatigue that follows a high-adrenaline event settling in with each step.

"Great job today, Chris," said Matthews.

"Thanks, Noodles," replied Cross. "First time I've used the gun on troops in the open. That went pretty smoothly."

"Textbook," replied Matthews.

The two pilots walked through maintenance, noted any issues with the aircraft, and then went to Aviation Life Support to get out of their flight gear.

"Let's do a quick debrief," said Matthews.

"Sounds good," said Cross.

The pair of aviators walked into a section of the building with four small rooms that had been set aside as briefing spaces. On the wall was a T.V. monitor, and on the table was a device that allowed a pilot to play recordings of a variety of sensors taken during their mission.

Matthews put her data brick into the device and forwarded it past the three hours of uneventful holding and the visit to the tanker and found the spot where they began talking to the troops on the ground.

She stopped and looked at Cross. "Any safeties?"

"None."

She looked at the notes on her kneeboard. "Okay, well, I don't have a ton. Communications were good. Weather was good. Fuel management was fine." She started the tape and proceeded through the entire twenty-minute engagement. "Pretty standard." When she got to the attack, she slowed the recording down and pointed out enemy silhouettes one by one. "I see…" She began to count. "Sixteen bad guys lined up along this ridge. It looks like they have two PKMs and at least one RPG." On the tape they could hear the two-point-seven-second burst from her cannon. In another second or two the rounds began impacting. "I guess I was a bit short," she said analytically as the first cannon rounds hit the dirt thirty meters in front of the targets. She began to count the bodies. "I'd say five KIA and probably another three WIA." She returned the tape to normal speed for a moment and then stopped it. "That's all I've got." She pulled her brick from the machine.

Cross placed his data brick in the reader. He forwarded it to the same time, listened to the same preliminary information, and watched the video from his SNIPER pod as Matthews' rounds impacted the enemy. The tape then transitioned to his gunsight. He heard himself call "Two is in hot" and watched as his pipper approached the bad guys. Again, they could hear the sound of his three-point-two-second burst. Moments later, he watched as the rounds tracked across the men along the ridgeline, destroying them.

Matthews slowed the tape. "I see…" She began to count as

some bodies exploded into bright white chunks on the infrared display while others who hadn't died immediately writhed in agony. "That was a good run," she said dispassionately. "I think I'd call that eight KIA and three WIA." There was a pause as she wrote a note for the after-action report.

She looked up at Cross. He had turned very pale. "You okay, Chris?"

Cross felt lightheaded and almost dizzy. He urgently looked around the room, picked up the trashcan, and puked.

9

ON THE GARDEZ-KHOST HIGHWAY - KHOST

Once he got onto the highway, Hamid continued up the road as quickly as he could until he found the spot that he was looking for. The burned-out hulk of the ANA truck was in the riverbed where it had been left, and the remains of the firefight were clearly evident; brass casings from the machine guns and rifle fire were scattered along with trash that had spilled from the trucks. As he walked around the wreck it was also clear that someone, probably the locals, had picked over the hulk and taken anything that might be useful.

He knew that the Americans had begun to exploit the remains of the explosive devices that were being used around Afghanistan. He had experienced the fact that some of the triggering devices that he had been using were now ineffective, either because they were being jammed or somehow being located before they could be detonated. He had zero opportunity to take advantage of this exploitation effort, but that was about to change. He walked to the hole in which the IED had exploded. Bending down, he found two small parts of the circuit board that had triggered the device and some of the wiring. He picked up the evidence, put it in a pocket, and then walked back to his pickup.

Before returning to the wreck, he surveyed the entire area for a moment, trying to visualize how the Americans would approach the site. He considered where they might walk and where they would park. The previous bomb had been planted at the edge of the ragged tarmac. He knew the Americans would be wary of the graveled areas around the destroyed vehicle. He then slowly walked about a dozen meters down the paved part of the road until he found a pothole. He stared at it for a few seconds, thought about the likelihood of civilian traffic, and then decided to take the risk. He returned to the truck, grabbed a spade, and dug the pothole about twenty-five centimeters deeper. He then returned to the truck and pulled up some of the lumber that covered his real payload. He carefully withdrew the components for a pressure-activated IED from its styrofoam container. After replacing the lumber, he walked to the pothole and set up a new pressure plate IED. He placed the device in the hole, filled it until it was level with the road, and then carefully camouflaged it with nearby gravel and sand.

He stepped back and looked at his work. The pothole now blended in very well with the rest of the scenery. He then turned around and walked up the road towards the wreck for a few meters. He found a large rock, an old burlap sack, and some other trash. He placed the garbage in a way that would suggest that it might be hiding something. He then reached into his pocket and pulled out a two-meter piece of thin copper wire. He placed one end of the wire underneath the rock and half disguised it with sand, making it look like an antenna.

Finally, he went to the cab of the truck and retrieved the grenades and three of the handy Chinese kits that turned grenades into boobytraps. He walked around the truck and placed two grenades with tripwires in fairly obvious places and then walked across the riverbed and placed one among some low trees that had grown along the bank opposite the wreck.

Finished, he stepped back and reviewed the scene one last time. It looked good. He walked back to the Hilux, started it, and headed further into the mountains to meet his contact.

* * *

SPECIAL OPERATIONS COMPOUND - BAGRAM AIR BASE

"Hey Nancy, you guys want to head to the big exchange?" asked Briggs. He had run into two FBI agents on his way across the compound. "I need to get some stuff and think a piece of pizza would be a good idea. I need a break from the DFAC."

"Briggs, this is just the excuse that I was looking for," replied Reams. She looked at Lawson. "Have you been to the big store yet?"

Lawson shook his head.

Reams turned back to Briggs. "Yeah, we'd be happy to go."

"Well, follow me," said Briggs. They walked to the Ops B-hut and stopped in front of a white Ford extra-cab pickup truck that was parked outside. "Wait here for a minute," he said, and walked inside to get the keys.

After signing out a set of keys, he walked from the B-hut to the truck. "Go ahead and get in," he said as he sat in the driver's seat and started it up. Reams sat next to him, and Lawson sat in the back.

"What have you heard about the explosion this morning?" asked Briggs.

"A Vehicle-Borne IED at the front gate," replied Reams. "A big one."

"Any casualties?" asked Briggs.

"Four truck drivers died, several were wounded. The gate guards had some minor injuries. The bomber had parked with the other trucks and then pulled out and attempted to run the gate. One soldier saw it happening and opened fire. He deserves a medal," said Reams.

"Yeah, they all do," replied Briggs.

Briggs came to an intersection, stopped, and then turned onto Disney Drive. He drove slowly down the potholed avenue that was a mixture of pavement, gravel, and hard-packed dirt. Along the way they drove past the large Allied Headquarters building, a few buildings further down was the infamous prison that held numerous Afghan combatants, and an inflatable hangar-like structure that several commands used as a place to host their unit ceremonies. After a hundred more meters, Briggs turned right into the parking lot of the shopping plaza. As usual, the area was busy. Briggs found a spot between a pair of MRAPS, turned the engine off, and put the key in his pocket.

The trio climbed from the pickup and walked across the gravel lot. In front of them were two large trailers; one contained a Burger King, the other a Subway. Slightly to the left was a large building with a familiar sign of the Army Air Force Exchange Service, or AAFES.

"Holy crap," said Lawson as he looked around. "This is almost like being in the States."

"Yeah," replied Reams. "Except for all of the people with guns, the dust, and the smell. That said, it's kind of nice to come down here every once in a while to get out of the compound. My only advice is that you'll probably regret going to the Burger King," she finished with a laugh.

Reams then pointed out the rows of small shops. "There are several local vendors back there. Most of what they sell is crap, but there are occasionally interesting items." She pointed to a longer covered walkway that was to their right. "If you wander down that way, there is a pizza joint, an ice cream store, and a handy place that will make plaques, or mount flags, or whatever you want."

"There needs to be a bar," said Lawson a bit sourly.

"Yeah, general order number one gets in the way of that," replied Reams. "No booze in Afghanistan or Iraq, I'm afraid." She paused. "Or a least, none that is legal."

Briggs turned to the two agents, "Let's split up for a bit. I am going into the big store and get some stuff. I'll meet you at the pizza place in fifteen minutes."

"Done," said Reams. She turned to Lawson. "You should go in and see what they have. Plenty of souvenirs to send home even if you don't need anything. I am headed over to a little booth where an old man sells gemstones. I've got a good collection of garnets going." She pointed to one of the trailers behind the Burger King.

* * *

AIR FORCE FACILITIES - BAGRAM AIR BASE

"Sir, I am fine," said Captain "Chris" Cross. "For some reason, things just got overwhelming for a second, but I'm okay now." Cross was sitting in the office of the squadron's DO, Major Jim "Boom" Calloway.

"I am sure you feel fine, Chris," said Calloway. "What I think I'd like you to do before we put you back on the flight schedule is talk to the flight surgeon and maybe the pastor."

"Sir..." began Cross.

"Chris, this is okay," said Calloway. "There is absolutely nothing derogatory about this. Nothing goes in your record. And I guarantee that nobody here will give you shit. We are killing people every day. It's the people who don't show any sign of humanity that I worry about. The rest of us will just bottle this shit up and live with it for the rest of our lives. You'll thank me when you do your VA paperwork in fifteen years. Go see the doc."

"Yes sir."

* * *

ROAD BETWEEN KHOST AND ALIZAI, PAKISTAN

When his meeting with Nabil Hamid had been complete, Zayan Shah checked out of his hotel. He had changed his clothes so that he looked more like the itinerant truck driver that he was pretending to be, walked into the market, and found the cargo truck that his team regularly used to bring bomb parts and other illicit goods across the border. He opened the passenger side door and pulled himself into the truck. In the driver's seat was a young ISI agent who had been running this route for two years and who was familiar to all the Afghan border agents in the area.

"Let's go," said Shah. "I need to get back for a meeting in Alizai"

"Yes sir," said the young man.

As they drove along the dusty road outside of the city, Shah thought about Hamid. As the ISI chief for this small part of the border, he had more than a dozen operators working in Afghanistan. Some of them were spying on the Americans, some were watching the Afghans, and two, including Hamid, had gotten close to the Taliban.

The meeting with Hamid had been good; he was getting results. However, Shah just couldn't shake a feeling that Hamid was losing his connection to Pakistan. It happened to some agents, it wasn't that they had changed ideologically, but their identities were just gradually abraded away by stress. For a moment during the lunch Shah had honestly considered bringing Hamid back with him and giving him a break. The only thing that had stopped him was a tiny voice in his head that said there was a small chance that Hamid had turned and was now working for the Taliban.

Shah spent an hour considering options until the low rumble of the diesel and the warm spot in the sun led to him falling asleep. His last conscious thought before succumbing to the fatigue was, "Time to find a replacement."

* * *

BASE EXCHANGE AREA - BAGRAM AIR BASE

"This pizza isn't too bad," said Lawson.

"I mostly put it down to the atmosphere," said Reams. "I mean, the pizza is okay, but it is nice to sit in an actual restaurant."

"Yup, it's a little bit of home," said Briggs. He gestured vaguely to the shopping area. "When I sit here, I always think of the line from Apocalypse Now when they are barbequing on the beach. The Captain says something like 'The more they tried to make it just like home, the more they made everybody miss it.'"

"Yeah, I can understand that," said Lawson.

Reams was quiet for a second and then smiled. "That is way too profound for me Briggs. You are a helo pilot, not a philosopher. Don't go and get all melancholy on us like some college kid who has just discovered that life isn't fair."

"Not moody, just tired," replied Briggs. He reached down and grabbed the last slice of pizza, and took a bite. As he did so his mobile phone rang. He stood up, pulled it from his pocket, and walked a few feet away from the table, making brief responses that were impossible to hear.

"Is that a local phone?" asked Lawson.

"Yeah," said Reams. "I need to get you yours. It's a simple phone on a cell network that only covers the base, but it is nice to have."

"I'll bet," said Lawson.

Briggs walked back over. "Sorry, that was Ops. Looks like I might go flying tonight, so I need to get back."

"I thought you had the day off," said Reams.

"Never a day off here," said Briggs.

The trio rode back to the Special Ops compound in silence,

the truck rattling along the road. They pulled up to the gate in front of the compound, had all of their IDs checked, and were let inside. Briggs backed into a spot next to the B-hut and turned off the truck.

Reams turned to him, "Thanks for the ride and the pizza."

"Yeah, that was great," said Lawson.

"No problem," said Briggs. "See you guys around."

* * *

ON THE GARDEZ-KHOST HIGHWAY - KHOST

The lead MRAP halted on a paved section of the highway, bringing the entire convoy to a halt. After a few moments, the radio came to life. "We are going to stop here and send EOD out for a look," said Lieutenant Johnson. "I want gunners up and aware."

There were acknowledgements from all seven of the vehicles in the convoy.

In Lancer Four, Grayson turned to talk to Flynn. "Can you hand me one of those Gatorades?"

Flynn reached into the small cooler that they had brought with them, grabbed the drink, and handed it to Grayson. He then returned to the screen, where he was using the camera system to look around the wreckage and the surrounding hillsides.

"We need to get to the next event earlier," he said. "Looks like the locals have picked over the wreck."

"They aren't looking for chunks of circuit board, though," said Jenkins. "They are looking for food or things that they can sell."

"Maybe," said Flynn.

"Lancer Six, this is Blade. We are dismounting," came the call from the EOD lead. "We are going to run the robot down there and take a look."

"Copy Blade."

In their MRAP, the forensics team watched as the EOD team

pulled a six-wheeled robot from the back of their MRAP. The robot was about the size of a picnic cooler. It had three large rubber wheels on either side, a couple of cameras, a claw arm, and a shotgun device that could be used to disarm unknown devices. One of the EOD techs pulled out a handheld controller and began to drive the device past the first two MRAPs in the convoy and out onto the open tarmac. The other two technicians grabbed some folding chairs, binoculars, and a pelican case. They walked to the front of the convoy, unfolded the chairs, sat down, and watched as the robot operator drove the machine down the road.

Flynn got on the radio. "Lancer Six, this is Tracer. Requesting to dismount and assist Blade as required."

"Tracer, if you need to get out there, it's your call," came the response from Johnson.

"I'm going out," said Flynn. "I'll call you if there is something interesting." He grabbed his rifle and helmet, opened the door, and stepped out.

Jenkins looked at Grayson. "The Lone Ranger rides again."

Grayson picked up a control pad for the MRAP camera. "Yup. Say what you want about him, but the man is consistent."

* * *

AT A ROADSIDE MOSQUE - NEAR THE GARDEZ-KHOST PASS

Nabil Hamid finally made it to the mosque as it was approaching midday. He had driven hard, trying to extend the distance between himself and the location of the trap that he had laid for the Americans. In his imagination, a Predator UAV followed him the entire way. When he stepped out of the truck, he shaded his eyes and searched the horizon, but didn't see any aircraft.

"The Americans are not overhead, brother," said a voice from behind him. "And even if they were, you would never hear a thing before you died."

Hamid turned to see a skinny young man walking from around the corner of the mosque. He had on the baggy clothing of a villager but wore a black Amamah, or turban, that was common among Taliban and al-Qa'ida militants.

"One never knows," replied Hamid.

"Indeed," said the young man. "I am Asif. Your escort and bodyguard."

"I am Hamid."

"I know. I have your picture," replied Asif. "We will not travel much farther today. I joked about the Americans, but they have been stirred up by several attacks in the area and will certainly respond soon. We will keep a low profile for now. While we wait, you can teach me your trade."

"I am always pleased to share my skills," replied Hamid.

"Give me a moment," said Asif. He turned and walked around the corner of the mosque.

Hamid tensed. For a moment, he considered grabbing his rifle from the truck, but by the time he had decided it might be a good option, Asif walked back into sight. An old backpack over his shoulder and an AK-47 in his hands.

"Do not worry, brother," said Asif. "If the Sheikh had wanted you to die, you would be dead. But because he wants you to live, I will guard you with my life."

Hamid nodded. He walked back to the truck and got in. Asif slung his pack into the bed of the truck, opened the door, and got in.

"We need to go back to the highway for another five kilometers, then we will turn south," said Asif.

Hamid started the truck.

* * *

ON THE GARDEZ-KHOST HIGHWAY - KHOST

Sergeant Marcus Blake pulled his binoculars from his eyes and turned to Specialist Caleb Foster. Foster was the youngest man in the EOD team and had been deemed to be the best robot operator due to his skills with a Nintendo. "Take a look at that trash on the right side of the road. It doesn't look like something that the wind would do."

"I see it," said Foster. He maneuvered the robot close to the garbage, seeing a few bags, something that looked like a potato sack, and some rocks. He turned the machine to get a better look.

While Foster worked with the robotic claw to pull some of the material away and Blake watched with binoculars, Flynn walked from around the MRAP and over to the EOD tech, who was sitting in a folding chair.

"This is a good way to work," said Flynn, gesturing to the chair.

"Yeah, looks lazy. But I fucked up my back in an IED strike a couple of weeks ago," said Staff Sergeant Wes Evans. "Can't stand for extended periods."

"Why the hell are you still out here?" said Flynn.

"They tell me that nothing shows up on the x-ray," replied Evans. "I'm operating on ibuprofen and hope. Typical Army medicine."

The conversation was interrupted by an excited outburst from Foster. "I've got a wire." He looked closer. "Definitely a copper wire that comes from under that rock."

"Let me take a look," said Blake as he took the controller from Foster. He maneuvered the camera a few times. "Yup, that looks like something." He turned to Evans and Flynn. "What do you want to do, boss?"

Evans stood, walked over, and briefly looked at the display. "Foster, what do you think?"

"Blow it in place," said Foster. "No reason to try to dig it up."

"I agree," said Evans. "Let's set it up." He reached for the handset of his radio that was hanging from his gear. "Lancer Six, Blade."

"Go, Blade," replied Johnson.

"We've got an exposed wire and a possible IED. We are going to blow it in place," said Flynn.

"Copy," said Johnson.

"We are going to need you to move back another fifty meters or so," said Evans. "We will pull our vehicle out of formation and to the side."

* * *

SPECIAL OPERATIONS COMPOUND - BAGRAM AIR BASE

Briggs walked into the Ops B-hut and found Fletcher sitting at the planning table with McCoy.

"How was your shopping trip?" asked Fletcher. He was wearing an unmarked Army-style two-piece flight suit and his normal ballcap.

"Got what I needed," replied Briggs. He placed his bags down and sat next to Fletcher.

"What's up?" asked Briggs.

"You and Fletcher are going flying with the Army tonight," said McCoy. "Since both of you are current in the H-60, we need you to get some time in MH-60Ms."

"Great," said Briggs.

"Just an easy night drop," said Fletcher. "Not a raid. Something to get us back in the groove."

"Not sure I want to get back in the groove," said Briggs.

"Well, make the call so we can decide how to move forward," said McCoy, a hint of impatience clear in his voice. "I appreciate your reluctance, but this is where we are heading."

"Got it. I'm in," said Briggs. "When's the brief?"

"2030," replied Fletcher. "But we are meeting with a guy

named Major Knutson at 1930. He is the Detachment OIC and kind of wants to see what they are getting into before they let us into a cockpit."

"Understandable," said McCoy. "Oh, and we've also got a meeting tomorrow at 1000 with Winters and the action team. I think Winters is going to put it all together and get us going."

"You know what they say about that," said Fletcher.

"No, what?" replied McCoy.

"If a military effort comes together smoothly, you've likely invaded the wrong place," said Fletcher.

Briggs laughed. "I'll see you in here at 1915." He stood up, grabbed his bags, and walked out.

McCoy looked at Fletcher. "You think he is okay to fly?"

"Yeah, Briggs is fine," replied Fletcher expansively. "He is wrestling with the fact that he probably should be a total stress case, but doesn't feel like he is. Which sets up a shitty feedback loop of self-doubt. Get him back in an MH-60M with NVGs so that he can go zooming into the mountains with a bunch of killers in back and he will be right as rain."

"Great analysis," said McCoy doubtfully.

* * *

ON THE GARDEZ-KHOST HIGHWAY

"It's all ready," said Foster.

"Lancer Six, we are going to set off the charge," said Evans on the radio.

"Copy."

All three EOD techs and Flynn were standing behind the EOD MRAP, staring at a screen that displayed the stick of C-4 high explosive that Foster had placed on the site where they believed there was an explosive.

"Blow it," said Evans.

Flynn plugged his ears, and Foster yelled, "Fire in the hole! Fire in the hole! Fire in the hole."

There was a loud "Crump" from the charge and a brief sprinkle of gravel and sand that had been thrown up into the air.

"Didn't sound like there was a secondary," said Blake.

"Yeah, I didn't hear anything either," said Evans. He turned to Foster. "Get the robot down there."

After a few moments of looking, it was clear that there had been nothing under the rock. Foster even found the copper wire a few meters away.

"It was a decoy," said Flynn. "They wanted us to stop and look."

"Could have been just trash," said Evans.

"Nobody around here is going to leave copper wire sitting around," replied Flynn. "You should send the robot for a look around the wreckage. There is more here."

"It was next on the list," said Evans. "Foster, go sweep for booby traps."

Foster moved back around to the front of the MRAP and began to drive around the wrecked ANA truck. Evans went back to his chair, and Blake disappeared into the MRAP for a bit.

Flynn stepped away from the MRAP and began to look at the surrounding scene. After a few moments, he was joined by Grayson and Jenkins.

"We saw the look," said Jenkins. "What's up?"

"We just blew up a decoy. It was set up to look like an IED. The bomber wanted us to stop. There is a chance that it was just done to irritate us. There is another chance that we are in the middle of an ambush and don't know it," said Flynn.

"Tripwire!" said Foster excitedly. "I've found a grenade and a tripwire on the truck."

"Fuck," said Jenkins.

"Yup," said Flynn." He walked over to Evans. "There are more surprises around here, we need to be really careful."

* * *

ARABKHEL VILLAGE - OFF THE GARDEZ-KHOST HIGHWAY

Hamid drove into another little village in the mountains and came to a halt under a shelter that Asif had pointed out.

"This is our home for a few days," said Asif. "You will be safe here."

Hamid turned off the truck and the two men climbed out. A few of the braver children from the village began to quietly collect around the strangers. Two older men with henna colored beards walked up and nodded.

"I am Hamid, this is Asif. I understand our stay has been arranged."

"You are welcome here," replied one of the men. "This house," he said, pointing to a small house near the shelter where they had parked the truck. "There is some food inside. You will not be disturbed."

"Thank you very much," said Asif, who had walked from around the truck holding his rifle casually. "We appreciate the kindness."

"It is as God wills it," said the man who had not yet spoken. He looked at Hamid. "We have heard of you. You will be aware that there are families in the valley who are seeking satisfaction. Blood requires blood."

"I am aware," said Hamid simply.

"Please," said Asif. "We are all working against the invaders." His voice lowered, "And the Sheikh will not tolerate revenge in this circumstance."

"Our ways are as old as these hills," said one of the two men dismissively. "This is our path."

"Well, let's hope that God grants those who may seek revenge the strength to ignore these temptations," said Asif.

"Inshallah," replied the man.

* * *

ON THE GARDEZ-KHOST HIGHWAY

"Fire in the hole!"

There was a sharp crack as Foster used the robot to disarm the second booby-trapped grenade that they found.

"All clear," said Foster.

"That was good work guys," said Evans. "Let's get the forensics team in here and get the hell out of town, we are running late as hell."

Evans jumped on his radio. "Lancer Six, Blade. The forensics team is cleared in."

"Good," came the voice of Lieutenant Johnson. "Tracer, you can go to work. I would appreciate it if you hustle."

"Tracer copies. I'm nearly certain the area has already been cleaned of evidence," replied Flynn on the radio. "We should at least be able to get the tripwires for the grenades; that will be something."

Flynn motioned to Grayson and Jenkins, "Let's take a look around. Be careful, I can virtually guarantee that there are more surprises around here."

The three men split up to search the area around the truck. Evans followed Flynn.

Flynn heard the door from two or three of the MRAPS open and saw that six or seven of the escorting troops get out and stretch.

"So, what are you looking for?" asked Evans.

"What we really want are the electronics," replied Flynn. "We can tell a lot about the supply chain from the circuit cards used in the IEDs that are triggered by some kind of radio."

"Cool," said Evans. The two men walked to the crater.

"See the footprints?" said Flynn as he pointed to the tracks of someone wearing soft-soled shoes of some kind. "Someone already swept this spot." He grabbed the small digital camera that he always carried and took a few shots of the prints.

"That is a pretty sophisticated move," said Evans.

"Yeah, this guy is probably not homegrown," replied Flynn. "Could be one of our Arab friends from Saudi or Egypt." He paused and looked closely at the crater again. "Most likely from Pakistan, though. They are more comfortable working along the border area here." He stepped into the crater, pulled out a non-magnetic tool from his belt and knelt down. He dug for a second. "Ha, that fucker missed this." He pulled out a one-inch square piece of circuit board. "This is exactly what we are looking for." He placed the fragment in a clear plastic evidence bag.

Grayson walked over to the two men. "Hey boss, we found the tripwires for the grenades. Both of them are cheap Chinese kits. Nothing else to see."

Flynn looked up. "Gotcha. I scored a piece of circuit board." He stood and looked around the area. "This is a good ambush site. Lots of cover on the terrain to the northeast and shitty sight-lines for anyone down here in the road."

Flynn noted that two of the troops from the 173rd had walked to the other side of the riverbed. One approached a collection of bushes, clearly with the intent to relieve himself. He was about to tell them to be careful when there was the sharp blast of a grenade.

After the explosion some of the troops dropped to the ground to seek cover, others ran to the trucks. Flynn began to run toward the soldiers who had been injured to the blast. One was motionless and the other was just now beginning to writhe on the ground and scream in pain.

"Fuck," said someone on the radio. "That was a grenade. Two down. Two down."

"Medic!"

Evans, Grayson, and Jenkins were close behind Flynn, moving towards the downed soldiers.

"I'm going to do a quick sweep for anything else," said Evans.

"Roger," said Flynn. He reached the motionless body and knelt next to the man. Flynn had seen a lot of graphic violence in his time on the force, but there was nothing that prepared him for what he saw. The soldier had absorbed the bulk of the blast and despite his body armor had been opened from waist to sternum. He reached for an arm and checked for a pulse. He felt nothing.

Five feet away, Grayson, Jenkins and now Blake were tending to the injured man. Much of the flesh of his right upper thigh had been shredded and he was moaning with pain.

"Hang in there man. Hang in there! We got you," said Grayson.

Blake began fitting a tourniquet over the man's upper thigh. The soldier screamed when it began to tighten, and Grayson did what he could to hold him down.

A medic who had run from the trucks skidded to a halt and dropped next to the wounded man. "I've got it." He looked the soldier over and saw Blake with the tourniquet. "Keep tightening that." He leaned close to the injured man's head. "Brother, you are going to be okay. We need to do a quick survey on you and look for other holes. This is going to hurt."

Flynn looked up as Lieutenant Johnson stopped next to the dead man.

"Shit," said Johnson. "Is he gone?"

Flynn nodded.

"Shit." He grabbed his radio. "First Sergeant, let's set up security and clear an LZ. We are going to need a dust-off. One KIA and one WIA."

"Roger, sir. In work." The radio was quiet for a moment. "We are going to reposition Lancer two and three for more cover."

"Get it done," said Johnson.

Two of the MRAPs began to maneuver. One made a sweeping

three-point turn and pointed back down the highway the way they came. The second was in the process of moving around the stationary EOD MRAP when it ran over the IED in the pothole.

There was a massive explosion that deafened everyone standing by the injured soldier. A rain of gravel and sand began falling. Grayson and the medic covered the injured man with their own bodies. Johnson, Flynn, and Evans stood and ran towards the site of the explosion. The damaged vehicle was obscured behind the EOD truck, but when they made it to the other side, they saw the truck leaning to the right by about fifteen degrees, the right rear wheel assembly had been blown off.

As they approached the truck, the radio started to crackle. "This is Lancer two. We are okay. Bruises and contusions."

The rear door of the MRAP opened, and two soldiers spilled out, along with smoke and dust from inside. One of them looked as if he might fall. Johnson stepped up and steadied him.

"Umm, thanks, Lieutenant," said the soldier uncertainly. "I feel like shit."

"Concussion," said Evans as he looked around the damaged truck. "It fucks you up."

Johnson got on his radio. "First Sergeant, let's report the IED strike. Going to need some help out here."

The voice of the First Sergeant came over the radio, "Got it sir. We've called it in. A QRF is on the way."

Evans looked at Flynn, "We need to kill this clever motherfucker."

"Yup"

Across the riverbed, Jenkins walked back to the dead soldier and knelt next to the body. "Fuck this fucking place."

10

BAGRAM AIR BASE FLIGHTLINE

The Big Voice came alive at nine A.M. "All hands will participate in a Fallen Comrade ceremony at zero-nine-thirty. All hands will participate in a Fallen Comrade ceremony at zero-nine thirty." This countdown was repeated every five minutes. As the ceremony got closer, the soldiers, sailors, airmen, and marines on the base began walking from their facilities, lining up along the side of Disney Drive or next to the taxiway on the flight line.

Out in the middle of a lonesome parking spot and positioned with its rear ramp open, a C-17 Globemaster awaited its solemn cargo. The crew were prepared and somber, standing in the rear of the aircraft. A delegation of the senior officers from all the armed services stood in formation behind the aircraft, creating a pathway from the tarmac to the ramp.

At nine-thirty, the Big Voice klaxon went off, and the base was called to attention. Everything came to a halt. The silence of the normally busy wartime base was palpable. A Humvee pickup truck rolled slowly from the base hospital and out onto Disney Drive. On the back of the Humvee was a single silver casket covered with an American flag. Leading the Humvee was a small convoy of military police, blue lights flashing but otherwise silent.

Along the roadside, the troops of the base all saluted their fallen comrade as the vehicle passed by.

The Humvee turned off of Disney Drive and towards the flightline entrance. It drove past the air terminal, the Pat Tillman Morale Welfare and Rec center, and out onto the taxiway. When it reached the main taxiway, it turned left again and slowly drove past hundreds of service members lining the route. Fifteen minutes after beginning its drive, the vehicle came to a halt in front of the group of senior officers. An honor guard lifted the heavy casket from the truck and marched it into the back of the C-17, where it was carefully secured in the center of the cargo bay.

The delegation of senior officers then walked into the back of the aircraft. A pastor said a prayer. Some of the participants said goodbye by touching the casket, while others stood there, heads bowed. When it was time, the officers walked from the aircraft. The cargo ramp closed, and within minutes, the aircraft was taxiing for takeoff on a long trip to Germany and, after that, to Dover, Delaware, where the remains would be officially repatriated and handed to the family.

"Secure from Fallen Comrade Ceremony," came from the Big Voice, and the base went back to work.

11

JOINT COUNTER-IED TASK FORCE - BAGRAM AIR BASE

"Well, we dodged a bullet," said Colonel "Mel" Brooks. "If it wasn't for Specialist James, we might have had a different outcome." He turned to FBI Agent Nancy Reams. "Nancy, any insight on the attack from your end?"

"Not a lot. There are a few lessons learned. The most important of which is that you can't bulldoze the evidence into a pile and expect us to learn much," said Reams with a hint of exasperation.

One of the Lieutenant Colonels sitting at the table spoke up. "That was our mistake. We didn't get the order to preserve evidence until late. The EOD guys had declared the wreckage safe, and there was a convoy of diplomats coming in from Kabul to see the Commanding General. We could have opened one of the alternate entrances, but that just got lost in the excitement, and the team moved the wreck as fast as they could."

"Got it," said Brooks. "We will add this to our post-event checklist." He turned back to Reams.

"Despite the fact that it was bulldozed out of the compound, we did find the remains of the electronics from the bombs," said Reams.

"Bombs plural?" asked Brooks.

"Yes, one large radio triggered bomb in the back of the truck that was probably a few hundred kilos of plastic explosive. The driver was also wearing a bomb vest. We found the dead-man trigger and the remnants of a standard walkie-talkie," said Reams.

"What about the human remains?" asked Brooks.

"We took DNA samples to the extent that we could and gave the remains to an Imam from Kabul. They will be buried in accordance with the proper rites," said Reams.

"What friggin Imam?" asked a Major from Air Force intelligence. "Did he come asking for the body?"

"You've got his name in the email I sent to the group last night," replied Reams curtly. "He may be a sympathizer, or he may just honestly want to take care of the deceased. We don't really care."

"Doesn't a proper burial just make the sacrifice look justified or something?" asked the Major.

"Probably," replied Brooks. "But those are our orders. We need to be aware of Afghan cultural sensitivities," he said, using his hands to indicate 'air quotes.'

"There is no shortage of volunteers for suicide missions, no matter what we do," said Reams. "Might as well uphold our own moral standards. We gain nothing by keeping what was left of that kid in a freezer somewhere."

There was a moment of silence and then Brooks spoke again. "So, the forensic team we sent from J-bad to Khost got hit, or at least, their convoy got hit. One KIA and one WIA from the escort. They were surveying a recent IED strike and were looking for evidence when someone tripped a booby trap. As they recovered from that, an MRAP hit another IED. The team itself is fine, but Flynn says that it was the act of a professional."

"That's concerning," said Reams. "I'd like to take Agents Lawson and Khawar over to J-Bad to meet the guys and talk about what they saw."

"I'll sign the airlift request," said Brooks. "Just send it my way."

* * *

ARABKHEL VILLAGE, OFF THE GARDEZ-KHOST HIGHWAY

The two men were sitting in the courtyard of the house that they were staying in. An old woman from the village had come with food, placed it on a table, and left without a word. Despite the odd tension, it was a pleasant evening and Hamid thought that it would be a good time for the scotch whiskey that he favored, but hadn't been able to drink since he began working in Afghanistan.

"Where are you from Asif?" asked Hamid.

"I grew up near Asadabad," replied Asif. "But I went to school in Jalalabad."

"Oh, so you have some school," said Hamid. "That is a good thing."

"Is it?" asked Asif. "It hasn't seemed to help my life at all," he said with a flat voice.

"Knowledge can sometimes be dangerous, but knowing how to learn is a gift," said Hamid. "When this war is over, you should continue your education."

"Education is for the wealthy," replied Asif. "I am not wealthy and this war will never end."

"All wars end," said Hamid. "The invaders will leave as they have throughout history, and you will be free."

"You don't think that Afghanistan will still have issues with your Pakistan?" asked Asif.

Hamid looked up, "Who told you I was from Pakistan?"

Asif smiled. "Everyone knows you are from Pakistan and are

ISI. This is not a problem, as you well know many of the Taliban are from your country."

"Perhaps," said Hamid carefully. "This war has many sides."

"As long as you fight on the side of the Taliban, we fight together," said Asif. "Tomorrow, you teach me how to build a bomb."

* * *

FOB CHAPMAN - KHOST

"Fuck" said Grayson. "We are getting visitors."

"What?" asked Jenkins. "From where?"

"Gotta be the FBI from Bagram," said Flynn.

"You are correct," said Grayson, surprised.

"Is it Reams again?" asked Flynn.

"It is." Grayson looked at Flynn. "How did you know?"

"I saw that she was back in the country. She is like the rest of us, sometimes we are drawn to the places where we experienced traumatic events," said Flynn. "She was injured and medevac'd not far from here; she'll want closure."

Jenkins looked up from his Nintendo, "You fucking analyze us like that too?"

"I can't analyze the actions of handicapped people," said Flynn with a straight face.

"Fuck you Flynn," said Grayson with a laugh.

There was a knock on the door of the supply shed and Sergeant Blake walked in. "You guys are getting visitors from Bagram."

"We know," said Jenkins.

Taken aback, "How..." He saw Grayson on the classified computer. "Oh yeah, I always forget how connected you are." He looked around the room. "Battalion has VIP spaces for them."

"Good," said Flynn. "You'll want to treat them right."

"They want to go on a mission with you," said Blake.

"Of course they do," said Flynn. "We are part of the same team. Tell Lieutenant Johnson that he should recommend a trip to the latest IED strike that is anywhere other than the Gardez-Khost highway."

"Why is that?" asked Blake.

Grayson interrupted, "So we can show them the ropes and get them back to Bagram where they belong, right?"

"Yes," said Flynn. "That and because we don't want to get them killed."

* * *

FBI OFFICE, SPECIAL OPERATIONS COMPOUND - BAGRAM AIR BASE

"Our airlift has been approved," said Reams. "We get out of here on our own chopper tomorrow at seven A.M."

"Cool," said Lawson. "What do we bring?"

"One small backpack," said Reams. "You are going to be humping a rifle, body armor, and a helmet. One backpack and maybe a Camelbak for water. It's going to all add up, believe me."

"Shit," said Khawar. "We carried all that stuff and an eighty-pound pack when I was in Kandahar."

"And it sucked, didn't it," said Reams with a smile.

"You bet your ass it did," said Khawar. "I'm sure I did permanent damage to my back." He looked at Lawson. "Try on everything tonight. Find out where shit rubs and where it doesn't. Make sure you have a first aid kit and everything on the list."

"It's worth doing," said Reams. "Ideally we won't be humping through the mountains, but we are on tap to ride to an IED strike north of Khost and do some site exploitation. The last site exploitation the team did lose a soldier. This is the real deal."

"It's what I volunteered for," said Lawson. "I'll go put everything on and walk around the compound."

* * *

ARABKHEL VILLAGE - OFF THE GARDEZ-KHOST HIGHWAY

"That is good work, Asif. You have steady hands," said Hamid as he watched the young man build a bomb, copying the steps that he had watched earlier that morning.

"I do not fear death," said Asif. "Why should I shake?"

Hamid didn't say anything for a moment. He connected the Chinese circuit board to the RCIED that they were constructing. When he was done, he placed the device in a foam case.

"In my experience, the shaking is not about fear of death," said Hamid. "It is about a lack of faith."

Asif was quiet, but Hamid could see that he understood the compliment.

"We should go on a reconnaissance trip this afternoon," said Hamid. "We need to choose a series of new ambush points. Now that the Americans are attempting to track me, it is time to think a few moves in advance."

"We will need to be careful near the pass," said Asif. "There is at least one group of smugglers who is not interested in any interruption in their trade. They live without honor and would turn you in to the Americans without a thought."

"I understand," said Hamid. "So, I understand that will we be coordinating these bombings with ambushes by your Taliban soldiers. It is always a good time to attack when one of the American vehicles is disabled."

"Yes, but they will not talk to you directly. You plant the bombs. I will give them the transmitters. They will attack when they see fit," said Asif.

"I see," said Hamid. "That is fine." He placed the foam box into a hole in the dirt floor and covered it with a rug. "I should be able to plant ten devices before I have to return to Khost and resupply." He looked at Asif. "We will go for a ride and see what we see."

* * *

ISI COMPOUND - ALIZAI, PAKISTAN

The driver of the Jingle truck had dropped Zayan Shah off outside the small Pakistani border town and had driven off without a word. Shah pulled out a phone, sent a text, and stood next to a tree at the side of the road. Within twenty minutes an unmarked sedan pulled up next to him. The passenger side window rolled down. Shah walked over, put his hand on the roof, and bent down so that he could talk to the young Pakistani Army soldier inside.

"Are you Lieutenant Colonel Shah?"

"I am," replied Shah.

"Sir, the General sends his regards," said the trooper. "Please get in."

Shah pulled open the rear door and sat inside. Without another word the driver proceeded on the short drive to Alizi Fort, an old walled facility that pre-dated the current conflict by many decades. The car pulled up to the outer gate of the fort. A guard walked from the post, checked the driver's papers, and waved them in. Once inside, the gate closed, and they found themselves waiting for a second barrier to open. When it did, the soldier drove to the front of the headquarters building and parked.

"Thanks for the ride," said Shah.

"Yes, sir."

Shah got out of the car, walked to the front door of the two-story concrete facility and opened the door. As he entered, he experienced the welcome coolness of an air-conditioned breeze. It took a moment for his eyes to adjust to the lower light level inside, but when he did, he saw a Sergeant sitting at a desk by the door.

"Ah, Lieutenant Colonel Shah," said the Sergeant. "Welcome back." He gestured to the stairs. "The General is waiting for you in his office."

* * *

INDIAN SPRINGS AIR BASE - NEVADA

Captain Harper Reeves sat in the control trailer for the General Atomics MQ-1 Predator Unmanned Aerial Vehicle. Outside, it was seventy-five degrees and dark; inside, there were few lights other than the glow from several screens and control panels. In the trailer with her was one General Atomics technician and a junior intelligence officer from the UAV Wing.

In the trailer, Reeves sat in an operating station that looked somewhat like a flight simulator. She was casually watching a display that showed the scene from the high-powered camera system that the aircraft carried and eating a bag of popcorn. While the sophisticated UAV did most of the flying on its own, she could command it to fly between waypoints in order to account for weather or give it new targeting guidance. Most importantly, she was the one who operated the sensor system when they had a target and was the one who employed ordnance at the direction of the CAOC. While she was thousands of miles from the battlefield and had never flown an aircraft herself, she had logged more lethal attacks on insurgents than most pilots in the Air Force.

"Why are we here today?" asked Reeves as she watched the screens.

"We are looking for a new bomber," said 1st Lieutenant Jacob Bryant.

"Do we have anything more to get the search started than 'just another bomber?'" asked Reeves.

"We have one location report from a CIA paramilitary team. We also have generated some good signals intelligence that indicates that we are probably looking for a single foreigner who drives a white Hilux pickup," replied Bryant.

"That narrows it down," said Reeves sarcastically. "'Foreigner' could mean anything from a person that lives in the next village, to one of our arab friends from Egypt or Saudi."

"It's a start," said Bryant. "The more this guy works, the more the villagers will talk about him."

"So, NSA is listening to gossip now?" asked Reeves.

"It gives us good data for a search like this," replied Bryant. "Based on what we are hearing, it seems like someone is angry at him and might even be trying to track him down. He's operating under the protection of the Taliban, so that is unlikely to happen. But we will find him."

"Ah, never thought that small town politics would have any benefits," said Reeves. She leaned forward and changed the display to a different screen. "We are at 'bingo' fuel. It's time to send this bird home." She turned to the tech and reached into the popcorn. "Bill, you've got it."

* * *

SPECIAL OPERATIONS COMPOUND - BAGRAM AIR BASE

"When was the last time you flew an MH-60M model Briggs?" asked Captain Hal Knutson.

"I'd have to look in my logbook," said Briggs. "But it was probably about two years ago."

"How about you, Fletcher?" asked Knutson.

"Oh, just under ten months," replied Fletcher.

"But you've both been flying here in Afghanistan, right?" asked Knutson.

"We are getting about sixty hours a month," said Briggs. "Not all of that is in the H-60; some of it is fixed wing time."

"So, you are both definitely current but not necessarily qualified," replied Knutson. "That's good." He paused and looked at his notes. "Well, tonight should be an easy one. We are heading up to FOB Kalagush and back. It will give you a chance to work the sensors, fly on NVGs, and get back in the saddle."

"Sounds good," said Briggs. "This is a two-ship?"

"Three. Two MH-60Ms and an Apache for cover," replied Knutson.

"Now that's something I want to fly," said Fletcher.

"I'm sure we can arrange it," said Knutson a bit absently.

"Cool," said Fletcher.

"So," said Briggs, interrupting the discussion before it could go off track. "How many passengers in each bird?"

"Six," said Knutson as he looked at his notes. "And some equipment. The FOB has been taking rounds from a really persistent sniper, someone with some decent training. There have been a couple of WIA, so we are dropping in a team of hunters."

"You think it is a foreigner or just a talented local?" asked Fletcher.

"I think that it is some suicidal al-Qa'ida dude, but don't have any evidence to support that," said Knutson. "We aren't really in the loop on this mission, its mostly just a high-speed delivery to get the team there after dark."

"A perfect opportunity to get back in the saddle," said Fletcher.

"Absolutely," replied Knutson. "We will brief at 2030 and then go fly."

* * *

FOB CHAPMAN - KHOST

"Hey Flynn, we got some preliminary analysis back on that circuit fragment you found," said Grayson.

"What do we have?" asked Flynn.

"It's Chinese," replied Grayson. "The intel team thinks it was part of a shipment made to Pakistan about eight months ago."

"So…" said Flynn.

"So," said Grayson. "They are ninety percent sure that it is one of those car-alarm mods. When it is shipped from China the board is packed with a key fob that has been modified with a larger battery. Range of about two hundred meters."

"All right, so the Pakistani ISI is a part of this," said Flynn.

"It sounds like it. But it could just have easily been shipped to some Taliban contact and then moved across the border without their knowledge," said Jenkins.

"I doubt it," said Flynn. "That last setup was not Taliban style. They like to place one bomb, set it off, and then use it as the start of a small arms attack. They don't like to leave shit around that might hurt a random traveler. The villagers would stop supporting them."

"Okay," said Grayson. "So we might have an ISI agent in the field…"

"Or someone trained by one," said Jenkins.

"Or someone trained by one," continued Grayson. "They are rolling up and down the Gardez-Khost highway hunting Americans."

"That's about the size of it," said Flynn.

* * *

AIRBORNE NEAR MEHTAR-LAM AFGHANISTAN

"So, did you miss this?" asked Major Knutson. He was in the right seat of the MH-60M. Briggs was in the left seat and was flying the aircraft. Both men were wearing NVGs. The cockpit was glowing with a very weak green light that was amplified by the goggles, but was very difficult to see with the unaided eye.

"Honestly, not sure how I feel yet," replied Briggs. "I love this bird, but it brings back a lot of memories."

"I understand," said Knutson. "I don't get the sense you are having any difficulty."

"Nope," replied Briggs. "I think I'd want someone who knew what they were doing up here with me for a few hours. It's going to take a while to get back into the flow of managing the comms, the sensors, and avoiding the ground. I wouldn't even consider this for a minute in an environment were there was a real anti-aircraft threat."

"Well," said Knutson. "We are flying missions every night, so there is plenty of opportunity to get some hours."

"Yeah, I understand."

Briggs clicked the mic button to transmit to the second MH-60M that was flying behind them. "Hey Fletcher, how you doing over there?"

There was a pause before Fletcher answered."Feels just like the old days. It's good to be back."

The three helicopters flew to the west of the largest town that would be on their route, called Mehtar Lam. The NVGs enabled them to see even the weakest light sources, making the city look more like a metropolis than the dusty medium sized town that it really was.

"Why don't you take the controls for a while so I can work the systems for a bit?" said Briggs.

"I've got the controls," said Knutson.

Briggs went through the systems of the helicopter; not much had changed since he had retired. The terrain-following radar that the helicopter was now equipped with was awesome, but he didn't anticipate needing to fly Nap of the Earth anytime soon. He looked over his shoulder. The two crewmembers in the back were both monitoring the world below them, each with a minigun that could spray thousands of rounds a minute at anyone who was foolish enough to shoot at them. The passengers, six Army Rangers who were riding in the nylon jump seats, looked hard as nails and ready for a fight.

He turned back to the cockpit, went through a few checklists, and looked through the infrared sensor that was in the ball turret that stuck out of the front of the aircraft along with the refueling probe. While the NVGs amplified light, the infrared sensor was like magic. He could see everything via its heat signature and it was sensitive enough that you could see the footprints of a person walking on the dirt.

After about another thirty minutes of relative silence, Knutson jumped on the ICS. "Why don't you fly us into the FOB?"

"Sounds good," said Briggs. "I've got the controls."

"Let's keep an eye out for ground fire," said Knutson. "A couple of helos have taken rounds here the last few weeks."

Knutson switched to the radio, "FOB Kalagush this is SHADOW42. We are a three-ship about twenty miles out." There was silence. Knowing that terrain sometimes blocked the radio. Knutson called again. On the third attempt, he received a response.

"SHADOW42, this is FOB Kalagush. You are cleared inbound; report five miles out."

"SHADOW42 Wilco."

The flight continued towards the FOB.

"VENOM14 will take high cover," said the crew of the AH-64 that was accompanying them.

"Copy all Venom," said Knutson.

"Well, as briefed, we won't run this as if it is a combat drop, but we won't spend a ton of time on the ground either," said Knutson.

"Got it," said Briggs.

"FOB Kalagush, we are five miles out for a quick drop," said Knutson.

"SHADOW42, the first bird is cleared to the landing zone in the northeast corner of the FOB. We recommend the other helicopters orbit to the southwest, there has been ground fire reported close to the mountains."

"SHADOW42 Wilco. LZ in sight," said Knutson.

"Got it," said Briggs.

* * *

SPECIAL OPERATIONS COMPOUND - BAGRAM AIR BASE

It was just after two A.M. when Fletcher and Briggs walked back into the Ops B-hut after their flight.

"Good flight?" asked McCoy. He was sitting behind the counter with a Sports Illustrated magazine in one hand, and a soda in the other.

"Why the hell are you still at the desk?" asked Fletcher. "It's way past your bedtime."

"Ha ha, funny," replied McCoy grumpily. "We had a flight get delayed in Kandahar. They should show up any minute."

"Gotcha," said Fletcher. "I haven't made up my mind about the hop yet. I mean, it was fine, but I was definitely behind the aircraft." He turned to Briggs, "What did you think?"

"Good mission. Good flight," replied Briggs. He went to the refrigerator, reached in and pulled out a bottle of water. "Felt pretty rusty. Not the flying part, those birds almost fly themselves. I was behind on all the important stuff, like managing the mission, comms, sensors. You know the hard part."

"It'll all come back," said McCoy. "Get a few more hours in the seat and things will start to click."

"Yeah, I suppose," said Briggs. He sat down at the planning table, opened the plastic bottle of water, and drank half.

"When are our new choppers showing up?" asked Fletcher.

"They were supposed to be here already, but it looks like we are still working on the logistics," said McCoy. "A lot of the parts and shit are showing up though, so that is a positive sign. We got two entire shipping containers full of gear today."

"Great," said Fletcher. His tone then got serious. "You guys know that there is more that we need to do if this is going to be real, right?"

"Seems like we are working our way down the checklist," said McCoy.

"What he means," said Briggs. "Is that we need to get to the range and start shooting. We need to start thinking about combat survival stuff. We can't just be bus drivers. Everybody is an operator on these missions. This shit is dangerous and success will depend on the fact that we aren't amateurs."

* * *

AL-QAEDA MILITANTS CROSSING THE WHITE MOUNTAINS - AFGHANISTAN/PAKISTAN BORDER

The lights of the valley around Jalalabad were clear from the mountain's upper ridge where they had stopped. "I haven't been on this mountain for years," said Khalil Al-Sudani. "It is as beautiful as I remember."

"It's just as cold as it was before," replied Abu Hamza sourly as he pulled his cloak tightly around his body. "This wind cuts right through my clothes."

"You are a creature of the summer desert, not the mountains," laughed Al-Sudani.

"It gets cold in Kandahar too," said Hamza reproachfully. "A mountain top is just an unnatural place for me." He looked at the valley below. "It does feel good to return. It was cowardly to run from here the way we did."

"We did what we had to do, and the Sheikh survived," replied Al-Sudani. "That was our goal."

Hamza was silent for a moment and then he pointed to the men who were gathered around two fires they had built in a small depression along the mountainside. "There is still a great deal of snow in this area. Must we stay hidden here?"

"We will warm ourselves for an hour and then make the crossing before the morning arrives," said Al-Sudani. "It is still a long walk, and we will be increasingly exposed to attack as we go. The invaders will surely be keeping an eye on the area. He looked at his watch. I want to be in the tunnel in thirty hours."

"What of the locals?" asked Hamza. "There will be more than a few who will be unhappy that a group of Arabs has returned to the mountain."

"We have agents who have prepared the way," said Al-Sudani. "If anyone objects or threatens us, we will silence them."

* * *

FOB KOGYANI - NEAR TORA BORA, WHITE MOUNTAINS

"Sir, we just had a confidential informant stop a patrol on its way back into the base and give them some tipper," said Sergeant Dan Robins.

Irritated at being interrupted, Captain James Vasquez looked up from the crossword puzzle he had been working on. "And?"

"He says that there are a large number of Arabs crossing back over the mountains from Pakistan and towards Tora Bora," said Robins.

"Any specific identities on these Arabs?" asked Vasquez, knowing that the local Pashtun tribes referred to almost every al-Qa'ida member as an "Arab."

"No," replied Robins. "Just that there are dozens of them."

"Well, someone in intelligence ought to be able to confirm that if it is true," said Vasquez. He thought for a moment. "Okay, you know what headquarters is going to ask. Write me up something for the contact report. Who the informant is, what they have given us in the past, and how we feel about this message. I'll send it up the chain as soon as it's done." He returned to his crossword.

"Got it, sir," said Robins. He walked out of the Captain's office and decided that he would get lunch first and then write up the report. He walked across the compound to the DFAC, grabbed a burger and some fries, and then shot the breeze with some of his buddies. After returning to the office, Robins leaned back in his chair and rubbed his eyes. He cracked open the can of dip, packed his lower lip, and exhaled as he turned his attention to the next task. He looked at the intel report for a second and then slid it to the side, deciding that he needed to complete an overdue supply requisition first. A series of interruptions kept him busy for the rest of the afternoon and into the early evening. When he finally typed it up and got the Captain to sign the release, it had been nearly thirty-six hours.

12

FOB CHAPMAN – KHOST

"Agent Reams, welcome back to Khost," said Staff Sergeant Daniel Flynn.

Reams, who had arrived with her two fellow agents an hour prior, smiled and held out her hand. "Not sure that I am happy to be back, but it is nice to see you again, Flynn." They shook hands and Reams pointed out the other two agents, "This is Derek Lawson, and that is Ethan Khawar."

Both agents stepped forward to shake hands.

Flynn said, "Jenkins and Grayson are out doing some work on the MRAP; they will be back in a while." He pointed to the table and chairs that they had put up in their bunk area. "Please have a seat." The FBI agents sat, and Flynn dragged over a chair. "Well, I suppose you heard about our adventure the other day."

"We did," said Reams. "Very sorry to hear about the soldier that was killed. How is the wounded soldier doing?"

"We haven't heard much," said Flynn.

There was an awkward pause.

"So, it sounds like there is a professional bomber working along the highway," said Reams.

"Yeah. Maybe," replied Flynn. "We really don't have a ton of data yet, but the tactics used in that last event were unusually aggressive."

"Not the Taliban's normal hit and run, right?" asked Reams.

"Yes and no," said Flynn. He stood up and walked to a map that had been hung from the plywood wall. He pointed to the spot where a Special Forces team had been hit. "This was the first attack that we know of. Although the site was not searched for evidence, it shows all the hallmarks of what I would describe as a standard radio-controlled IED." He pointed to a second spot. "About ten klicks further down the road, the CIA team was hit two days later." He looked up. "This was the typical Taliban style attack. An RCIED was triggered that destroyed a truck and a small group of insurgents sprayed the area with gunfire to harass the survivors."

"That was the site where you guys got hit the other day, right?" asked Lawson.

"Yes," said Flynn. "When we went back, the site had been swept by someone trying to keep us from identifying anything. In addition, there were multiple booby traps and at least one new IED, except this time it was a pressure plate."

"Did you collect anything useful from the pressure plate? asked Lawson.

"No," said Flynn. "As far as I could tell, the parts were just the standard components we find all the time. I sent them to Quantico to see what they can find."

"I did see a report about a piece of circuit board you recovered from the earlier strike," said Reams. "Chinese."

"And delivered to Pakistan," said Khawar.

"Not sure how significant those facts are yet," replied Flynn. "Sure, it could mean ISI. However, the truth is that nobody operates in those mountains without the Taliban knowing and approving."

"So, kind of a worst-case situation," said Reams.

"Kind of," said Flynn. "We are mobilizing now. Whoever it is, we will get them."

* * *

AIR FORCE FACILITIES - BAGRAM AIR BASE

"Welcome back, Chris," said Major Matthews. "I hear you are cleared to fly."

"Yup, I'm all good," said Captain Cross. "Don't tell ops, but it was nice to get off the flight schedule for a bit."

"We all need a break every once in a while," replied Matthews. "We will be back on the schedule tomorrow. It's time to get back into the groove."

* * *

NEAR THE GARDEZ-KHOST PASS

Hamid had pulled the truck to the side of the road at a promising ambush site and had gotten out to take a look. The first thing he noted was that the road had a well-maintained and level gravel surface. On one side of the road was a steep drop off that went about fifty meters down to a roaring creek. The other side of the road contained a dry creek bed that rose steeply up the mountain for a hundred meters and then became a shallow valley. The hillside around the creek bed was covered with pines, giving an attacking force some concealment and cover.

He turned to Asif. "Where would you place the bomb?"

Asif looked thoughtfully around the site. "Well, even though they are driving large trucks, the Americans tend to stay on the right side of the road, so probably right around there," he said, pointing to a spot where there was a large boulder that almost protruded into the lane of traffic.

"You have a good eye," said Hamid. "What of the ambush? What would be best for them?"

Asif eyed the hillside. "This is a good place to fight from, but you must escape to the west. The upper part of the valley is exposed to American aircraft." He pointed upwards. "What you cannot see is that the trees end a few hundred meters up. A team cannot run to the east without being seen."

"Do you think this location would be acceptable to your leadership?" asked Hamid.

"I do," replied Asif.

"Good, then we will return tomorrow night and set up an explosive," said Hamid. "We only need to find one more location before we return to the village to prepare."

* * *

INDIAN SPRINGS AIR BASE – NEVADA

"Captain Reeves, we have pop-up tasking," said 1st Lieutenant Jacob Bryant.

Reeves, who had been leaning back in her chair, feet up on the console watching video from another Predator feed, let her feet drop and sat forward. "Good. I'm bored as crap. What do we have?"

"The pattern recognition software thinks it has a hit along the Gardez-Khost highway," replied Bryant. "There is a vehicle of some kind that may be doing reconnaissance."

"Ahh, great," said Reeves with a sigh. "One of those again. Send me the coordinates, and we will go take a look."

The program that Bryant was referring to was a version of a "data fusion" product created by one of the world's largest defense contractors. It was collecting information from a variety of sensors and applying a range of algorithms that were intended to cut the amount of human interaction down to a minimum. In this case, it was looking for vehicles that were constantly stopping along the highway. However, there were many false alarms. One of the challenges for the software was that most of the vehicles that traveled the Gardez-Khost highway were heavy and slow, frequently triggering the software that had difficulty managing this issue.

Reeves went to her console, checked the status of REAPER55, one of three MQ-9 Reaper drones that were in orbits over Afghanistan at the time, and directed it to a location over the Gardez-Khost highway.

"It is going to take about thirty minutes until we get overhead," said Reeves. "Why don't you do a little digging and see if you can find out what triggered it? That will help me a ton."

"Will do," said Bryant.

* * *

ISI COMPOUND - ALIZAI, PAKISTAN

"Zayan, how are you, my friend?" said General Qadir Sharif. The General was leaning back in a reclining office chair, he held a glass that contained an inch of whisky in one hand. There was a sheen of sweat on his brow and a thin smile on his face.

Shah saluted and then walked to a chair. "I'm fine, sir. May I sit?"

"Absolutely," replied Sharif. He waited for Shah to sit. "How is your prodigy in Khost?"

"He is very busy," said Shah. "And he has had some early success."

"I would say so," replied Sharif. He sat the glass down on his desk and picked up a folder. "I hear that he has already caused several casualties."

"He has," replied Shah.

"He understands that what we really wanted him to do was to become integrated with the Taliban, not necessarily kill Americans. We told him that we did not want him to expose our operation, did we not?" asked Sharif. He tossed the folder across the desk; it slid smoothly to the edge and stopped. "Take a look at the intelligence report on the top page."

Shah leaned forward and picked up the folder from the General's desk. Sitting back for a moment, he read the report. It described an ISI contact with an American CIA operative in Islamabad who was fishing for information about several bombings along the border and a shipment of Chinese-manufactured IED detonation devices. Shah looked at the General. "We knew this effort would attract the attention of the Americans; that was always a risk."

"As I said at the beginning, the Americans are not necessarily our enemy, this operation was a means to an end," said the General. "This report tells us that we have been complacent about managing the supply chain for these bombs and have underestimated the Americans' ability to collect information. They know these bombs are built here."

"They don't know this for sure. This still could have been the work of the Taliban," said Shah. "We don't have much left of that shipment. The agents in the field will use the remainder, but we can destroy the material we still have on hand here."

"It has already been destroyed," said the General simply. He drank the rest of the whisky and then leaned forward. "The man broke tradecraft when he set up an ambush for the Americans around the wrecked vehicle. That was not the work of the Taliban." He looked Shah in the eye. "How do you feel about this agent?"

Shah was quiet for a while. "Honestly, I am not sure. I think he has been in the field too long."

"Is he turning against us?" asked the General.

"No," replied Shah. "Not exactly. I think he is just numb to the whole thing. He seemed to be lost." Shah looked at the floor. "He did ask to come home. I told him that it might be possible in a couple of weeks."

It was quiet again, and then the General cleared his voice.

"Well, now there is an additional problem. Our contacts among the Taliban have suggested that one of the local tribes is seeking revenge against him."

"One of his initial explosives killed a civilian family," said Shah. "He requested money to honor the loss, but it was denied."

"Of course it was," said the General. "If we paid for every civilian death along the border, we'd be broke."

"So, let's bring him home," said Shah. "We can send him further up into the FATA, or even to Kashmir to fight the Indians."

"If we remove him without the village getting satisfaction, will we ever get an operative into the Taliban?" asked the General.

Shah was quiet.

"I have a new agent for you to teach," said the General. "You can take him back to Khost when you return. As for Hamid... well, we will see."

* * *

FOB CHAPMAN – KHOST

"So, Agent Reams, what would you like to see?" asked Lieutenant Johnson.

"I need my guys to get a perspective of how a site exploitation is done," said Reams. "I'd like to follow Flynn and his team to one of the latest IED strikes."

"If Colonel Brooks hadn't cleared you to come on a mission, I'd say no," said Johnson. "Things are definitely heating up around here. You know I lost a soldier the other day, right?"

"I do," replied Reams. "I am truly sorry about that, but that is the best reason for us to come with you. We want to help with this as much as we can."

"I still don't understand why the FBI is in a combat zone," said

Johnson. "You have no jurisdiction, and the thought that we might put any of these guys in jail is ludicrous."

"Tell that to the prisoners in Guantanamo," said Reams. "I know this is odd, but we are here on the basis that there was a crime conducted in the United States on 9-11. We are pursuing all of those who are culpable."

Flynn interrupted. "They will be fine, Lieutenant. Just think of this as a cop thing."

"Got it," said Johnson. "Well, we will be heading out tomorrow at 0400. We are going to drive north to Khalbest, a town about twenty klicks from here. There was a strike at a road intersection there yesterday. No injuries and only light damage to the MRAP that got hit. Might be some pretty good leftover bomb parts from that."

"Sounds great," said Reams.

"Agent Reams can ride with Flynn," said Johnson. He looked at a little notepad that he had in his right hand. "Agent Lawson can ride with the EOD team." He looked at Khawar with a smile. "And Agent Khawar, who I hear was in the Marine Corps, can ride in my truck and tell me why he was stupid enough to come back."

* * *

CIA SPECIAL ACTIVITIES DIVISION B-HUT - BAGRAM AIR BASE, AFGHANISTAN

The B-hut was full. The seven members of team ATLAS, along with Briggs, Fletcher, and McCoy, all waited for Winters and Barnes to show up.

"You guys want some coffee?" asked Dan Reyes.

"No thanks, said McCoy. "My hands are already shaking from the three cups that started my morning."

The rest of the men all declined.

The B-hut door opened and Winters walked in, followed by

Barnes. "Sorry I am late. Got a last-minute call from Dr. Reynolds that I had to take."

"As long as he wasn't adding anything to our to-do list, that is fine," said Fletcher.

"He knows what the challenges are here," said Winters. "For those of you who haven't been introduced, this is Matt Barnes. He is here representing the aviation team back in Langley." He walked over to the two chairs that were clearly intended for them.

"You need anything to drink?" asked Scott.

"I'm good," said Winters. "Let's get started." He sat down and gestured for Barnes to sit. "So, you are all part of a new effort. You have all heard about the surge. You know about our efforts to find Bin Laden. You know about our Counter Terrorism Pursuit Teams. What you don't know is that Dr. Reynolds has gotten some input from the DDO about the need for some specific actions that can be taken outside of the larger effort. He offered to create a scalpel, a small unit that can conduct night raids when necessary, can do important reconnaissance, and who can conduct strategic kinetic actions when required."

Jack O'Connor laughed. "What the fuck are strategic kinetic actions? Can't we just use the word assassinate?"

"O'Connor, don't be an ass," said Scott with an exaggerated tone of irritation. "They make up words in D.C. so that they can isolate themselves from the fact that they are ordering us to kill people."

There were a few chuckles from the group.

Winters held up his hands in surrender. "Yes, you got us. As always, D.C. is the real enemy." His tone got serious. "Yes, we are likely to generate a list of targets that need to be eliminated. However, I don't anticipate it being lengthy; plenty of people are dying here as it is. As I am pretty sure I mentioned the other day, leadership wants these actions to be delivered in a specific way."

"You mentioned a bombing," said Delgado.

"Yes," replied Winters. "There is at least one target folder being worked on right now where the boss would like a bomb to be used. You'll understand as soon as the folder gets released."

"It doesn't take much of an imagination to guess," said Amir Patel.

"No, I suppose it doesn't," said Winters. He paused for a minute. "You know, I do think a cup of coffee would be good."

Reyes got up, poured a cup, and handed it to Winters.

"Thanks," said Winters as he took a sip. He then looked up. "So ATLAS has been together as a team for quite some time. Our aviation component of this effort has not." He nodded to Barnes. "Matt can explain that aspect."

Barnes cleared his throat. "So, we have two MH-60M aircraft inbound, they should be here any hour. Due to our operating tempo, we currently only have two pilots qualified to fly them. We'd usually borrow some folks from the Army, but they can't spare any bodies right now due to the surges in Iraq and Afghanistan, so we are going to start slowly."

"You know that the Taliban doesn't do 'slow,' right?" asked Briggs. "We will either be combat effective or not."

"I understand," said Barnes. "But this doesn't mean that you have to be combat effective at all your mission sets all at once. And you know that is not unusual for a unit to crawl, walk, and then run."

"Oh, it definitely sounds like we'll be crawling," said Scott.

There was an awkward silence.

"Maybe," said Winters. "But that is one of the hazards of the job. Now, I've got to head back to Kabul today. Your first operation will be replacing a couple of sensors on ridgelines near the border. That should take a couple of nights. By the time you are done with that we should have the first target folder ready."

* * *

NEAR THE GARDEZ-KHOST PASS

"Stop here," said Asif.

Hamid pulled the Hilux to the side of the road. They were at the inner curve of a very steep switchback. There were no easy places to park the truck, but Hamid maneuvered to the rocky shoulder. Part of him was concerned that the stop was more than just a place to set up a bomb, but Asif's body language was relaxed, so he decided there was no threat.

"You think this would be a good place for a bomb?" asked Hamid.

"I do," replied Asif. "There is no room for their vehicles to maneuver here." He pointed to the steep hillsides on either side. "There is also no easy way for the Americans to attack us from the air without threatening their own troops."

Hamid looked at the location again. This time with a more discerning eye. "You are right. They would need those attack helicopters to have the best chance at causing casualties."

"And while they are hovering, we can attack them with a DSHKA machine gun, or even a Strela hand-held missile," said Asif.

"Yes, but those kinds of attacks are very dangerous," said Hamid. "The Americans are relentless when an aircraft is lost."

"Which brings more targets," said Asif. "They need to be reminded that this is our home."

"I understand," said Hamid. He looked at his watch. "Let's go back to the village. We can prepare the weapons and maybe consider an extra surprise or two."

* * *

INDIAN SPRINGS AIR BASE – NEVADA

"I can't find out much about what triggered the alert," said 1st Lieutenant Bryant as he stepped back into the control van. "The algorithm just looks for vehicles that stop several times along the highway. It's up to us to see if there is anything worth tracking."

"Too late" said Captain Reeves with a grin. "I think I found something."

Bryant walked over to the operator's console. Reeves pointed to a vehicle parked along the highway. "This is a white Hilux. It has stopped and parked twice on the Gardez-Khost road since I've been watching." She reached for the controls and zoomed in. "There are two men inside. I don't see any weapons, but they are doing something unusual."

"You think they are looking for places to bomb?" asked Bryant.

"I'd bet a beer on it for sure," said Reeves.

"Can you tell if they are placing bombs right now?"

"They haven't while I've been watching them," replied Reeves. "Granted, that's only been a little while, but I get the sense that this is a recon trip."

"So, what are you going to do?"

"If I see them planting a bomb, I will request permission to strike. If not, I will follow them back to their base," said Reeves. "And you are going to send a situation report up the chain of command so that we can explain why we need to keep an eye on them."

13

OPERATIONS B-HUT, SPECIAL OPERATIONS COMPOUND - BAGRAM

"The new helicopters are here," said McCoy with a smile on his face. "They are in great shape."

"That's good," replied Fletcher, the irony clear in his voice. "Find anyone to fly them yet?"

"Why, yes I have," said McCoy. "The Army Task Force guys are going to take them out for a post-maintenance check ride this afternoon. You," he said, pointing to Fletcher. "And you," he continued, pointing to Briggs. "Are both going out as co-pilots for these hops. We need you to get your quals back and the only way to do it out here is to fly."

"Great," said Briggs. "I suppose that you'll want our first mission to be tonight, too."

"I do, but it's a real quick one," said McCoy with a thin smile.

"I was kidding," said Briggs, his voice edged with annoyance.

"I wasn't," replied McCoy. "You need to take ATLAS over to a spot near Mt. Sikaram so that they can set up a couple of those persistent sensors on a ridgeline and then come home."

Fletcher stood up and went to the chart that was spread out on the wall. "Fuck that. The mountain is fifteen thousand feet tall."

"You aren't going to the top," said McCoy, exasperated. "Scott has the location for you, but the border follows a ridgeline to the south. The infill point is about nine thousand feet. The exfil is about eight."

"Was anyone going to ask us about this?" asked Briggs.

"No. I needed you guys to get your beauty rest," said McCoy. "Don't worry, Scott is waiting for you over in their B-hut so you can hammer out the details. The biggest part of this has already been determined by the location of the old sensors, so rest assured that someone who is a much less skilled pilot than you did this same thing more than six months ago."

"Which is why returning to the location breaks every rule in the book," said Briggs. "The people that live in those hills remember stuff like this."

"Well, I suppose that is part of the risk," said McCoy casually. He handed Fletcher a piece of paper. "Here is the schedule for your maintenance flights. Go talk to Scott and do what you need to do about the mission, and then go sign our helicopters off."

* * *

NSA INTELLIGENCE FUSION CENTER - FT. MEADE, MARYLAND

"Ma'am, we are seeing a spike in activity in one of our key surveillance locations," said Bob Fiser, the civilian duty officer on the NSA operations floor.

"What you got?" asked Colonel Brit Holmes as she walked over to Fiser's console.

"Some comms traffic that seems to be related to several members of al-Qa'ida who are moving into the area near the White Mountains," replied Fiser.

"Tora Bora?" asked Holmes, a note of excitement in her voice.

"Not yet," said Fiser. "They are still in Pakistan, but it does sound like they are headed to the Afghan side of the mountains." He paused for a moment and pulled up a second intelligence product. "Before they stopped using them, several of the phones in the group started their trip in Peshawar. Others started as far south as Kandahar."

"Okay, that's really interesting," said Holmes. "I'll put an alert on this and send it to the front office. You know what everyone will want to hear, right?"

Fiser nodded. "I know. I know. I had the comms group go over our intercepts twice. Right now, there is no discussion of UBL, there was only a single mention of the Sheikh, but that could be about anyone. There is nothing that would indicate that he might be heading back into the area."

"Okay," said Holmes. "Well, this will be enough to retask some sensors so that we can take a better look. Set me up with some options that I can recommend to the boss. We will definitely need to ratchet up the priority."

"Yes, Ma'am," said the Fiser as he turned back to his computer.

As Holmes was walking away, she stopped and turned. "Hey Bob, do me a favor and put this in the JSOC network. They will be interested."

"Will do," replied Fiser.

* * *

CIA SPECIAL ACTIVITIES DIVISION B-HUT - BAGRAM AIR BASE, AFGHANISTAN

"So, it sounds like the boss wants us to take you into the mountains tonight," said Fletcher.

"I guess so," said Scott. "It's not ideal timing wise, but we need to be in motion to stay sharp, and this will give us something to do."

"Hell of a way to cure your boredom," said Briggs. "That area is fucking full of every type of bad guy that would be happy to take your scalp. Taliban, al-Qa'ida, Pakistani, and every flavor of village gunfighter who would love to collect the bonus on your head."

"Stop," said Reyes in a monotone voice. "Don't get me excited."

"Shit, Briggs. We know you are an operator. You understand this shit," said O'Connor. "We've got a job to do."

"Yeah, I'm an old operator. I've seen a lot of operations go wrong because of complacency and a lack of planning," replied Briggs. "We don't have backup, we haven't trained together, and that is about as sketchy an area as it gets."

"Consider this to be training," said Scott. "There is no other place to get this experience here."

"Who is going to be in the JSOC Operations Center?" asked Briggs.

"I will," said Amina Khan. "I'm the lead spook and all-around action officer for the team."

"Okay," said Briggs. "Let's get the mission on the Air Tasking Order under one of our unit's normal names. We use ATHOS during the daytime; let's use PORTHOS for tonight."

"Can do," said Khan. "I'll call it an 'emergent resupply mission,' since that is what it is."

"Sounds good," replied Briggs. He looked across the room. "Fletcher, get over here. If we are going to do this, we need to agree on the Infil and Exfil points, look at the timeline, and plan our fuel."

"I knew you'd come around," said Scott.

"I will still be sending a note up the chain about the risk," said Briggs. "But we will get you where you need to go."

"And if you are nice," said Fletcher. "We might even pick you up."

* * *

ARABKHEL VILLAGE - OFF THE GARDEZ-KHOST HIGHWAY

"That was a good trip," said Hamid. "I think we have three or four suitable locations for the next series of strikes."

Asif was quiet for a few seconds and then spoke. "Yes, I think that they will be acceptable to Ahmad."

"Who is Ahmad?" asked Hamid.

"He is my team leader. He is responsible for the Gardez-Khost pass," replied Asif.

"Will I be able to meet him?" asked Hamid. "I have much more that I can offer to you and your team."

"I think so. He is interested in meeting you and hearing about your backers," said Asif. "He has been consulting with other groups in the valley before he decides what to do."

"You know that I do this work on behalf of Afghanistan and the Taliban, right?" said Hamid.

"We know that is what you say," replied Asif. "But you know that this area has always seen friction between your nation and mine, even before the Americans were here."

"Yes, we helped you against the Soviets too," said Hamid.

"So they say," said Asif. "I was not even born in those days."

"Asif, I am not an outsider. We are neighbors, we share common interests. This is the only truth of this matter," said Hamid sincerely.

"I am only a student of war," said Asif. "I do not decide what we do, or where we go." He looked at Hamid. "I have already recommended that we extend an offer to help your effort here along the road."

"I appreciate that," said Hamid. "I hope that Ahmad agrees with you." He walked into the house, followed by Asif. "Let's pack the truck up and fill it with petrol for tomorrow. That way we do not have to do it in the morning."

* * *

INDIAN SPRINGS AIR BASE – NEVADA

"The truck stopped next to a house in a village called..." Reeves looked down at a chart on her monitor. "It's called Arabkhel."

"Got it," said 1st Lieutenant Bryant.

"Two men got out of the truck and went into the house. They have been visited by at least one villager since I've been watching," said Reeves. "That person was there about five minutes and left."

"I'm on the SIPR chat with the CAOC," said Bryant. "They have approved the request to maintain surveillance on the location."

"Great," said Reeves.

It was quiet in the control room for several minutes as both officers attended to their mission-related tasks.

Reeves looked back up at her screen. "Wow, you'll never guess what they are doing now."

"Fifty cents says they are loading the truck," said Bryant.

"You are quicker than you look, Bryant," replied Reeves. "I can't be sure what they loaded, but it went under some material in the bed. So they are hiding it. One of the men is now fueling it up from a gas can."

"Won't be enough to get a strike approved," said Bryant.

"That's okay," replied Reeves. "I'd bet this means that they are going to leave early in the morning and go back to the highway and set the explosives in place." She made some notes on the computer that was part of her console. "I'll make some notes for the next team and am going to try to come in early just in case."

"You want to be the one that conducts the strike?" asked Bryant.

"Of course I do," said Reeves seriously. "That's what we are here for."

* * *

ALONG THE AFGHANISTAN-PAKISTAN BORDER - NEAR NARAY

The briefing had been thorough. The risks were discussed, and a mitigation plan was agreed upon. At the end of the briefing, Amina Khan had departed to go sit in the Joint Operations Center so that she could monitor events from there.

Briggs and Fletcher had walked to maintenance, read the log book for the helicopter, and signed for the aircraft. At 2230, the six members of team ATLAS walked across the flight line and climbed into the MH-60M. They had transformed from a casually dressed group sitting around a table in the B-hut to a well-armed team comfortably carrying a variety of high-tech weapons, dressed in a mixture of uniforms, helmets, night vision goggles, radios, and two medium-sized Pelican cases that contained the sensors they were delivering.

Briggs and Fletcher were at the controls, Briggs as the pilot in command and Fletcher as the co-pilot. There were two crew members manning the door-mounted mini-guns, Kyle Holland on one side and a former Marine named "Bud" Daniels on the other.

Fletcher turned to look into the cargo area. "We good?"

"I'm up," said Holland.

"Good on this side," said Daniels.

"ATLAS is belted in," said Scott. "Let's go get'em."

"Great," said Fletcher. He switched to the radio. "Bagram Tower, PORTHOS12 is on the north ramp for takeoff."

"PORTHOS12, you are cleared to take off from the north ramp. Winds 314 at 10, altimeter 29.97."

"PORTHOS12 is cleared to take off, 29.97."

The MH-60M climbed into the early evening dusk.

"Well, I don't know how to say this, but it kind of feels good to be back in the saddle," said Fletcher to Briggs over the ICS.

"Yeah, don't tell that to McCoy," replied Briggs.

"Definitely not," said Fletcher.

The flight continued smoothly. There was occasional chatter on the radios between the AWACS overhead, a KC-135 tanker aircraft, and a few of the fighters that were on call to provide air support for any forces that required it.

After about twenty-five minutes, Hunter Scott transmitted from his headset. "How we doing up there?"

"All good," replied Fletcher. "Looks like fifteen more minutes until the infill."

"Cool."

Ten minutes later Fletcher spoke. "Lights are off and we are now on IR."

"Copy," said Briggs.

"We are five minutes out," said Fletcher on the ICS.

"Got it," said Scott. The team unbuckled their seatbelts and readied themselves for a quick exit.

"There is the ridge," said Fletcher. "The LZ is clear. I don't see any light and there is nothing on the sensors. We are good for the drop."

"Concur, inbound," said Briggs as he began a descent to the ground.

Fletcher began calling out altitudes. "Fifty feet, forty feet, thirty, twenty, ten." The landing zone was temporarily obscured by dust. "Contact. Deploy. Deploy."

"See you guys in a few hours," said Scott as he took off his headset and got out with the team.

It took twenty seconds for the team to jump from the helicopter and run into the dark. When he was sure they were clear Briggs quickly added power and pulled on the collective. Fletcher called "Airborne." They continued the flight towards FOB Chapman along the same route of travel, hoping that nobody on the ground would be able to tell that they had done anything other than fly by.

On the ground, Scott had dropped his NVGs over his eyes and switched to his Inter-Team communications radio.

"Let's move."

14

AFGHANISTAN-PAKISTAN BORDER NEAR MT. SIKARAM

It was amazingly quiet on the ridgeline, thought Hunter Scott as he walked with his team through the dark. They had been dropped onto the side of the mountain over an hour ago and had been carefully patrolling down the ridgeline ever since. The good news was that the weather was perfect. It was cold at the 3000 meter level that they were traversing, but there was very little wind, and the stars were spectacular in the clear sky. Other than the occasional patch of shale-like loose rock, or large boulders, the hard-packed terrain wasn't too difficult to move across. In places, there were animal trails created by the sheep that lived in the area that they could follow for a few dozen meters, making their lives easier.

They had planned the mission so that they would be dropped off and would walk downhill towards the spot where they would exchange the sensor. The exfil location was even further down the ridge on a broad outcrop that would be the perfect place for Briggs and Fletcher to land. So far, their pace had been excellent, and they had already made it nearly five kilometers.

. . .

"CONTACT FRONT," said a quiet voice that Scott recognized as Jun Park, his best scout and the man who was walking point. "A long way off, maybe a thousand meters down the mountain."

The team stopped and took a knee. Scott crouched and slowly moved to Park's position. When he arrived, he took a knee next to the scout.

Park pointed out the sighting. Scott pulled out a pair of expensive thermal optics with a better zoom than their goggles. He looked where Park was pointing and could see two human-sized spots near a roaring creek at the bottom of the ridge. He could also see two dozen sheep grazing in the grass around them.

"Shepherds," said Scott. "Shouldn't be a factor. Let's keep going."

The team stood up and continued their movement. After another two kilometers of travel, Scott looked at his GPS just in time to hear Park say, "We are at the objective and I found the old sensor. You probably aren't going to like this."

The rest of the team smoothly took defensive positions around the objective while Scott and Yri Ivanov, the team's tech specialist, went to Park's location. He was standing next to a smashed pile of aluminum that was barely distinguishable from the camouflaged camera system that it had been when it was originally planted.

"Doesn't look like it was the weather that got this one," said Ivanov quietly.

"No," replied Scott. "Well, you know the drill. Let's clean up the parts." He checked his GPS again. "We won't leave the replacement here. Once we get this mess packed up, we will head to the exfil point. We will be early, but that is okay. We'll just call this a dry run."

"Gotcha," said Ivanov. He broke out a bag and started collecting the broken pieces. In five minutes, he was done.

"Let's go," said Scott.

"Moving out," replied Park.

* * *

ARABKHEL VILLAGE - OFF THE GARDEZ-KHOST HIGHWAY

The two men had agreed to get up well before the dawn to complete their preparations. Asif was the first up. When he dropped a tin cup to the floor he saw Hamid wake with a start.

"Good morning," said Asif.

"Good morning," replied Hamid tiredly. He hadn't slept well and was still fatigued.

"Too early for you?" Asif asked with a smile.

"The older one gets, the less sleep one manages," Hamid said tiredly.

Asif chuckled. "My grandfather could sleep past dawn."

"Worn out by his grandchildren, no doubt," Hamid replied with a small smile. "I'll be okay with some tea."

The two men moved about, preparing for the day. As dawn approached, Hamid stepped outside to the spot he had chosen for prayer. Asif joined him, and when they were done, both rolled up their prayer mats and returned them to the house.

Hamid checked his watch. "We should go. I'd like to start at the spot farthest along the road, near the steep switchback. We can work our way back down the highway from there."

"I'll get the thermos of tea," Asif said, disappearing into the house.

Hamid walked to the truck, lifted a canvas cover, and inspected their cargo. The bombs were still in place, carefully arranged in their shock-resistant packing, and his AK-47 remained where he had left it. Before Asif returned, Hamid reached between the stacked lumber that concealed their load and pulled out a compact 9mm pistol, slipping it into his waistband.

A moment later, Asif emerged from the house carrying his own AK-47 and the thermos. "We're ready."

"Yes, we are," Hamid said. "Let's get going."

* * *

FOB CHAPMAN – KHOST

"If he says 'mount'em up' again, I'm going to puke," said Grayson as he took his place in the driver's seat of the MRAP.

"What do you want him to say?" asked Flynn.

"How about start your engines?" said Jenkins jokingly.

"I don't really care, but that calvary crap just irritates me for some reason," said Grayson.

"That's because you are a city boy," said Jenkins.

"Well this ain't a damn horse," said Grayson slapping the dash of the MRAP.

Flynn turned to Reams. "You settled in?"

"I think I am good," replied Reams. She looked around. "This is probably the newest MRAP that I've ever been in."

"Yeah, it's awesome," said Grayson.

The radio crackled, "Mount'em up, Lancers. Remember to keep your distance as we head north."

"Fuck," said Grayson. "That's the kind of day it's going to be."

* * *

FOB SALERNO – KHOST

"It's about time," said Fletcher.

"Yeah, let's go pick them up," said Briggs.

The two prepared the helicopter for takeoff. They had been sitting on the ground for three hours, having flown from the infiltration point to FOB Salerno, where they had topped off with fuel and then listened to the radios, waiting. It was still dark, but there was now a weak glow beginning to show along the eastern horizon - light that could not be seen with the naked eye but was apparent through their NVGs.

"We are ready to go back here," said Kyle Holland.

"Copy."

Briggs requested to taxi and take off from the tower, and within moments, they were airborne and headed to the northeast to pick up ATLAS and take them home.

* * *

MRAP CONVOY - OUTSIDE KHOST

The MRAP convoy had left the FOB without incident and had been traveling on the narrow dirt and gravel roads for more than an hour. They drove at about twenty-five miles an hour, which was a speed that allowed them much better control, allowed them to stay in formation, and kept them from running over the numerous civilians that also used the road.

As the truck rumbled along, Agent Lawson looked at the EOD operators he was riding with. Evans had a heavy-duty laptop computer open and was looking through the roof-mounted camera system, scanning for threats. Blake was sitting in the passenger seat staring out the window, headset on, and listening to music. Foster was casually driving the MRAP, humming inaudibly to some inner tune that only he could hear.

He turned to Evans. "So, we just drive around in these monster trucks and hope nobody shoots at us?"

"Pretty much," Evans replied. "Most of the job outside the wire is spent in these things."

"That seems pretty stressful," Lawson said. "Like a horror movie, just waiting for a jump scare."

"Ah, it's not that bad," Evans said. "These things are tough as hell. The biggest risk is hitting something big and getting slammed around inside." He nodded toward the harness Lawson was wearing. "That's why you're strapped in like you're in a fighter jet. If one of these things hits an IED, getting banged up is pretty common."

"What about rocket-propelled grenades?" Lawson asked.

"They might penetrate if they hit the right angle," Evans admitted. "But we don't see a ton of them." He tapped the thick armored glass. "This stuff is almost as good as steel. Unless they bring out some serious cannons, we'll be fine."

Lawson decided to change the subject. "How long have you been an EOD tech?"

"Six years," Evans said. "It's a great job."

"You don't worry about handling ordnance every day?" Lawson asked.

"Nah," Evans said with a shrug. "We're about as safe as any job out here. If we find something, we blow it up. We don't take risks. It's the shit you don't see that should worry you."

"That's why that ambush the other day was so deadly," Lawson said.

"Yeah," Evans agreed. "If they start getting really sneaky with their bombs, then things are gonna get stressful."

* * *

INDIAN SPRINGS AIR BASE – NEVADA

"They are on the move," said Reeves.

"I just got the note from CAOC. If you see an imminent threat, you are cleared to fire," said Bryant.

The MQ-9 Predator that Reeves was controlling was circling fifteen thousand feet above the terrain, flying in slow circles to the south of the target area. It was armed with two AGM-65H Maverick missiles that employed an Electro-Optic seeker. The weapons were lethal to personnel in the open, could easily destroy local buildings, or stop light-skinned vehicles.

"I understand," said Reeves. A veteran of many such hunts, Reeves generally tried to maintain the surveillance orbit downwind of the targets, in this case to the south. The engine of the Reaper was not particularly loud, but it sometimes echoed in the steep valleys and could spook their quarry.

She watched as the pickup truck was driven carefully along the rocky road that led through the valley and towards the Gardez-Khost highway. It was very early morning and the sun was just creeping towards the horizon, so the headlights of the truck were easy to follow.

It took thirty minutes for the truck to arrive at the intersection with the highway. The vehicle stopped for a moment and then turned north.

"They are going back up to those same spots, aren't they?" asked Bryant.

"Absolutely," replied Reeves. "As soon as they break out a shovel, they are done."

* * *

AFGHANISTAN-PAKISTAN BORDER NEAR MT. SIKARAM

"PORTHOS12, this is ATLAS. We are at the exfill point. Strobe on," said Scott on the radio.

"I see your strobe," said Briggs, who could see the IR strobe through his goggles.

"I don't see any threats," said Fletcher. "You guys in the rear, stay sharp."

"Will do," said Holland.

"ATLAS, we are inbound," said Briggs.

The aircraft swooped towards the large flat shelf that nature had carved out of the ridgeline. On any other day they all would have been astonished by the scenery. The glow in the east was now exaggerating the rugged nature of the mountain. The tall pines and massive boulders that were scattered nearby provided a confusing perspective in the dark. The scale of the mountain range just made everything seem small.

"Fifty," called out Fletcher. "Forty, thirty, twenty, ten, contact."

The helicopter settled on the shelf. Within seconds, ATLAS began peeling from their protective positions and boarded the helicopter calmly and in single file. Within twenty-five seconds, they heard Holland call out. "All six onboard."

"Roger," said Briggs. He increased power and launched the helicopter back into the sky. He maintained the climb for two thousand feet and turned north towards Bagram.

There was some broken static as a headset was plugged into the ICS system, and then they heard Scott's voice. "Thanks for the pickup."

"No problem," said Fletcher. "We just happened to be on the way home and had some room."

"Well, we appreciate it," said Scott.

"How'd it go?" asked Fletcher.

"It was a bust," said Scott. "The previous sensor had been smashed by a rock or rifle butt, not disabled by the snow. We recovered it and brought the new one back with us."

"I told Winters that the villagers would notice this shit," said Briggs.

"Just part of the game," said Scott. "It was a good dry run for us anyway."

* * *

NEAR THE GARDEZ-KHOST PASS

They arrived at the difficult switchback that Asif had chosen as a good spot for an attack and parked on the side of the road. They had momentarily stayed in the Hilux while a small convoy of Jingle trucks drove past on their way to Khost. When the vehicles were clear Asif had gotten out and gone to the rear of the truck. Hamid checked his pistol and then got out and walked back to join him. He stopped when he found Asif standing there holding his AK-47.

"Ahmad would like to talk to you," said Asif.

"That is good," said Hamid. "It is what I was asking for."

"He will talk to you now. You may put your pistol back into the truck, you won't need it," said Asif. "Ahmad's bodyguards will only take it from you."

Hamid hesitated. "You would disarm me?"

There was a voice from the tree line. "We have been tricked by you Pakistani operatives before, we won't be again."

A tall man in baggy Afghan clothing carrying an AK-47 stepped from around a large tree. "I am Hafiz. I will lead you up to our meeting."

"I am honored to have the escort," said Hamid. He grabbed the pistol from his belt and went to the back of the truck. He pulled back the canvas cover and returned the pistol to its previous hiding place. For a moment, he looked at the AK-47 that was lying there but knew that if he reached for it, he would die by the side of the road. He stepped back.

"Asif will guard this truck," said Hafiz. "You will come with me."

* * *

NEAR YAKUBI - AFGHANISTAN

"Okay, Lancers, this is the location we were looking for," came the voice of Lieutenant Johnson. "Let's organize this convoy so that we can head home. Circle, and let's point this formation to the south. Then we will let EOD do their job."

After two hours of driving, the evidence recovery convoy arrived at the site. The seven-vehicle convoy of MRAPs each followed the lead vehicle as it swung around in an empty gravel lot and pointed south. When they had settled into place and parked, they found themselves next to a large walled compound on the west and open fields to the east. Along the eastern side of the road was an irrigation ditch lined with trees. The previous attack had happened at the intersection of two roads that were just to the north of the convoy. It took twenty minutes to get rearranged, but when they were done, there was another radio call.

"Okay, Blade, you're up," Johnson said. "Let's try to make this expeditious. I'd like to be moving again in an hour or less." He paused. "The rest of you, keep your eyes peeled. There was a full ambush here just last month."

In the second-to-last MRAP, Sergeant Evans glanced up at the radio and shook his head. "It takes as long as it takes," he muttered. He turned to the FBI agent seated next to him. "So, Agent Lawson, Blake and I are going to get out and take a look around. We'll come back for you when it's safe."

"Sounds good to me," Lawson replied without hesitation.

"You can watch through these ports," Blake added. "And the back doors will be open in a minute."

"Yeah. And if you happen to see Flynn and your boss out there with us, don't assume it's clear," Evans said. "It just means they're jumping the gun."

"Got it," Lawson said.

The EOD team gathered their gear and climbed out of the MRAP. Foster swung open the rear doors, giving access to the robots and other equipment.

"You see the crater?" Evans asked.

"Got it," Foster replied.

"Take a sweep around it with the robot, and then we'll decide our next move," Evans instructed. Just as he did, Flynn appeared around the end of the truck, Agent Reams following close behind.

"I told the guys you wouldn't wait until we cleared the site," Evans said, shaking his head.

"It's a calculated risk," Flynn replied. "Worth it to watch you guys work."

Evans sighed. "Everyone thinks they're special."

Foster deployed the robot, guiding it toward the crater at the roadside. As it rolled forward, Lieutenant Johnson and Agent Khawar stepped into view.

"Fuck," Evans muttered under his breath. "Start the circus music." He turned to Blake. "Might as well go get Lawson."

* * *

JOINT COUNTER-IED TASK FORCE - BAGRAM AIR BASE

"We have some more details on the new generation of IEDs being used around Khost," said Colonel Brooks. He glanced down the conference table, noting the absence of the FBI agents. "They are being assembled in Pakistan."

Several task force members shifted uncomfortably in their seats.

"Sir," one of the Lieutenant Colonels from the DIA spoke up. "I've only been here six weeks, but that seems like a pretty big deal. Pakistan is supposed to be our ally."

At the far end of the table, a contractor laughed, then quickly turned it into a cough.

Brooks looked at the contractor, then back at the intelligence officer. "There are no allies in this region - except maybe the ones from NATO."

"That's pretty cynical," the Lieutenant Colonel said.

"There's a difference between cynicism and realism," Brooks replied. "And this region is the ultimate test of realism. We're fighting in the middle of relationships that have existed for thousands of years - relationships we're culturally blind to. Add to that a religious framework we don't understand, and you have a situation where our assumptions rarely match reality."

The room fell silent.

"Look," Brooks continued, "I'm not defeatist. But the thousands of PowerPoint slides churned out of this headquarters every day are built on a fundamental misunderstanding of how this place works. You think we're fighting a counterinsurgency only because that's the one doctrinal manual on the Army's bookshelf that seems to fit."

"If it's not a counterinsurgency, what is it?" asked one of the EOD NCOs.

"What do you call getting caught in the middle of a tribal war that's been raging since the Dark Ages?" Brooks asked. "I don't think we even have a word for it."

"I think we do, sir," the contractor said. "It's called 'mistake.'"

There were a couple of low laughs from around the table.

"It may be a mistake," Brooks admitted. "But our original intent was punitive - and that's something this culture understands better than almost anywhere else on the planet." He leaned forward. "That's what we should have stuck with. Ride in with vengeance, kill our enemies, and leave."

The Lieutenant Colonel leaned back in his seat, clearly dissatisfied.

"Don't worry," Brooks said with a thin smile. "I'm trying as hard as anyone to win. Our job is to mitigate the IED threat. And based on the information I opened this meeting with, I think it's time we take a hard look at our allies."

* * *

INDIAN SPRINGS AIR BASE – NEVADA

"There's something weird going on here," Reeves said. "They stopped at the same location as yesterday, but now they're talking to a couple of guys in the woods."

"They're not planting a bomb - at least not yet," Bryant said. "But they sure look like militants."

"They're armed," Reeves confirmed.

The two watched the video feed as the conversation unfolded. Then, one of the men from the truck left with the group. The way he was being escorted made it clear - this wasn't a casual departure.

"The SIPR chat from the CAOC says to observe for now," Bryant said. "They want to see where those guys go."

"Wilco," Reeves acknowledged. She refocused on the screen. "So, now we've got a group of five heading up the mountain on foot. I wonder what the hell just happened."

"The CAOC has directed us to maintain surveillance on the pickup truck. They're bringing in another asset to track the group on foot," Bryant said. "They pulled another Predator down from the north. It's almost on station."

"What feed is it using?" Reeves asked.

"Predator Feed 3," Bryant replied.

"That's Captain Moran's feed, right?" Reeves asked as she checked the flight schedule for the three other Predator control stations in the Indian Springs compound.

"Looks like it," Bryant confirmed.

"Gotcha," Reeves said. She turned back to the screen. "Well, this guy looks like he's settling in for a while." The man left behind with the truck had found a spot in the trees and sat down.

"Looks like he's gonna take a nap," Bryant said with a laugh.

"Can't blame him," Reeves replied. "It's a beautiful day."

The room was quiet for several minutes. Reeves, preparing for a long surveillance stint, grabbed a cup of coffee from the counter and a snack from her bag.

"Whoa," she said suddenly. "The CAOC must think they know what's going on. They just vectored BONE18 to hold nearby."

"BONE18?" Bryant asked.

"A B-1 bomber," Reeves said. "This one is carrying a couple dozen 2,000-pound JDAMs."

* * *

NEAR YAKUBI - AFGHANISTAN

"The area is clear," Evans said. "Doesn't mean there isn't a booby trap or something we missed."

"I understand," Flynn replied. He turned to the three FBI agents. "Okay, time to forget you're in Afghanistan for a minute."

"What do you mean?" Lawson asked.

"You need to look at this as a crime scene, not a battlefield," Flynn said. "Most of the guys planting these bombs aren't experts. They're just kids or junior fighters; the Taliban pays to bury them. They ride up here on a motorbike in the middle of the night, bury the bomb, and take off."

"If they were professionals, they'd pull the kind of shit we saw up on the highway," Evans added. "Booby traps, secondary devices, ambushes."

"Absolutely," Flynn agreed.

He gestured to the scene around them. "Start by looking at your surroundings. We're at a crossroads. This building provides cover and concealment - for us and for an adversary. We're looking for places with a good line of sight. The Taliban love filming a truck getting blown up and posting it online." He pointed across the road. "That field over there? Useless for an ambush. But this ditch? That's as much of a trap as anything."

Lieutenant Johnson turned to the agents. "What you can't see is that these irrigation ditches and fields are muddy as hell. Tough to maneuver through. You really want to go around them, but those trails? Easy ambush points."

"Right," Flynn said. "Thanks, Lieutenant."

He walked slowly toward the crater. "Now, what do we see when we look at the blast site?"

"The explosive was buried at the edge of the road," Khawar noted. "Not under it."

"Yup," Flynn said. "That tells us a few things."

"It was a hasty emplacement," Khawar continued. "They didn't want to dig into the road itself."

"Or they were lazy," Grayson added.

"Could be," Flynn said. "Either way, it shapes what happened here."

"I'd guess that's one of the reasons the MRAP didn't take much damage," Reams said. "The blast got funneled away by the packed dirt of the roadbed."

"Good," Flynn said. "What else?"

"It wasn't that large," Lawson observed. "If it had been a bigger bomb, the packed dirt wouldn't have mattered."

"Probably less than a kilo," Flynn confirmed.

The group walked along the road, stopping about ten feet from the crater. Flynn raised a hand. "Now, stop and look again." He scanned the area, the others following his lead.

"Was this an RCIED or a pressure plate?" Flynn asked.

"I'd guess pressure plate," Khawar said.

"Why?"

"Because of the remaining wires I can see from here," Khawar replied.

The group laughed.

"Good eyes," Flynn said. "Most of the time, when you see a bomb at the edge of the road like this, it turns out to be a pressure plate."

He stepped aside and continued. "Okay, I'll take a few pictures. If I notice anything unusual, I'll diagram it." He paused. "Let me check the site before anyone else steps in. We don't want to screw up the scene."

Carefully, Flynn stepped into the shallow crater, crouched, and examined the site. After a moment, he stood up and walked back.

"Let's do a drill like we used to back on the force," Flynn said. "One at a time, walk to where I stopped and take a look. Don't touch anything. You have three minutes to survey the scene. Then come back and tell me what you see." He pointed at Lawson. "You first."

* * *

SPECIAL OPERATIONS FLIGHT LINE - BAGRAM AIR BASE

"How did it go?" asked Matt Rathbine.

Rathbine oversaw maintenance for the detachment. It was unusual to see him standing at the maintenance desk when Briggs and Fletcher walked in, but not surprising.

"It was fine," Fletcher said.

"Wasn't asking about the mission," Rathbine replied. "What about the new bird?"

"No real gripes," Briggs said. "Had some issues with the radar. I wrote them up for you." He glanced at his notes. "Might be operator error - it's been a while."

"Good," Rathbine said. "It's gonna be a few days before I can get into the parts pipeline for them, so don't break anything. I hate begging for shit from the Army."

"Understandable," Fletcher said.

"Thank the team that worked their asses off today," Briggs added. "They did a great job."

"Will do, thanks," Rathbine replied. "You look exhausted - go to bed."

"I am," Briggs admitted. "But I'm not sure sleep's gonna help right now."

Briggs and Fletcher left, walking across the base to the operations B-hut. Inside, they found McCoy sitting at the briefing table.

Fletcher checked his watch. "McCoy, it's four-thirty in the morning. What the hell are you doing here?"

"Couldn't sleep," McCoy said. "First mission with the new gear." He looked up expectantly. "How'd it go?"

"It was a bust," Fletcher said. "Helo was fine. Drop and pickup were smooth. The team found that the first sensor had been discovered and destroyed, so they didn't bother putting in a new one. Basically they just went for a short hike in Indian country."

"Fuck," McCoy muttered. "Well, that sucks." He stood up. "Briggs, what'd you think?"

"As much as I hate to say it," Briggs said, "it was a good dry run."

"That's what I was looking for," McCoy said. He stretched. "I'm gonna grab a couple hours of rack time. You guys should, too. I don't have anything solid yet, but something's bubbling over at the JSOC Ops Center. We might get busy all of a sudden."

"Fuck," Fletcher groaned. "We need a bar."

* * *

NEAR THE GARDEZ-KHOST PASS

"Brother, this does not feel like the welcome of an ally or a guest," said Hamid. He was slightly out of breath and sweating. They had been climbing through the mountain valley for more than an hour, and nobody had said a word.

"You are not restrained," said Hafiz. "If we thought that you were an enemy, we would only be carrying your head."

There was some rough laughter from the other guards.

"May I ask where we are going?" asked Hamid.

"You may," said Hafiz. It was silent for a few moments and then there was more laughter.

"I am not a mountain goat like you," said Hamid. "I am a city boy."

"That would explain why you talk so much," replied Hafiz. "We have thirty more minutes of walking until we reach the compound. Even a Pakistani city boy should be able to manage this. Until then, you will be quiet."

* * *

NEAR YAKUBI - AFGHANISTAN

"Okay, round them up and move them out," Lieutenant Johnson said over the radio. "Let's go home, troop."

"I'll give the Lieutenant credit - he's relentless with that cavalry crap," Grayson muttered.

"Shit," Jenkins said. "At least we're leaving."

"Yeah, I suppose so," Grayson replied. "Doesn't matter to me - I'm just ready to get back."

Any further conversation was drowned out as Grayson got the truck moving. The radio crackled with convoy updates, but soon, the chatter settled into the monotonous rhythm of their low-speed ride across the Afghan countryside, heading back toward FOB Chapman.

"I know this wasn't exactly what you wanted to be doing, but it was great exposure for my team," Reams said. "It'll help us going forward. Thank you all."

"You're welcome," Flynn replied. "Hope you got something out of it."

"Well, we got to see how you processed a crime scene in a combat zone. We collected a small selection of IED parts from the site. And my guys now have a better sense of what it feels like to be trapped in this metal box, driving through bomb country," Reams said.

"All good things," Flynn said.

"You know," Reams added, "the FBI is always looking for seasoned law enforcement personnel."

Flynn glanced across the truck at him. "Yeah, I looked into it once. Too much like the Army. New agents just get sent wherever the government wants them. It might be exciting for young guys looking for adventure, but me? I just want to go home."

"I get that," Reams said. "It does come with some costs."

"All these jobs do," Flynn said tiredly.

* * *

NEAR THE GARDEZ-KHOST PASS

The group broke from the trees and Hamid and the four Afghan militants walked towards a decrepit old farmhouse nestled in an open meadow. There was a low wall around the house and the roof of the building had a gaping hole. As they got closer, he could see fifteen or more armed militants in the compound. Some were sitting, some were lying down and napping. As they got closer, there was a shout and everyone stood up to see the visitors.

"Ahmad is waiting in the building," said Hafiz.

They walked through the gap where there had once been a gate and over to the house. Hafiz gestured for Hamid to lead the way. Inside, it was much darker, despite the hole in the roof. There were four men sitting at a wooden table. Three of them were wearing the black turbans customarily favored by the Taliban. One was dressed like a farmer.

"You can stand there," said the eldest of the Taliban, gesturing to a spot about two meters from the table.

Hamid stopped. "You must be Ahmad."

"And you must be Nabil Hamid, bomb maker and member of the ISI," Ahmad replied.

"I work for myself these days," Hamid said. "I saw a cause worth supporting and decided to do what I could to help."

"Is that why you meet with Zayan Shah every few weeks?" Ahmad asked.

"The Pakistanis supply me as long as I can fulfill both our objectives," Hamid said. "I am not loyal to them. Only to God."

A murmur of discontent rippled through the Taliban fighters in the room.

Ahmad raised a hand, silencing them. "That doesn't sound very convincing. In fact, given what we know about you, it might even be seen as blasphemy."

"I am a true believer," Hamid said calmly. "And I have done you no harm."

A man at the table stood abruptly, turning to face Hamid. His body trembled with barely contained rage. "But you have done me harm," he spat. "And I will have justice if Allah allows it."

"This is Adil," Ahmad said. "Brother to Farid - a man you killed with your bombs."

"I did no such thing," Hamid said firmly. "There are a million bombs and mines in this area. I have only attacked the Americans."

"Normally, I might agree. After all, war is war," Ahmad said. "But we know this bomb was yours. My team saw you place it." His dark eyes locked onto Hamid's. "Can you pay the blood debt that this requires?"

"Not now," Hamid said. "But now that I am aware of the injury, I can ask."

Ahmad shook his head. "The village elders told you about this when it happened. You said the same thing then. You were warned. You had a chance to make good."

"As you said, it is war," Hamid replied with a shrug. "I have done more damage to our enemy than most. I do what I can to limit the risk."

"Yet, it was not enough," Ahmad said coldly. He turned to Adil. "What would satisfy this debt?"

"It would take three lives for the three that are gone," Adil said. "But I will be satisfied with one."

"And if I grant this justice, you will join us?" Ahmad asked.

Adil hesitated. "But my farm..."

"We all have farms. We all have homes," Ahmad said, sweeping a hand toward the others in the room. "Like these men, you will operate here in the valley. You will not be far from your village."

Adil bowed his head. "For my brother, I would do this."

Strong hands suddenly grabbed Hamid's arms, wrenching them behind his back. Someone produced a roll of tape and bound his wrists and elbows together.

"Come, Pakistani," one of the men said. "Let's take you to meet God."

* * *

INDIAN SPRINGS AIR BASE – NEVADA

"Have you been watching the other feed?" asked 1st Lieutenant Bryant.

"Not for a while," replied Captain Reeves. "What's up?"

"They took that guy to a house about three kilometers away. He was inside the building for about twenty minutes. Now it looks a lot like they are lining him up in front of a wall," he replied.

"Shit!" said Reeves. She pulled up the other feed as a split screen. She saw that there were about twenty militants gathered in the courtyard. One man was braced up against a wall, and another was surrounded by a semicircle of militants.

The SIPR chat became active. Bryant looked down from the scene to read it. "Wow."

"What?" asked Reeves. "The CAOC director just cleared the compound for a strike. As soon as BONE18 comes around, they will drop."

"Well, one thing is clear," said Bryant as he watched the armed men on the mountainside. "It isn't a wedding party."

* * *

NEAR THE GARDEZ-KHOST PASS

"Do you wish to pray?" asked Ahmad.

"No, God knows me," said Hamid. "And I will not beg. I am a warrior of God just like you."

"You are a bomber and a coward," said Adil.

The men had marched Hamid to the tallest remaining portion of the adobe wall and left him there. Hamid knew that there was no point in trying to run, not with twenty armed men within ten meters.

"I am a lot of things," replied Hamid. "But I am no coward. I am fighting the infidel, just like you."

"You killed my brother, his wife, and their daughter," said Adil. "This is God's will."

"Yes, it is written this way my brother," said Ahmad. He turned to Hamid. "Any last words, Pakistani?"

"No, my friend," replied Hamid. "I do not fear death."

TWENTY-FIVE THOUSAND FEET ABOVE THEM, the crew of BONE 18 had completed the weapons release checklist. They were flying one of the B-1Bs that had been newly equipped with the SNIPER targeting pod and had the sensor slewed to the compound. They could clearly see the collection of militants gathered in a semi-circle in the compound. They didn't need the sensor system to guide the weapons because they were set to drop two GPS-guided GBU-31, 2000-pound JDAMs. In this case, the SNIPER pod just enabled them to record a good Bomb Damage Assessment.

The copilot looked at the pilot. "We are good. Time of fall is about forty-three seconds."

"Pickling," replied the pilot.

The bomb-bay doors opened, there was a bit of a shudder in the jet, and the two weapons began to fall.

IN THE CONTROL room in Indian Springs, Captain Reeves received a message from the CAOC. She read it and turned to 1st Lieutenant Bryant. "We've just been directed to destroy that pickup. Can you confirm?"

Bryant went to his console and saw the same direction. "Yup, take it out."

Reeves slewed the target seeker onto the truck and made sure it was locked. "I need the Predator to come through about another twenty degrees of turn and then I'll fire."

AHMAD HANDED AN AK-47 TO ADIL. "It is loaded."

"This is for my brother." Adil shouldered the weapon and aimed at the man who was standing ten meters away. He was just about to pull the trigger when the world went black.

"GOOD IMPACT. GOOD EFFECTS," said the pilot of BONE 18. The SNIPER pod's display clearly showed the explosion of the two weapons. One landed inside the compound, and one just outside. The two-thousand-pound warhead had a lethal radius of more than 150 meters and would do damage well over three times that distance. As the smoke and dust cleared from the scene, the militants who had once been standing in a semicircle in the compound were all gone.

"The CAOC has eyes on via a Predator," said the copilot. "They concur, good effects."

"Great," said the pilot. He turned to his copilot. "Hey, what do we have in the cooler? Any of that soda left?"

ASIF HAD BEEN LOUNGING at the foot of a tree, waiting for one of Ahmad's men to tell him what to do next when he was startled by the sound of two massive explosions in the direction of the farmhouse. He stood up and grabbed his radio. "Brother, what was that? Are you well?"

There was no response. He knew that he should climb the ridge and go see if he could help, but couldn't bring himself to do so. He had seen the effects of bombing in his own valley and was not ready to face the results. Not yet, anyway.

He tried again on his radio with no luck. After considering his options, he walked to the pickup truck. He thought that there was a more powerful radio in the cab, one that the Pakistani agent used to talk between valleys. He opened the door and sat on the passenger seat while he tried to figure out how to make the radio work.

"RIFLE," said Captain Reeves as she pulled the trigger on the Predator's joystick. The AGM-114 Hellfire missile lept from the rail under the wing of the Predator and accelerated towards the targeted Hilux. "Time of flight, twelve seconds."

It was quiet in the control room.

"Good hit," said Bryant. "Target destroyed."

15

NSA INTELLIGENCE FUSION CENTER - FORT MEADE, MD.

"Brit, that was a good catch the other day," said Brigadier General Mack Parker, leaning back in his chair. "We've confirmed at least a couple dozen al-Qa'ida operatives working their way over the White Mountains into Afghanistan."

"Thank you, sir," replied Colonel Brit Holmes. "But that wasn't my call. Bob Fiser was on the duty desk - he caught it."

"Well, you both did a great job," Parker said. "And boy, have you stirred up a hornet's nest."

Holmes frowned. "Sir?"

"Our Bin Laden cell is already working overtime," Parker said. "Someone thinks they heard 'the Sheikh' mentioned in an intercept from one of these phones. That set off alarms up the chain. The Director wants another shift stood up inside the Bin Laden cell - effective immediately."

"Another shift?" Holmes echoed.

"Yeah." Parker folded his arms. "A lonely one. You're going to be on from midnight to 0800, pulling everything we've collected the day before and turning it into the slides for the morning briefs - including the Presidential Brief."

Holmes tilted his head. "Don't we already have a team that does that?"

"We do," Parker acknowledged. "But as of today, all Tora Bora-related intel is in its own special compartment. Not saying anybody will leak it, but the Director's sure the rumor mill is about to explode, so we're locking it down. You're the only one who'll see it."

Holmes exhaled. "Shit."

Parker's eyebrow shot up. "That's hardly the response I expected."

Holmes looked grim. "I doubt it leaks to the public, but you know damn well word will travel through every agency and department in the government. And it sounds like I'll get the blame if it does."

Parker studied her for a moment, then nodded. "I see your point. But orders are orders. I'll pass your reservations up the chain, but your job is to keep this locked up tight. We can't control what the other agencies do."

Holmes straightened. "Yes, sir. I understand."

* * *

NATIONAL SECURITY COUNCIL - WASHINGTON, D.C.

"I heard Bin Laden is heading back to Tora Bora," said Eleanor Grayson, Deputy Assistant National Security Advisor for Counter-Terrorism.

Robert Calloway, the Assistant National Security Advisor for Southeast Asia, barely looked up. "Who told you that?"

Grayson shrugged. "Just talk around the water cooler."

"Well, it isn't true." Calloway slid a thick three-ring binder across the desk, its TOP SECRET label stark against the dull cover. "Scan this, then go downstairs and tell those morons in the basement to shut the hell up."

Grayson flipped open the binder and skimmed the NSA summary, her brow furrowing. After a moment, she muttered, "Yeah… hardly seems like a lock. But it's interesting that this group is moving back over the mountains. You'd think they'd had enough of getting blown to pieces."

Calloway leaned back in his chair. "It's late spring, the snow's melting. It's finally possible to walk over. Honestly, we don't know if this is new or if they've been doing it every year, and we just happened to catch them this time. Hell, we really don't even know who they are. We're working off intercepts from a couple of phones linked to al-Qa'ida. It could be a bluff. Could be intentional misdirection."

Grayson nodded. "I get it. But man, wouldn't it be something if Osama really was heading back to Tora Bora? It'd be pretty damn nice to put that bastard down on our watch."

"Which is exactly why people won't stop talking about it," Calloway said. "Go remind the team downstairs about OPSEC. Tell them to ignore the churn. No leaks from the NSC, or I'll fire them myself."

Grayson grimaced and closed the binder. "Will do." She handed it back. "So… what's the plan?"

Calloway exhaled. "More surveillance and some trigger-pullers. JSOC's prepping to send a couple of teams to the mountain, along with some CIA assets. If nothing else, when these terrorists get near Tora Bora, they're gonna get a warm welcome."

* * *

JOINT CHIEFS OF STAFF J-3 JOD, PENTAGON - ARLINGTON, VA.

"Osama is on the move," said Lieutenant Colonel Ethan

Sharpe excitedly. "He's heading back to Afghanistan, walking over the mountains."

Commander Tom Henshaw looked up, incredulous. "What the fuck are you talking about?"

Sharpe leaned against the doorframe. "I was in the J3's office, trying to track down that memo, when the General came out and told the Deputy."

Henshaw frowned. "Yeah, that sounds like a rumor to me. I haven't seen anything in the intel stream."

Sharpe crossed his arms. "You know the J-3 Special Operations Division has been spooled up for the last twelve hours. I'll bet you five bucks that this is what they're working on."

Henshaw exhaled. "Maybe. But maybe not. You do remember there are two wars still going on, right? There are lots of less exciting reasons to get people moving."

Sharpe shrugged. "Well, I'm gonna walk down to the intel spaces and see what I can find out. Would be pretty damn cool to finally catch that guy."

* * *

CENTRAL INTELLIGENCE AGENCY - LANGLEY, VA.

"Sir, we've got some unconfirmed intel from NSA that says a bunch of al-Qa'ida militants are walking back over the mountains toward Tora Bora," said Dan Katz, the Special Activities watch officer.

Dr. Marcus Reynolds leaned back in his chair. "That sounds interesting. What's the basis of the intel?"

"Phone intercepts and some imagery," Katz said. "Sounds like they're tracking a few familiar phone numbers."

"I'll bet that has everyone excited," said Reynolds with a knowing look.

"It's causing some discussion," Katz admitted. "But we've all been through this drill before."

"Yup." Reynolds was quiet for a moment, his fingers tapping lightly against his desk. "I'm sure they're already aware of this at the DDO and Director level, right?"

"They were the first to know," Katz confirmed.

Reynolds smiled. "Well, if that's the case, I bet my phone rings any second." He glanced at it, as if daring it to prove him right. He looked at "Do me a favor - dig up whatever you can on this report. I want to know what the other agencies are doing to chase it down. I expect some overreaction, at a minimum."

"Will do, sir," Katz said. "Want me to loop anyone else in?"

Reynolds nodded. "Send a note to Winters. Tell him not to get excited, but there might be a job for ATLAS in the next few hours."

The phone on Reynolds' desk rang.

"Well, that didn't take long," Reynolds muttered, reaching for it. Before answering, he covered the mouthpiece and shot Katz a knowing look. "You should escape while you can."

"Will do," Katz said, already halfway to the door.

* * *

JOINT SPECIAL OPERATIONS OPS CENTER - BAGRAM AIR BASE

Amina Khan stepped into the JSOC Operations Center. Mid-morning was usually slow - most operations took place at night - but today, the air practically buzzed with energy. The action officer positions were nearly full, an unusual sight at this hour. She made her way to her assigned desk, logged in, and scanned her inbox. Nothing special. Just the usual emails and briefing slides.

The permanent CIA action officer, Alex Ramirez, strolled over with a cup of coffee and dropped into his chair.

"Hey, Amina. I heard your mission was a bust," he said.

She swiveled her chair toward him. "Yeah. Turns out people

who live in the mountains pay attention to their surroundings and don't appreciate us putting up cameras to spy on them. We'll have to find another place for those sensors." She gestured to the unusually busy room. "What's going on? Feels different in here."

"Oh, they're all jumping through their ass about some rumor that Bin Laden is back in town," Ramirez said, taking a sip of his coffee.

Khan's eyebrows shot up. "What?"

"Yeah," Ramirez said with a shrug. "I poked around this morning. There are reports that some al-Qa'ida dudes are on a camping trip headed toward Tora Bora. Everyone's acting like that means UBL is back." His tone was dismissive, like he'd seen this kind of overreaction before.

"You don't think it's real?" Khan asked.

Ramirez leaned back in his chair. "How stupid would the guy have to be? We own that area."

"Maybe he wants to go out in a blaze of glory," she suggested.

Ramirez smirked. "Unlikely."

Khan's eyes narrowed and her smile got thin. "You're pretty salty for a guy who sits at a desk all day."

"I'm a professional observer," Ramirez said with a grin. "And my observation? The bureaucracy is gonna spool this up, get everyone excited, and then find out it was all bullshit."

Khan exhaled, considering that. "I don't know whether to hope you're right or wrong." She pushed back from her desk. "Either way, I'll let the guys know so they can prepare."

* * *

CIA SPECIAL ACTIVITIES DIVISION B-HUT - BAGRAM AIR BASE

"Amina just sent me an email on the high side," said Hunter Scott, eyes on his screen.

"She got any tipper on our next mission?" Reyes asked.

"No," Scott replied. "Just a rumor that Bin Laden is heading back to Tora Bora."

"Bullshit," Amir Patel scoffed. "Remember the great Saddam hunt? We jumped through our ass for months because the intel guys got all excited over some call, email, or text they intercepted. We'd gear up, hit the target, and find jack shit. Old Bin Laden is a wily one - he ain't climbing those cold-ass mountains just to come back to a place we can bomb the crap out of."

"Probably not," Scott admitted. "But now I've got an email from Winters." He clicked it open. "Winters says Dr. Reynolds has heard the same rumor and wants us to prepare, just in case."

Reyes rolled his eyes. "What does that even mean? Every time shit like this happens, the boss tells us to 'get ready.' We don't need to prepare. All our stuff is in this B-hut. If somebody gave me the chance to snuff UBL, I'd be out the door in a second. We all would."

"He knows that," Scott said. "This just means if we get a call, it's the real deal."

"It's always the real fucking deal for us," Jun Park muttered from the back corner. He was leaning against the wall, flipping pages in a tattered paperback. "Being in the goddamn mountains of Afghanistan, surrounded by hostiles the other night - that was the real deal. There ain't no make-believe in this fucking place."

Scott smiled. "Go back to your book. We all get it."

Park didn't look up. "I'm just sick of everyone making a big deal over one raghead," he muttered. "If we're patient, he'll surface, and we'll pop him - just like we've done a thousand times in these stupid wars."

Reyes set his jaw. "As cynical as I am these days, he isn't just another raghead," he said. "If there's even the smallest chance to take that motherfucker out, the chain of command will do whatever it takes to make it happen."

"Which is why we'll be in the mountains freezing our asses off inside of twelve hours," Patel said. "You can count on it."

* * *

FOB KOGYANI - NEAR TORA BORA, WHITE MOUNTAINS

"Sir, Lieutenant Colonel Robinson wants you to get in touch," said Specialist Jones.

Startled out of his attempt to set a personal record on the New York Times crossword, Captain James Vasquez blinked. "What?" He swung his feet down from the desk. "What does he want?"

"No idea, sir," Jones replied. "Brigade sent me an email. That's all I got."

Vasquez sighed, logged into his computer - something he hadn't done in over twelve hours - and immediately saw several unread emails from Robinson. He quickly opened the most recent one.

"Shit," he muttered, the word dragging out in one long syllable.

Grabbing his government-issued cell phone, he dialed Robinson's number. The connection was almost instant.

"Sir, this is Vasquez. I heard you wanted to talk to me."

"Where in the hell have you been, Captain?" Robinson barked. "I've been trying to hunt you down for four fucking hours."

Vasquez winced. "Uh, well, sir… You know we're rebuilding the FOB perimeter right now. I hate sitting in my office, so I figured I'd keep an eye on things out there."

Out of sight, Jones rolled his eyes.

"Right," Robinson said slowly, his tone thick with doubt. "Brigade wants to know why the fuck it took you almost two days to forward a solid HUMINT report that a bunch of al-Qa'ida fighters are climbing the mountains toward Tora Bora?" His voice rose. "You do realize that's the entire fucking reason we're here, right?"

Vasquez swallowed hard. "Uh, yes sir. As I recall, I signed it out for release as soon as it came in."

"Shit. Captain, that is the kind of thing you follow up with a phone call," Robinson snapped. "For fuck's sake, it's the kind of thing you run a hundred miles for and hand deliver if you need to."

A pause. Vasquez could hear muffled voices in the background but couldn't make out the words.

"Captain, you still there?" Robinson asked.

"Yes, sir," Vasquez said quickly.

Robinson's next words were clipped and cold. "Brigade just called. Pack your shit and prepare to be relieved."

Vasquez stiffened. "What?"

"You heard me," Robinson said. "Your replacement is on a helo right now. When he gets there, hand over the FOB and report to me immediately."

"Yes, sir."

The line went dead.

Vasquez slowly lowered the phone, staring blankly at Jones.

"I guess you're getting a new boss," he said flatly.

* * *

THE LANDING ZONE, SPECIAL OPERATIONS COMPOUND - BAGRAM AIR BASE

The El Zed was alive with activity. Pool tables were crowded, televisions blared, and two dozen special operators - sporting different uniforms, accents, and patches - unwound with rare downtime.

Briggs and Scott lounged in a pair of overstuffed chairs, each nursing a fake beer while watching a taped replay of a football game from the previous fall.

"You hear the latest rumor?" Scott asked.

Briggs didn't look away from the screen. "Yeah. But we've

seen this before. I was part of the great Saddam hunt. We jumped through our ass for months."

"That's exactly what Patel said," Scott said.

Briggs shook his head. "Yup, there's too much chatter out in public for this to be real. If the administration actually thought UBL was heading back to Tora Bora, one of the Tier One units would already be in the mountains hunting him."

"Yeah, well, that won't stop people from jumping through their ass on a rumor," Scott said. "Even if it's just a bunch of al-Qa'ida guys, it means we get some payback. I think everyone's sick of fighting the Taliban. We want to kill the assholes that actually conducted or supported the attack."

"Maybe," Briggs said, finishing his beer. He looked at the empty bottle and frowned. "This fake shit tastes like soap. I'd kill for a real one."

Scott smirked. "That probably could be arranged. There's always contraband somewhere."

Briggs shook his head. "Appreciate it, but no thanks. My liver enjoys deployment - it's a good break from booze."

Scott's eyes flicked toward the door. "Oh, here it comes."

"What?" Briggs followed his gaze.

Amina Khan and McCoy had just walked in, scanning the room. Within seconds, they were making a beeline toward them.

"I told Amina we'd find you two here," McCoy said, arms crossed. "You know your phones are off, right?"

"They're not off," Scott corrected smugly. "We're just ignoring them."

"What's the drill?" Briggs asked, already sitting up.

Amina folded her arms. "You need to be in the air in three hours." She gave them a knowing look. "And I think you already know why."

* * *

KHOST - AFGHANISTAN

The evening air in Khost was warm. Zayan Shah sat in the shaded courtyard of the hotel restaurant, the same one where he had met Nabil Hamid just a few days before. He liked the place - the food was good, and the hotel's owner knew not to ask too many questions. Tonight, he had chosen a table in the far corner, partly for the solitude and partly to maintain a view of the entrance.

Shah's return from Pakistan had been uneventful. After meeting with the General, he had departed the ISI facility as soon as he could, knowing that the Taliban might be watching. He had crossed the border before dawn, changing vehicles twice. Ironically, he believed that Khost was safer than his own nation, but only by degrees.

Before leaving the ISI facility, he had sent an agent to check the Gardez-Khost highway for signs of Hamid, and the news that had come back was troubling. The agent had reported finding the burnt wreckage of Hamid's truck on the roadside. The Americans had hit it with a missile, likely a drone strike. There had been signs of death in the blackened crater, but no body. Later, in a roadside mosque, the agent had heard rumors that Hamid was dead, along with a group of Taliban leaders. If true, the timing was truly convenient. The General had wanted to dispose of Hamid and the Americans seem to have handled it directly. But now the other agent had gone silent.

Shah had assumed he was in Gardez as planned, but silence could also mean two things; he was dead, or he had been taken. Neither option was particularly good. Shah was running out of agents in the local area, and if the Taliban was behind the move, he might be in trouble himself. He'd have to set up a meeting and make peace.

The hotel owner emerged from the kitchen, wiping his hands on a towel. "Sir, would you like the dinner special?"

Shah nodded. "As always."

The owner smiled and disappeared back inside.

He reached into his satchel and pulled out a copy of the Islamabad Express Tribune. Even after years away, he liked to keep up with news from home. He unfolded the paper, scanning headlines. Elections, power shortages, an op-ed about corruption in the intelligence services. Nothing surprising.

The entrance to the courtyard was visible around the edge of the paper, but his attention was on the article in front of him. If he had glanced up, even for a moment, he would have seen the two men enter.

The first man was older, with a face hardened by years in the mountains, wind-carved and scarred by sun. His companion was younger, nervous energy radiating from him in barely contained bursts. The older man moved methodically around the courtyard, speaking in low tones to the few other patrons. Whatever was said was enough - within moments, they abandoned their meals, gathered their belongings, and slipped out without looking back.

When the restaurant was clear, the young man pulled a long, curved blade from his waistband. He crossed the courtyard quickly, stepped up to Shah's table, and with a quick motion, grabbed the newspaper, yanking it down to face the intelligence agent.

"Die, you Pakistani spy..."

Two gunshots cut the words short. The young man dropped as if a switch had been flipped, his body crumpling into a heap on the tiles.

At a speed that was surprising for his girth, Shah began moving before the young man had dropped, pistol in hand. The older man reacted faster. He pulled up the AK-47 that had been hidden beneath his loose-fitting tunic and fired a short burst from the automatic weapon.

The impact sent Shah staggering backward, the force of the rounds hammering into him, throwing him against the low wall behind his seat. The pistol slipped from his grasp. As he lay on the tile floor his breath came in short, uneven gasps, lungs failing, blood spilling out onto the bricks beneath him.

The older man stepped forward, rifle at the ready, the steel barrel only inches from Shah's face.

He pulled the trigger.

"Allah Akbar."

16

Al-QAIDA MILITANTS - APPROACHING TORA BORA

The group of al-Qa'ida militants crested the final ridgeline. Before them lay the entrance to the tunnel complex, nestled in the barren landscape like a scar from an old bullet wound. The men were exhausted - bodies aching, stomachs hollow, nerves frayed - but they pressed on, driven by the weight of their mission.

Al-Sudani stopped for a moment and scanned the valley, his expression unreadable. "Nothing has changed," he murmured.

"Other than the fact that we are sneaking into a place we ought to proudly own," Hamza muttered, his voice laced with bitterness.

"Perhaps," Al-Sudani allowed. He reached into his vest and retrieved a folded topographic map, tracing the contours with a calloused finger. He studied it for a long moment before tapping on the paper. "The Sheikh believes the item is in this tunnel," he pointed.

Hamza leaned closer. "Was he sure?"

Al-Sudani didn't hesitate. "Of course he was sure," he said, the reproach clear in his voice. "We will find the item and then immediately prepare to return."

Hamza frowned. "You expect trouble?"

"I expect to be discovered," Al-Sudani corrected. "It is only a matter of time. When it happens, I want us to be a few hours march from the border."

Hamza shook his head. "Surely you don't think the invaders will honor the border this time." His voice carried skepticism, thick with the memory of past battles.

Al-Sudani's eyes darkened. "I do. At least with their aircraft. But I am also sure they will send their soldiers to pursue us."

A slow, grim smile spread across Hamza's face. "Good. We can send some to hell before we return."

Al-Sudani exhaled, the weight of the mission settling on his shoulders. He looked out at the valley, then at his men - tired but resolute.

"Inshallah," he said.

Without another word, they continued their descent into the shadows.

* * *

JOINT COUNTER-IED TASK FORCE - BAGRAM AIR BASE

"That was a good meeting. Thanks for giving us a look at how things are going on in the field," said Colonel Brooks.

"No problem," said Agent Nancy Reams. "It was worth the trip."

The rest of the people in the room stood up to leave, Brooks leaned forward, "Hey Agent Reams, can I get a minute with you alone?"

"Sure," said Reams.

The two waited as the rest of the group filed out.

When they were the only ones in the room, Brooks looked at

Reams. "So what did you think of Flynn and his team? Are they as good as I think they are?"

"Well, let's put it this way - I tried to convince him to apply for the FBI academy," said Reams. "All three are solid, but I think Flynn will be running a detective branch at some point if he wants to."

"Good," said Brooks. "Can't tell you why, but I got a request for some forensic help. I told them I didn't have anyone, but then I remembered Flynn. It doesn't sound like IED work, though."

"He'll be fine doing almost anything," said Reams.

"Okay, thanks. I'll let them know."

* * *

CIA SPECIAL ACTIVITIES DIVISION B-HUT - BAGRAM AIR BASE

"I told you we'd be jumping through our ass inside of twelve hours," Patel muttered, stuffing gear into his oversized pack.

"Yes, you were right," Reyes admitted. "Too bad your wisdom doesn't work on the stock market."

Patel smirked. "That's what I let you think. I'm really a millionaire."

Reyes snorted. "Dude, you are so poor that the last time someone broke into your house to steal your money, you offered to help them if they would split it with you."

Laughter rippled through the room.

"I hate to interrupt this touching moment," Jun Park cut in, "but there's one big difference between this and the Saddam hunt."

Patel glanced up. "What's that?"

Park deadpanned. "It's in the fucking mountains, dumbass." He gestured vaguely toward the landscape beyond. "Did you see the size of the mountain we were patrolling the other night? We're about to be humping our asses through deep-ass valleys and steep fucking ridgelines in the damn dark, and when we stop to set up an OP, we're gonna freeze."

Reyes grinned and tapped his temple. "Dude, you sound like a quitter. The cold is all in your mind."

"Fuck you, Reyes," Park shot back. "Don't tell me about your resistance to cold. You're a wetback from southern Mexico - I've seen you shivering in a damn sauna."

The room erupted in laughter. Reyes grinned and chucked an empty water bottle at Park, who batted it away with a smirk.

From across the room, Scott's voice cut through the noise. "We brief in an hour." The laughter died down as everyone turned toward him. "Hate to say it, but Jun's at least partially right."

Park made a show of nodding smugly.

Scott ignored him. "Based on what I got from Amina, we're not dropping in as shooters - we're spotters. That means we hike in, find good observation points, and call in airpower if we see the bastards."

"So pack warm," Patel muttered.

"Yes, pack warm," Scott confirmed.

* * *

INDIAN SPRINGS AIR BASE – NEVADA

"New mission just in," said 1st Lieutenant Bryant. "A hot one."

"What is it?" asked Captain Reeves.

"We are looking for some al-Qa'ida who are on their way to Tora Bora," said Bryant, the excitement clear in his voice.

"No shit," said Reeves. "That is cool." She pulled up a chart on her display. "Is there anyone on the ground yet?"

"No," replied Bryant. "The CAOC is running the air plan for now. We have REAPER32. It has about four hours of fuel remaining."

"Switching," said Reeves as she pulled up the Predator in her control panel. "Well, let's start looking for terrorists."

* * *

AIR FORCE FACILITIES - BAGRAM AIR BASE

"Hey, Chris," said Major Sarah Matthews as she stepped into the ready room. "We're on alert tonight."

"Really?" Captain Ben Cross frowned. "What's up? I don't remember anything from the ops brief this morning."

Matthews shrugged. "Everyone's pretty quiet about it, so I'm not entirely sure. Last time this happened, it was some special ops thing that lasted a couple of days."

"Cool," Cross said. "How does this work? I haven't done one of these before."

"We're on the schedule from 2000 to oh-dark-thirty," Matthews explained. "We brief at 1900, get our gear on, and then just sit in here watching TV, reading a book, or whatever. If they call us in, we need to be airborne in ten minutes or less."

Cross nodded, processing. "Do we know where the operation is?"

Matthews glanced at him. "Northern side of the White Mountains."

Cross raised a brow. "What, south of Jalalabad?"

Matthews gave a tight nod. "Yup. Near Tora Bora."

* * *

CIA SPECIAL ACTIVITIES DIVISION B-HUT - BAGRAM AIR BASE

The entire ATLAS team was gathered with Briggs, Fletcher, and McCoy. Bags were packed, weapons prepped, and everyone's attention was on a large map spread out on the table.

Amina Khan, the unit's intelligence analyst, was leading the briefing. She pointed to the location of Tora Bora. "Tora Bora is a complex of several caves in this area here," she said, circling a valley on the north side of the mountain. "We haven't located the terrorists yet, but we're pretty certain we'll have their position pinpointed within the next couple of hours."

"Pretty certain?" Patel asked.

"They don't want to be found," Khan said dryly. "And they've had some practice."

"No shit," Patel muttered.

"They're likely holed up in one of these caves right now," said Khan. "Based on past patterns, they'll send out patrols and possibly a recon team or two. That was their pattern when there were militants here before."

"How good do you think they are?" Scott asked.

"Hard to say without knowing exactly who is in the group, but we expect this is a highly skilled team," Khan replied. "It's no small feat to make that trip over the mountain in a couple of days. And if this is a critical mission assigned by UBL, they probably sent their best."

"Shit," said Reyes. "When has their best ever been good enough?"

"As I recall, they've gotten close a few times," said Jun Park.

"Oh, fuck that," replied Reyes. "The only advantage they've ever had is some occasional luck."

KHAN WAITED for the banter to stop and then continued. "You are one of three teams deploying into the area," she said. "FANG consists of eight SEAL team members. They're jumping in tonight to take a position here…"

Park cut her off. "They're parachuting into the fucking mountains? In the dark? Are they suicidal?"

The room erupted in rough laughter.

"They like the drama," Patel said. "Makes a good story for the leadership books they'll write when they get out."

More laughter.

"As I was saying," Khan resumed, "FANG will cover the western edge of the fight." She pointed to another spot on the map. "TALON will be inserted by helo and hold the upper part of the valley from here."

"Which leaves us with the eastern side," Reyes said.

"What about the south?" Patel asked. "What if they run down the mountain toward Jalalabad?"

"Airpower and a reserve force from the 75th Rangers," Khan replied. "They won't be headed south. When they run, we expect them to try and make it back to Pakistan. You'll be chasing them uphill."

An uneasy silence filled the space.

"I've got a stupid question," Reyes said. "Why don't we just start fucking bombing them right now?"

"We don't want to destroy whatever they are looking for. There is strong evidence to suggest that they are recovering something from one of the caves," Khan explained. "If it's a recovery mission that's important to Bin Laden, we'd rather get our hands on whatever it is first."

"Seems like Bin Laden could've just hired local help to find whatever they left behind," Scott said.

"Depends on what it is," Khan replied. "Remember, al-Qa'ida and the Taliban aren't exactly allies. Their objectives don't always align, other than the fact that they both hate us."

"Didn't we search those caves a couple of years ago?" Scott asked. "I know several guys who spent a lot of time up there after the first big Osama hunt."

"As you can imagine, it's tough to do a thorough search in the dark," Khan said. "We ran dogs through and collected a lot of intel, but if we weren't looking for the right thing, it would've been easy to miss."

"What if they're just drawing us into a trap?" O'Connor asked from the back of the room.

"Using themselves as bait?" Patel's exasperation was clear.

"Hey," O'Connor said defensively, "Suicide attacks are their thing."

"It's a good question," Scott said. "But we'll have a ton of airpower overhead. We're not about to engage a force six times our size. If they try something suicidal, we'll just sit back and let the Air Force pick them off."

* * *

FORENSICS TEAM - FOB CHAPMAN

The three forensic IED investigators were lounging in their temporary supply-shed home when the *ding* of an arriving email broke the silence. Sergeant Ty Jenkins sat up from his cot and moved to check their SIPR computer.

He scanned the email account. "Well, this is weird," Jenkins said.

"What is that?" asked Staff Sergeant Dan Flynn.

"We're heading back to Jalalabad - on a priority basis, no less," replied Jenkins.

"Fuck," Private Eli Grayson muttered. "That can't be good."

"Maybe not," Jenkins admitted, "but at least we'll get back to our stuff. I need to do laundry in the worst way."

"I'll agree to that," said Grayson as he mimed smelling his own pits and passing out.

"What's in the orders?" Flynn said as he placed the book he was reading on the floor beside his cot and sat up. "Anything that'll give us a clue about the task?"

Jenkins read silently for a moment before speaking again. "Ah, yeah, this one is different."

"What?" Grayson asked.

"We're temporarily attached to the Special Ops teams. Sounds like we need to report as soon as possible," Jenkins said.

"That doesn't sound like IED work," Grayson pointed out.

"It's probably not," Flynn agreed. "My bet is that somebody doesn't want to make a formal request for forensic or investigative support from outside the theater. We are the closest thing they could find. "

"Who'd have thunk that being a cop would have benefits here in Afghanistan?" Grayson said with a grin.

"Yeah, don't start thinking this is a good deal until proven otherwise," Jenkins cautioned. "It sounds to me like we get stuck with a bunch of superstars as they climb through the mountains. I prefer life in an MRAP myself.

"Well, let's start packing up," Flynn said. "Sounds like they're in a hurry."

"You ain't kidding," Jenkins replied, his expression shifting to surprise as there was another *ding* from the computer. He took a moment to read it. "We just got another email. We have ninety minutes until our helo shows up."

"Great."

* * *

SPECIAL ACTIVITIES DIVISION AVIATION B-HUT - BAGRAM AIR BASE

"Sounds like a simple drop," Fletcher said.

Briggs snorted. "Another ridgeline delivery on a dark-ass mountainside with bad guys waiting for us. Simple, but not easy."

"At least we won't be alone this time." Fletcher scanned the Air Tasking Order. "Two JSOC teams are being dropped to the north and east of our LZ. And get this - there'll be not one, but two B-1B bombers in holding patterns somewhere nearby. Plus, the usual A-10 support. We'll even have an airborne jammer."

Briggs shook his head. "Yup. It's gonna be a circus."

The door swung open, and McCoy stepped into the B-hut. "When are you guys launching?"

"In about forty minutes," Fletcher said.

McCoy nodded. "Just got word from Amina in the ops center. After the drop, they want you repositioned to Jalalabad. There'll be five other JSOC MH-60Ms at the field with you. You're on call as the priority dust-off if the shit hits the fan."

Briggs frowned. "Are we getting a medic?"

"You will if you need to launch," McCoy said. "Normal medevac will be there too. This is just if an especially hairy situation develops. This also means that you won't have two door gunners, just Holland."

"Great," Fletcher muttered.

Briggs shot him a look. "Told you this would happen."

McCoy grinned. "Oh, come on, Briggs. You love this shit."

* * *

SPECIAL OPERATIONS FLIGHT LINE - BAGRAM AIR BASE

Briggs and Fletcher left the ATLAS briefing and made their way to the flight line to prepare the aircraft. As they approached the helicopter, Kyle Holland was already there waiting for them.

"The helo is good," Holland reported. He was decked out in fresh fatigues, a new helmet with NVGs, a Kevlar face guard, and a heavy plate carrier.

"You think you can handle this by yourself?" Briggs asked.

"Sure," Holland said with a grin. "We're just dropping the team off and heading to Jalalabad, right?"

"That's the plan," Briggs confirmed. "But if shit hits the fan, we'll be right in the middle of it."

"I'll be fine," Holland assured him.

Briggs and Fletcher did a walk-around of the helicopter,

checking everything over. They were soon met by the maintenance crew chief, Kody Bishop.

"Don't get any holes in this one tonight," Bishop said, resting a hand on the fuselage. "It's nice having two brand-new birds to take care of." He shook his head. "Not to mention, we don't have any spare parts."

"So we've heard," Fletcher said. "Don't worry, we are just dropping the kids off at school."

"Yeah, right," Bishop scoffed. "See you in a couple of days."

"Will do," Fletcher said as he climbed into the cockpit next to Briggs.

"You ready for this?" Fletcher asked.

"Sure," Briggs replied. "Feels like I'm back on the task force treadmill. Doesn't even seem like I left. My ex would be shaking her damn finger at me, saying, 'I told you so.'"

"That's what I mean," Fletcher said. "It doesn't feel like I left either." He started working through the switches on his side of the MH-60M's cockpit. "I know I gave you shit before, but I think I'm done after this."

"Don't think about it now," Briggs said. "We'll chat with McCoy when we get back."

"Here comes the team," Holland called out.

Briggs looked up and watched the seven members of ATLAS approaching the aircraft. They look like a bunch of action movie stars or superheroes, he thought.

"Let us know when you're all secured back there," Fletcher said.

"Will do," Holland replied.

17

AL-QAIDA MILITANTS - TORA BORA CAVES

"This is the right cave," said Al-Sudani. "I remember it well." He turned to Hamza. "Set up a defense here. Detail eight men for observation posts. The rest of us will look for the item and decide what we will do when we find it."

"What are we looking for?" asked Hamza.

"A box or crate that is probably near the rear of the cave. It will be buried," replied Al-Sudani. "There will be some sort of graffiti or other marking on the wall over it."

Hamza walked away and found one of their most seasoned fighters. "Farid, pick eight men. Establish two overlooks, one north and one west. We will rotate out replacements as soon as we figure out what is next."

Farid nodded. He selected his men and walked out of the cave and into the dark.

Hamza turned to the rest of the men, "The rest of us will begin searching for a crate that is buried somewhere along this cave. Always operate in pairs. We are looking for a place where there is graffiti on the wall."

"Are there any mineshafts or holes in this cave?" asked one of the men.

Al-Sudani turned, "No, this not a mineshaft. It is a refuge. There are some branches and walkways that lead from the main tunnel, but they do not go far."

The militants fanned out, their flashlights sweeping across the cave's rough walls. Dust swirled in the stagnant air, disturbed by their movements. The cave smelled of damp stone and decay, thick with the residue of old battles. Bullet holes pockmarked sections of the rock near the entrance, a rusted ammunition belt lay half-buried in the dirt. A skeletal hand, likely belonging to some forgotten fighter, protruded from the debris.

One of the men nudged the remains with his boot. "Americans?" he asked.

"No," said Al-Sudani, barely glancing at the bones. "One of ours."

Deeper inside, the cave opened into a wider chamber. Scattered shell casings glinted under the dim light, and fragments of old radios, shattered by gunfire, lay in a heap near the back wall. There were charred marks on the ground, remnants of a grenade explosion.

"This place has seen war," Hamza muttered.

"This battle was intense," said Al-Sudani.

He stepped forward, his boot crunching over spent brass. "They fought to the last man in here."

A rusted AK-47 leaned against the wall, its barrel warped by heat. Nearby, a broken radio, the plastic melted from fire.

Hamza exhaled. "And the Americans?"

"They pinned the fighters in the cave with bombs. Then they waited outside and picked off any who attempted to escape," said Al-Sudani. "When the fighters could take no more, they made an attempt to run in the middle of the night. Only a few made it." He paused. "I was part of the group watching from the upper ridge, we wanted to assist but the Sheikh demanded that we save ourselves and escort him to safety."

It was quiet for a long time. The search continued for more than an hour. Al-Sudani was clearly becoming less certain of the location. As they went further into the cave, the headlamps cast wavering beams across the jagged rock, creating ghostly shapes that flickered among them. The cave seemed deeper than it should be, the darkness pressing in, swallowing their movements.

* * *

TEAM FANG - TORA BORA

The red jump light inside the C-130 cast a dim glow over the eight men of team FANG, their faces masked behind oxygen rigs, their gear strapped tight. The cargo bay rattled with turbulence as the aircraft powered through the thin Afghan air at 30,000 feet. Outside, the vast black expanse of the mountains stretched below, jagged and merciless in harsh contrast of their NVGs.

"Thirty seconds," came the voice over the headset.

Chief Petty Officer Logan Kane checked his altimeter one last time. He glanced at his team. No words were needed. They had done this before.

The ramp began to open, and a howl of wind filled the bay.

One by one, the SEALs shuffled to the open void and waited.

"Green light."

The first SEAL stepped into the void, vanishing into the abyss. Stacked behind him, the rest of the group piled out of the aircraft in less than five seconds.

Kane leapt last. As soon as he cleared the ramp, the world exploded into a maelstrom of wind and cold. The roar of the C-130's engines vanished the moment he left its belly, replaced by the deafening rush of thin air tearing past his body. The night sky stretched in every direction, a void of black and stars, the ground beneath him nothing more than a vast, unseen abyss.

He spread his limbs, stabilizing himself in freefall. The cold bit at his exposed skin, the mask pressed tight against his face, feeding him oxygen in the thin, frozen air at 25,000 feet. His altimeter blinked - time to deploy.

Kane pulled the ripcord.

The chute snapped open, yanking him upward in a sudden, bone-jarring deceleration. The harness bit into his shoulders, and then the world slowed. Below him, his team followed, their canopies unfurling like silent phantoms in the night sky. They spread into formation, gliding forward with barely a sound.

This was the reason for a High-Altitude, High-Opening jump - stealth, distance, and surprise.

By deploying their parachutes at extreme altitude, they could glide for miles, infiltrating enemy territory from far beyond detection range. The aircraft had never needed to come close to the valley where the caves were located, reducing the risk of spooking their quarry. To anyone below, the SEALs did not exist - there was no sound, no helicopter flying nearby to put them on edge.

Below, the ridgeline west of Tora Bora stretched out like the spine of a great beast. The terrain was treacherous - sheer cliffs, loose rock, and deep ravines. The kind of place where a bad landing could snap a leg or send a man tumbling into darkness.

Kane adjusted his toggles, steering toward the LZ marked on his HUD. He spotted movement - his team, already drifting toward their landing spots.

The wind shifted. A downdraft caught him, and suddenly, he was sinking too fast. He gritted his teeth, flaring his canopy to slow descent. Not enough. The rocks rushed up to meet him.

Shit.

He braced, knees slightly bent, absorbing the impact as his boots slammed into the uneven ground. He rolled, keeping momentum, his chute collapsing beside him. Pain shot through his ankle; he felt something snap, and then his leg was flooded with pain.

As soon as he could, he unclipped his harness and stowed the chute. He scanned the darkness. The others were landing, their forms emerging in the green hue of NVGs.

"Status?" asked Kane as he limped to the group.

One by one, they checked in. Each team member reported that they were fine.

"Well, I hate to be the one to fess up, but I am pretty sure I busted an ankle or something." He made his way to a boulder and sat down. "Renner, how about wrapping me up and I'll gimp my way along."

"You got it Chief," said Renner. The medic helped Kane remove his boot. "Nothing protruding, Chief. It's definitely swelling, though." He wrapped the limb tightly and helped Kane put his boot back on."

"Thanks," said Kane. He stood, gripping his suppressed HK416. He inhaled the thin, freezing air. He knew that they would have to walk eight or nine kilometers and he would be wincing every step.

"Sharpe, let the ops center know we are on the deck. Report one injured, but mobile," said Kane.

"Gotcha Chief," said Sharpe.

"Move out," Kane whispered.

The shadows swallowed the SEALS as they melted into the night.

* * *

AL-QAIDA MILITANTS - TORA BORA CAVES

After another hour of frustration Hamza adjusted his rifle. "Are we sure this is the right place?"

Al-Sudani hesitated. "It should be. I am sure it is the one the Sheikh identified."

At that moment, one of the fighters ran his fingers over the scrawled Arabic on the cave wall. He found the words "Allah Akbar" scratched into the stone with the tip of a blade. The letters were jagged, hurried. A final prayer before death.

Frowning, he kicked at the dirt beneath it. The ground shifted unnaturally. Loose.

His heartbeat quickened.

"Hamza," he called, stepping back. "Come look at this."

Al-Sudani and Hamza walked to the location. Hamza kneeled beside the disturbed ground. He ran his hand over the uneven surface, then dug his fingers into the dirt.

Something was buried here.

"Get the others," Hamza said.

They dropped their rifles and began scraping away dirt with their hands. The loose gravel gave way easily, and within minutes, one of them hit something solid.

"I have it," one whispered.

The men cleared the remaining dirt, revealing a weathered wooden crate. Its edges were rotted, and a faint scorch mark stretched across the lid, a sign that it had barely survived whatever battle had raged here. Al-Sudani knelt, prying it open. Inside, wrapped in decayed cloth, was a dusty, battered laptop.

"This is it," he murmured, brushing away the grime. He looked at his watch. "Now we have a choice to make."

* * *

TEAM TALON - TORA BORA

The MH-60M Black Hawk thundered low over the jagged peaks of the Hindu Kush, its rotors cutting through the thin mountain air. Inside the darkened cabin, the eight men of TALON sat packed together, rifles across their chests, their gear cinched down tight. The only light came from the faint glow of instrument panels in the cockpit and the occasional flicker of green from their night vision goggles.

Captain David "Hawk" Bennett gripped the overhead strap as the helicopter bucked in the turbulent air. He glanced at his team - seven hardened Green Berets, silent and ready. No chatter, no nerves, just the steady, controlled breathing of men who had done this before.

"Two minutes," the crew chief called over the intercom.

Bennett gave a single nod. He turned to his second-in-command, Staff Sergeant Miguel Ortiz, who flashed a quick thumbs-up.

Outside, the ridgelines below were nothing but shadows, steep and unforgiving. Somewhere beyond those peaks lay their objective - an observation point above the caves. If the militants tried to escape back to Pakistan, TALON would be waiting.

The Black Hawk banked hard, dropping lower.

"One minute!"

Bennett shifted his weight, reaching down to check the sling on his suppressed MK17. The wind was about to hit them hard.

The side doors slid open, and the roar of the rotors became deafening. The cold night air blasted into the cabin. Below them, the LZ was a small clearing barely big enough for the bird to set down. Sharp rock outcroppings flanked the sides.

"Go! Go! Go!"

Bennett was out first, boots hitting the rocky ground. He moved fast, peeling left as the others followed, rifles up, scanning. The helicopter held just long enough for everyone to disembark before lifting off, its engines screaming as it banked away into the dark. Within seconds, there was nothing to be seen or heard.

Silence.

Only the wind remained, a stiff breeze blowing through the mountain pass. Bennett crouched, scanning the area through his NVGs. The LZ was clear. He keyed the mic on his radio. "Check in."

One by one, the others responded. All accounted for.

Bennett gestured forward. "Move."

They began their ascent, climbing the narrow path toward the ridgeline that overlooked the pass. The terrain was brutal and was difficult to walk on quietly, consisting of loose shale, jagged boulders, and an occasional patch of ice. They moved carefully, knowing one wrong step could send a man tumbling into darkness.

He signaled for the team to spread out.

"Ortiz," let the operations center know we are on deck and proceeding to our overwatch.

"Will do sir."

* * *

AL-QAIDA MILITANTS - TORA BORA CAVES

The eight militants assigned to set up the observation points moved like shadows, splitting into two teams as they left the mouth of the cave. They spoke little, their breath visible in the cold night air as they adjusted their gear and began the climb.

The northern team, led by a combat veteran named Faisal, scaled a jagged rock face, using narrow ledges and deep cracks for leverage. The mountain was unforgiving - loose stones skittered beneath their boots, tumbling down the hillside. Faisal took point, his AK slung across his back, guiding his men upward towards the overlook.

THE WESTERN TEAM, led by Umar, a militant who had joined the group all the way from Kandahar, moved along a narrow ridgeline, navigating a treacherous ascent over slick, uneven ground. The rock was brittle, crumbling underfoot, and more than once, someone had to steady themselves to avoid slipping.

After nearly fifteen minutes of climbing, both teams reached their positions. Each observation point sat within 100 meters of the cave, perched high enough to give them a commanding view of the valley below. The cave entrance was a black void in the moonlight, barely distinguishable from the surrounding cliffs.

Faisal knelt behind a cluster of boulders, pulling his radio from his vest.

"We are in position in the north," he whispered.

He heard the mic click, and Umar also reported in, "We are set in the west."

A moment later, Hamza's voice crackled through the earpiece. "Understood. Keep your eyes open."

Faisal clicked the mic in acknowledgment, then settled in. The others followed, positioning themselves behind rocks or in natural depressions, rifles resting in the crooks of their arms. They scanned the valley below, watching for movement, but there was nothing, only the wind.

Time crawled.

Umar's team, watching from the west, was equally motionless, their eyes flicking between the cave and the moonlit ridges beyond.

"Nothing," one of the men muttered. "No one knows we are here. We are safe."

"You are a fool," Umar whispered back. "The Americans are watching you every time you pick your nose or scratch your ass."

There was a chuckle from the others.

One of the younger fighters shifted uncomfortably. "They are very difficult to hear. A single drone can kill a man from thousands of meters away. We saw it in Ghazni. One second, Abdul was walking. The next, he was gone."

The younger fighter turned to Umar. "Why do they fight like this? They send bombs from nowhere. They do not even see who they kill."

"They see," said Umar. "They capture each death on video and play them for entertainment." He gestured to the mountainside around them. "There will be Americans on this mountain right now. They will want to know why we are here and won't bomb us until they find out."

Silence settled over the teams again.

Time passed. Fatigue gnawed at them, the exhaustion of the long journey over the mountains creeping into their bones.

* * *

EC-130 OVERHEAD TORA BORA

The EC-130 Compass Call droned high above the rugged peaks of Tora Bora, circling at altitude, its large antenna arrays sweeping the spectrum below. Inside the dimly lit fuselage, rows of consoles flickered with data, operators hunched over screens, listening, searching.

Staff Sergeant Kyle Mercer adjusted his headset, fine-tuning the frequency scanner. Most of what they picked up was chatter between the local tribes. The transmissions from distant villages were common as they had no phones but only handheld radios to communicate. As they came closer to the mountain, he could hear the occasional chatter of Pakistani border troops.

A faint transmission cut through the interference.

"We are in position."

Mercer stiffened. The voice was barely above a whisper, but it was there. Arabic, Pashto? No - this was Urdu-tinged Arabic. He glanced at his screen, marking the time and frequency.

"Understood. Keep your eyes open."

Another voice. Different speaker. A response. Mercer quickly tapped out a log entry, then patched the feed to the linguist seated nearby.

"I've got something," he called out.

The analyst leaned in, listening, adjusting his own headset. "That's a check-in. Short-range comms. Could be line-of-sight."

Mercer nodded. "They're close. Somewhere in the mountains, north or west of Tora Bora."

The mission commander stepped over. "Get a fix if you can."

Mercer worked fast, triangulating the rough direction of the signal. "Can't do that yet, but it sounds like they're in a ridgeline position, likely overwatching something."

The commander keyed the intercom. "Send this to JSOC. We may have a lead."

Outside, the EC-130 continued its silent hunt.

* * *

TEAM ATLAS - TORA BORA

The MH-60M lifted off from Bagram, the rotors carving through the cold Afghan night. Inside, the seven men of ATLAS sat in silence, checking weapons, adjusting gear, mentally preparing for what lay ahead. The dim green interior lighting bathed them in an eerie glow, adding to the surreal atmosphere.

From the cockpit, Fletcher glanced out at the mountains below, dark and endless beneath the moonlight. His thoughts drifted. "This almost feels like a scene from Apocalypse Now."

Beside him, Briggs was unusually quiet, focused on the instruments. "ETA, 20 minutes," he said over the intercom.

"Copy," replied Scott. His voice was calm, controlled.

Down below, rugged ridgelines stretched into the darkness, untouched and treacherous. At five minutes out, Briggs and Fletcher gradually started descending, scanning for the LZ.

"There it is," Fletcher called, spotting the clearing - a small, rocky plateau nestled against the mountain. It was tight but manageable.

"Copy," Briggs acknowledged.

Inside the cabin, Scott and his team shifted forward, rifles slung, rucks secured.

"One minute!" said Fletcher. As they got closer, he started

calling altitudes. "One hundred, seventy-five, fifty, thirty, twenty, ten."

The Black Hawk flared, the downdraft kicking up dust and loose rock as the wheels kissed the earth. ATLAS moved fast. One by one, the operators leapt from the helo, fanning out, weapons at the ready.

Briggs and Fletcher wasted no time. The MH-60M lifted into the sky banking hard, its silhouette vanishing into the night as it headed for Jalalabad to wait.

Silence returned, except for the whisper of wind through the mountains.

Scott turned to his team. Patel, Reyes, and O'Connor were kneeling near him, and the others moved into a loose formation. The next task was a seven-kilometer hike to their overwatch position - a vantage point above a key pass where they would observe enemy movement.

"Let's move," Scott said quietly.

They set off, navigating the rocky terrain with careful precision. The moonlight cast long shadows, making every boulder and outcrop look like a potential threat. They kept their pace steady, conserving energy for the long trek ahead.

FAR BELOW, in the darkness of another ridgeline, al-Qa'ida militants in their listening posts stirred.

They could hear the faint thump-thump of helicopter rotors echoing through the valley, barely audible over the wind.

Farid turned to his comrade. "Helicopter."

The other nodded. "Americans."

Farid picked up his radio, "We have heard helicopters; they are here."

They listened as the sound faded into the distance. Then, silence.

* * *

INDIAN SPRINGS AIR BASE – NEVADA

Captain Reeves sat hunched over the controls of REAPER32, her eyes locked on the video feed. The screen displayed the jagged terrain of Tora Bora in a stark palette of black and white - cold rock formations, patches of sparse vegetation, and heat signatures moving across the ridgeline.

"There," she muttered, zooming in. Eight distinct thermal figures clustered in two positions, watching the valley below.

"Got 'em," said 1st Lieutenant Bryant as he leaned closer to his monitor. He began typing rapidly. "Two observation teams, approximately 100 meters from the cave entrance. Transmitting coordinates now."

Reeves fine-tuned the feed, adjusting the contrast to get a clearer picture. "They're dug in. No sign they've detected us."

Bryant confirmed receipt from the CAOC. "HQ is tracking. They're pushing this to JSOC now." He glanced at Reeves. "If one of the teams moves in, we will have eyes on them."

Reeves nodded, keeping her gaze fixed on the figures. "It's a shame we can't just light them up, or maybe call BONE in to plaster the area."

"Yeah, I'm not sure what they are waiting for," said Bryant.

* * *

AL-QAIDA MILITANTS - TORA BORA CAVES

The cave was cold, damp, and unforgiving. Al-Sudani crouched near the first laptop, its dust covered casing barely visible in the dim glow of a flashlight. The others had gathered nearby, exhaustion weighing heavily on them. They had found their objective, but the most difficult part of the mission lay ahead.

"We will rest here for five hours," Al-Sudani announced, his voice calm but firm. "Then, before dawn, we move back up the ridge to our last camp. It is only eight kilometers away. We need to be gone before the Americans turn this cave into a trap."

Some of the men grumbled, but no one objected. Hamza, however, folded his arms. "Five hours is a long time to sit still. We should go now. The listening posts heard a helicopter. The Americans are always watching."

Al-Sudani looked at him evenly. "And we are tired. Running now without rest would result in chaos." He turned toward the entrance, where the two observation teams remained at their positions. "Rotate the guards every ninety minutes. Fresh eyes will keep us alive."

Hamza hesitated. "As you said, they are tired. We all are."

Al-Sudani's expression hardened. "Fatigue makes mistakes. Rotate them."

Reluctantly, Hamza nodded and disappeared into the darkness outside. The others took their cue and began settling in near the cave's entrance, wrapping themselves in blankets, weapons within reach. A few spoke in low whispers, but most simply closed their eyes, trying to steal a few precious moments of rest.

The cave focused sound in strange ways. Every shuffle of boots, every whisper, every distant gust of wind echoed slightly as if the earth itself was listening.

Then, a new sound. A low, distant thrum.

Al-Sudani's eyes flickered open. He turned his head slightly, listening. The others noticed too - men stirring, some instinctively gripping their rifles.

"A helicopter," someone muttered.

"A drone," another replied. "Above the valley."

They strained their ears. A hum overhead. Almost imperceptible. The sound of aircraft at altitude - circling in the vast darkness above.

Al-Sudani slowly exhaled. Yes, a drone.

"They are watching," he murmured. "The plan has not changed. We leave here in five hours."

No one spoke. The militants stayed still, weapons clutched tight, as the unseen hunters loomed high above.

* * *

TEAM ATLAS - TORA BORA

The ridgeline was brutal. Every step sent loose gravel skittering down the slope, the crunch of boots against rock echoing into the empty night. Team ATLAS moved in silence, the only sounds being their controlled breathing and the occasional crackle of radio chatter in their earpieces.

Scott hated this kind of terrain - a treacherous mix of jagged stone, uneven ground, and patches of leftover snow that made every step a gamble. Even with NVGs, the contrast between shadow and ice was deceptive. A bad foot placement could mean a twisted ankle or worse. But they pressed forward, picking their way through the ridgeline, climbing steadily toward their overwatch position.

Scott heard Patel grunt behind him as he used his rifle for balance on a particularly steep incline. "Couldn't we have picked a mountain with a paved road?" he muttered.

"We could have dropped in like the SEALS," said Park.

Scott ignored him, eyes scanning ahead. The moon cast a faint glow over the peaks, but beyond that was nothing but darkness.

Then, the radio came alive.

"TALON is moving into position," came a hushed voice over the secure channel. "FANG is on schedule, expected to reach their OP soon."

Scott acknowledged with a click of his mic. Everything was unfolding as planned.

They climbed for another hour before reaching their designated OP, a narrow plateau with a clear vantage point over the valley below. Scott called for a halt, and the team immediately went to work.

"Confirming location," Patel muttered, crouching next to the satellite communications terminal, the small screen casting a dull green glow onto his face. He keyed in a few commands, then nodded.

"We've got movement on the eastern side of the cave complex," he whispered. "ISR confirms that's where the militants are holed up."

Scott's jaw tightened. That was a few hundred meters closer than expected.

"Better for us," Reyes murmured, setting down his M110 sniper rifle and beginning the process of setting up his shooting position. O'Connor knelt beside him, unzipping a pack and laying out his own rifle, a MK22 ASR.

Scott took one last scan through his binoculars, adjusting for the distance. The caves below were barely visible, just black voids cut into the stone, but the intelligence was clear - the enemy was there.

"Patel, get set up with comms. I want updates every 30 minutes," Scott ordered.

Patel nodded and got to work.

Scott turned to Reyes and O'Connor. "We sit tight and wait. If anything changes, I want to know immediately."

Reyes locked in his scope. "Roger that. Let's see how the night plays out."

The wind whispered around them, but Team ATLAS was in position. Now, they watched. They waited.

* * *

JALALABAD AIR BASE

Jalalabad was only a twenty-five minute flight from the LZ.

When they were fifteen miles out, Fletcher pressed the mic

button for the radio. "Jalalabad Tower, PORTHOS 16 is ten miles out for runway one-three."

"PORTHOS 16 is cleared to land, runway one-three, winds are calm. Altimeter 29.95."

"PORTHOS 16 is cleared on one-three, 29.95," replied Fletcher.

They swooped in low over the town along the outskirts of the base and hover taxied from the runway to the parking area.

"PORTHOS 16 is clear of the active, taxi to parking," said Fletcher.

"PORTHOS 16, follow your director," replied tower.

"I've got him," said Briggs, spotting a man with a pair of flash-light wands waving him to a parking spot.

After a few minutes, they completed their taxi and brought the Black Hawk to a stop alongside five other MH-60Ms. They sat motionless on the tarmac at Jalalabad air base, their rotors still, their dark silhouettes blending into the night. Now, they waited. Waiting for the mission to play out. Waiting to see who would come back.

Briggs exhaled, unstrapped, and leaned back in his seat, stretching his fingers before resting them on the cyclic. He stared out at the dim air base, lights glowing faintly along the perimeter through his NVGs.

"This is the hard part," he muttered.

Fletcher gave a tired chuckle. "Flying a Black Hawk through mountain passes at night? No problem. Sitting here with nothing to do but listen to the radio? Pure hell."

Briggs grunted. It wasn't the flying that stressed him out. It was the waiting.

The cockpit radio crackled with routine check-ins from Bagram, JSOC, and the CAOC, but there was nothing urgent. Everything was unfolding out there, in the mountains.

Holland, their door gunner, stood up from his seat and leaned into the cockpit.

"I'm making a run to ops," he said. "Want anything?"

"Yeah, I'll take a Coke," Fletcher said.

"Make that two," said Briggs. "Even though I'll eventually have to piss."

Holland unplugged his intercom and disappeared into the night. He returned a few minutes later with three cokes and several small bags of chips. He handed the sodas to Briggs and Fletcher and sat down in one of the webbed seats in the back of the aircraft.

"How long are we going to wait here?" asked Holland.

"Just till they get to their observation point," said Briggs. "Then we will hang out in ops until something happens or they need to exfill."

"Great," replied Holland.

After about thirty minutes, a figure emerged from the darkness, walking toward their helicopter.

The shape turned into a voice, "Are you guys PORTHOS 16?"

"We are," said Fletcher.

"I'm Staff Sergeant Buckman, a SF medic. I was told to come out here and wait with you until it is time to wrap things up for the night."

Briggs and Fletcher exchanged glances.

"We thought we were only a backup in case the regular medevac couldn't handle things," said Fletcher.

"Apparently, they want a dedicated dust-off capability for the next couple of hours. If anything goes sideways, we will be up first," said Buckman.

Fletcher sighed, rubbing his face. "Shit. Grab a seat."

"Cool," said Buckman. He looked around the helicopter. "You guys aren't Army, are you?"

"Nope."

Buckman threw a large backpack full of medical gear into the chopper and then climbed in and sat down.

Outside, the air base remained quiet.

18

TEAM ATLAS - EAST OF TORA BORA

The forested ridgeline above Tora Bora was deathly quiet. Even the wind, which had come whipping through the valley earlier in the night, had faded. The seven men of Team ATLAS had settled in for a long, silent vigil.

Their observation post was perfect; it was high above the al-Qa'ida militants working in the cave below, nestled in a dense patch of trees and boulders, with commanding views of the valley. Reyes and O'Connor, the team's designated snipers, were stretched out behind their rifles, keeping watch on the cave entrance with spotting scopes and night optics. Their thermal sights clearly highlighted the militants below, who had just begun rotating their own observation points.

The rest of the team had formed a perimeter, keeping their eyes on the surrounding hillsides. There was no talking, just the occasional traffic on the radio or the scratch of a gloved hand adjusting clothing.

Two hours passed.

The tension of the swift movement from Bagram to a rocky

outpost a hundred miles away had dulled into the slow, grinding patience of a long overwatch mission.

JUN PARK SAW SOMETHING MOVING.

He was making a routine sweep of the opposite ridgeline through his NVGs, and saw four men. He looked closer. The figures were carefully working their way up the steep terrain of the ridgeline's eastern slope toward their observation post. All were armed with Ak-47s. If they weren't part of the al-Qa'ida group in the caves, it likely meant they were local fighters - Taliban. He watched them for several more minutes before triggering the mic on this radio. If they kept moving at their current pace, they would reach ATLAS within twenty or thirty minutes.

"Contact. Four militants moving up the ridgeline on the trail. Six hundred meters."

The easy rhythm of a lengthy observation changed in an instant.

Scott was at Park's side in seconds, lowering to a crouch as Park guided him onto the threat. He pulled out his thermal binoculars and watched as the four fighters moved in single file up a trail, navigating the rocky terrain deliberately and with the occasional assistance of a weak flashlight. They clearly did not anticipate the fact that any Americans might be in the area.

Scott exhaled slowly. "They don't seem very tactical." He watched them for a few more moments. "But they're going to be a problem."

He switched to the team radio, his voice just above a whisper.

"Everyone listen up. We have four hostiles approaching our position up the ridgeline. If they keep moving this way, they'll be on top of us soon. We need to adjust now and get ready to take them out."

Patel moved to Scott's side, whispering, "After we engage, will we hold or fall back?"

"We hold until we see what happens," said Scott. "Once we initiate we will move based on what the guys in the tunnel do." He turned to Patel. "Let TALON and FANG know that things are going to get noisy. Worth letting the Ops Center know too."

"Will do," replied Patel.

Park, still watching the enemy patrol, whispered, "They're stopping."

Scott looked through his thermal binoculars. The four Taliban fighters had halted near a cluster of boulders, whispering among themselves. One gestured up the hill, as if debating their next move.

"Let's see what they do," said Scott.

* * *

TEAM FANG - WEST OF TORA BORA

Chief Petty Officer Kane adjusted his NVGs, scanning the valley below. He and his team had settled into their overwatch position west of the cave complex, perched along a natural rock formation that gave them a commanding view of the terrain. Unlike the grueling insertion, this was comfortable, at least by SEAL standards. The team was well-hidden and had solid cover should things turn kinetic; the only problem was his leg. It hurt miserably and was swollen so badly that he had to cut his boot open at the top to keep the blood flowing.

The radio crackled in Kane's ear.

"FANG, TALON, this is ATLAS. Be advised, four tangos pushing up the ridge towards our location."

"Copy, ATLAS," he responded. "Do you anticipate contact?"

A pause. "Unclear," came Patel's reply. "Boss says that if if pops here, the jihadis in the cave will probably try for a jailbreak and head towards TALON."

Kane understood immediately. If a firefight broke out on the eastern approach, the al-Qa'ida's fighters would likely abandon the cave, moving uphill, north towards the border and Team TALON's observation point. While FANG would have a good position for harassing fire from their current overwatch, if the militants pressed to up the ridge, they would quickly be at risk of directing friendly fire into TALON's position.

He tapped Graham, his second-in-command, signaling him to come over.

"We need to be in a better position to support TALON," said Kane. "If this gets hot, the guys in the cave are going straight for Pakistan."

Graham shifted slightly. "If we move about two hundred meters further up, we will have a better angle."

Kane nodded. "Exactly."

He turned to the rest of his men, speaking low and calm.

"If ATLAS makes contact, expect movement from the cave." He pointed up the trail to the north. "We will move two hundred meters north. If the militants move up the ridge we let them get into open terrain before we engage. After that if we need to, we link with TALON and ATLAS."

A few nods. No unnecessary chatter. These were SEALs, men who had spent their careers preparing for moments like this.

Graham keyed his own mic. "CAOC, this is FANG. Requesting ISR refocus west of the cave complex. If hostiles move up the ridge, we need eyes on them."

The Combat Air Operations Center responded immediately.

"Copy, FANG. Standby."

Kane checked his watch. The night was deep, and the cold had begun to settle into his gear. Five kilometers away, something was happening.

* * *

TEAM TALON - NORTH OF TORA BORA

"Fuck," said Ortiz. "We are stuck right in the middle of a shit sandwhich."

He glanced at Captain Hawkins, who was listening intently to the transmission from ATLAS.

"Possible contact on our end," came Patel's voice over the radio. "If it happens, expect movement from the cave."

The men of TALON crouched along the rocky overwatch position, staring down at the cave complex directly below. The night was cold and still. Ortiz shifted slightly, his eyes locked on the valley below. The numbers weren't in their favor. The intelligence suggested nearly forty al-Qa'ida fighters were down there. TALON had eight men. They were established in a good overwatch position, but a poor defensive one, and any movement would silhouette them against the ridge once the sun began to rise.

Hawkins' face remained unreadable. If ATLAS got into a fight, the al-Qa'ida fighters would do one of two things; fight back and hold the cave, or cut and run - straight for the border. And if they ran? They would run right up the mountain at TALON.

Hawkins keyed his radio. "Understood, ATLAS. We'll be ready."

He switched channels, connecting to his own team. "Alright, listen up. If the enemy breaks for the border, they'll be coming up this ridgeline in a hurry. We've got elevation, but we don't have anywhere to fall back to without exposing ourselves. If they swarm us, we can't hold."

Ortiz exhaled sharply. "So what's the move? We ambush and reposition?"

Hawk nodded. "If they leave the cave we will hit them hard and then move east towards ATLAS. We can't get bogged down here. No hero shit. There will be plenty of aircover to take care of things if we need it."

The others absorbed the plan without question.

Jackson O'Neal, the team's combat engineer, ran a hand over the small pack of explosives at his side. "We can leave them a gift," he muttered. "Delay their movement, buy us some space."

Hawkins nodded. "Do it. Claymores will give us time."

O'Neal nodded. He quietly moved forward about twenty meters and set up the charges along the trail from the cave.

Liam Tate, one of TALON's marksmen, shifted his rifle slightly. "We could take their observation posts before they even realize what's happening."

Hawkins shook his head. "Let's not encourage them to flank us early. I don't want to have to run up that motherfucking mountain."

The radio crackled again.

"If there is contact, FANG will move north two hundred meters. If the tangos head to the border, we'll pick them apart on the way up and give TALON time to move," Kane's voice came through.

That was some relief. But TALON was still in an exposed position. If the enemy charged straight up the mountain, they would be pinned between the cliffs above and the cave below.

* * *

TALIBAN PATROL, EASTERN RIDGELINE - TORA BORA

The four Taliban fighters moved carefully up the rugged mountainside, their boots crunching softly over loose stone and dry earth. They had been climbing for over three hours and were only now beginning to feel the effort. The truth was that they weren't in a hurry. This was not their fight.

They were walking to the cursed caves because their leaders had heard rumors - an al-Qa'ida group had returned to the old cave complex. Hassan, the eldest of the four men, adjusted the strap on his AK-47 and glanced at Latif, who walked beside him.

"If the Arabs are back in the caves, the valley will soon be crawling with Americans."

"There is no doubt that Arabs are in the caves and the Americans are already here," said Latif. "You've already heard their aircraft above us."

"They might even have soldiers on the mountain now," said Hassan, the concern clear in his voice.

"Maybe. If they aren't, they will be soon," replied Latif. He walked a few more steps. "What do you think the Arabs are doing there?"

"The elders think that they are searching the caves," said Hassan. "There must be something they left behind when the Americans chased them off."

The truth was that they did not trust the Arabs. The Taliban was fighting for their land, their villages, and their people. Al-qa'ida fought for something else - a war without borders, a jihad without end.

Harun, the youngest, adjusted the old Russian radio slung across his chest, checking the battery. "If we find the Arabs, what do we tell the commander?"

Hassan exhaled slowly. "We just confirm their presence; that is all. Then we watch."

Latif was blunt. "If they see us and we do not say anything, they will assume we are hostile."

Hassan nodded. The Arabs were paranoid. If they knew the Taliban were watching them, they might think it was a betrayal. They had killed many men for less.

"That is why we were told to find a place to watch without being seen," Hassan said.

Latif stopped for a moment on the steep incline, looking up into the dark and considering the terrain ahead. He knew that the caves were still further up, and across the ridgeline to the west. They were hidden by rock formations and thin lines of scraggly trees. If they pushed just a little further, they might be able to find a place to observe from above - high ground without exposure.

Harun wiped sweat from his brow. He was overheating despite the cold. "What if the Arabs somehow discover us?"

"Then we greet them as brothers and guests," Hassan said simply. He looked at the others. "We will not help them. But we will not betray them, either."

The men nodded. That was enough of a decision for now.

Without another word, they continued climbing.

* * *

INDIAN SPRINGS AIR BASE – NEVADA

Captain Reeves sat in the dimly lit control center, fingers steady on the joystick as she adjusted REAPER32's angle over the Afghan mountains. The infrared display on her screen was a grainy grayscale of ridgelines and caves, ghostly figures moving through the night.

Her headset crackled as the conversation between FANG, TALON, and ATLAS played out.

"If ATLAS makes contact, expect movement from the cave. They'll push up the ridge, likely heading west," Kane's voice came through, cool and steady.

Scott followed. "TALON, you're in a bad spot if they run. What's your plan?"

A pause.

"We will ambush them and run to the east," Hawkins said. "We can link up with you, or hold a spot further along the ridge and wait for air cover."

Reeves frowned, letting the conversations unfold while she kept scanning the terrain. Then, something new. Her infrared sensor picked up four distinct heat signatures - separate from the main al-Qa'ida group. They were moving up the ridgeline, slow, deliberate. Different formation. Different intent.

She zoomed in, adjusted contrast, and keyed her mic.

"All stations, this is REAPER32. I've got four unknowns moving up the ridge, 500 meters east of TALON's position."

Scott's voice came back first. "We are visual, thanks. Once there is contact, be prepared to assist."

"REAPER32 copies."

She watched as the four Taliban continued their slow ascent, unaware that they were walking into danger.

* * *

AIR FORCE FACILITIES - BAGRAM AIR BASE

Major Matthews walked into the ready room from the squadron's operations space. "We are launching Chris. Let's get moving."

Captain Cross, who had been engrossed in a video game, stood up abruptly. "Cool. Let's go."

The two pilots grabbed their helmets and moved briskly out the door, crossing the tarmac toward their waiting A-10 Thunderbolts. The aircraft sat armed and fueled, their massive GAU-8 cannons glinting under the floodlights.

The ground crew was already moving, pulling safety pins and running final checks. No time for delays.

Matthews climbed into the cockpit. Her crew chief helped her get strapped in and then slapped her helmet lightly as good luck. He dropped back down and folded the ladder up.

Matthews turned on the aircraft battery and keyed her comms. "TUSK flight, check-in."

She received the minimal response expected from Cross: "Two."

It took three minutes for Matthew to fire up the twin turbofans; she felt the low vibration as his bird came alive.

"Two's up. Let's go hunting," Cross said over the tactical frequency radio.

Matthews looked down at her kneeboard card, reminding herself what her ATO callsign was for the event.

"Tower, TUSK10 and 12 for taxi," said Matthews.

"TUSK flight cleared to taxi to runway three one, altimeter 30.02. Winds calm," replied the tower.

"TUSK is cleared."

The two A-10s trundled to the hold short. Cross gave Matthews a thumbs up through the canopy with her NVGs.

"Tower, TUSK 10 is a flight of two for takeoff, runway three one."

"TUSK flight is cleared for takeoff, runway three one."

Seconds later, the two A-10s rolled onto the runway and thundered into the Afghan night.

* * *

TEAM ATLAS - EAST OF TORA BORA

"Ah, fuck," said Park quietly. "They are heading this way."

"So be it," said Scott. "I want Reyes and O'Connor to stay on the cave, this is going to generate some activity down there. Can't lose track of those guys."

"Got it," said Reyes.

"Patel, Park, you guys slide down the hill about twenty meters," said Scott as he looked at the layout of the path that the militants were following. "You'll have clean up. Me and Delgado will initiate."

Without a word, Patel and Park moved into the darkness in a crouch and disappeared.

"I'll take the lead, you take dash-two," said Scott as he settled down next to a tree and brought his rifle to bear.

"Done," said Delgado. He then moved five meters away to a small rock formation that would give him better cover.

. . .

THE FOUR TALIBAN fighters moved up the ridge. They had all grown up in these mountains and knew these ridgelines like the backs of their hands, but it felt different now. They were worried about the unpredictability of the al-Qa'ida militants and the possibility that the Americans might be watching.

The air had become very still.

Every so often, Latif, the first in the group, clicked on his small flashlight, cupping it with his hand to control the beam. It cast a narrow cone of weak yellow light, illuminating the trail that ran between jagged rocks and steep inclines before being switched off again. The use of the flashlight was risky; they knew they couldn't afford to be seen - but they also couldn't afford to misstep that would alert the enemy or injure one of them.

Hassan, second in line, but leader of the patrol, felt the weight of his responsibility increasing as they got closer to the caves. He had been proud that he had been selected to lead the group, but now the weight of that task was increasing with every step. He scanned the hillside ahead, but the darkness seemed to press back against his vision.

Behind him, Harun whispered, his voice tight. "I can hear the drone above us again."

"There is nothing we can do about that," said Hassan. "If they wish to strike it is God's will."

They continued their slow walk up the ridge.

Latif stopped and turned to the men behind him. "We are only a short distance from the best overlook…" His voice was interrupted by the sound of a suppressed rifle firing from thirty meters ahead.

AS THE FOUR militants came into the kill zone, Scott took aim at the man in the lead. He was just about to pull the trigger when the man stopped and turned to the group behind him. The militant said something and was turning back around when Scott pulled the trigger. The sound of the suppressed HK416 was quite loud in the stil mountain air. His target dropped immediately and did not move. Delgado fired within a fraction of a second and took the second militant with similar effectiveness. The third and fourth militants had only moments to respond, and neither managed to do more than take a single step before all four members of ATLAS unleashed a short burst of controlled rounds at them. Within seconds, all four were down.

"CONTACT. FOUR TANGOS DOWN," said Scott on the radio. He switched to the team channel. "Patel, Park, do a quick search and see what you can find on the bodies," said Scott. "Reyes, there is no way the dudes in the cave didn't hear that. What do you see?"

* * *

AL-QAIDA MILITANTS - TORA BORA CAVES

The night had been still, the mountains hushed in a heavy silence. The monotony of the night was broken by the muffled sound of gunfire. The noise came from above them and to the east. There were only ten or twenty rounds fired, the echo quickly bouncing off the valley walls and disappearing. The quick silence following a single volley said everything; it had been an ambush, not a skirmish.

At both al-Qa'ida observation posts, the radio operators tensed, exchanging uneasy glances with the men around them. One of the outpost leaders, Nadim, grabbed his radio and pressed the transmit key.

"Commander, we have heard gunfire from the east. Orders?"

In the cave below, Al-Sudani had heard the same gunfire. Americans. It had to be. No other force moved efficiently at night. If there were American troops on the eastern ridgeline, more were likely circling around to block them in.

A second transmission.

"Commander, this is the northern post. We also heard the shots. We see nothing, but the night is too dark. What do we do?"

Al-Sudani took a slow breath and keyed the radio.

"Hold your positions. Keep scanning. Do not engage unless they come to you."

He turned toward Hamza, who was standing near the laptop, his rifle slung over his shoulder. The others in the cave were awake now, alert and tense.

Al-Sudani spoke low, but firmly.

"The Americans are here. We cannot stay."

Hamza's face was hard to read, but he nodded. He had expected this moment.

Al-Sudani gestured to the laptop, their reason for being here. "The Sheikh sent us for this. We cannot allow them to take it." He handed it to Hamza. "Gather twenty men and take this over the mountain to him. Do not engage the Americans."

Hamza hesitated, glancing around at the fighters in the cave. "And you?"

Al-Sudani met his eyes.

"We will hold them here and buy you time to escape. If we can, we will follow. If not..." He let the sentence hang.

Hamza clenched his jaw but said nothing.

This was how it had to be. Al-Sudani turned back to the radio.

"All units, listen carefully. We are dividing forces. Twenty men will take our objective across the mountain. The rest will prepare for battle."

There was a pause. Then, crackling confirmations from the observation posts.

"Understood."

"We will hold."

Al-Sudani turned back to Hamza. "We will need to move before they call in air power. We will move lightly; move fast."

"We will move as quickly as we can," said Hamza.

Al-Sudani turned to Hamza. "If they overwhelm you, burn the computer."

Hamza nodded. Then, without another word, he began to gather his men.

Al-Sudani exhaled and unslung his rifle. He would erase the shame that he felt from the last time he had been here. He would fight.

* * *

TEAM FANG - TORA BORA

The gunfire from the opposite ridge was distant but distinct. Controlled, precise. Team ATLAS had engaged.

"Contact. Four tangos down," said Patel on the radio.

Kane didn't hesitate. "That's it, let's move."

The SEALs collected their gear and left their overwatch position. They weren't running - they were hunting. Every step was calculated, boots placed carefully on rock and loose gravel, minimizing noise.

It took valuable time, but Kane found the spot two hundred meters up the ridgeline and kneeled. It was a location that wouldn't endanger TALON with friendly fire. He had left two men behind at the original post, but as soon as they were established, called them up. He took stock of the view. Their new position was better - higher, with better lines of fire.

This was good ground. If al-Qa'ida tried to escape, this was where they would stop them.

* * *

AL-QAIDA MILITANTS - TORA BORA CAVES

The twenty men selected to escort Hamza and the computer to Pakistan gathered at the mouth of the cave, their breath visible in the cold air, rifles slung, gear strapped down tight. Some shifted restlessly, others stared into the darkness ahead. No one spoke.

Hamza stood before them, voice low but urgent.

"This must reach the Sheikh. Nothing else matters." He placed a hand on the canvas-wrapped package, held tight by one of the fighters. "We move fast. We fight only if we must."

The men nodded. They understood. Fighting the Americans was secondary. Escape was the mission.

Al-Sudani stepped forward, his calm presence anchoring them. "We know the Americans are to the east. They will come to bottle us in soon." He swept his gaze over the men, measuring their resolve. "We cannot let them close in. We must move first." He paused for a moment. "Fifteen of us will start with Hamza's group. If there is an ambush, we will buy you time. No hesitation."

Hamza's jaw tightened, but he said nothing.

Al-Sudani turned to the last ten men in the cave, their faces shadowed. "You ten will stay. If there is nothing left, you make them pay."

The men gripped their rifles, nodding. No words were needed.

Then, Al-Sudani gripped Hamza's hand, pulling him in close.

A brief silence. Then a bear hug.

"Go with God."

Hamza stepped back, eyes hard. "Let's move."

Then, without another word, they moved into the night.

* * *

TEAM ATLAS - TORA BORA

Reyes adjusted his scope, his breath steady despite the bitter cold. It had been nearly twenty-five minutes since they had ambushed the Taliban patrol and there had been no visible activity at the cave.

Something shifted in the darkness. Then, movement. A lot of it.

He clicked his mic. "We've got movement at the entrance."

In a low voice next to him, O'Connell, who was also observing through a scope, said, "Here they come."

Scott came up in a crouch and knelt beside him, peering through his own optics. One, two, five - no, more. "Well, that's it. They're leaving."

From the cave entrance, thirty militants spilled into the open, their dark figures silhouetted against the rock face. They moved with purpose, forming into a rough column, heading up the trail toward the border.

Scott keyed his mic, his voice measured. "FANG, TALON, this is ATLAS. We've got approximately thirty hostiles moving up the trail, headed west toward the ridgeline. This is the main element. We recommend that TALON initiate the ambush and withdraw. ATLAS will press up the mountain and link up with you to the east."

There was a brief pause, and then Hawkins replied. "Copy, ATLAS. We'll hit them hard when they're in the kill zone and then retrograde towards your position. You be ready."

Kane came on the radio. "Copy all. We've got them after that. Nobody is getting past us tonight."

Scott shifted his focus back to the cave. The movement of the main force had also drawn down the security - only two militants remained at the eastern observation post. He tapped Reyes on the shoulder. "You take the one on the left. O'Connor, the right. As soon as you take the shot, we will move straight up the hill to link with TALON."

There was a few minute pause.

Once again, the sound of suppressed rifle fire echoed through the night.

"Let's go."

19

HAMZA'S GROUP - TORA BORA

Hamza stood among his men, the mountain air biting through his clothes. He turned to the four scouts he was sending up the mountain in advance of the main party, their faces set with quiet determination.

"Push hard," he ordered. "The Americans are likely above us. Move fast, but be aware. Do not be careless."

The scouts nodded, gripping their rifles tighter. They knew the risk.

Hamza hesitated. The Americans wouldn't strike first. Not yet. They would wait, watch, let the scouts pass, and then hit the main force. That's what he would do.

He exhaled and adjusted his orders. "They will not attack you, so do not stop. Keep climbing, but watch below. The moment you hear gunfire behind you, you flank them. Hit them hard."

The scouts exchanged quick glances. One of them, a man named Kareem, gave a sharp nod. "Understood."

Hamza studied them for a moment, then waved them off. "Go."

The four men melted into the darkness, moving fast up the slope.

Hamza watched them disappear, his mind already shifting to the larger problem. He turned to his second in command, a rough man named Tariq. "The moment we are engaged, the Americans will call for air support."

Tariq's expression hardened. "Then we must move fast."

Hamza nodded. There was no outrunning the drones. The only chance was to break through before the Americans locked them in place.

He looked up the steep mountain path. The real fight was coming.

* * *

TEAM TALON - TORA BORA

"Fuck," whispered Hawkins. "Here it comes guys."

The team watched as the militants left the cave and began climbing the rocky mountain trail.

The night was deep, the mountains still. Hawkins adjusted his NVGs, scanning the valley below. Movement.

Four figures separated from the shadows near the cave entrance, their pace deliberate but rapid. Scouts, pushing up the mountain as hard as they could. The main force would follow.

Tate whispered, "Do we let them pass?"

Hawkins considered it. Letting them move up meant avoiding an early fight. But if they got too high, they'd be above them and able to flank their position - bad news. He exhaled. "We hit them now. Then we move and let FANG finish the main group."

The team adjusted positions, shifting along the rocks. O'Neal set the final Claymore and gave a quick nod. Ready.

The four militants worked their way up the slope, scanning for evidence of the Americans. One carried an RPG. Hawkins watched. The timing had to be perfect. Closer. Closer.

"Take 'em."

Tate fired first. The lead scout crumpled. The others hesitated - half a second too long. A burst from Ortiz's suppressed rifle dropped one more. O'Neal's Claymore erupted, a brutal blast that shredded another. The last militant dove for cover, rifle up, spraying blindly. Hawkins barely felt a bullet whiz past before the fire stopped for a moment. Hawkins couldn't see what the man was doing until he got to his knees with a RPG.

"Finish him—"

There was a loud "woosh" and a streak of fire. The RPG slammed into the rocks a few meters from Hawkins. The explosion punched the air from his lungs, sent him sprawling. He hit the ground hard, ears ringing, chest burning.

A man to Hawkins' right fired a burst that dropped the militant who had fired the RPG.

"Hawk's hit!" Ortiz was already there, dragging him behind cover.

Hawkins groaned. Everything hurt. His leg - wet, hot pain. Not good.

O'Neal crouched beside him, checked his leg for a moment and pull out a bandage. "You're lucky, boss. Could've been worse."

Hawkins gritted his teeth as the bandage tightened. "Yeah. Feels great."

The radio crackled. Kane's voice, low and steady. "TALON, you good?"

Ortiz answered. "Four tangos down. We've got a WIA. We're moving."

The valley below stirred. More shadows. The larger force was coming.

"Time to go!" Tate said urgently.

Hawkins forced himself up, wincing. No choice. "East. Now."

They moved fast, weaving through the rocks, keeping low. No stopping, no looking back. The militants wouldn't wait long before swarming their old position.

Ahead, the ridgeline dipped. Beyond it, ATLAS.

They just had to get there.

* * *

HAMZA'S GROUP - TORA BORA

Hamza moved in silence, his group spread out along the narrow trail. Ahead, the scouts climbed steadily, dark figures against the jagged rock.

Then - gunfire. Short bursts. Controlled. A grenade or mine exploded.

Hamza froze. The scouts had walked into an ambush. Shouts echoed through the valley. Another crack of suppressed fire. A detonation. Then, silence. Al-Sudani emerged from the rear, rifle slung, face unreadable. He took in the darkness ahead, listening. Then, quietly, "My men will pursue the Americans. Go with God."

Hamza said nothing. This had been expected. Al-Sudani's warriors - all hard men - lived for this fight. He raised a hand, signaling his own group to hold as Al-Sudani's fighters broke off, moving fast and low across the ridgeline. They disappeared into the black, heading towards the Americans.

Hamza exhaled. He turned to his own men. "We keep moving."

They advanced cautiously. Minutes passed before they found the bodies.

Four of their own, sprawled in the dirt. The Claymore had torn one man apart. Another lay face down, head twisted unnaturally. Blood darkened the ground.

Tariq cursed under his breath. Hamza's hands clenched into fists. The others stood still, eyes burning in the dim light. Hamza waved them forward. He stopped for a moment by one of the bodies, brushing dirt from a bloodied sleeve. He knew these men. They had fought together. Eaten together. Laughed together.

Now they were dead. There was no time for anger. The Americans were running like cowards, but he needed to climb the mountain.

Hamza saw his men hesitate, drawn to follow al-Sudani into battle.

"We must continue," said Hamza.

Tariq's jaw was tight. He pointed to the bodies. "We just leave them?"

"We avenge them by completing the mission," Hamza said, voice steady. "We deliver the package to the Sheikh. That is why we are here."

A long silence. Then, grudging nods.

Hamza stood, adjusting the strap on his rifle. "Move."

They left the bodies behind, rage burning in their chests, discipline keeping them in motion. The trail stretched upward, toward the high ground.

* * *

TEAM ATLAS - TORA BORA

Scott crouched low, scanning the darkness. The hilltop was narrow and covered with trees, but the clearing ahead gave them just enough elevation to see the slope below. He heard the sound of gunfire, it continued for a few minutes then stopped. TALON should now be moving.

He keyed his radio. "Hawkins, this is ATLAS. What's your status?"

Static. Then a voice - Ortiz, not Hawkins.

"Hawk's hit. We're moving east, but they're coming up behind us fast." Ortiz's breathing was heavy.

"Copy. Hold tight. Three of us will head your way and bring you in," replied Scott.

He turned to the team, eyes locked on Reyes and Patel.

"TALON's in trouble. We're moving to link up. Reyes, Patel, you're with me. The rest of you hold here. If this goes sideways, we will need cover fire. Delgado, see if you can arrange some air support."

O'Connor gave a quick nod, already shifting position. "We'll keep eyes on."

Scott dropped to a knee, looking through his NVGs. A faint flicker of light cut through the black - a pulsing IR beacon, two hundred meters down the slope. TALON's lead man.

Reyes adjusted his rifle, whispering, "I can't count them, but there are a few jihadis moving lower on the ridge, trying to flank."

Scott didn't hesitate. "Then let's move."

The three of them slipped from the tree line, descending fast. Scott's ears strained for movement, for voices, for the sound of enemy fighters closing the distance. The valley was alive now. Somewhere beyond the ridgeline, the militants were pushing up, hunting.

A hundred meters.

Another burst of gunfire cracked through the night. Closer now. Scott could hear American voices, controlling their fire, pointing out the enemy.

Fifty meters.

Reyes caught movement ahead - figures shifting against the rock. Friendlies.

Scott keyed his mic. "Ortiz, we see you. Coming in from your west. Don't shoot us."

A pause. Then, "About fucking time."

They closed the final distance in seconds, sliding into position behind TALON's battered group. Ortiz was kneeling next to Hawkins, pressing a bloodied bandage into place. The Captain was pale but conscious, jaw clenched against the pain.

Scott took a quick glance at the wound. Leg hit, bad and

bleeding but not fatal. He clapped Ortiz on the shoulder. "We've got you."

Ortiz exhaled. "We need to keep moving. They're coming."

Scott turned, looking back up the slope toward ATLAS' position.

He keyed his radio. "ATLAS, we have TALON. Get ready. Things are about to get loud."

* * *

AL-SUDANI'S GROUP - TORA BORA

Al-Sudani moved swiftly, boots skimming over loose rock as his men advanced across the mountainside. The Americans were trying to slow them down, forcing hesitation with intermittent fire. They would try to employ air power. He would not allow it.

The Americans were predictable. They would probe, assess, and then summon their aircraft to attack them from the sky. His job was to keep them from seeing the whole picture - to close with them before they could call down fire.

He signaled his men to push harder. The group moved fast, skirting the base of the ridgeline, angling north. If they could flank the Americans, they could take advantage of their weakness.

A faint sound.

Al-Sudani halted, dropping to a crouch. The others followed, vanishing into the folds of rock and scrub. He listened. The wind moved through the trees above, whispering through branches. Then - footfalls, barely audible over the mountain's hush.

The Americans were near. Moving ahead of them, higher on the slope.

Al-Sudani signaled again, hand cutting low and then pointing forward. His men understood immediately. They surged forward along the slope, intending to get ahead of the Americans and set up a hasty ambush. They were the hunters now.

* * *

TEAM TALON AND ATLAS - TORA BORA

Ortiz tightened a tourniquet around Hawkins' leg, the Captain grimacing but staying silent. Blood was still seeping through, but it wasn't gushing. He'd hold, for now.

Scott knelt beside them, eyes scanning the dark slopes. "We can't stay here. We need to move east now."

Ortiz nodded, already hauling Hawkins to his feet. The Captain gritted his teeth, leaning on Ortiz and O'Neal for support. "Don't slow down for me," he muttered.

Scott glanced at Reyes and Patel, who were already checking their mags. "We'll cover the rear," Patel said.

"Give us thirty meters," Reyes added, settling behind a fallen tree, rifle braced. "If they come, we'll slow them down."

Scott hesitated a fraction of a second - leaving two behind felt risky - but they needed to keep moving. He nodded. "Catch up when you can."

The rest of the team pushed east, slipping through the trees. The ridgeline loomed ahead, where the rest of ATLAS was waiting, perched on the crest of a small hill. Good high ground, a place to hold while they could get aircover in to help.

Behind them, Reyes adjusted his night optics, scanning the valley below. Movement flickered. Not enough to shoot.

"They're coming," Patel murmured.

Reyes exhaled, settling into position. "Then let's make them regret it."

* * *

TEAM FANG - TORA BORA

Kane lay prone behind a slab of rock, rifle nestled against his shoulder. Through his NVGs, he watched the scene unfold below. TALON's initial ambush had been swift, brutal. The al-

Qa'ida scouts never had a chance. A few short bursts, an explosion, and it was over. The other American team had moved quickly, slipping east into the ridgeline's folds, out of sight from Kane's position.

Kane didn't need to say a thing. There was no need. They all knew what was coming next. The militants thought that the Americans were running from the fight. Now, they would resume their efforts to move back up the mountain and head to Pakistan.

Graham, his second-in-command, shifted beside him. "You sure they'll come this way?" he asked.

Kane nodded. "It's the only direction they can move. They picked up something in the cave and are trying to make it over the border. They will be in a hurry to avoid our air support."

BELOW, on the lower slopes, movement stirred in the darkness. Hamza's group pressed forward, climbing with purpose. They were tired. Worn from several days of rough travel and distracted by the battles around them.

Hamza wiped sweat from his brow, barely feeling the cold anymore. His legs burned. His lungs ached. The climb was brutal, the slope steep and unforgiving. Every man in his group felt it. But no one complained.

The bodies of their fallen scouts were behind them on the trail. No time to mourn, no time for revenge. He had not put new scouts out in front. There was no point. The Americans had struck and vanished east. Their only mission now was to escape. To get over the ridge, into Pakistani territory before the drones came.

Hamza hated the drones. Silent, patient, watching. Their bombs came without warning, without mercy. His men feared them more than gunfights, more than American soldiers. A bullet could be outrun, hidden from. A drone was death from the sky, inevitable and final. It was all he could think about. Every step upward, every ragged breath. He slowed, scanning the darkness ahead. The jagged terrain leveled slightly, forming a natural funnel between two rocky outcrops - a bottleneck, dangerous.

KANE SQUEEZED HIS TRIGGER.

The first shot punched through the night, dropping the lead militant mid-step. A half-second later, the entire ridgeline erupted.

Muzzle flashes bloomed in the darkness. The SEALs unleashed hell.

Hamza's men never had a chance. They were exposed, bunched together on a steep trail, and there was nowhere to run. The first volley cut down half of them before they even got their weapons up.

Hamza dove for cover as rounds snapped past him, shattering stone, thudding into flesh. Men screamed. Some fired blindly into the darkness, spraying rounds upward, but the SEALs had the high ground. They were ghosts in the shadows, methodical, ruthless.

Hamza gritted his teeth, crawling behind a boulder. He clutched his rifle, breathing hard, chest heaving. He peeked over the edge, saw the carnage.

It was over.

His group was in ruins. Bodies littered the mountainside, the survivors scrambling, panicked. There couldn't be more than four or five left. Gunfire continued, snapping through the air, cutting them down one by one. There was no escape. Then, he remembered the computer. His breath hitched. It was still with him, secured in his pack. The reason they had come to these cursed caves. The reason Al-Sudani had sent men to die. The Americans must not capture it.

He couldn't let that happen. Hamza ripped open his gear,

fingers closing around the phosphorus grenade. His last option. Bullets tore through the air around him, ricocheting off stone. He ignored them, pulling the pin on the grenade, feeling the lever press into his palm. He took a deep breath. Then, with a final burst of motion, he yanked the pack off his back, shoved the grenade deep into it, and pressed it against the ground.

White-hot fire erupted. The pack flared, smoke and flames licking the air. The heat was blinding, searing. He saw the fabric melting, revealing the laptop, its plastic warping, circuitry frying.

A bullet struck his shoulder. Another hit his side. He collapsed, gasping, but he didn't care.

The computer was gone. The Americans would get nothing.

He rolled onto his back, staring up at the dark sky. The stars were bright. Peaceful.

Then everything faded.

* * *

INDIAN SPRINGS AIR BASE – NEVADA

Captain Reeves leaned forward, gripping the joystick as she tracked the chaos unfolding on her screen. The Predator's sensors painted the mountains in shades of black and white, a shifting tableau of figures darting between rocks, muzzle flashes blooming in stark contrast.

She keyed her mic. "CAOC, this is REAPER32. We're tracking multiple engagements across the ridgeline. TALON and ATLAS are engaged. FANG just hit a large group moving up the slope. Standby for updated SITREP."

1st Lieutenant Bryant typed rapidly, relaying fresh coordinates. "Special Operations Command has eyes on the feed. No CAS request yet."

Reeves frowned. The troops on the ground were taking hits, moving hard, but no one had called for air support. She listened to the chatter, switching frequencies, keeping her focus sharp.

Then, something new.

A separate cluster of heat signatures, distinct from the main fight, moving along the shoulder of the mountain below TALON and ATLAS. Fast. Coordinated. Flanking.

She zoomed in. "Shit. CAOC, REAPER32 has a breakaway element maneuvering on TALON's blind spot." She switched to the team's frequency, cutting in. "TALON, REAPER32. Urgent. You have a hostile element moving on your position from below - bearing one-eight-zero. Less than fifty meters."

Ortiz's voice came back, tight. "Repeat?"

"They're right under you. Standby for contact."

Even as she spoke, her screen flared with fresh muzzle flashes. The ambush had begun.

* * *

TEAM TALON AND ATLAS - TORA BORA

The night exploded.

Al-Sudani's men struck first, their initial volley hammering into Team TALON and ATLAS with brutal force. Gunfire cracked through the trees, bullets slamming into rocks, sending shards of stone flying. The militants had the element of surprise, and they used it well.

An RPG screamed through the air, detonating just short of the American position. The shockwave sent Reyes and Scott sprawling, their bodies peppered with hot shrapnel. Scott groaned, rolling onto his side, pain flaring in his ribs. Reyes clutched his arm, blood soaking into his sleeve.

Already injured, Hawkins barely had time to react before a burst of gunfire tore into their group. A round struck him in the chest, just inches from his chest plate. He went down hard, without making a sound. Ortiz was on him instantly, dragging him behind a thicker outcrop.

Nearby, Patel screamed as a round went through his ankle. He fell hard, rifle slipping from his grasp. Gritting his teeth, he yanked his sidearm free, still in the fight.

The militants kept up their assault, firing from below, their gunfire relentless. Al-Sudani moved among them, barking orders, driving them forward. He knew they had to press the advantage before the Americans recovered. But that window was closing.

Scott, bleeding and furious, shoved himself upright. He sighted down his rifle, ignoring the sharp burn in his side, and squeezed the trigger. His first burst dropped a militant mid-sprint, his body folding over itself. The second cut down another who had been preparing to lob a grenade.

Reyes gritted his teeth through the pain and followed suit, his shots snapping through the trees. Patel, despite his injury, fired from the ground, hitting a fighter in the chest and sending him tumbling back down the slope.

TALON and ATLAS had regrouped. The higher ground and their superior firepower began to shift the fight. The militants who had started with an advantage were now being systematically cut down. Their desperate flank had turned into a fatal trap.

AL-SUDANI REALIZED IT TOO LATE.

He turned to give an order, but a round snapped through his skull, sending him crumpling into the dirt. His death was fast, unremarkable. No dramatic last words, no desperate final stand. Just another body among the fallen.

With their leader gone and their attack faltering, the three remaining militants knew they had only one option - one final, desperate push.

They charged, yelling, firing wildly, trying to break through before they were completely overwhelmed.

They didn't make it ten steps.

From the crest of the hill, the rest of ATLAS opened up. Their coordinated volley shredded the charging fighters before they could reach cover. Bodies tumbled backward, rolling down the slope, lifeless. The last man managed to fire a burst before a bullet struck him clean through the chest, his rifle slipping from his hands as he collapsed.

Then, silence.

The mountain, which had been alive with the chaos of battle just seconds ago, was suddenly still.

Scott took a deep breath, his body aching, the adrenaline starting to wear off. His radio crackled.

"O'Connor to Scott. Clear down here."

Scott exhaled, nodding to himself. "Copy. We're good up here, too."

Ortiz crouched next to Hawkins. "We need a dust-off. Now."

Scott switched frequencies, calling it in. "Overlord, this is ATLAS. Multiple wounded. Request immediate casevac."

"Copy, ATLAS," came the reply. "Dust-off is inbound. ETA twenty-five minutes."

Scott looked around, they needed a good LZ, or at least a spot to drop a basket. The terrain was rough, but they could make it work.

Ortiz knelt beside him. "We hold here 'til the bird comes?"

Scott nodded. "Let's keep security tight. The last thing we need is some stragglers with a death wish. Let's move to the hill and send two back down fifty meters to keep an eye on things."

Reyes sat down hard, pressing a rag against his bleeding arm. "Yeah, I'm good with staying put."

Patel leaned back against a rock, grimacing as he watched a member of TALON placing a tourniquet on his lower leg. "Guess I'm not walking out of here."

* * *

BASE OPERATIONS - JALALABAD AIR BASE

Briggs was half-asleep on a cot in base operations when a Sergeant walked into the room and said, "I'm looking for the crew for PORTHOS 16."

Briggs sat up. "That's us. What's up?"

"We have a dust-off for you sir. It's urgent," replied the Sergeant. He handed Briggs the details on a briefing card. "This is what we have, you can expect more information when you get airborne."

Across the room, Fletcher was already swinging his legs off his cot, reaching for his boots.

"We are on it," said Briggs.

Holland burst into the room, zipping up his flight vest. "We got a call?"

Briggs shoved his feet into his boots, lacing them fast. "We're up. Tora Bora. Casualties in ATLAS and TALON."

Buckman, the SF medic, was already throwing his med pack over his shoulder. "Any idea on the nature of the casualties?"

"No details yet. Just 'multiple wounded.'"

Fletcher yanked on his flight helmet as they sprinted toward the Black Hawk, its silhouette dark and silent on the airstrip. The ground crew rushed forward, pulling safety pins and removing tie-downs.

The team climbed in, Holland taking his seat behind the M134 minigun as Briggs and Fletcher settled into the cockpit and began working their way through their checklists. Within ten minutes the helicopter was ready to fly.

Briggs keyed his mic. "Tower, PORTHOS 16 ready for immediate departure."

"PORTHOS 16, Jalalabad Tower, cleared to take off from spot delta. Winds 110 at 10, altimeter 29.94."

"PORTHOS 16 is cleared to takeoff from spot delta, niner-niner-four."

The helicopter lifted off, banking sharply as they sped toward the mountains.

* * *

HILLSIDE ABOVE THE CAVES - TORA BORA

The cave was deathly silent.

Nasser sat with his back against the cold stone, gripping his PKM, heart hammering in his chest. The firefights had raged for what felt like hours. The echoes of distant gunfire, the thunder of explosions - now all gone.

Nothing but silence.

The radio on the ground crackled faintly, but there was no voice, no contact. Hamza had fallen silent. Al-Sudani had vanished.

Nasser exchanged glances with the other nine men in the cave. Some avoided his eyes entirely, gripping their weapons with white-knuckled hands. Others simply stared at the floor, lost in thought.

Then, they heard it. The low hum of rotor blades in the distance. Growing closer. A helicopter.

Nasser clenched his jaw, his mind racing. The Americans were extracting their wounded. That meant the battle was over. And they had won.

The realization settled in his chest like a stone.

"This is over," one of the men muttered. He pulled his scarf up over his face, adjusting his rifle. "We need to leave."

Another stood. "If we go now, we can move south. The villages around Jalalabad... someone will take us in."

There were nods.

Cowards.

Nasser's grip on his PKM tightened as he watched the other men prepare to flee. They were ready to abandon the fight, abandon their brothers who had died on the mountain.

He rose to his feet. "Run if you want," he spat. "I will not."

The others hesitated, their eyes flicking to the dark tunnel behind them, then to the distant sound of the helicopter. They had already made up their minds.

Without another word, the nine men slipped into the night, vanishing into the rocky terrain, heading south, toward the promise of safety.

Nasser watched them go, disgust curling in his gut.

Then, he turned toward the hillside and began to climb as fast as he could towards the sound of the helicopter.

* * *

PORTHOS 16 - TORA BORA

The flight was quick. The terrain below them was all jagged ridges and shadowed valleys, the cold peaks of Tora Bora glowing in the infrared displays. The sun was just barely starting to illuminate the eastern horizon, giving them a better sense of the terrain below.

CAOC's voice crackled in their headsets. "PORTHOS 16, contact TALON-Two."

"Copy," said Briggs. "Switching." Fletcher switched frequencies and Briggs got on the radio. "TALON-Two, this is PORTHOS 16. We are five minutes out for a dust-off."

As they closed in, their radio crackled again - this time, Ortiz's voice, tense but steady. ""PORTHOS 16, this is TALON-Two. I have you inbound from the southeast. Be advised, your LZ is hot - engagements recently concluded, but potential enemy presence in caves below. Terrain is steep, loose rock. Best approach is from one-three-zero. Recommend one-wheel or hover extraction. You are danger-close to friendlies - watch your rotors against the obstacles."

Briggs adjusted his grip on the controls. "Roger that. You got a marker?"

Ortiz continued, "IR strobes are active. Winds are from the north at ten knots. Expect reduced visibility at touchdown. No immediate movement seen from hostiles, but we've taken sporadic small arms fire from the caves - possible RPG threats. Keep your heads on a swivel."

The Black Hawk banked, dropping toward the figures on the ridgeline. Through his NVGs, Briggs spotted the strobing IR markers - the only sign of the battered, waiting operators.

Briggs eased the aircraft lower, the tires barely scraping the loose rock. The helicopter shuddered, the angle precarious, but it held.

"Go, go, go!"

Buckman was out first, dropping onto the uneven ground with his med pack. Two operators rushed forward carrying Captain Hawkins' limp form, his uniform slick with blood.

"Help me with him!" Buckman shouted.

Scott, limping, shoved Reyes and Patel toward the bird. "Get on!"

Reyes was bleeding, shrapnel still lodged in his shoulder, but he pushed forward. Patel hobbled with a rifle slung across his back, his ankle wrapped hastily.

Holland reached down, pulling them up into the cabin. "You're good, I got you!"

* * *

HILLSIDE ABOVE THE CAVES - TORA BORA

The mountain loomed above, jagged and steep. The air was thin, cold against his skin. He climbed with the desperation of a man who knew he was already dead. His boots scraped against loose rock, sending pebbles tumbling into the void below. He pressed forward, his breaths coming in ragged gasps. The helicopter was close now. He could see the silhouette against the night sky, hovering just above the ridge. Dust and loose gravel swirled beneath its rotors, kicking up into a violent storm.

Nasser gritted his teeth. It was a very long shot, if only he could get a little further.

He reached the crest of the hill, dropping to a knee. He could barely make out the figures of American soldiers on the hillside - wounded, struggling, climbing aboard the helicopter. This was his moment. He braced the PKM against his shoulder, eyes narrowing as he lined up his sights. The recoil would be brutal, the muzzle flash a beacon - but none of that mattered. He pulled the trigger.

THE FIRST BURST tore through the air, several heavy 7.62 rounds slamming into the side of the Black Hawk. Sparks erupted as bullets ripped into metal.

Inside the cockpit, Briggs jolted as pain flared across his chest. The helicopter lurched as he gasped, struggling to keep control.

"Shit!" Fletcher shouted, eyes darting to the instruments. "We're hit!"

Holland reacted instantly. The minigun spun to life with a deafening roar, spitting a relentless stream of rounds down the slope.

Nasser had slipped backwards down the steep hill after the recoil of the machine gun had pushed him from his precarious position. He desperately tried to fire again. The bullets from the mini-gun shredded through his body, punching him backward. His vision blurred and his limbs went numb. He collapsed onto the rocks, his PKM tumbling from his grasp.

BRIGGS GRITTED HIS TEETH. "Fletcher, you need to take the controls."

"I got it," said Fletcher. "Where'd you get hit?"

"Chest or shoulder," said Briggs. "Can't tell. My left arm is useless."

Holland came over the intercom. "We've got them all. It ain't pretty, but it's time to fucking go!"

Fletcher kept his eyes on the instruments, checking for more damage. "We've got fuel loss, but we're stable. No catastrophic hits. I think we can get back to Jalalabad."

"Let's give it a shot," said Briggs. "We can set it down on the way if we need to."

"TALON, PORTHOS 16 is departing to the southeast at this time," said Fletcher.

"Take care of our guys," said Ortiz simply.

The helicopter lifted from the landing zone. Once they were clear, Fletcher dumped the collective, overbanked, and swooped down towards the valley.

In the helicopter cabin, Scott sat against the cabin wall, cradling his shrapnel wounds, watching as the medic struggled over Hawkins.

Patel, still clutching his injured ankle, exhaled sharply. "He doesn't look good."

Reyes, leaning against the bulkhead, nodded. "No"

The Black Hawk continued, carrying its battered crew toward the Jalalabad.

* * *

INDIAN SPRINGS AIR BASE – NEVADA

Captain Reeves hunched over the Predator controls, eyes locked on the grainy infrared feed streaming from REAPER32. She zoomed in, adjusting contrast. Nine figures spilled from the cave entrance, moving quickly, weapons slung across their backs. They weren't engaging. They were running.

"Squirters," she muttered.

Bryant, sitting beside her, caught it too. He tapped rapidly on his keyboard, marking targets and relaying the data. "Confirm, nine militants moving south from the cave. Bearing one-seven-five. Heading toward lower elevation." He switched frequencies. "CAOC, this is REAPER32. Be advised - elements from the cave are breaking contact and moving south."

The response was immediate. "Copy, REAPER32. Tracking."

Reeves exhaled sharply. "Let us take the shot. We're armed and in position."

Bryant keyed his mic. "CAOC, requesting immediate engagement authority. We have a clear shot."

A brief pause. "Negative, REAPER32. Standby. We are tasking TUSK 10."

Reeves leaned back in her chair. The A-10s. They'd been loitering overhead for some time, watching helplessly as the fight played out below. Now, it was their turn.

"TUSK 10, this is CAOC," the radio crackled. "Militants moving south from the cave complex. REAPER32 has them marked. You are cleared hot."

A new voice came over the net, calm and steady. "TUSK 10 copies. Engaging."

CIRCLING ABOVE, Major Matthews nudged her A-10 Thunderbolt II into a shallow descent. She squinted at the infrared targeting pod display - there they were, a cluster of figures moving south in the darkness, unaware that death had just been called in from 15,000 feet.

"TUSK 12, you see 'em?" she asked.

Her wingman, Captain Cross, was locked in. "Got 'em."

Matthews toggled her AGM-65 Maverick missile system. The targeting reticle locked onto the fleeing militants, the infrared contrast painting them as bright white against the cold desert floor.

"Rifle," she called.

The Maverick rocket detached from the wing with a dull thunk, its motor igniting as it streaked toward the target. Seconds stretched. Then - impact. A white-hot flash erupted in the valley. When the smoke cleared, half the militants were gone.

Cross followed up immediately. "Rifle."

A second Maverick streaked through the night, striking the remaining figures. When the explosion cleared, nothing moved.

REEVES WATCHED as the heat signatures on her screen turned from shadowy outlines of humans to indistinct blobs on the forest floor. "That's it."

Bryant confirmed the kill. "CAOC, REAPER32. No further movement. Targets eliminated."

The radio crackled. "Solid copy. Good hits."

* * *

TEAM FANG - TORA BORA

An hour later Kane moved carefully through the dark, his rifle steady as he led FANG up the ridgeline. Ahead, he spotted movement, friendly silhouettes shifting against the rocks. The remnants of TALON and ATLAS were waiting.

Graham, moving just behind Kane, whispered, "They look good, considering."

Kane agreed. Despite their injuries, the team members left behind after the medevac were in surprisingly high spirits. Some sat against the rocks, weapons still in their hands, watching the ridgeline. Others were quietly talking, catching their breath after a long night.

Ortiz spotted them first. He rose, rolling his shoulder to shake off fatigue. "About time," he said with a tired grin. "Figured you'd gotten lost."

Kane smirked. "Didn't want to rush back to the party. You boys alright?"

Delgado, bloodied but upright, nodded. "Lost some, but we're still standing."

Kane exhaled. "Good. What's the word?"

"Command says need to move back to the ambush site," said Ortiz. "The forensics team is inbound in an hour or so. They want us to hold security for a Sensitive Site Exploitation."

"They want us to walk back across the mountain again? What the fuck," said Kane.

Graham raised an eyebrow. "SSE? What do they think is there?"

Ortiz shrugged. "They want to see if we can find whatever the militants were trying to deliver. That and take DNA samples."

Kane groaned and rolled his neck, adjusting his gear. "Alright. As long as you guys can handle it, we'll move out now before the sun comes all the way up."

FANG AND THE REMAINING TALON/ATLAS operators moved across the mountainside in silence, retracing their steps across the rugged terrain. The sun was now peeking over the horizon, and although the valley was still in the shadow, NVGs had been stowed.

Every so often, the team would pause, scanning the valleys below, checking for movement. Nothing. The enemy was either dead or gone.

As they neared the ambush site, Kane took in the aftermath, now visible in the daylight. Bodies littered the slope where FANG had cut down the retreating militants. Shell casings glinted in the dirt, weapons scattered beside lifeless hands. The fight had been quick, decisive.

No one spoke as they set up a perimeter, placing men at key points along the ridgeline.

Kane pulled out his radio. “Overlord, this is FANG. Perimeter set. Standing by for forensics team.”

A brief pause.“Roger, FANG. Hold position.”

Kane sat against a rock, exhaling slowly. “Fuck this place.”

* * *

COMBINED AIR OPERATIONS CENTER - AL UDIED AIR BASE

Six hours after the fight had ended, the Air Force Lieutenant General stood in the dimly lit Combat Air Operations Center at Al Udeid Air Base, arms crossed. He stared at the live drone feed on the massive screen before him and watched as the last of the helicopters removed the forensics team and their special forces escorts from the mountainside, carrying all of the exhausted operators from the battlefield and towards Jalalabad.

After hours of combat, the radio chatter went quiet. The mountain was still.

The red phone next to his left arm rang twice. He picked it up and listened. “General, the boss wants that cave sealed for good.”

“Got it.” He hung up the phone and looked at the Air Tasking Order that was displayed on the screen before him. Two B-1B Lancers from Diego Garcia were still circling in positions nearby waiting for any calls for assistance. The bombers were loaded with full bomb racks of 2,000-pound JDAMs.

He picked up STE phone and dialed the watch commander on the operations floor.

“Re-task BONE 64 and 68. I want the cave where that battle took place cave sealed tight. Put everything they have on the entrance.”

The young Lieutant Colonel on the other end of the phone replied quickly. “Yes sir, that will collapse it for sure.”

Thirty minutes later the General watched the Predator feed that had been switched to the center display over the CAOC floor. He heard the B-1B crews call "bomb's away" and then watched as several minutes worth of shattering explosions blasted the side of the mountain over the cave entrance. When the explosions ceased, there was no sign of the tunnel, just a smoking pile of rubble.

The General watched in silence, then said to no one in particular, "That ought to do it."

20

MILITARTY HOSPITAL - BAGRAM AIR BASE

Scott shifted uncomfortably in the hospital bed, adjusting his arm to avoid jostling the bandages wrapped tightly around his shoulder. Across from him, Reyes sat slumped against his pillows, eyes half-lidded, exhaustion still clinging to him despite the painkillers. Patel sat at the foot of his own bed, his left pant leg folded up over the thick gauze where his foot had been.

The room was quiet except for the occasional beep from the machines monitoring their vitals.

Scott exhaled. "Hell of a fight."

Patel snorted. "Hell of a week." He ran a hand through his hair before forcing a smirk. "On the plus side, I get out of ruck marches now."

Reyes chuckled. "Yeah, but good luck learning to dance again."

Patel pointed a finger at him. "Joke's on you, I couldn't dance before."

They all laughed, but it was short-lived. The weight of the night before still hung in the air.

The door opened, and a doctor stepped in, flipping through a clipboard. He was an older, tired-looking Army Colonel.

"Hey Doc," said Scott. "Any word on Hawkins?"

The doctor's expression barely changed, but the pause said everything.

"I'm sorry," he said quietly. "Captain Hawkins didn't make it."

The air in the room seemed to vanish. Patel closed his eyes. Reyes swore under his breath. Scott's jaw tightened as he let out a slow breath, nodding.

The doctor gave them a moment before clearing his throat. "Your C-17 is leaving this afternoon. You'll be transported back to Germany for additional treatment."

Scott nodded again, but no one said anything. The doctor lingered for a second, then gave a small nod before stepping out of the room.

Finally, Patel sighed. "I really thought he was gonna pull through."

Reyes shook his head. "The man survived half a dozen deployments, only to get hit last night. It's not fucking fair."

Scott swallowed the lump in his throat. "None of this is."

BEFORE THE MOMENT could settle too deep, the door opened again. McCoy walked in, looking as rough as the rest of them, his eyes bloodshot from lack of sleep.

He nodded at them. "Glad to see you ugly bastards are still breathing. Winters sends his regards and wishes he could be here." He looked at them solemnly. He pulled up a chair and sat down. "Just so you know, the SSE team didn't find much. There was a laptop that had been slagged by a phosphorous grenade and that was about it."

Reyes sighed. "Figures."

"But," McCoy continued, "we confirmed multiple ranking AQ

operatives among the dead. You boys took out some real players last night." He leaned forward, eyes hard. "You did good work."

Scott gave a weary nod. "Not sure it feels that way right now."

McCoy exhaled, rubbing his face. "Yeah. I hear that." He shifted in his chair. "Look, I know it's not much, but at least you're headed to Germany. Decent hospitals, actual beds, cute nurses - hell, maybe even some good beer if you play your cards right."

Patel let out a weak chuckle. "Shit, at this point, I'd take a lukewarm Bud."

McCoy smirked. "That's quitter talk. You boys better not disgrace America by drinking anything weaker than a liter of the good stuff."

Scott shook his head, the faintest hint of a smile tugging at the corner of his mouth. "I'll drink anything that isn't warm bottled water."

* * *

CIA SPECIAL ACTIVITIES DIVISION B-HUT - BAGRAM AIR BASE

Ty Fletcher sat alone at the briefing table, absently turning a pen between his fingers. The dimly lit CIA Special Activities hut was quiet. He had just come from the hospital, checking in on Briggs and the team with McCoy. They were alive - that was what mattered. But nothing about the past 48 hours felt like a win.

Across the room, McCoy stood behind the counter, a thick stack of papers in front of him that would account for the mission they had conducted. He was flipping through the forms with the slow, deliberate movements of a man who had done this job a thousand times before.

Fletcher finally broke the silence. "What's the final damage assessment on the bird?"

McCoy didn't look up. "Bad." He flipped another page. "Unflyable."

Fletcher sighed, rubbing his face. "Figured as much."

McCoy continued, "Rotor assembly's shot, fuel system's punctured." He leaned against the counter. "They're gonna disassemble it and ship it stateside."

Fletcher let that sink in. The MH-60M had taken them through the mountains, pulled out the wounded, and taken rounds for them. Now, it was a casualty, just like the men who had bled inside it.

McCoy cleared his throat, flipping another page. "Oh yeah, Winters called."

Fletcher glanced up. "And?"

"They're sending someone to replace Briggs." McCoy barely looked up from his paperwork. "Mike Gray."

Fletcher froze. He stared at McCoy, eyes narrowing. "Bullshit."

McCoy smirked, finally meeting Fletcher's gaze. "Yeah, figured that'd get you." He leaned back, arms crossed. "Just yanking your chain."

Fletcher exhaled, shaking his head. "Christ, man. You had me ready to walk out of here. I won't fly with that idiot."

McCoy shrugged. "Well, lucky for you, it's not him." He flipped to the next page in his stack. "Some new guy - just left the 160th. Should be here in a day or so."

Fletcher leaned back in his chair, rubbing his eyes. "Great."

The hut fell back into silence, the only sound the rustling of paper as McCoy resumed his work. Fletcher sat there a moment longer, thinking about Briggs, the team, the ruined Black Hawk - everything that had gone down.

He sighed. Another mission. Another rotation. The wheel never stopped turning.

* * *

THE LANDING ZONE, SPECIAL OPERATIONS COMPOUND - BAGRAM AIR BASE

The El Zed was dimly lit, packed with operators from every unit that had fought in the mountains just nights before and more from the operations center across the compound. The door to the B-hut was blocked so that no one would disturb the evening.

A few dozen men stood around the room, illicit beers in hand, quiet conversations murmuring beneath the low hum of country music playing from an old speaker in the corner. The remaining members of FANG, ATLAS, and TALON had all gathered, along with others from the compound: DevGru, Delta, and the OGA guys who never gave their real names. They had all lost men before. They all knew the ritual.

At the center of the room, Ortiz and the remnants of TALON stood together. Their battered bodies still bore the signs of war - stitched-up wounds, bruises, bandages barely hidden beneath their shirts - but they were here, alive, with a fifth of bourbon making the rounds.

At the far end of the room, a pair of boots and a green beret sat on a table, Captain Hawkins' unit patch on the front.

Ortiz cleared his throat and stepped forward.

The room fell silent.

Everyone turned, waiting, knowing. Ortiz held his glass up, his face unreadable but his voice steady. "To Captain Hawkins, warrior, hero. May we meet again in Valhalla."

There was a beat of silence, a collective breath held. Then, as one, every man in the room raised their glass.

"To Hawkins."

They drank. The burn of bourbon hit hard, but no one flinched. The room stayed silent for a moment longer, letting the weight of the toast settle. Then, slowly, conversation returned, hushed at first, then louder, as stories began to flow.

Ortiz stepped back, taking another drink, his eyes lingering on Hawkins' beret.

Gone, but not forgotten. Never forgotten.

21

BAGRAM AIR BASE FLIGHTLINE

The Big Voice came alive at ten thirty A.M. "All hands will participate in a Fallen Comrade ceremony at eleven hundred hours. All hands will participate in a Fallen Comrade ceremony at eleven hundred hours." This countdown was repeated every five minutes. As the ceremony got closer, the soldiers, sailors, airmen, and marines on the base began walking from their facilities and either lining up along the side of Disney Drive, or next to the taxiway on the flight line.

Out in the middle of a lonesome parking spot and positioned with its rear ramp open, a C-17 Globemaster awaited its solemn cargo. The crew were prepared and somber, standing in the rear of the aircraft. A delegation of the senior officers from all the armed services stood in formation behind the aircraft, creating a pathway from the tarmac to the ramp.

At eleven o'clock, the Big Voice klaxon went off and the base was called to attention. Everything came to a halt. The silence of the normally busy wartime base was palpable. A Humvee pickup truck rolled slowly from the base hospital and out onto Disney Drive. On the back of the Humvee was a single silver casket covered with an American flag. Leading the Humvee was a small convoy of military police, blue lights flashing but otherwise silent.

Along the roadside, the troops of the base all saluted their fallen comrade as the vehicle passed by.

The Humvee turned off of Disney Drive and towards the flightline entrance. It drove past the air terminal, the Pat Tillman Morale Welfare and Rec center, and out onto the taxiway. When it reached the main taxiway, it turned left again and slowly drove past hundreds of service members lining the route. Fifteen minutes after beginning its drive, the vehicle came to a halt in front of the group of senior officers. An honor guard lifted the heavy casket from the truck and marched it into the back of the C-17, where it was carefully secured in the center of the cargo bay.

The delegation of senior officers and a small group of special forces members then walked into the back of the aircraft. A pastor said a prayer. Some of the participants said goodbye by touching the casket, while others stood there, heads bowed. When it was time, everyone walked from the aircraft. The cargo bay closed almost immediately. Within minutes, the aircraft was taxiing for takeoff on a long trip to Germany, and after that, to Dover, Delaware, where the remains would be officially repatriated and handed to the family.

"Secure from Fallen Comrade Ceremony," came from the Big Voice, and the base went back to work.

22

THE TANK - PENTAGON, ARLINGTON VIRGINIA

"So, no Bin Laden?" asked the Commandant of the Marine Corps.

"No," replied the Chairman of the Joint Chiefs of Staff. "Best we can reconstruct, there were somewhere between thirty and forty al-Qa'ida militants who went back to Tora Bora for reasons we still haven't figured out."

"Did the forensic team find anything useful?" asked the Chief of Naval Operations.

"No," the Chairman said. "The DNA samples match some mid-level al-Qa'ida operatives, good kills but not headline news. Doesn't sound like there was much in the way of electronics lying around. The remnants of a laptop were recovered, but it had been fried with a phosphorous grenade."

"Shame," said the Chief of Staff of the Army. "If it was worth the lives of more than three dozen men, there was probably something on it we could have used."

"Maybe there is more to find," suggested the Commandant. "Have we searched those caves thoroughly enough?"

The Chairman exhaled. "Unless we want to fly in a billion

dollars worth of mining equipment and the personnel to support it, we're not getting back into that cave. The Air Force dropped a hundred thousand pounds of ordnance on that area after the last troops left the mountain in order to seal up any survivors."

"Holy shit," the Commandant muttered.

"Holy shit is right," said the Chief of Staff of the Air Force. "We might need to restock the magazines at Diego Garcia before we do this again," he said jokingly.

"How about our casualties?" asked the Chief of Naval Operations.

The Chairman glanced at his notes. "You already know about the SEAL who broke his leg in the jump. We had one Army special operator KIA, and three wounded in the team that was ambushed."

"And from the CIA?" asked the Commandant.

"Three wounded operators, including a helicopter pilot who was shot during a medical evacuation," the Chairman said. "That was the bird that pulled out the Army team. From what I hear, they'll all recover."

The Chief of Staff of the Army shook his head. "Give those men a medal. That was some ballsy shit."

"I've already called the CIA Director," the Chairman replied. "We're working on it."

* * *

CENTRAL INTELLIGENCE AGENCY HEADQUARTERS - LANGLEY, VA

"Briggs says he quits," Terrance Winters said as he briefed Dr. Marcus Reynolds.

"He can't quit," Reynolds replied flatly. "The Director wants to give him a medal."

Winters smirked. "I'm not sure that'll convince him. The profanities I heard were... uncharacteristic, to say the least."

Reynolds exhaled. "The process will take time. As soon as he's released from Bethesda, put him on leave. Give him some space to cool down - send him to a nice beach for a couple weeks or something."

"I'll try," Winters said. "His ex-wife is visiting him in the hospital now. That might do the trick." He chuckled.

"Alright," Reynolds said, shifting gears. "What about the others?"

Winters glanced at his notes. "Reyes and Scott should be fine. They're both on their second or third surgery to remove shrapnel." He flipped a page. "Patel lost his left foot. Docs say he should be able to use a prosthetic and regain almost full mobility."

Reynolds nodded grimly. "Could've been worse." He leaned back. "And the chopper?"

"Riddled with holes," Winters said. "Fletcher called it a miracle that it even made it to Jalalabad. They're stripping it down to see if it can be salvaged."

"Gotcha." Reynolds opened a folder on his desk, scanned the contents, and tapped his fingers against the paper. "Now we need to do something about our friend in Pakistan who is ferrying IEDs across the border."

"I've got a target package ready and a second team in the theater," Winters said. "Just need the green light."

Reynolds didn't hesitate. "The DDO has already approved it. We want it done with a bomb if possible. If that's too difficult, fine. Only restriction - no American fingerprints."

Winters nodded. "I think we can make that happen."

"I'm counting on it."

EPILOGUE

ALIZAI, PAKISTAN

General Qadir Sharif stood near the window of his office, hands clasped behind his back, watching the lights of Alizai flicker in the darkness. The room was dim, the faint hum of a ceiling fan the only sound as he turned toward the man seated across from him. The operative - a lean, sharp-featured man in his late thirties - sat with perfect posture, his expression unreadable. He wasn't ISI, not officially. But he had proven to be skillful in the past, and Sharif needed someone he could trust.

Sharif exhaled, finally speaking. "Zayan Shah is dead." He paused. "We need to have a conversation with the Taliban who work in the mountains between Gardez and Khost. The situation with Hamid and Shah was regretful for both sides, but we need to move forward."

The words hung in the air. There was no shock, no reaction from the operative - he had already heard.

"Shot in the restaurant in Khost." Sharif's eyes narrowed and he shook his head. "The Taliban sent a clear message. They have gotten their blood price, we now need to re-establish the connections he had built."

The operative nodded, waiting. Sharif stepped away from the window, moving to the desk. He pulled open a drawer and retrieved a small USB drive, sliding it across the polished wood.

"This contains the last messages Shah exchanged with our contacts in Khost. He was arranging another shipment - components, detonators, timers."

The operative picked up the USB, turning it between his fingers.

Sharif leaned forward. "You will take his place."

The man nodded, unsurprised.

"There is a truck being prepared. Weapons, bomb-making materials, explosives. You will drive it to Khost and deliver it personally. There is no cost. Tell them we are still their friends. We have not abandoned them."

Sharif studied the man closely. "They will not trust you. Zayan was a known operator. You are not."

The operative smirked. "Gifts soften hearts."

Sharif allowed a faint smile. "Yes. And a truckload of weapons speaks louder than words."

He stood, straightening his uniform. "Once you have made contact, you will do what you can to reestablish the link. The Taliban need to believe we are still committed to their war." His expression darkened. "And I need you to confirm who killed Shah. If it was the Taliban, we will move forward. If the Americans had something to do with it, I need to know."

The operative pocketed the USB drive and stood. "Understood."

Sharif gave a satisfied nod. "Good. You need to leave as soon as the truck is loaded."

* * *

18,000 FEET ABOVE THE COMPOUND, a CIA-operated Predator drone circled in silence. The infrared camera tracked the movements of everything in the compound, its sensors capturing the figures entering and leaving the headquarters building. The AI tagging system highlighted the truck that was clearly being loaded with weaponry. The operator watched as the vehicle pulled away from the compound and headed towards the border, and presumably Khost.

The drone maintained its position over the compound, seeking to track the General.

The Americans were listening. And they were patient.

GLOSSARY

SOME TERMS USED IN THE NOVEL:

- **A-10 WARTHOG:** A heavily armored close-air support aircraft designed for attacking ground targets, particularly tanks.
- **AK-47:** A widely used Soviet-designed assault rifle known for its durability and reliability.
- **Al-QAEDA:** A global militant Islamist organization responsible for the 9/11 attacks and other terrorist activities.
- **ANA (Afghan National Army):** The military force of Afghanistan, trained and supported by NATO forces.
- **ATO (Air Tasking Order):** A document outlining air operations, missions, and coordination for military aircraft.
- **B-1B:** A supersonic heavy bomber used for strategic bombing and close air support.
- **B-HUT:** Basic wooden living quarters used on military bases in Afghanistan.
- **BIG VOICE:** A loudspeaker system used on bases to issue emergency alerts and warnings.
- **C-17:** A large military cargo aircraft used for troop transport and logistical support.

- **CASEVAC (Casualty Evacuation):** The urgent transport of injured personnel from the battlefield to medical facilities.
- **CENTCOM (U.S. Central Command):** The unified command responsible for military operations in the Middle East and Central Asia.
- **CIA Special Activities Division:** A covert operations unit of the CIA that conducts paramilitary and intelligence missions.
- **CIA (Central Intelligence Agency):** The U.S. agency responsible for foreign intelligence and covert operations.
- **CJTF-82 (Combined Joint Task Force-82):** A U.S.-led military task force operating in Afghanistan.
- **CONUS (Continental United States):** The 48 contiguous U.S. states, excluding Alaska and Hawaii.
- **DFAC (Dining Facility):** A military cafeteria where service members eat on base.
- **DIA (Defense Intelligence Agency):** A U.S. military intelligence agency responsible for analyzing foreign threats and providing intelligence to defense policymakers and combat forces.
- **DRMO (Defense Reutilization and Marketing Office):** A system for redistributing or disposing of excess military equipment.
- **DUST OFF:** A term for medical evacuation (MEDEVAC) missions using helicopters.
- **EA-6B:** An electronic warfare aircraft used to jam enemy radar and communications.
- **EC-130:** A military aircraft used for electronic warfare and psychological operations.
- **FATA (Federally Administered Tribal Areas):** A semi-autonomous tribal region in north-western Pakistan.
- **FOB (Forward Operating Base):** A military outpost in a combat zone for supporting operations.
- **GENERAL ORDER #1:** A strict regulation prohibiting alcohol, fraternization, and other activities in combat zones.

• **GREEN BERET:** A highly trained U.S. Army Special Forces soldier specializing in unconventional warfare.

• **IED (Improvised Explosive Device):** A homemade bomb commonly used by insurgents in asymmetric warfare.

• **ISI (Inter-Services Intelligence):** Pakistan's military intelligence agency, often accused of supporting Afghan insurgents.

• **JDAM (Joint Direct Attack Munition):** A GPS-guided bomb used for precision airstrikes.

• **JINGLE TRUCK:** A highly decorated Afghan or Pakistani transport truck often used for logistics.

• **JSOC (Joint Special Operations Command):** A secretive U.S. military command overseeing elite special operations forces.

• **KC-135:** A military aerial refueling aircraft used to extend the range of combat jets.

• **KIA (Killed in Action):** A term for military personnel who die in combat.

• **LZ (Landing Zone):** A designated area for helicopters to land and extract or deploy troops.

• **M-4 Rifle:** A lightweight, selective-fire carbine used as the primary weapon for U.S. troops.

• **M-240 Machine Gun:** A belt-fed 7.62mm machine gun used for suppressive fire.

• **MAVERICK:** An air-to-ground missile used for precision strikes against armored targets.

• **MH-60M:** A special operations variant of the Black Hawk helicopter used by U.S. forces.

• **MRAP (Mine-Resistant Ambush Protected):** A heavily armored vehicle designed to withstand IEDs and ambushes.

• **NATO (North Atlantic Treaty Organization):** A military alliance that led operations in Afghanistan through the ISAF mission.

• **NSC (National Security Council):** A U.S. government body that advises on national security and foreign policy.

• **NVG (Night Vision Goggles):** Optical devices that allow soldiers to see in low-light conditions.

• **OPSEC (Operational Security):** Protecting sensitive information to prevent adversary exploitation.

• **POTUS (President of the United States):** The commander-in-chief of the U.S. armed forces.

• **PKM:** A Soviet-designed 7.62mm belt-fed machine gun widely used by insurgents.

• **POG:** A term referring to paper coins used in the forward areas to reduce the weight of shipping currency.

• **PREDATOR:** A remotely piloted drone used for surveillance and airstrikes.

• **QRF (Quick Reaction Force):** A rapid-response military unit prepared to deploy at a moment's notice.

• **RCIED (Radio-Controlled Improvised Explosive Device):** A remote-detonated roadside bomb.

• **RPG (Rocket-Propelled Grenade):** A shoulder-fired anti-tank weapon commonly used by insurgents.

• **SEAL (Sea, Air, and Land Team):** An elite U.S. Navy special operations force.

• **SCIF (Sensitive Compartmented Information Facility):** A secure area where classified intelligence is handled.

• **SIPR (Secret Internet Protocol Router Network):** A classified U.S. military communication system.

• **SNIPER POD:** A targeting system used on military aircraft for precision strikes.

• **SPECIAL ACTIVITIES DIVISION:** A covert CIA unit responsible for paramilitary and intelligence operations.

• **SENSITIVE SITE EXPLOITATION:** The collection of intelligence and materials from high-value enemy locations.

• **TALIBAN:** An Islamist militant group that rules Afghanistan and fought against U.S. and Afghan Government forces.

• **THE TANK:** The Pentagon's secure briefing room for top military leaders.

- **UH-60H:** A Black Hawk helicopter variant used for combat and medical evacuations.
- **WIA (Wounded in Action):** A designation for soldiers injured in combat.

ABOUT THE AUTHOR

J. P. Springett II is a retired Navy pilot, combat veteran, author, teacher, and part-time farmer. He lives in the Shenandoah Valley along the Shenandoah River and writes full time.

ABOUT SELF PUBLISHING

PLEASE LEAVE A REVIEW OR RATING!

Thank you so much for reading this book!
Reviews and ratings are really the lifeblood of self-publishing. If you enjoyed this book, please leave a review and/or rating on Amazon, TikTok, Barnes & Noble, Google, or any of the social media sites of the day.

editor@commodoresridge.com
www.commodoresridge.com

ALSO BY J.P. SPRINGETT II

"Cease Buzzer!" is the author's description of the world of tactical Naval Aviation from the perspective of a career EA-6B pilot. Embark on a three-decade long journey with the author as he navigates through flight training and his first several fleet squadrons, takes command of an EA-6B squadron, and ultimately steers the Electronic Attack Wing of the U.S. Pacific Fleet. Discover life aboard a carrier, amusing port visits, engaging training detachments, and an array of high-intensity liberty experiences. Beyond the personal anecdotes, this book also sheds light on combat actions in Serbia, Kosovo, and Iraq, and provides a distinctive viewpoint on land-based EA-6B combat support in Afghanistan.

FIND IT ON AMAZON!

ALSO BY J.P. SPRINGETT II

In this gripping saga of NSA intelligence and CIA operations, we meet Thomas Harrington IV - son of a high-ranking U.K. intelligence officer and a battle-hardened ex-Marine. Defying his father's wishes, Harrington charts his own course as a CIA operative. Sent to Europe, he partners with MI-6, the SAS, and Ukrainian intelligence to uncover proof of Russia's hidden agenda in Ukraine. With time running out, the CIA gambles, and Harrington joins four elite Ukrainian Spetsnaz soldiers. Backed by Team Argos and the British SAS, he embarks on a high-risk mission into the Syrian civil war with his "Ukrainian Lions."

Made in the USA
Middletown, DE
17 March 2025

72748801R00186